LUCK OF THE DRAW

Stuart Blackburn

First published in Great Britain in 2025 by
The Book Guild Ltd
Unit E2 Airfield Business Park,
Harrison Road, Market Harborough,
Leicestershire. LE16 7UL
Tel: 0116 2792299
www.bookguild.co.uk
Email: info@bookguild.co.uk
X: @bookguild

Copyright © 2025 Stuart Blackburn

The right of Stuart Blackburn to be identified as the author of this
work has been asserted by them in accordance with the
Copyright, Design and Patents Act 1988.

All rights reserved. No part of this publication may be
reproduced, transmitted, or stored in a retrieval system, in any form or by any means,
without permission in writing from the publisher, nor be otherwise circulated in
any form of binding or cover other than that in which it is published and without
a similar condition being imposed on the subsequent purchaser.

This work is entirely fictitious and bears no resemblance to any persons living or dead.

Typeset in 11pt Adobe Garamond Pro

Printed and bound by CPI Group (UK) Ltd, Croydon, CR0 4YY

ISBN 978 1835740 996

British Library Cataloguing in Publication Data.
A catalogue record for this book is available from the British Library.

PART ONE

1

White peaks in the distance drew him forward, straight ahead, like an arrow shooting through space. He'd forgotten that part of it, the adrenalin-fuelled exhilaration, the pure sensation of movement. The little boy energy that had propelled him through high school and college. The compulsion to make progress and achieve something. That memory was all he had left now.

The gap between the mountains narrowed, leading him on, through dense forests. Under a lowering sky, everything was muffled, even the roar of the road. It was almost noon on a mid-March day. The hard winter hadn't finished yet. Crusty snowbanks lined the roadside, and people wore Russian-style fur hats with long ear flaps. They moved with short steps or stood and watched. One or two seemed to stare. He wasn't sure. Anyway, he was out of sight within seconds.

It surprised him, how close to the surface it all was. And how quickly he had reacted. As if the intervening years had never happened. It was probably just "second nature", an instinct that had lain dormant for decades and sprung back up at the slightest scent of danger.

She rested her head against the window and looked across at him. The tired jaw and brooding eyes. After days of arguing, she'd given up trying to understand why they were suddenly going so far away. 'I'm supposed to graduate in a few months, you know,' she'd pointed out when he first told her. 'How am I going to do that now? I know you said this hick town has a high school, but maybe it's just a big cow shed.'

She couldn't explain it to her friends and had to invent a "fantastic job" that her father was taking up. 'Why couldn't I stay behind?' she'd asked. Graduate and join him in the summer? But he'd been adamant. Unbending, yet pleading. And he said something she had not realised – that he needed her, needed her to be with him.

She reached over and changed the station from local news to pop music.

'At least the radio works out here,' she said without much sarcasm.

The road crested and dipped down into a valley, with a river frothing white on one side.

'Just crossed the watershed,' he said, turning to her. 'Should be easier from now on.'

They rumbled on at a steady speed, only passing when the car in front was "a crawler", as she liked to call them. A major highway, two lanes in each direction, separated by a snow-dusted median and hemmed in by forested hills. It was tunnel vision until they climbed high enough to see again those white-capped peaks, where the snow lay in deep crevices untouched by the sun.

She felt trapped inside the chocolate-brown Volvo with its faded interior, enormous steering wheel and gear shift that stuck out at a ridiculous angle. She'd stared too long at the dark face of the dashboard, its white numbers and silver dials. Directly in front of her, she saw the air vents set into moulded plastic, the pushed-in ashtray and a glove compartment. Had she brought her gloves? Yes, of course, they were packed in the suitcase in back.

The old Volvo. A rusting rattletrap with bits falling off, but safe as a battleship. She had loved driving it around Vancouver, just guiding it really. No one could touch her. But now it had become oppressive.

She looked over at him again. He was straining forward, checking the rear-view mirror, his face rock hard. A moment later, he sighed and slumped back.

That was it, she realised. The thing that had bothered her for as long as she could remember. He was always looking out for something. He'd pick up the binoculars from the windowsill in the kitchen and train them on the driveway that curved down to the road.

He said he was birdwatching. 'Lots of robins around here,' he'd say, still holding the heavy black field-glasses to his eyes. There were jays and crows, too, but she didn't pay attention and couldn't tell one from the other in any case.

One day, she must have been twelve or thirteen, she'd watched him watching. And when a bird, maybe a robin, flew across and perched on the branch of a tree near the house, he didn't move the binoculars from their fixed position.

'Dad! Over there,' she cried.

'What?'

'It's over there.'

'Oh, thanks,' he said and shifted the glasses to where she pointed.

Maybe he just hadn't seen it, but the same thing happened too many times.

2

The road narrowed again, squeezed hard between dark hills. Up ahead, the surface glistened and, fearing ice, he slowed down. Going around the bend, though, they emerged into sunlight so bright he had to pull down the visor above the windshield.

'You'd look good in shades,' she said. 'Only I'd recommend shorter hair.'

'Noted,' he said and returned her smile.

It's not so bad, she thought. I'll have to go to this new school for a few months. But after I graduate, I'll go to university back in Vancouver, where I'll be with my friends, and everything will be like it was before. She leaned over into the back seat, stuck her finger through a small metal grill and wiggled it.

'Yes. It'll all work out, but you won't be with me, will you?' she cooed. 'No, you'll keep Daddy company.'

Tuxedo pushed his nose up against the grill and uttered a squeak. A cry of pleasure or discomfort, she could never tell. She'd found the black-and-white cat four years earlier when it was a kitten, crouching in a corner of their garage. Now, it was her constant companion. Almost like a little brother. And just as fractious.

'Hungry?' he said.

'Yeah.'

'Great. There's a good-sized town just ahead.'

'Oh, boy! More than ten houses?'

'Maybe even fifteen.' His smirk had no sting. 'Anyway, it should have a half-decent café or restaurant. I'm starved.'

'Don't look it,' she chided, angling her head down at his ample waistline.

He was handsome, she had to admit, even for a father. Dark brown hair, a little too long, but bright blue eyes and eyebrows as thick as paint. She wondered why he never remarried or even had a girlfriend. 'You're enough for me to handle,' he joked whenever she brought it up.

So what happened to me? she wondered, unhappy with her frizzy hair and eyes that she knew were too small. Could be my mother, though I've never even seen a photo of her. Anyway, I probably won't have much competition out there. All fat farm girls.

She toyed with a French fry before tossing it into her mouth. After hours of moving at speed over concrete, she felt dull and heavy. But the café was pleasant enough. Someone, probably a friend of the owner, had painted garish garden scenes on the walls. Enormous sunflowers, very black bees and crouching frogs with protruding eyes.

Her father was finishing his second BLT sandwich, with the bacon removed. He was a vegetarian, sort of. Chicken and fish were OK. She could have pointed out the contradiction but didn't because she hadn't thought the whole thing through herself. And because he didn't make a big deal of it. If he tried to control her eating, it was only to tell her to cut down on butter, sugar and salt. In other words, everything she liked.

Overall, she thought he looked pretty healthy. She knew he'd played football in high school and college, a small place somewhere in New England. He didn't talk about it, but she'd seen his collection of photographs and awards. 'Big fish in a little pond,' he'd told her, with feigned self-deprecation. 'Not a pond, actually. More like a puddle.'

'So, tell me again. Why are we going to the boonies?'

'The what?'

'Boondocks. You know, way out there. Remote, without control.'

He looked at her and wondered, not for the first time, how much she really knew.

'Like I said, I lost my job. "Restructuring" they called it. And this one came up. Not much choice, really. Besides, you'll like it in Castlegar. It's beautiful and there's lots to do.'

'Oh, right. Hiking and fishing. My favourite activities.'

Now the mockery was clear, yet still not caustic.

'Look. I'm really sorry about the timing, but the job wouldn't wait. It was now or never.'

'Never would have been better.'

'I'll make it up to you, Rosie. Something nice after you graduate.'

'How about something right now? I'd like some of that cherry pie for starters.' She pointed toward a plastic dome on the counter. 'And some ice cream.'

'Sure, why not? I'll have some, too. It's a special kind of day.'

They both enjoyed the pie, even though, as she pointed out, the fruit had been flown in from thousands of miles away. He ordered coffee and she got the ice cream.

'I'm serious,' he said, brushing hair from his forehead and resting his eyes on her. Fatherly and boyish at the same time. 'We should do something really nice together for your graduation present. A long vacation, anywhere you like.'

Anywhere in Canada. She knew that without him saying.

'Like where?'

'I don't know. Montreal?'

'Paris?'

'You know we don't have that kind of money. But we could…'

'It's all right, Dad. We don't have to go anywhere. I might spend the summer in Vancouver anyway.'

Seeing his crestfallen face, she wanted to reach across the table and take his hand.

'I'll visit you a lot. You know, vacations and Christmas. And like you said, it's beautiful in Castle-whatever.'

While they waited, he pulled a folded piece of notebook paper from his jacket pocket and spread it on the table. He liked making hand-drawn maps. That way he could include only essential information – towns, rivers, highways – the things he needed to get to his destination.

Sipping his coffee, he saw it was National Highway 3 all the way now. Skirting the US border, turning up north, cutting through the Kootenays and sloping down to Castlegar, where two rivers met. Four or five more hours.

The view changed from hills to a valley that widened out into farmland, cold and barren except for distant tractors and power lines overhead. They passed through a string of small towns, each defined by a single traffic light. Houses were set back from the road and screened off from each other by fir trees, the Christmas tree type. They didn't see a person for a long time. Only a wooden statue of a bear, standing on hind legs and wearing a wide-brimmed hat.

She frowned as they climbed mile-high mountains and drove under arches hewn straight through rock. It was another kind of watershed. No longer leaving Vancouver, she was going to Castlegar.

For most of the final hour, she listened to her Walkman, and he listened to the local news. This is one consolation for being a single parent with an only child, he reflected. They were together a lot and had learnt to be content without having to talk. What went on in her head, he didn't know and didn't think he needed to know. He just wanted her to be happy and hoped she felt the same. One day, though, he would tell her.

'Civilisation!' she cried when they reached the end of a twisting descent and stopped at an intersection with lights controlling traffic in four directions.

Welcome to Castlegar. Pop. 5,906.

The sign was as high as a one-storey building and featured streaks of electric-blue water slashing across bright green mountains. It had, she admitted, a certain panache.

'See over there,' he said. 'That's the Columbia. Starts somewhere further east and goes all the way down to the US. It's the biggest river in…'

'I know. We did it in geography.'

He glanced at her, lips compressed, confident. A little like her mother, he thought.

He tried again. 'I know it's small, but it's got more than you'd think. There's a regional airport, a vocational college and the high school, of course. Plus an independent bookshop and a cinema.'

'No castle?'

The hint of mockery made him hesitate.

'No. The name comes from a place in Ireland. With a castle.'

They both laughed.

Before the town proper, he turned sharply onto a road that climbed, curved and flattened out. Bungalow-style houses lined one side of the short street that ended in a cul-de-sac. On the other side, facing the eight houses, snow was banked up at the foot of a tree-covered hill. The street was part of a property development scheme in the 1960s, before the area had been hit by a decade-long economic decline.

Each front lawn, uniform in size and carpeted with crusty snow, was flanked by a driveway leading to a two-car garage. He pulled into the last driveway, separated from the next house by cypress trees. Not bad, though the dead-end might be a problem.

'Well, what do you think?'

Rosie had jumped out and was stretching her body, legs wide

on the pavement, while surveying their new home. There was no one in sight, no movement anywhere. Only a stiff wind.

'It looks big,' she said.

'Yeah, bigger than we need, but a nice spot. Don't you think?'

'Spot?'

'Quiet, I mean. Peaceful.'

They carried their suitcases inside and set them down in the vestibule. The house was furnished, and far from shabby, but the all-white décor gleamed with disregard. He was drawn toward the picture window that took up the entire back wall. A good view of the main road and the town below, cradled in a bend of the Columbia River where it joined the Kootenay River. He could also make out a bridge crossing to the other side and a road running north into the mountains. Perfect.

When he turned around, Rosie was coaxing Tuxedo out of his cage. First the head, diamond-shaped and downy white except for the black mask covering his eyes and some of his cheeks. Freed, he reconnoitred, sniffing around the perimeter of the kitchen, the hallway and other areas, before relaxing in front of bowls of water and food, with Rosie maintaining her distance.

'All good,' she announced. 'Now we can explore.'

The central section of the house was open plan. The living room area had a white leather couch, glass-topped coffee table and easy chairs facing a fireplace to the right of the picture window. There was also a good-sized kitchen, dining area and small study, or "den" as he called it. From the vestibule, the hallway led to two bedrooms with a bathroom on one side, and a larger ensuite bedroom on the other.

She selected the small bedroom at the end of the hall. Lots of light, but also privacy, though she sensed she would never be at home in that room. Not even when her things arrived in the moving van. It was temporary, a forced necessity. She would help her father settle in – he seemed happy enough – then graduate and, with any luck, be off to university in Vancouver.

She put away her clothes and shifted the bed so that she would see the trees when she woke in the morning, though she calculated that the rising sun would be blocked off by the high hill across the street. The pinewood desk looked more suited for a dollhouse and lacked a chair. She decided to pinch one from the kitchen.

'There you are,' he said, poking his head through the doorway. 'I'd have gone for this one, too.'

'Right, my liege. Now, let's see your chamber.'

Across the hall, with another large window facing the river and town, it boasted a king-sized bed, built-in closet and recently refurbished tiled bathroom.

'Looks comfy,' she said. 'I might want to put a few plants in here.'

'Sure. Make it a garden, if you like. Sleeping with slugs and ants has been my lifelong ambition.'

His smile was not returned. Anything that suggested she would stay a long time cheered him, while she was thinking that someone should be sharing that room with him.

After an early dinner in town, they picked up breakfast provisions at a late-night store and drove home. At the end of the cul-de-sac, a single streetlight flared in the darkness piled up at the base of the hill.

Walking up to the front door, two powerful beams shot out from the eaves.

'Jesus!' Rosie cried and shielded her eyes. 'What are we, thieves or something?'

'Some kind of sensor, I guess,' he ventured.

'Can't we turn them off?'

'Yeah, but they're there for a reason.'

She shook her head and mumbled something while stamping her feet in the cold.

'At least we're allowed inside,' she said when he'd managed to find the key and push the door open.

They both slept heavily and spent most of the morning unpacking the boxes of kitchen things they'd brought with them in the car. After a big breakfast, she went back setting up her bedroom and he did the same for the kitchen.

'When does the job start?' she asked, coming into the living room, where he was standing in front of the panoramic window. Something told her he was making a calculation. Then she noticed the binoculars lying on a small table in a corner.

'Monday. But I have to go in tomorrow for the paperwork and an interview.'

'Interview? I thought…'

'It's just perfunctory.' He had turned around to face her. 'You know, a formal requirement. I have the experience and the manager here knows my old boss. So it was a shoo-in.'

Especially since he'd his eye on it for months. Always having an escape plan was one of Sharon's rules.

By late afternoon, after their first substantial shopping foray, the kitchen was stocked, the electricity, gas and telephone had been connected, and the moving van had arrived. The house was an obstacle course of half-unpacked boxes.

No television, but she'd learnt to live with that. 'My dad's an ex-hippie,' she said whenever a friend asked if she'd seen a particular programme. To compensate, he'd bought her a high-quality radio. CBC came in clearly and she discovered a local station that played decent music. When the time was right, she would ask him about a telephone extension in her room.

"Leaving on a Jet Plane" played in her ear as she arranged her plants, most of which had survived the journey from Vancouver undamaged. The small purple orchids went on one windowsill and the cacti on the other. A spider plant dangled from the ceiling in the corner between the windows, and a terrarium sat on the little desk.

Next came her books, a mixture of textbooks, novels, science fiction and natural history. They fit neatly into her oak bookcase, which she placed against the wall facing the foot of her bed, now warmed by a canary-yellow duvet and pillow covers. Large, framed photographs, reproductions bought in a museum shop, were hung on the walls. Lions and tigers above the desk, mysterious moonshots overlooking the bed.

'C'mon, Rosie. It's ready!'

He had been in the kitchen, working up their staple: a spaghetti dish with onions, garlic and chopped tomatoes.

From the round, wooden dining table, they had a view of the hill across the street. Too close to see the top, it loomed solid and black. She gave a tiny shudder.

'Looks cold out there, doesn't it?' he said, bringing the plates to the table and sitting down.

'Colder than Vancouver, that's for sure.'

'Yes, but the snow's melting. You can see that.'

She offered him a dry smile. Just like Dad, she thought, doing his best.

3

He left for work before she got up. That was another thing that bothered her. He drove a garbage truck. It was embarrassing, no matter how hard she tried to tell herself that it didn't matter. 'He works for the city' had been her standard answer whenever someone asked in Vancouver. It would have to do here, too. But it just didn't seem right. He was intelligent, graduated from a prestigious college and read books. Whenever she'd suggested that he should try something "better", he shrugged and said he liked the work and the people he worked with. And it paid well, he claimed, with a good pension. She didn't believe any of it.

For one thing, he never seemed to do anything with his so-called "buddies". None had ever come over to their house in Vancouver, at least not for anything social. A few times, someone had stopped by to pick him up if the car had broken down or to take him to a hockey game.

She always thought he'd have more friends and do more if he were married. Or even had a girlfriend. How many eligible women is he going to meet driving a smelly truck around a small rural town? In Vancouver, he had come to school events – the annual play, Parents Night, the awards ceremony – during which she had, with what she considered great finesse, engineered casual contact with attractive and unmarried female teachers. Once or twice, she'd detected sparks and waited for the flames to rise, blowing gently on them with hints at home and innuendoes at school. Disappointment had not dimmed her desire, but she accepted that now there would be fewer targets to aim at.

At least it was Spring Break. She spent most of those days at home, reading in her room, fussing with her plants and making sure Tuxedo adjusted to his new environment. After experiments in various rooms, she chose the kitchen as the location for his meals and placed the shallow bowl on a mat with a grinning image of Felix the Cat. She also did some of the shopping. A large natural food store was a welcome surprise, as were the independent bookshop and a garden centre called Green Thumbs.

The school, located outside the town and surrounded by spacious playing fields, was not what she had expected. She parked across the street, as if waiting for someone, but felt ridiculous since it was vacation time, and no one was around. Should have brought Dad's binoculars, she joked to herself.

Getting out, she crossed the street and stood in front of the single-storey, modern-looking building with flaring wings. I can do this, she told herself, zipping up her jacket against the bitter wind.

A plaque on the wall behind the principal's desk was emblazoned with the school motto: Carpe Diem. Rosie wasn't sure what it meant but decided it wasn't the right time to ask.

'Yes,' Mrs Stipanovich was saying to her father, 'all Rosa's school records from Vancouver have arrived.'

'That's good. So, she can begin without hiatus?'

Rosie supressed a smile. He might wear scuffed boots and drive a garbage truck, but he was no hick. Could be a teacher in this or any school, if he wanted.

'That's right. And we're really pleased to welcome such a good student. Especially someone with a strong interest in languages. Now, what about an elective?'

'I was wondering,' Rosie said, speaking for the first time, 'do you have a creative writing class?'

'We do. Tuesdays and Thursday afternoons.'

'Fantastic.'

'Any sports interest?' Mrs Stipanovich asked. Her dimpled cheeks as soft as dough.

'No, not really,' Rosie answered. 'That's my father's department. If you need a coach for the football team, he…'

'You'll have to excuse her impetuosity,' he cut in. 'I will certainly be an enthusiastic supporter, but I am fully and happily employed.'

'What is your occupation, Mr Williams?'

'He works for the city,' Rosie answered.

'Admirable,' Mrs Stipanovich said with a sweet smile.

Too bad she's married, Rosie thought.

At the weekly mid-morning assembly, Rosie was introduced to the school, squeezed in between congratulations for the girls' volleyball success and an announcement about new cafeteria hours. Then, she was on her own. Most of the students paid scant attention to the "new girl", and she was reluctant to ask questions about classrooms, lockers and schedules. Twice found herself lost in the maze of corridors and had to ask directions. Otherwise, in jeans and baggy pullover, she blended in.

Within a week, she was enjoying herself. It wasn't Outer Mongolia, and some teachers were actually a notch above those in Vancouver. And there was something else. She felt like she was looking in a mirror all the time, watching herself react, adjust, absorb. Seeing herself from the outside made her less self-conscious, creating a distance that was both protective and pleasurable. The only conscious change she made was to paint her nails a dark red used by the girls who seemed most popular.

On a sunny day, she took her tray from the cafeteria and sat on a bench in the courtyard. Boys and girls milled around in the wind-sheltered space, talking and giggling, jostling each other and sneaking cigarettes. From the courtyard, she could see across the river to the dark green hills, flecked silver by the sun. He was right. It is beautiful.

So was Miss Blanc, the creative writing teacher, whose shoulder-length blonde hair framed an oval face. The perpetual smile on her taut lips gave the impression that she knew exactly what you were thinking. And when she spoke, never quickly and never wasting a word, she wrapped you up in a conspiracy of two. Rosie was transfixed and couldn't understand why the dozen other students, mostly girls, passed notes, chewed gum and gazed out the window.

After two weeks, she decided to make a move. They had been told to write for twenty minutes, describing any scene they wanted. She started on something romantic, possibly even sensational, to grab Miss Blanc's attention and draw her in. But that was risky. During each session, one or two students were asked to read aloud what they'd written. What if she were handed that poisoned chalice? Biting her lip, she crossed out the love scene on the beach and began to describe a ship crossing the ocean. Lots of sails. Very nineteenth century.

A fierce storm whipped up the waves, tossing the vessel and its desperate crew from side to side. Water lashed their faces, their hands gripped thick ropes and…

'All right, time's up.'

She listened to a boy read his portrait of a girl in a crowded shopping mall. Not bad, but lacks verve, she thought and tried to come up with a clever "intervention". That's what Miss Blanc called suggestions for revision.

'You could tell us what she's wearing. You know, give it some more colour,' she said, selecting another one of Miss Blanc's favourite words.

'But I don't want colour,' the boy replied. 'I want to show a crowd in chaos. Does chaos have a colour?'

'Smart alec,' she whispered, drawing a look of disapproval from Miss Blanc, who steered the discussion toward the question of point of view.

4

'I think we've got something for you, Mr Gill.'

'OK, let's hear it.'

The caller paused to check his notes. 'Right. A hotel clerk in Seattle saw someone fitting the description. Can't be sure, given the time lapse, but he was pretty confident. Seemed like a regular sort of guy. The clerk, I mean.'

'When was this?'

'Wednesday. My agent was working the downtown area up there. You know, the usual beat. Taxi stands, train station, bars, restaurants, hotels. And this guy says he saw him.'

'Alone?'

'Yes.'

'Where?'

'In the hotel lobby.'

'You said he was confident. How confident?'

'As sure as can be. He was wearing a hat, but the clerk recognised the face right away. Different name, of course. A Mr Mathews. So he said.'

'He's still there?'

'No. Checked out yesterday. Said he was going to Spokane. I sent my man there, to follow up on this "Mathews". Spokane's not that big, so he'll probably get something.'

'OK. Let me know what you find out.'

'Will do, Mr Gill.'

Ronald put down the phone and stared out into space.

He wanted to feel optimistic, but he had learnt not to get ahead of himself. After all, he'd been at it for eighteen years now.

With the fine tip of a marker pen, he wrote "106" on the head of a plastic push-pin and walked over to the map on the wall of his office. Seattle was already obscured by a half a dozen pins, so the new one had to go a little south of the city. Pushing it in, he heard the reassuring "pop" when the metal point pierced the paper. He stepped back and scanned the map, with its rash of pins, from the Canadian border to Mexico, and California to New York. Shaking his head, he went back to his desk, entered "106" in the notebook and added the relevant details. All his life, Ronald Gill had been haunted by a sense of incompleteness, that something was missing, or perhaps had never been there.

5

His hand came down hard on the alarm clock and sent it flying. It was Tuesday and Rosie wouldn't be up for another half an hour or so. Rosie. She'd be gone in a few months, off to university. She said she'd come home on holidays. Then, who knows? A job in Vancouver. Or Ottawa or Montreal. Gets married and moves away.

He dressed and dragged himself to the kitchen, prepared stove-top coffee and cut slices of wholemeal bread. He turned off the kitchen light and looked toward the big window at the back. The peaks were pink-tinged, the rest in shadows. He had no doubt that coming to Castlegar had been the right decision – never can be too cautious – but it had shifted things between them. Although he couldn't put a finger on it, she had changed and seemed to look at him anew in this new place.

'The toast's burning!'

Pyjama-clad Rosie rushed in and switched off the unreliable toaster.

'Mustn't set the house on fire, you know,' she said over her shoulder and retreated back to her room.

It had been smoother than he'd feared, getting out of Vancouver, but he did miss the life they'd built up there. Didn't have any real friends, but he liked going to the cinema and the parks, and the occasional hockey game. And he knew all the staff in the local bookstore and organic food store. They were his friends, the people he chatted with week in and week out.

He also missed the house in North Vancouver. Small, warm and comfortable, it was set back from the road, almost in the woods. More cover than here, but Castlegar is more isolated. That was important.

He buttered his half-burnt toast and sipped his coffee. It'll all work out fine, for both of us. It's warming up now. Only one night below freezing last week, and the snow has retreated to the hillsides.

The locker room at the Castlegar depot was already familiar. Men sitting on benches, dressing and undressing, joking and complaining. All the guys were friendly and accepted him right away, especially after he told them he was a Canucks fan. They didn't ask about his past, though they joked about his stubborn American accent. No one, as far as he could remember, had mentioned that in Vancouver.

'Morning Wilson,' he said when a wiry man, a good ten years younger, entered the locker room. He wondered if that was his first name. Wilson was his "swamper", the guy who stood on the footplate at the back of the truck and jumped off to collect the bins. After two weeks, they'd gotten used to each other, but he was mostly alone in the cab, listening to music.

In the thin light, they crossed the yard to their truck. It was bigger than the ones in Vancouver and equipped with snow-chains. It was also a different type, a front-loader modelled on a forklift. It had taken him a few days to get used to the new set of controls, the larger size and wider turning arc. But old habits kicked in and, despite the unwieldly truck, the job was more or less the same as in Vancouver. Except that some of the containers had been gnawed by raccoons, overturned by deer or smashed by bears.

After a couple of hours, they went to a café for sandwiches and coffee. Wilson lit a cigarette and, for the first time, began to talk about himself. He was from a small town ("even smaller than this one") further north, married with two young kids. His parents were divorced, and his married sister lived in Calgary.

'I have a daughter,' is all he said. 'In high school.'

Back in the truck, Wilson directed him to a bridge over the Columbia and along a rough road running parallel with the river.

'This is a bit different,' Wilson said. 'We only come here on the second Tuesday of the month.'

They passed a string of widely separated bungalows and came to the end of the road, where he saw an old house with a wrap-around white porch. Off to the side, a weather-beaten barn and idle farm implements.

'It's a sort of museum, for the Doukhobors,' Wilson explained.

'The who?'

'Doukhobors. Came over here from Russia. Something to do with religion. That's what they say. Sort of like Quakers.'

'Pacifists?'

'That's the word.'

'When was this?'

'I don't know. My grandfather says he remembers them coming. So, a long time ago.'

'Are there many of them?'

'Thousands back then. Only a couple of hundred now. More of them, a little north of here.'

'Do they come into town and, you know, go to the schools here?'

'Yeah. And they produce the same amount of trash as the rest of us. Sometimes more, when they have events.'

Listening to the metal arms crank up and over with the heavy-duty plastic bins, he shook his head and smiled. He'd chosen a town with pacifists from Russia.

When he got home, the sun had burned away the early dusting of snow. Rosie would be back soon. She had her creative writing class that day, so a little later than usual.

He made himself a tomato-and-cheese sandwich, and the mug of black coffee he'd been thinking about ever since the tepid one at their break. Sipping, he read the previous day's edition of a Vancouver newspaper, glancing at stories about campaigns for elections that fall. He spent more time on the international news: a huge oil spill in Alaska, the continuing collapse of the Soviet Union and the bombing of a US army club in Naples, in which five civilians died.

Turning quickly to the sports pages, he concentrated on every detail of every game. It didn't work. He moved to the dining-room area and picked up the binoculars. He could see down their street to where it met the main road, only a hundred yards away. By now, he knew which cars were regularly parked in the seven other driveways. Seeing nothing unusual, he went to the large window at the back of the house, found the main road and traced it into town. He doubted he could spot anything there, though he always felt better after his "full sweep", as he called it.

When the door opened, he put the binoculars away and waited for her hello. He heard only the rustle of a coat and her footsteps coming toward him.

'Anything the matter, sweetie?'

'Yes. Yes, there is.'

Earlier that day, the boy from the creative writing class had sat next to her in the cafeteria. They talked about Miss Blanc, complained about the soup and laughed when a well-known bully dropped his tray. That broke the ice. Where was she from? Vancouver, that must be incredible. No, he was from Kelowna. When his father died of cancer, they moved to his grandparents' house in Castlegar. What did her father do? Local government? That's good. His mother worked in the library. What about her mother?

She skipped her next class and went for a walk along the fast-flowing river. In the distance, she counted seven white peaks, four on one side of the gap and three on the other. Below them, the carpeted hills sloped down until the fir trees became separated, countable even, and trickled down to the rocky shore where she stood.

She wasn't sure when she'd first noticed it. Probably years ago, but you don't think about those things when you're young. Besides, he was both father and mother. Protective and firm when she needed boundaries. He was normal in most ways, but secretive. Careful and controlled. "Wary" is the word she settled on. Never spoke about his past. She knew he was born in the American Midwest, moved to Southern California, went to college in New England and met her mother in San Francisco. That's what he said.

Her mother. He got tight-lipped whenever she asked about her. Now that they'd made this ridiculous move away from Vancouver, it was time she found out more. Carpe Diem.

'Why don't I know anything about her?' she asked when she found him in the living room.

'You know I don't like to talk about it.'

'But what about before the accident? What was she like?'

He didn't answer.

'And your family. Why don't we ever visit them, or they come up here?'

'As I've told you before, we just don't get along, so...'

'*So*,' she mocked him, 'I've never met my grandparents and I probably never will, even though they live not that far away, somewhere in California.'

'Listen, I really do not want to talk about this.'

'But you're going to. Because I won't stop until you do.'

'Rosie!'

'Please, Dad! I don't even know how you guys met and all that.'

She was in front of him now, almost in tears.

'Please.'

He knew it would come some time, and this was as good as any.

'OK,' he said, putting an arm around her shoulder and guiding her toward the sofa. 'There is a lot you don't know.'

PART TWO

6

He could see why it was called a *mesa*. At the back of the house, behind the swimming pool and the mesh-wire fence, the land dropped off. It wasn't a high cliff, maybe fifty feet, but enough for a view across a new housing development bordered by what was left of the orange groves. To his right, he could see Mount Baldy – the name made him smile – topped with snow, even now, in March.

He swallowed hard. He didn't like heights: never got up on a diving board and avoided looking down any flight of stairs.

Everything was so open here. That's what had struck him right away. Four-lane highways, wide streets, sprawling houses, spacious lawns and all those groves spreading over tracts of land. A world away from the prim suburb he'd grown up in. It had taken him months to get used to wearing short-sleeved shirts and jeans to school, where he'd been mocked for his leather shoes.

The family had already moved twice before. Each time, his father had been offered a better job. This last move, though, had been difficult for his dad, who left a well-paid position. As a twelve-year-old, he didn't understand it, only that it had to do with his dad's boss, who looked like a gangster in the movies. Heavy jowls, expensive cars and big cigars. Something about a lack of respect shown to his father. Anyway, his dad quit and was unemployed for several months, setting up a tiny office at the back of the house and applying for a new job. The man who always wore a sunny face became haggard and short-tempered, bickering with his mother and filling the house with gloom. Routines were altered, plans put on hold, and nothing was certain. He never forgot that fear of failure gripping his father.

Coming home from school one afternoon during that terrible ordeal, he found his parents in the front room, having a glass of sherry.

'Westward ho!' his father cried.

The uprooting was disruptive, packing a hundred boxes that went into a moving van and having to live out of suitcases. It was chaos, but it had a destination, a goal to be achieved, and that was all he needed. Later, he would reflect that it seemed inevitable, moving from east to west, as if guided by an atavistic instinct.

His father had gone ahead of them, to hunt for a house. Two months later, he and his mother drove out to California. He was the navigator. He loved studying the route marked in red pen on laminated road maps, each one covering a few hundred miles and all of them bound in a booklet prepared by the AAA. Following the red route, he called out city names and highway numbers, estimated times and distances to each landmark. Six or seven hours, with a lunch break, until they reached the recommended motel. Five whole days, and they got lost only once, on the first afternoon, trying to bypass Chicago.

They made a side trip to the Grand Canyon. Vast, ancient and barren, it left him feeling joyless, standing well back from the edge. And the final day of borderless desert did nothing to lift his spirits, until they crossed the Cajon Pass and descended into a valley of citrus groves. Rolling down the window, he smelled Southern California. It wasn't the ocean he would come to love. It was the oranges.

At San Bernadino, they headed due west, still on Route 66, to a place about sixty miles east of Los Angeles. A small town, with a college, lying at the base of the San Gabriel range, and close to his father's office.

The soaring aviation industry was financing an economic boom, pulling in families like his from the rust-belt cities in the Midwest and housing them in sun-kissed valleys in the shadow of mountains. Only an hour from Los Angeles and the beaches of the Pacific.

They turned off the highway and onto Indian Hill Boulevard, a wide road with orange groves on one side. Why "Indian"? he wondered. Minutes later, after passing more groves, they climbed up and found Mesa Drive. That, he knew, was Spanish.

All the houses were one-storey with ample, well-trimmed front lawns and a driveway. But no garage. 'Don't need them here, son,' his grinning father explained later. All the houses and their front doors were beige, off-white or sand coloured. Blue or red or green would fade in the sun, he was told. All the cars were parked on driveways, none on the street.

His father rushed out of the house when he heard the car approaching. As the family of three hugged on the asphalt driveway, he noticed that his parents clung to each other for an extra few seconds.

'C'mon, son. Let's get everything inside.'

His dad, in an open-neck shirt and wide grin, was his old self.

'Lord, it's hot,' his mother said, dabbing her face with a handkerchief that seemed to come from nowhere. Her dark hair and grey-green eyes looked out of place in the intense sun.

'Nice, isn't it?' his dad said, standing with feet splayed, arm around his son's shoulder and looking at the house.

Two wings stuck out, like skinny legs, on either side of a peaked entrance. Inside, he found few doors in the central area, just adjoining spaces. Through a floor-to-ceiling window at the front of the house, he saw enormous cactus plants. At the back, sliding glass doors opened out to a patio and a pool, and the wire-mesh fence at the edge of the cliff. It was odd, all of it.

Hallways to the left and right of the central area led to bedrooms and bathrooms. The ensuite master bedroom had access to the pool and patio through its own sliding door. He reckoned it was a hundred yards from one end of the house to the other. A football field, in fact.

Not everything, he discovered, was so spacious or exposed. He'd been watching the sprinklers in the neighbour's front lawn. Little cones of water leapt up and died down when the man stuck some pronged thing into the ground. He also noticed that one small section of the lawn was not watered.

Walking over, he saw a metal surface about the size of a manhole cover, with a handle. He reached down.

'Hey, what are you doing?'

The man came toward him, across the damp grass.

'Ah, nothing. I just saw this and…'

'You're from next door, aren't you? The new family.'

'Yes, sir. I'm Stephen.'

'Nice to meet you, Stephen. Where are you from?'

'Detroit.'

'Like it here?'

'Oh, yes, sir. Very much.'

'Well, welcome to the mesa. And say hello to your parents for me.'

Steve smiled and nodded.

'But don't play around with that. It's not for kids.'

At dinner, he spoke about the encounter on the grass.

'What is it, Dad?'

His father looked at his mother, who didn't dissuade him. 'I was going to tell you anyway, sooner or later. It's a fallout shelter.'

'Fallout?'

'Where you go to protect yourself, in case of an attack.'

'A nuclear attack?'

His father hesitated. 'Yes.'

'Like in school, Duck 'n' Cover?'

'That's right. Mr Simpson built it a few years ago, he told me.'

'Wow! Can we go in and see it?'

'No.'

He squeezed his face into a ball.

'You can look into it sometime, if you like,' his father said. 'That's what he told me. But we can't go down there.'

'Never?'

'That's right. It's for his family. Only them.'

'Are we going to build one, too?'

His parents looked at each other.

'That's enough questions for now. I'll get the desert,' his mother said and rose to collect the plates.

The next day, after school, he stood on the driveway, waiting.

'Good evening, Mr Simpson.'

The man was bending down with his forked tool. He walked closer.

'Is it OK if I have a look at your shelter?'

Mr Simpson straightened up and regarded him, unsmiling.

'You want to look?'

'Yes, please.'

'All right. But as I told your father, no one goes down there. Understand?'

Mr Simpson led him to the centre of the lawn, to the metal lid hinged to a concrete ring set into the ground. The handle had a lock on it, which Mr Simpson opened with a key.

'Stand back,' he barked and hauled the lid up. 'OK. Come and look.'

Standing at the edge, he saw a metal ladder bolted to one side of a concrete shaft that dropped down into darkness. Dizzy, he stepped back and took a second to recover.

'What's down there?'

'Oh, we've fixed it up really nice. Bunk beds, lanterns, kerosene stoves and lots of water and canned food. Air vents and a pump system. We'd be all right for two or three weeks.'

In bed that night, he tried to imagine what it would be like living underground. Safe, but the possibility of suffocating was terrifying.

By age fifteen, he had his future mapped out. College and then law school. First, though, there was Citrus Valley High School, where his Russian history teacher had just been dismissed because it was said he was homosexual, and where his white-haired Latin teacher entertained classes by enacting scenes from Pyramus and Thisbe. On winter nights, he and his girlfriend parked in orange groves warmed by hundreds of little flames in smudge pots. The Cuban missile crisis, Kennedy's assassination and race riots in nearby LA did not distract him. The war in Vietnam was too far away.

He was thrown off track only once. Riding in the school bus, books and lunch box on his lap, he was eager to start the day. He tried to block out the noise from the other kids as the bus rattled down the road at the base of the foothills. What did it mean? he kept wondering, *The Grapes of Wrath*? He was certain it would be the main question on his English test. Mrs Peacock always set one broad thematic question followed by several simpler ones, like what's the name of someone's wife or son. In his head, he was repeating the famous line, 'Mine eyes have seen the glory,' when a fight broke out between two Chicanos directly across from him.

One boy fell heavily in the aisle, the bus stopped, and the other boy ran off. The fallen boy had a knife in his stomach. Not much blood and he wasn't screaming, but he was looking up at him.

'Please help!' The voice squeaked like an old man and the eyes ran wild with fear.

He froze, staring down, until the driver pushed him aside and lifted the boy onto a seat. The driver told everyone to get out and drove straight to the hospital. He was still shaking as he watched the bus rumble away. OK, he wasn't trained in first aid or anything, but he should have done something. The kid might die.

The injured boy was back in school a week later but never took the bus again. Each time he saw him, he shrunk back inside himself, trying to forget his panic and his humiliating incapacity.

He was named "Most Likely to Succeed" and offered an athletic scholarship at Stanford. Instead, he chose a small liberal arts college, where he studied Russian language and English literature, captained the football team and let his hair grow. In the spring of his final year, he joined a NAACP march, and he clapped when the speaker at his graduation condemned the war in Vietnam. Otherwise, he kept his head down and moved forward.

Toward Harvard Law School. He applied and was accepted but deferred for a year so that he could get some experience in the "real world". A friend who'd graduated the year before was teaching at a boys' school and recommended him. Two hours north of Boston, in a small town on the Maine coast, a large house with five acres had been converted into classrooms and offices. Most of the teachers lived in town, but he was given a bedroom on the third floor. Thurgood Academy was about as far as you could get from Citrus Valley High School.

For the first time in his life, he was lonely. His girlfriend came up one weekend from New York, didn't like the set up and decided to break it off. He was no longer playing sports, but he enjoyed teaching. It was the challenge, trying to do a little better each day, leading a discussion on a short story or explaining restrictive and non-restrictive modifiers. Obsessed with commas, he felt he was in control.

Until the first day of December 1969.

7

The revolution might not be televised but the draft lottery was.

He could have watched it on the communal TV room at the school, but he wanted to be where no one knew him. The small television mounted on brackets in a corner of the bar was in colour. People began to grumble when it was announced that the scheduled programme was being pre-empted by a special broadcast from Washington DC. He sat by himself, with a beer and pretzels.

The ceremony began with modest fanfare. Officials stood in a large office, an American flag prominent in the background and microphones everywhere. A grey-suited, grey-haired, bespectacled man spoke and stepped aside. A black wooden box was brought in and placed on a high table. It looked like the one in *The Lottery*, the short story his juniors had just read. He shuddered, remembering the gruesome ending, and watched as the box was unlocked, turned upside down and shaken over a large glass bowl, until all 366 blue capsules in the box had fallen into the bowl. Transparency was key.

A second man stepped forward, reached into the bowl and swished around – it also had to be seen to be arbitrary – before plucking out a capsule. The first man opened it and drew out a small piece of paper inside. Facing the cameras, he cleared his throat and said, 'September 14.' The paper with that date was stuck up on a large board opposite the number 001.

All men born on September 14 in the years 1944 to 1950 were now assigned number one in the draft.

More capsules were drawn out, papers extracted, dates revealed and posted on the board in numerical order. Your birthday was your destiny. It was widely known that if your birthday was assigned any number up to about two hundred, you would almost certainly be drafted and probably sent to Vietnam.

His beer and pretzels had disappeared by the time they'd reached fifty. So far, so good. Might get lucky, he thought. He ordered another beer and wiped away the wet mark on the tabletop. Then he heard it. May 19 was given number seventy-five.

He watched in numbed stupor as more dates were posted on the board. Four older men, sitting at the next table, continued playing checkers. A middle-aged couple on their second bottle of wine laughed. Young men cheered when their birthdays got numbers in the two hundreds. The voices sounded muffled, as if he were under water.

The glass bowl emptied, the board filled up and the men in suits said goodnight. When the news came on, people left the bar, but he sat alone, afraid to move. As long as he stayed, it all remained just a television programme. Tomorrow morning he'd discuss Ann Rand with his seniors and after lunch he'd coach them on their SATs.

He drove back to the school through a blackness thickened by snow flurries. His wallet held the dreaded 1-A classification card. 'Available for service.' He knew there were exemptions, but he wasn't a father or a Quaker, and the graduate student deferment had been eliminated.

Rising at daybreak, he hunted around in the library until he found an atlas. He was surprised to see how close it was to China. And how small. He didn't understand what it was about anyway. North and South, Communists and Catholics, unpronounceable names and places. He tried to convince himself that it wouldn't happen. Some bureaucratic error or detail he wasn't aware of.

He called his parents in California and told them not to worry. His lottery number was high, so he'd never be drafted. After finishing his year of teaching, he would go to Harvard Law School. It wasn't exactly a lie because he still thought that could happen.

Christmas came and went. Maybe there had been a mistake or maybe they had changed the system. More likely, the prediction about the numbers was wrong. Then, in early February, he received a letter from his draft board, forwarded by his parents. He was to report for a pre-induction physical at the end of the month. At 7:15am.

Still holding the letter, he looked out at the school grounds. After a thaw, everything was snow-crusted again. At least another month before lacrosse practice would begin. He could get a doctor's letter saying he had a medical problem, like diabetes. He could say he was homosexual or just act weird during the physical.

He drove down the coast to Portland on a blustery, cloudless day. He'd told his headmaster he had a hospital appointment to check on an old heart murmur. He'd combed his longish hair, more out of habit than design, and put on casual clothes, like he was going to class. Beside him, on the front seat, was yesterday's *New York Times* with news of another attack on a US base in Vietnam. Thirteen GIs dead, sixty-three wounded. He couldn't picture it any more than he could the battle between Israel and Egypt reported on the same front page.

The red-brick building rose like a fortress, covering an entire city block. Directly opposite, he saw an equally large public garden, its paths deserted and fir trees stunted. He walked up a flight of shallow steps to a wide door, topped by an eagle sculpted in white stone. Above it, an American flag was whipping in the wind.

Yellow plastic signs pointed around corners to the Armed Forces Examining and Entrance Station, where he met his first uniformed soldier. He was wearing a hat with a wide brim, like a forest ranger. He handed over his letter, had his name checked and was told to wait in a large room. It resembled a school gym, barren except for rows of folding chairs. A hundred other men were already there, facing the front.

He looked at the person next to him, a skinny guy with big ears, wearing a suit that didn't fit. He seemed even more scared than he was.

'Where you from?' he asked.

'Here, in Portland. You?'

'California. But I'm working in Bath.'

'California,' the young man repeated and nodded slowly. 'So you'll be used to the heat, then.'

He saw that he was serious. 'Yeah, I guess so. If I ever get there.'

'Me, I'm going to fly helicopters. Already got a pilot's licence, so I figure I can help out that way.'

The skinny guy tugged on an ear.

'Only, I might get turned down cause I'm too light.' He stood up and faced him. 'What do you think?'

'Sit down, son!' shouted the soldier at the front of the room. 'And keep quiet, all of you.'

'I think you'll be fine,' he whispered.

Half an hour passed. An officer with a face like a car engine appeared at the front. 'Listen up! You're going to take a written test. And if any of you college boys think you can get out of the army by failing it, you're wrong. I'll keep you here until you pass.'

The test, he told people later, wouldn't have screened out third graders. It consisted of one hundred multiple-choice questions, such as "What is the capital of the United States?"

After the written test, the men were given a large paper shopping bag and told to strip down to their underwear. But to keep their socks and shoes on. Their clothes and any letters from doctors, psychiatrists or priests went into the bag.

He'd been in many locker rooms, but nothing could match this. More than a hundred men standing in their underpants and shoes, holding paper bags. He tightened his lips but couldn't suppress a smile.

In groups of four, they trooped into a small room and sat along the back wall. A doctor, clipboard in hand but no white coat, examined them one by one.

The man sitting next to him turned and hissed through a corner of his mouth. 'You worried?'

'No, not really. You?'

'Don't know. I've got flat feet. Sort of. Tried to make it worse by jumping off a bench.'

He stared at him.

'Day after day. It hurt, but better than… you know.'

'OK, who's first?' the doctor asked.

The guy with the flat feet approached the doctor and mentioned his problem. The doctor made him walk around in a circle, stand on tiptoes and bend his knees.

'Right, you're out,' the doctor said and handed him a piece of paper.

Leaving the room, flat-feet grinned at him and gave the thumbs-up.

'Next.'

He rose and stood in front of the doctor.

'Any health problems?'

He had thought about faking a hearing problem but had no documents to support it.

'Not really.'

He'd also practised speaking with a bad stutter but lost his nerve in front of the doctor. His height was measured, body weighed, eyes and ears checked, blood pressure recorded. He turned his head and coughed while the doctor put a finger on his testicles. He bent over and touched his toes.

'Pass. Next.'

Back in the half-filled holding room, he was handed a sheet of paper with the names of organisations listed in alphabetical order, from the Abraham Lincoln Brigade to the Young Communist League. At the bottom it read: "If you have never been a member of any of the above, sign here". He signed and rose to hand it in.

'Sit down,' the officer barked.

More men trickled in, sat down and read the form. They all signed. When the last man was in, the officer told one of them to collect the papers and bring them to him. Putting the stack of papers to one side, the officer called them to attention.

'Successful candidates will be contacted within two months. Then you have ten days to report back here for induction,' he said and waited for the men to calculate. 'Don't plan any trips to Las Vegas.' Deadpan, not even a twisted smile. 'Dismissed.'

Driving back up the coast, he felt his body go limp. He'd been tense ever since entering that building. Scared, disoriented and humiliated. Nothing blatant or physical, just the quiet terror of helplessness.

He had no army in his family history, not unless you counted a great-great-grandfather who survived the Civil War because a diary in his breast pocket stopped a northern bullet. In 1941, his father had been summoned to Washington to work in some office connected to the War Department. Korea meant nothing, and he didn't know anyone who'd been to Vietnam. A friend's brother had enlisted and, as far as he knew, come back.

He'd been paying more attention to the news, though, especially on television. The whirling helicopters, soldiers in rice fields and flag-draped coffins. A recent issue of *Life* magazine featured the faces of 242 Americans killed in a single week. Some were official army photos with dress uniform or combat fatigues, helmet and rifle. Others were from high school yearbooks, suits and ties, maybe the night of the prom. He had thought he was different. Looking at them, he knew he wasn't.

He turned off the highway and onto the road leading into Bath. Mid-afternoon, in mid-winter, in a small town once famous for shipbuilding. A few shoppers about, otherwise dead quiet. He passed through the town's two intersections without having to stop and reached the school on the crest of a hill. The sun was out, and he walked across the grounds toward the ocean. Standing back from the cliff edge, he squinted into the light glinting off the water.

He had two months, maybe less, before he'd have to report for induction. Raise his arm, take the oath and get bussed off to some place for basic training. He could go to Canada. It was in all the papers, the thousands of "draft dodgers" who'd done that. Montreal was only a few hours away. But it probably wasn't that easy to get across the border. Besides, it seemed desperate. Too final.

The conversation with the headmaster proved difficult. He'd never really liked the man but felt a loyalty because he'd given him his first job and, despite the gap in years, had treated him with respect. The bald head on top of the tall man dipped as he explained that he had to go home because his father was seriously ill. One lie necessitated others, but he told the truth when he said he wouldn't be coming back.

8

He felt better when he was on the road and back in control. The headmaster had said he "didn't really have a choice", but he knew that wasn't true. He had too many choices, and he picked one a lot farther away than Montreal. Pulling out to pass, he came face to face with a speeding Greyhound bus and retreated back into his lane. The window wipers were just about winning the battle with the clinging sleet. Take it nice and slow, he kept saying. This'll stop soon and it'll be clear sailing. Nothing lasts for long here on the Maine coast.

Sleet turned to slush as he eased into Massachusetts. The next exit was for Boston. He could go straight to Charlestown and register for his law degree in the fall. And who's to say that wouldn't happen when this was all over? He wasn't really running away. Just being smart. The irony was, he could use a little legal advice right now. Did you go to prison for not showing up? Could be, but they're not going to send the FBI, for god's sake!

Slush and sludge in New York gave way to green-budding trees in rural Pennsylvania. A good end to a long day. Bending over to sign the motel register, he hesitated, wondering if he should use another name. In the box-like room that night, he thought about money. Road tolls, gas, food and the motel room had already eaten into the $215 he had managed to bring with him. He figured it would take four more days, driving about ten hours a day.

Pennsylvania, Ohio, Indiana and Illinois. Farmland as far as the eye could see, fields flat as pancakes, four-lane highways and two-block towns. He remembered driving across country with his mother, when everything was still possible. Speeding through those same open spaces, he now felt his world shrinking. He focused on the decisions he could still make. When to pass, where to turn, how far to roll down the window.

In the Great Plains, abandoned wooden water towers stood under a big sky, while tractors churned soil and spread fertiliser before disappearing into barns as wide as airplane hangars. Billboards advertised shaving cream, toothpaste and beer. Near the big cities, he heard the familiar voice of NPR, a welcome sound amid the babel of local stations. Glenn Campbell and folk rock replaced Stevie Wonder and Motown. He also heard about a bombing at an army base in New Jersey, said to be revenge for the police shooting of a Black activist in Chicago. No one was killed, but the injuries were severe.

He avoided the snow-bound Rockies, swung north and sped through the plateaus of Wyoming and the deserts of Utah and Nevada. Smooth sailing, all the way, until the fifth and final day. Rounding a mountain curve, just over the California line, he stopped. Rocks were bouncing off the road and traffic was at a standstill in both directions. He imagined the trickle of stones becoming an avalanche, blocking his path. No way forward. The taste of panic rose in his throat, and he thumped the steering wheel with both hands, screaming so loud he didn't hear the horns blaring behind him. Someone knocked on his window and said that the road was clear.

Crossing the Donner Pass, he rode down the western slope of the Sierras, past pine-covered hills and spacious shopping malls, past Sacramento and spreading agricultural land. He stopped for lunch at a café surrounded by drab brown hills. On the other side of the road, cows munched scrub grass. Beyond them, he saw rows and rows of stunted trees, which the café owner said was a vineyard.

At the northern reaches of San Francisco Bay, he felt a tingle of excitement. From the rush-hour freeway, however, he could see only storage tanks, industrial parks and tract houses. But he knew it was there and was soon rewarded with a view of the burnt-red towers of the Golden Gate.

He swung down an exit into Berkeley and onto a main thoroughfare. Shops and restaurants, mostly single storey, like any other town he'd passed through during the long journey, though the traffic divider was a garden of green grass and flowering bushes. And up ahead, he saw the trees of the campus.

Dwight Way was on the south side, the student quarter, with cheaper rents. The 1920s building, thin with a fire escape, had mustard-coloured stucco walls. Inside, the narrow hallway was painted lime green.

'Welcome to Bezerkely,' John said with a wide smile.

The ground-floor apartment was roomy and sunny. Windows overlooked a scruffy back yard and the grass strip separating that building from the adjacent one.

'Nice place,' he said, putting down his suitcase. 'Thanks for letting me stay.'

'It's great to see you.'

It had been a sudden decision, after the physical in Portland. He needed to get away as soon and as far as possible. Could have gone to Southern California, but he didn't want to be anywhere near his parents. The Bay Area, with its counterculture, seemed a better choice. He knew John was a graduate student there, and he'd gotten his telephone number from a mutual friend.

They looked at each other, a little apprehensive. They hadn't been close, just studied Russian literature together. But four years at a small college meant familiarity and, in their case, mutual respect, though not much insight. Sort of like brothers who didn't really know each other.

'Hey, you look exhausted,' John said. 'Let's get something to eat.'

John led him up the street, past a string of apartment buildings from different decades, mostly stucco, others brick, redwood or adobe. The few family houses looked out of place, as if they wished they were somewhere else.

'This is Telegraph,' John said when they reached a busy one-way street. 'The university's down there.'

It was getting dark. Cars moved down the street at the same speed as people on the sidewalk. They passed a corner store with windows for walls. Inside, students stood in front of bulky machines, copying pages, chapters and whole books, on an industrial scale.

John led him into Jenny's Kitchen, where the square wooden tables were so close you could hear what was said at the next table.

'So, what happened?' John asked in a low voice when they'd ordered. 'I heard you were teaching. But you didn't get fired, I'm sure of that.'

'No, nothing like that.' He fiddled with his knife and fork, making sure them were lined up. He'd been wondering what he should tell John. 'I got number seventy-five in the lottery.'

John blew out his lips and nodded.

'I had the physical. It was scary. Like you were already in the army.'

'But you weren't actually drafted, right?'

'Technically, no. But they'll send another letter ordering me for induction, when I'll be "led into" the army. What a stupid word.'

'So, you just left the teaching job?'

'Yeah. I decided I just couldn't do it. Told the school my dad was in hospital and drove out here. Gave them your address.'

'AWOL.'

He looked straight at John, at his unblinking eyes and untroubled face, which slowly broke into a smile.

'Right. I guess that's what it is.'

'I was lucky. I got 283.'

They both looked down, at the scuffed tabletop.

John spoke. 'You know, I heard some guys who want to go to Vietnam are trying to switch their numbers with people like you.'

'Is that possible?'

'I don't know. It's what I heard. The whole thing's crazy, isn't it?'

He mumbled in agreement and let himself get lost in the noise swelling around them. He almost didn't notice when their food came. A burger and fries for John, mushroom risotto for him.

'What are you studying?' he asked after a few bites. 'Something useful, I hope.'

'A hundred per cent. Comparative linguistics is the key to understanding human culture. Including world peace.' Again, a playful smile on his face. 'You see, the language we speak influences culture. It doesn't just reflect it.'

'Eskimos and snow, right?'

'Yes, but that's just vocabulary. There's new research showing how grammar actually affects how we think and act.'

'Such as?'

'Well, Hopi doesn't have tenses, which explains their fluid sense of time.'

'So, if I use bad grammar, I'm more likely to commit a crime?'

Now it was John who took a moment to make sure his friend wasn't serious. 'Absolutely correct,' he said in a bad mock-German accent.

Back in the apartment, they drank coffee.

'No one knows you're here, right?'

He nodded.

'What are you going to do? If I remember correctly, you don't exactly sit on the sidelines, waiting for something to happen.'

He took a deep breath. 'I don't know. It was difficult just coming here. Lying to the school and to my parents.'

'You could go to Canada.'

'I know, but I don't want to leave the US. Maybe I wouldn't be able to come back. Besides, I don't have an argument with the country, just the politicians and this stupid war.'

'OK, but are you against this war or all wars?'

It wasn't a question he'd asked himself, even during the long days on the road.

'I just don't want to kill someone. Or get killed. It's as simple as that.'

In the morning, he called his parents in Southern California.

'No, I'm in New York, staying with a friend... No, not Helen. That's over... Yes, I'm fine. We have an early spring break because it's so cold up there... I will. Bye.'

He put down the phone with a heavy clunk. He was alone in the apartment, a dull morning, with the threat of rain. He could keep on lying, he realised, because he always called them, never the other way around. Come the summer, though, when the teaching was finished, he'd have to think of something else.

9

His immediate problem was solved by a part-time job in a bookstore, enabling him to pay his share of the food and utility bills. He also found he got on well with John. They both liked a tidy apartment and took turns cooking in the evening. John spent a lot of time on campus, while he converted the couch and coffee table into his "space". John said he could stay as long as he wanted.

March turned into April, with warming days and little rain. During his lunch break, he often walked to the campus, where crowds on Sproul Plaza listened to speakers on the steps of the administration building. Anti-war, Free Speech, Black Panthers, Women's Liberation and Socialist Workers. Even when there was no rally, the plaza resembled a county fair, with tables set up to distribute leaflets and solicit signatures.

He picked up a flier with the photo of a helicopter hovering above a crowd.

'That was here last year,' said the young woman behind the table. 'We were protesting against the police killing of James Rector – you heard of him? No, well, they sprayed us with tear gas from that helicopter. Like in Vietnam. The war's come home.'

He nodded, recognising the phrase from somewhere.

'Want to sign our petition? We're calling for an immediate withdrawal of troops.'

He signed and turned to leave.

'We also protest against the army presence on campus,' she continued. 'ROTC, the officer training course. Every Friday at noon. Why not join us?'

'Ah… I'll see.'

Back at John's place after work, he found he had several leaflets stuffed in his pockets. One had a headline "50,000 GIs Dead" above a drawing of a soldier's helmet perched on a rifle butt, the bayonet stuck into the ground like a hastily erected cross. Another leaflet screamed: "Stop Militarism in Schools! Children Should Not Be Taught to Kill!" Can't argue with that, he said to himself. Should have discussed the war in class. At least, had them read something like *The Red Badge of Courage*.

He was about to get up when his attention was caught by the striking image of a broken rifle, the two parts held aloft by a pair of hands. In the small print, he read that the War Resisters League was holding an open house on Saturday.

Taking the afternoon off, he walked the short distance to an address in the Claremont district. A handsome early twentieth-century home, redwood shingles, deep front porch and mature rhododendron bushes. Not what he'd expected.

Stepping through the open door, he joined a bustle of middle-aged mothers, bright-faced students, bow-tied professors and barefoot hippies. Others were dressed as cowboys, clowns and cosmonauts. A long table offered leaflets and newsletters, while another sold books and buttons.

Above the fireplace, in the high-ceilinged room, he spotted that image again: two pieces of a broken rifle held in the air. He stared at it. Was he a "war resister"? "Draft dodger" was probably more accurate, though "draft evader" sounded better.

The large backyard was filled the acrid smell of cannabis and the sound of live music. Two male guitarists flanked a woman singer in jeans and high heels, hairband and sequins on her cheeks. The make-shift stage was sinking under the weight of mountainous speakers. He was offered a joint, took a toke and passed it to a thin man in a monk's robe, who was parading around the yard with a placard that read: "Don't let your Karma run over my Dogma".

A letter from the office of the President of the United States arrived two days later. It had been forwarded by his parents to Maine and redirected by the school to John's address. The eagle was there on top, arrows in one talon and laurels in the other. He was to report to the Armed Forces Induction Centre on S. Broadway in Los Angeles on the fifteenth of the month. The small print at the bottom informed him that transportation would be provided if required, that he should bring a change of clothes and that failure to appear meant a fine and imprisonment.

He slid the letter into a plastic folder, where it joined his draft card, birth certificate and social security card. Would he really go to prison? Don't be silly. No one was going to look for him, and even if they did, they wouldn't find him in Berkeley, with tens of thousands of students.

He would stay where he was and build a new life. At a "free box" on the sidewalk, he picked up a small, triangular-shaped bookcase that fit perfectly into a corner in John's front room. He arranged his books, the ones he'd bought now outnumbering those he'd brought with him. He got a library card, learnt to use a wok and saw a series of Japanese movies on campus. He and John planned a camping trip to Yosemite.

It didn't happen.

He watched the televised footage of the clash at Kent State. Soldiers with rifles chased protestors over swathes of green grass, while other students perched on hills, like spectators at a Civil War battleground. Smoke from tear gas cannisters obscured the scene, but the gun shots rang out with clarity. A woman bent down over a fallen body. Then stood up in disbelief.

Alone in the small room, he felt lost. Four unarmed students had been shot dead. He grit his teeth and still it didn't make sense. Staring at the screen, hearing but not listening to a news reporter, something broke inside him. The wall that had stood between him and the world – allowing him to believe that "things like this don't happen" in the United States, not among middle-class white people – that barrier collapsed.

By noon the following day, the main plaza on campus was filled with people waving banners and chanting anti-war slogans. Hundreds of helmeted police brandished batons and rifles with bayonets. At first, it was a spirited if chaotic stand-off, the protestors and police milling around, sizing each other up, like boxers. Protestors suddenly appeared on the steps of the administration building, shouting, 'Killers off campus,' referring to the officer training programme.

When the police moved in to disperse them, they huddled together. The police struck with batons and dragged away a dozen protestors. Urged on by the crowd, the remaining protestors fought back and engaged in running battles with the police, enacting a cops-and-robbers pantomime across the plaza, charging into the open and retreating behind trees. But the farce was belied by the army helicopters buzzing overhead and the rifles pointing down from roofs.

Standing at a safe distance, he saw cannisters of tear gas explode and heard wild shouting. A group of protestors swarmed around him and swept him up to the main building. The police had bunched up on the shallow stone steps to guard the doors, while the protestors surged forward. The police responded with more tear gas and beat anyone who mounted the steps.

He was coughing from the smoke when someone handed him a bottle. Before he knew what was happening, she lit the twisted cloth wick and yelled, 'Throw it!' He did, as hard as he could, and when it burst into flames, he felt a sickening sense of satisfaction. Seconds later, he was handcuffed and bundled into a van, along with a dozen others.

During the hour-long journey, he listened to them talk about "the people" and "the pigs" and how the university was "complicit in the killing". They sat on hardwood benches bolted to the floor along the sides of the van, the only air coming through a small wire-mesh window. Roughly half men and women, they looked like graduate students and seemed to know each other. The woman who'd given him the Molotov cocktail was directly opposite him, a purple bruise on her arm and a bloodied cut on her forehead.

'You OK?'

'Yeah.'

'Cheer up. We're going to one of the finest prisons in California. A disused military base. Ironic, isn't it?'

The others joined in her snickering, while he managed a wan smile.

'Don't worry,' she said. 'We have lawyer friends. We'll be out in the morning.'

One by one, they were fingerprinted, photographed and had their personal details recorded. After some kind of goulash was served in aluminium bowls, they slept on coir mats on the concrete cell floor. In the morning, they were given a banana and coffee before all charges were dismissed by a judge and they were released.

On the journey back, unshackled and emboldened, the others congratulated each other and began to plan their next "action". The jubilant voices and camaraderie grated on him. Two months ago, he was enjoying his teaching and gearing up for law school. Since then, he'd quit his job, lied to his parents and earned himself a police record. No charges, but suppose they checked with the army or his draft board?

'Where were you last night?' John asked when he heard the apartment door open and close.

'Long story.'

He came into the kitchen and sat down opposite his friend.

'God! You look like something the cat dragged in. What happened?'

He hung his head in silence.

'You weren't in that riot on campus, were you?'

'Afraid so. Spent last night in detention.'

'Detention?'

'Santa Rita Prison, near Dublin. They let us go this morning.'

He showered while John made them both breakfast. After the eggs and toast, they again faced each other, with mugs of coffee.

'What happened?'

'I don't know. Just got caught up in the chaos.'

'And?'

'I threw a Molotov cocktail at the admin building.'

'Jesus Christ!'

'Yeah, I didn't plan it. Someone handed it to me, and I threw it.'

John shook his head.

'It's hard not to want to do something. But you've got to be careful.'

He fiddled with the mug, turning it around and around.

'It's good you got out so quickly, but…'

'I know. That's what scares me. I don't know where this is heading.'

John started to say something about the "crazy lottery" but stopped when he saw the pain on his friend's face. He was the lucky one who would get a nice graduate degree and never have to worry about Vietnam.

'Don't blame yourself,' John said. 'The war is shit. We all know that.'

'Yeah, but now I'm in that shit and don't know how to get out.'

'Maybe you should talk to someone.'

The United Congregational Church stood on a corner, only a block from John's place. Studiously discreet, it was easily mistaken for a university building, except for the needle-sharp steeple rising above the sycamore trees. A large box, with "free" painted on the side and filled with clothes, squatted beside the walkway to the front door. Next to it, a wooden signboard nailed to a shoulder-high post announced the timetable for church services and secular meetings. On Thursdays from 4:00–6:00pm in the basement, the Berkeley Peace Cooperative offered help to "anyone seeking alternatives to military service".

There was no one there when he arrived, so he picked up a pamphlet from a table. "Clergy and Laity Concerned about Vietnam" was printed on cheap paper. The front page set out the group's stance, arguing that "the time for silence had passed" and advocating "an end to conflict and amnesty for draft resisters". Inside, short pieces covered the "Christian Response to War", "Our Vietnamese Brothers and Sisters" and "The Dangers of Nuclear Energy". The back page listed organisations, local and state, dedicated to social change.

'You might find that useful.'

He turned to face a woman not much older than himself and without any obvious clerical insignia.

'I'm Marjorie Fitzpatrick,' she said, coming closer and holding out a hand. 'I do counselling here. The secular kind, that is.'

'Hi. I'm Stephen,' he said, taking her hand.

She looked at him with large, bright eyes.

'Nice to meet you, Stephen. Here, take a seat and let's talk.' She gestured toward two chairs and a table partially hidden behind a folding screen.

The stone floor and stone walls were cold. A crypt stripped of its caskets, tombs and memorials. A place for the dead.

'I know,' she said, reading his thoughts. 'It can be a little creepy down here.'

He told her about his lottery number, the physical in Portland, the move to Berkeley, the induction letter and his participation in an anti-war rally, leaving out the night in prison. He spoke matter-of-factly, having rehearsed the chronology and wording. An orderly sequence of decisions and events, it made him feel better.

'There's nothing shameful in what you've done,' she said with a benign smile. 'I want you to understand that. I know it's hard, because we are trained to think that breaking the law or disobeying the government is wrong. But it's not wrong when your motive is to stop a greater evil. In this case, the killing of innocent civilians.'

He shrank back, unsure of his place in the landscape she had opened up to him.

'I don't want to kill anyone,' he stammered.

'Of course. And you don't want anyone to be killed. Is that right?'

He nodded.

'Have you thought of applying for Conscientious Objector status?'

'I… don't have any religious beliefs.'

'You don't have to say you believe in a Supreme Being, or in any god. Only that your religious background prevents you from fighting in a war.'

'I couldn't say that.'

'Never went to Sunday School?'

'Only as a little kid.'

'I see.' Again, a beneficent smile. 'There is a case before the Supreme Court right now that would allow you to claim CO status on the basis of your personal moral principles. Without any religious belief.'

'When will it be decided?'

'Soon, we hope.'

He looked down at his hands, clasped in his lap.

'There's also the Peace Corps.'

'You mean going to Africa?'

'Yes. You can get trained and work as a volunteer in lots of places. Not only Africa. For the two years that you're in the Peace Corps, you won't be drafted.'

'And afterward?'

'Who knows? The war might be over? Or the draft might be over. Or they might change the rules.'

Not fool-proof then. He said he'd think about it.

'Good. There's no rush.'

'But there is,' he said to himself on his way back to John's apartment. Sooner or later, the lies would catch up with him. Or maybe the police would. His earlier optimism had been shaken by the news that the FBI had set up a new force dedicated to tracking down draft resisters. Several thousand had already been arrested.

He wandered up to Telegraph, where he stood, motionless, as people flowed by him. People his age, who looked and talked like him, but with some idea of where they were going.

'I don't know,' John said as they ate dinner together that night. 'It's your decision. But I think it's best to fight the system from the inside.'

'Maybe,' he said, 'but I'm beginning to realise that I'm no longer in the system.'

'What does that mean?'

'I just have this feeling that I can't stay here. I'll get sucked into more and more… stuff. No idea where it might end.'

In a bookshop, looking at a shelf of large-format photography books, he picked out one on Africa. Glossy colour images of people dancing, hunting, crouching over cooking pots, sitting in front of straw huts and scratching in parched fields. Lots of beads and not many clothes. Sliding it back into place, his eye snagged on another book. *Discover Mendocino County.* Plate after plate of stunning landscapes, mountains, rivers and forests. He found it on a map, north of San Francisco, halfway to Oregon. Perfect.

10

The dark blue Vega got a tune-up and for the second time that year, he was on the move. He wrote to his parents, preferring to lie on paper this time, saying that he had met a girl, they were travelling to Europe together for the summer and he'd be back in touch in September. He smiled to himself, thinking that sounded nice.

John made him a special meal and they talked late into the night.

'Next time I see you,' John said in the morning, 'you'll have flowers in your hair.'

'And you'll be a professor with grey hair.'

Stuck in the Bay Area morning traffic, he reflected on how much he'd come to value John's friendship. And how much he'd miss him. All through high school and college, he'd been "popular" but never developed a close bond with anyone. Never really opened up, let anyone in. Not even his girlfriends, all two of them.

After Sausalito, he turned off Route 101 and cut through the hills to the coast road. An hour or two longer, John said, but nicer. He sailed past Muir Beach, Stinson Beach and Point Reyes, and into Bodega Bay, where the water sparkled.

He'd never seen the Pacific Ocean. It had been too far away during his high school years in Southern California, and to reach the beaches you had to drive through parts of LA known for race riots. Besides, they had a swimming pool. Still, he knew what those beaches looked like, and this northern coast could not be more different. All cliff and cove, and not a swimmer in sight.

It felt good, going north, wind whipping through the window and waves crashing not ten yards away. Ever since the campus riot and the night in prison, he'd been unsure, double guessing himself. This was another escape, he knew that, but it felt more directed than the flight from the east.

Running a hand through his hair, he leant back and sighed. It would be a big change, of course. A chance to clear his head. All that ferocious chanting and marching, that energy of conviction and urgency of action, had broken through his barriers and left him unguarded. Staying in Berkeley would only have led to another holding cell.

That was all behind him as he cruised along a road twisting between hill and water. Few cars and no trucks, just the wind and the waves and soft rock music on a San Francisco station. Would he ever go back?

He saw Mendocino on a headland in the midday sun. Crossing a low bridge at the mouth of a river, he turned onto a road that led past a white clapboard church, a stone-filled cemetery, a gas station and a disused water tower. In the centre of town, on his right, a row of shops sold jewellery, paintings, soaps, candles and glassware, all produced by local residents. On the other side, beyond an open field, the ocean spread out, its true-blue surface decorated with tiny white ribbons.

Mendocino was named after a sixteenth-century viceroy of New Spain but remained only a name on maps until the Gold Rush. In 1850, a shipwreck off the headland caught the attention of an entrepreneur who built the sawmill that started the timber industry in Northern California. The logging community soon developed into a town, populated mainly by New Englanders, Portuguese from the Azores and Chinese from Canton. The white church was erected, a post office established and a dozen more sawmills built, while the local Pomo Indians were driven onto a nearby reservation. After World War Two, the town declined until someone from San Francisco built an arts centre and turned it into a haven for artists, dissidents and dreamers.

He took a room in a B&B, painted daffodil yellow, facing the ocean. Collapsing on the lumpy bed, he woke up in late-afternoon silence and decided to take a walk. Down the porch steps and across the road to the field, where he found a headland path dotted with fragrant lilac bushes.

It reminded him of the Maine coast, except that the coves were sandy and even the rocks looked soft. He came upon a man sitting rigid on a fold-up canvas stool, fishing with an incredibly long pole. Raising his hand, he mouthed a greeting, but got no response. He continued along the sweep of the headland, passing couples on benches and solo walkers coming in the opposite direction. Their easy smiles and hellos underlined his solitude, and he was glad to see the flagpole of the local school, marking his return to town.

In the morning, after breakfast, he sat in the communal living room and got into a conversation with the owner, who sized him up quickly.

'There is one place I've heard of,' the man said. 'It's called River Ridge. Some kind of commune or farm. Ask Maggie in the bookstore, just down the street. She can tell you about it.'

Maggie was sitting behind the counter. Rimless glasses and white hair cut short with bangs.

'Any good?' he asked.

She showed him the cover. *Poems by Robinson Jeffers.*

'Wonderful writer,' she said. 'The Beatles used his lyrics, you know.'

'Never heard of him.'

'He lived a long way from here, south of San Francisco. But it's the same coast and he gets the feeling right.'

She produced a taut smile.

'You interested in poetry?'

'No. I mean, not really. I…'

'You're after local history, aren't you?'

'Well, in a roundabout way. You see, I was hoping you could tell me about a place called River Ridge. The guy over at MacIntosh House said you might know it.'

She stood up, took off her glasses and studied him with pale blue eyes.

'I've been there only once, to visit a friend. She liked it all right. But her kids didn't. Wanted regular school. So she went back to the Bay Area.'

'Do they welcome visitors? I mean, can I just show up?'

'They do and you can.'

She gave him directions. Ten miles or so up the coast road, then a dirt track through the forest to a clearing.

'That's where they keep vehicles. Most of them don't own cars, of course. They're the enemy,' she said with a hoarse laugh. 'From there, it's about a mile walk to the farm.'

'I guess I can manage that,' he said.

'Sure. But keep your wits about you. There's a few crazies up there.' Then she winked. 'And maybe some undercover people, too. Know what I mean?'

He drove past the church and water tower to the highway. After fifteen miles, he realised he must have missed the turning. Doubling back, he spotted it, hidden by foliage but more visible from the other side of the road. He bumped along a rutted track, crossed a shallow stream and entered dense woods.

Rocks spat out as he coaxed the Vega through the forest, rising all the time. Redwoods, pine and fir trees crowded close on both sides, making it difficult to see anything up ahead. The track narrowed, the trees thinned, and ferns brushed against the car. Only a few miles she'd said, but it felt like a lot more.

The car hit something, lurched and came to a stop. Getting out, he saw there was no damage, but standing there, in the middle of the forest, he had second thoughts. This is crazy. Probably took the wrong turn from the highway. Maybe the place doesn't exist anymore. And what's to say the bookstore woman didn't send him on a wild goose chase? Even if he did find the place, what are the chances he'd like it? A commune, whatever that was. Rain-soaked tents and children running around naked.

The light widened and he saw the clearing. A Jeep, an old Volkswagen, two pick-ups and a hand-painted sign informing him that he had entered River Ridge Farm and that no vehicles were allowed beyond that point. Having locked his suitcase in the car and checked the doors, he shouldered his backpack and found a path that led back into the woods.

Minutes later, he was in a smaller clearing, where teenage boys sat on a boulder, smoking what looked like cigarettes.

'This the way to River Ridge Farm?'

The boys nodded.

'Is it far?'

'No,' one said. 'Not if you stay on the path.'

The others snickered.

'OK. Thanks.'

'See you later, alligator,' the boy cried.

'In a while, crocodile,' the others said in unison.

He raised an uncertain hand to them and stared at the path that disappeared into the woods. He could go back to the car, return to Mendocino and find a job. The bookstore maybe. He felt the boys' eyes on him. No, that would be a retreat.

Shifting the pack higher up on his back, he plunged ahead, each step cushioned by crushed needles and woodchips. He heard voices, which seemed to come from a great distance but a minute later saw a river. Children splashed and paddled in shallow pools, while adults bathed and washed clothes, left to dry on exposed rocks. Some were naked, others in white underclothes, their faces serene. It reminded him of a Biblical painting.

He felt self-conscious. His hair was long now, twice the length as in college, but only half as long as some of these men. Dressed in beige chinos, a button-down shirt and brown leather shoes, he looked positively Ivy League. Out of place, just like his first day at Citrus Valley High School.

'You come to visit?'

A large man, probably in his fifties.

'Yes, if that's all right.'

'Come for a day, stay for a year. That's what I say.'

The man's roar was friendly enough, though he wasn't sure how to respond.

'I'll take you up to the farm. We're just getting cleaned up here before lunch. I'm Ted, by the way.'

The path through the trees rose slightly and brought them to a large open area. Bordered by the forest, it was a patchwork of vegetable gardens and flower beds, with a greenhouse, a barn, a cluster of cabins and a large house. Everything was neat and trim, the undergrowth cut back at the perimeter and the grass recently mowed. The path to the house, sitting on the highest point, was marked by small, white-painted rocks.

'That's where Gavin and his wife live,' Ted explained.

Gavin, he learnt, was a professor from San Francisco State who had "dropped out", bought the land and built the house about twelve years ago. He and his wife allowed friends to come and build their own cabins. Together they all worked the land and fed each other. More than half the group, about forty at present, had been there since the beginning.

'There are no rules,' Ted continued. 'Except that you can't use chemicals to grow food or flowers. And everyone has to contribute something. Gardening, cooking, cleaning, firewood. That kind of thing.'

Cash donations from guests were appreciated but not obligatory. Some members received unemployment checks, others got money from their parents, and a few worked part-time in Mendocino.

Ted's cabin resembled an igloo with a glass dome. Steve ducked down, waddled through the short tunnel and straightened up inside an octagonal space, with raised floorboards and wood-panelled walls. Four walls had window, the others mounted bookshelves. It was surprisingly large, containing a round table, two armchairs, a proper bed and a kitchen area with a sink and gas ring.

'Built it myself. With help from the Whole Earth Catalogue,' Ted said, running a hand over his close-cropped hair. 'Before that, the only wood I'd ever worked with was a pencil.'

'Cosy,' Steve said, choosing the only word he could think of.

'You can stay here, if you like. I've got a sleeping bag and a fold-up cot. No electricity or running water, but there's a shower and toilet outside, with a metal roof. I share it with two other cabins.'

'That's really nice, but you don't have to.'

'You want to stay or not?' Ted smiled, deepening the creases around his soft brown eyes.

'I do. Thanks.'

He chose a corner with bookshelves and Ted set up the cot and added a small side table.

'That all you got?' he asked pointing to the backpack.

'No. There's a suitcase, in the car.'

'You can get that after lunch. What's your name, by the way?'

'Stephen. Steve.'

They ate in the barn, sitting on benches at long tables. No prayers and little conversation until the dishes were brought out from the kitchen in the house. Barley soup, baked bread and pasta with asparagus, fresh from the garden. Ted introduced him to the people sitting at their table as "a visitor from Berkeley". After a few half-hearted questions, they ignored him.

He relished the good food and listened to the voices eddying around him. Quiet for such a big group, including children.

'Does the owner eat with you?' he asked Ted at his side.

'No. Gavin and Catherine eat in the house. And Sharon, the accountant. She lives in there, too.'

Ted started talking to a boy, about eight or nine. Something important, it seemed. He wondered if it could be his son.

'Yeah! Strawberries!'

A cheer went up when bowls of berries and pitchers of cream were placed on the tables. When his turn came, he spooned out very little, unsure how many others would use the same bowl, then passed it to a young mother, who hand-fed her toddler. Smiles all around until the child spluttered and spat, leaving a red stain on Steve's shirt.

'Oh, damn. Sorry,' the mother said. 'Xavier loves them but can't swallow yet. Give me your shirt and I'll wash it.'

'That's OK. I can do that at Ted's.'

'All right. Not a very warm welcome, though. It's your first day, right?'

'Yes. First meal, too.'

'But not the last. You know the saying.'

He looked at her.

'Strawberries are forever.'

He retrieved the suitcase from his car and lugged it back through the woods to Ted's cabin. The light from the dome lit up everything, except the recesses in the many corners. Feeling stuffy, he pushed open a hinged window and was about to turn around, when he heard a rapid hammering. He waited, listened and spotted a bird with a white neck and crimson crest, drilling into a tree trunk. 'Surely not at night,' he said to himself.

On the low pinewood table, his small travel clock, date diary and paperback of *Fathers and Sons* competed for space with the kerosene lantern Ted had supplied. When he got everything just right, he placed his toiletry kit next to the cushion doubling as a pillow and shoved the suitcase under the cot.

That's it, he thought with a chuckle, as he lay down. A cot in a cabin. No frills and communal meals. It's hippie boot camp. Despite the industrious woodpecker, he fell asleep.

When he woke, he went outside. Ted was sitting with a group of children by the barn, while other adults weeded in the gardens and chopped wood. All unhurried. He took the path behind the cabins, as Ted had advised, and found himself surrounded by moss-covered trees and leafy ferns. The gnarled roots of a redwood stood head high and he spotted the telltale holes but not the woodpecker. He listened to bird calls but couldn't see anything in the trees. Maybe Ted had a bird book.

As the path narrowed and rose, the sound of rushing water grew louder. At the top of the path, he saw a waterfall cascading down a rocky face and into a pool. He figured it was the same river he'd seen people bathing in when he'd arrived earlier that day. The river ran in all directions, he later learnt. From the waterfall, it headed south, curved north and twisted east before flowing west and emptying in the Pacific near Mendocino. Always on the move.

'So, why'd you come up here?' Ted asked.

After a light supper in the barn, they were inside the cabin, sharing a joint. He'd been wondering when he would ask.

'No reason, really. Needed a change. That's all.'

'OK, but why now?'

He told him about his past. High school and college. Teaching and the draft. Berkeley and prison.

Ted pushed out his lips and nodded.

'Course I'm too old to get drafted,' he said. 'But if I'd been in your shoes, I'd have done the same. Maybe more.'

Ted explained that he had come out to San Francisco in 1958 and lived in Haight-Ashbury, where he joined a collective that supported homeless people. He learnt carpentry and helped renovate poor-quality housing. After a bad acid trip with his girlfriend, they separated and he found his way to Mendocino and River Ridge.

'Seven years now,' he said, scratching his clean-shaven cheek. 'But I don't feel the itch.'

11

He blinked in the fractured light coming through the dome above him. It was quiet, just past eight in the morning. Ted was gone and he had to think for a moment about what he should do and how to do it. A funny kind of freedom.

He showered outside, shaved inside and changed his clothes. He wanted to tell someone what he was doing. That would make it more real, more believable even to himself. But also defeat the whole purpose. Besides, there was no telephone, except in the house. He could write it all down in a letter, to John, for example.

In the barn, only two tables were occupied, about a dozen people eating breakfast. It was served buffet-style on a massive sideboard. Hard-boiled eggs, granola, fruit, honey, yogurt, pitchers of milk and thermoses of tea and coffee.

He helped himself and sat down.

'Good morning,' he ventured.

The others mumbled a greeting and resumed their low-volume conversations and slow-motion feeding.

'There's bacon and scrambled eggs, if you ask in the house,' someone said.

'Thanks. This looks good by itself.'

'You vegetarian?'

'No, but I don't eat a lot of meat.'

'From Berkeley, right?'

'Yeah, I… drove up from there.'

'Student?'

'No. I'm, I mean, I was a teacher.'

Heads turned toward him.

'Teacher?' a middle-aged woman said. 'We need someone to teach the kids. Only nine of them now, but they're running wild.'

'That's no bad thing, of course,' a bearded man chipped in. 'My ten-year-old is a lot more self-sufficient than I was at her age. But she needs to read properly and learn how to write more than one sentence.'

'Ted tried for a while, but it didn't catch on,' the woman put in. 'Maybe you could try?'

Expectant faces were trained on him, forks in mid-air.

'Sure. I'd like that. Maybe I should get all the parents together first and work out a plan.'

'Good idea. Just make sure Ted's there.'

They held a meeting late that afternoon inside the house: four couples, two single mothers and a single father, a range of ages and dress styles. He asked them what they wanted and together they put together a syllabus and a schedule. Classes would start after breakfast at nine and run until noon, Monday to Friday. The emphasis would be on reading, writing and basic mathematics, with no grades or tests. Afternoons would be voluntary, either arts and crafts with Ted or tuition with him.

'What about some physical exercise? Like calisthenics or running?' he ventured.

'Learning to sit might be better,' a mother replied. 'They get enough running as it is.'

'OK. But something that teaches teamwork? Volleyball, for example?'

'No,' came a man's voice. 'Too competitive.'

In the cabin after dinner, he made an inventory of the books on Ted's shelves. Mostly history, natural history, geography, science fiction and a few battered novels, *Slaughterhouse-Five* and *Animal Farm* among them. Using his never-far-away notebook, he began to plan lessons, not for juniors and seniors in an expensive prep school, but for children aged five to fifteen in the woods.

Needing to get supplies for the kids, he volunteered for the commune's weekly drive into town to pick up provisions and run errands.

'If you see something good on Native Americans at the bookstore, get it for me,' Ted said.

'OK. I'm going there anyway.'

'And I'd consider getting a pair of boots for yourself. Those aren't much use here, especially when it rains.'

He looked down at his scuffed deck shoes. Same old problem.

'Get a cash advance from Sharon, in the house. And settle up with her when you get back.'

The house was sturdy yet elegant, with a white porch, slender railings and a peaked roof trimmed with fretwork. The door was open, as Ted had said it would be, and he found himself on a Persian rug in the front room, facing an enormous fireplace. His call was answered by young voice.

A teenage boy sprung out from a side room, wiping his lips. 'I'm Gavin's son, Michael. Can I help?'

'Yes. I'm looking for Sharon.'

'She's back there. First door on the left.'

A hallway, with rooms on both sides, led toward the back, where he knocked on the closed door.

'Come in.'

She swivelled in her chair to face him.

'Hi. I'm Steve. Ted said I should see you about getting cash for the town run today.'

'You're the teacher, then,' she said in a flat voice.

'Well, I'm going to see how it goes.'

She took him in. Tall, dark hair and soft brown eyes.

'I'm sure you'll do a good job.'

'I'm going to give it my best try. I like a challenge.'

'That's nice to hear.' She smiled at him. 'I'm Sharon, by the way. Have you got the list?'

She scanned it, reached down and took out a metal cash box. 'Fifty should cover it.'

'Ah, I might need more. I'm going to buy lots of school supplies.'

'Right. Let's make it seventy. Be sure to keep all the receipts.'

His companion on the short journey was one of the long-term residents, a man in his forties and the father of two. Under his guidance, they divided up the list. The older man would get all the food items, while he would go to the post office, drug store and hardware store.

'Don't forget to pick up Gavin's newspapers at the drug store,' he was told. 'He'll skin us alive if we forget.'

At the bookstore, Maggie greeted him with a twinkly smile.

'You're staying on, it seems.'

'Yes, it's peaceful. Just what I need.'

'Don't we all.'

He loaded up on notebooks, pens, pencils, erasers, drawing paper and an armful of storybooks and fiction for the wide range of ages. He added two novels for himself and a collection of California Indian folktales for Ted, keeping those receipts separate. At the last minute, he remembered to get a pair of hiking boots.

'Can't that stupid bird learn better manners?'

The staccato drilling on the nearby tree had him up before dawn.

'Now, now,' chided Ted, who was already shaving in front of an ornate mirror nailed to a wall. 'I know people talk about "bird brains", but did you know that woodpeckers have a larger cerebellum than…'

'Not this one,' he cried, sliding off the cot and trundling out to the toilet.

After breakfast, he joined everyone inside the house for the twice-monthly Sunday morning meeting. Every inch of the large front room was occupied, most people sitting cross-legged on the floor. Warm ripples of conversation ran through the group, and he returned smiles and nods directed toward "the teacher".

The meeting began with a moment of silent meditation led, it seemed, by no one. Gavin, tall with thick silvery hair, gave a short "state of the commune" statement, in which he welcomed Steve's teaching initiative and told everyone that a child who had taken seriously ill was recovering in Mendocino hospital. A birthday was acknowledged, and the celebrant responded by singing a song of her choice. Not very well. 'One of our traditions,' Ted whispered with raised eyebrows.

Gavin then asked Sharon to fill them in on finances.

'I'm happy to say that this month, we are in the black, thanks in part to the increase in our food production and decrease in energy bills. However, I have to remind us all that the energy savings is the result of an early spring.'

He noticed that most people didn't pay attention to her updates on the long-standing disputes with a timber company over land use and the county regarding building codes.

'Can't you just tell them off?' a young man said. 'I mean this is Gavin's land, isn't it? And he lets us stay. End of.'

'No, Jason. It isn't that simple. According to county regulations, every time a new structure larger than a shed is built, you have to apply for a permit. Then…'

'OK, OK.'

Next came the open-ended discussion, "Looney Tunes" as Ted called it, when many more voices were heard.

'I really think we should focus on candles. They sell well in Mendocino.'

'Not that again, Phyllis! It isn't worth it. Too much time for too little return. If we want to go into business, let's sell our fruit and veg in the whole food store in town. People would buy that.'

'Can't we focus on what really matters? Not profit but sustainability. We need to invest in new gardening tools, for one thing. And gloves, for Pete's sake. My hands are so full of callouses I can hardly lift a fork.'

'You do pretty well at the dinner table, though!'

Howls of laughter.

'Speaking of dinner, can we ask our esteemed chefs to vary the menu? Just a teeny, weeny bit? I mean, ratatouille is fine, but not every other night.'

The free-for-all ended with yet another call for an anti-war protest march in town, which was, as always, rejected by a vote.

'Gavin doesn't say much, does he?' he said to Ted as they made their way back to the cabin.

'No. Now and then, he will remind someone of "the vision" of River Ridge. Living off the land, communal sharing, non-violence and such. But you're right. He likes to stay in the background and let us talk among ourselves.'

'Sensible.'

'Yeah. It's all a bit silly anyway because everyone knows he'll bail us out if absolutely necessary. If we can't make ends meet.'

'Not exactly communal sharing, then.'

'You could say that. But so what? As long as it works and everyone's happy.'

Ted's radio was their source of news. They listened in the evening after dinner, and liked to chew over anything meaty, especially politics. One item sent him into the house the next morning, asking for a copy of Gavin's San Francisco paper. On an inside page, he found the story about the Supreme Court ruling that conscientious objectors no longer had to prove religious belief, only a moral objection to war. He thought back to the conversation in the Berkeley church basement. It might be possible, he thought, but then read more closely. It had to be an objection to all wars, not just Vietnam, and he wasn't sure he could convince a draft board, let alone himself, that he held such a principled view.

It was a way out though, a route back to his old life. Probably as much a legal as a philosophical issue. Maybe if he studied it and thought it through…

'How do you say that word?'

Seven-year-old Estella frowned and twisted her lips.

'Please!' she persisted. 'It's hard. I can't say it.'

All the children looked at him, expecting to hear an answer in his gentle voice. He was staring into the woods behind the barn.

'Are you OK?' one of the older boys asked.

No answer.

'Steve?'

He shook himself and produced a smile.

'Yes, I'm fine, Billy. Just a little tired, that's all.'

'Debbie says you should do some yoga when you're tired,' Estella said.

'I'll try that.'

The rest of the day passed off as usual and he took his walk up to the waterfall as the sun was beginning to dip. And now, thanks to Ted's books, he could identify some of the bird calls.

He sat on a flat rock, free from ferns and open to the light. The teaching was a success. Helping the kids with their spelling, sentence structure and pronunciation of difficult words gave him pleasure, especially because their progress was so rapid and evident. Every day, he looked forward to building up their worlds, little by little, and watching them gain confidence.

Listening to the water, he told himself that he was a good teacher. When this was all over, he could forget about Harvard and go back to teaching. Even start a school of his own. Something progressive. Not Montessori exactly, but a place where learning was a shared experience between teachers and students. River Ridge could be a stepping stone to the next stage of his life.

The next time he did the run into town again he didn't need a cash advance because Sharon came with him. She sat beside him in the sun-warmed car, her straw-coloured hair flying in the wind.

'Enjoying yourself in our little hideaway?' she asked. Not even a hint of a smile.

'Yes. It's taken a while, you know. I can't wait for my next bowl of granola.'

She looked at him, saw his raised eyebrows and laughed.

They hadn't spoken since the first time he went into town. But he had noticed her around the farm, in part because she didn't wear tie-dyed shirts and jeans, preferring slacks or a skirt and blouse.

'I hear the teaching's going well,' she said.

'Yeah. They're really good kids, so open and curious.'

'Must be hard, though, the different ages and lack of discipline.'

'That's what I thought, at the beginning. But each one of them seems to have a desire to be good at something. The trick is to find out what that is.'

'Yes. That's the key to everything.'

They bought in bulk at the natural food store, packed it all in the car and then split up. She went to the bank, hardware store and post office, while he picked up the newspapers at the drug store and browsed in the bookstore.

Driving back, they stayed silent for the few minutes it took them to clear the town and reach the highway. He felt she was waiting.

'So, the teaching's fine, but how about you?' she asked. 'How are you getting on?'

'Good. It's peaceful and healthy.'

'And isolated.'

He nodded but kept his eyes on the road.

'By the way, I think you did a brave thing,' she said after another interval, which felt like another moment of assessment. 'Refusing the draft.'

That much everyone knew, or anyone who wanted to know. More than that – especially his time in Berkeley – he'd only revealed to Ted.

'Not so brave, really. Just scared.'

'But your fear was justified, wasn't it? Fear of killing and being killed is normal. Moral, even.'

'I don't know. The war is immoral, that's for sure.'

'Exactly. And that's why we have to fight it.'

He looked across at her. At the rigid jaw and piercing eyes.

That evening, Sharon veered from habit and ate in the barn.

'So, we aren't going broke this month?' Ted asked.

'All depends,' she said, also deadpan.

'On what?'

'On whether or not you can get that roof repaired by the end of the summer. If not, we'll have to hire people. Not less $300.'

The barn roof had been a sore spot ever since a winter's storm had blown off shingles and let the rain in. Ted had promised to take charge of the project but found himself diverted by personal projects, like making a bookcase or a table for someone.

'There's still lots of time. I could use a new ladder, you know.'

She eyed him. 'Ten bucks, no more.'

'Your munificence is wondrous,' Ted said, pressing his palms together in prayer.

'Of course, you could always make your own. On the sly.'

'True, but it wouldn't work.'

Steve and Sharon looked at him.

'I'd need a fake receipt, wouldn't I?'

All three chuckled and resumed dipping chunks of homemade bread into their vegetable stew.

'By the way, I hear you're going to teach the kids about the Pomo Indians.' She had pushed her bowl away and lit a cigarette.

'Yeah. It was Ted's idea, really. But I'm working on it now, the lessons.'

'Tell me more.'

'I think I'll focus on history and mythology – Ted's got some good books on that. And he's going to do some days on Indian crafts.'

'Great. There's so much they can learn from Native Americans. Non-hierarchical structures, barter economy and…'

'Whoa. I'm just a humble English major.'

'I can give you some things to read. If you like.'

Gathered inside the barn on a hot morning, the children concentrated hard. Having listened to a Pomo myth read aloud by Steve, they set about making drawings of the story. That had been Ted's idea. 'Easier than writing,' he said. 'And more fun.'

Strange-shaped animals, blue rivers, red mountains and stick figures filled large sheets of drawing paper. One of the boys was explaining why he'd put a dog on the sun, when they heard shouting.

'Come! Quick!' Two of the older children, who hadn't come to the barn that morning, rushed toward them.

'What's the matter?' he asked.

'It's Estella. A snake bit her.'

'Where is she?'

'Near the river. We were just…'

He was on his feet and moving while the others stared, wide-mouthed. He sprinted down the path between the garden plots and into the woods, his mind racing to remember what he'd been taught as a Boy Scout.

She was sitting down, knees drawn up, holding back tears. He eased her onto her back, tore off his shirt sleeve and wrapped it tightly over the reddened wound near her ankle. Then made sure the leg was lower than her chest.

'You'll be fine,' he said, as calmly as he could. 'Just lie still for a minute, OK? I'll carry you back.'

He bore the young child inside the house and laid her on a

sofa in the living room. Gavin and his wife fluttered around until he told them to fetch a bowl of warm soapy water and a towel.

'Can you remember what the snake looked like?' he asked, his hand on her forehead.

'It was sort of yellow.'

'Did it make any kind of sound?'

'I don't know. I…'

'That's all right. You'll be fine. Just sit up a little.' Propping her up with cushions, he unwrapped the makeshift bandage and washed the wound, which didn't show much swelling.

'We'd better take her to the hospital in Mendocino. Just to make sure.' Sharon had been watching from the hallway and now took a few steps toward him.

'No, I don't think that's necessary,' he said. 'She'll be all right here.'

She looked at him and smiled. Nice to have someone else take control.

12

He was sitting on a stump by the side of the barn, reading one of Ted's books.

'Looks absorbing. What is it?'

Sharon had come from nowhere and was standing in front of him.

He held it up so that she could read the title. *Natural history of Northern California.*

'I usually read novels, but being here, it's great to learn about the wildlife, birds and plants.'

'A world we understand even less than our own.'

'And more beautiful.'

'More beautiful, but just as ruthless.'

She looked at him with steely eyed intensity. Even her hair, falling straight as if ironed, showed determination.

'I can show you that stuff now, if you like,' she said. 'You know, things that might help with the Pomo teaching.'

Her room reminded him of his college days. Single bed, crammed bookcase, pinewood table facing the only window and a spindle-back chair. Three-ring binders stood erect on the table, their spines labelled vertically for easy reading. Also a neat stack of pamphlets and a tall glass with cut flowers. Irises, he thought.

The only thing missing was a typewriter. That had been his pride and joy, a Remington electric, his parents' birthday gift, which he'd used to produce his senior thesis. "The Psycho-Sociological Aspects of the Black Revolution." That choice of topic had surprised him and, remembering it now, he realised that he hadn't been as politically naïve as he pretended.

She bent down and selected two hefty volumes from the bookcase.

'These give you a critical analysis of capitalism and the patriarchal state.'

He grimaced.

'Right,' she said with a tiny smile. 'They are hard going.'

Putting those back, she pulled out a pamphlet, the manifesto of a radical group well-known for its actions against the war.

'Try this,' she said. 'It sets out the underlying principles for social change.'

'Principles,' he repeated.

'Call them values if you like. The things that guide us. They are everything. Absolutely everything.'

Her eyes brightened as she spoke, releasing a warmth he had not felt before. They stood, looking at each other, and he saw that she was beautiful. Not the features themselves, but the whole radiant face, smooth as porcelain. When she lowered her eyes, he knew for sure.

'OK, I'll read it,' he said, taking the well-thumbed pamphlet.

'Good. Let me know if you find it useful.'

In the cabin after dinner, he asked Ted, 'Where's Sharon from?'

'Not sure. She doesn't talk about her past much. Like a lot of us.'

'Seems like a good person to have around.'

'No doubt about that. Sharp as a tack. I think she went to law school and worked as a civil rights lawyer.'

'What brought her here?'

'Not sure. It was about a year ago. Maybe burnt out. Or just wanted out.'

He nodded and picked up the pamphlet she'd given him. Cyclostyled on poor-quality paper, the sixteen pages were difficult to read in the lantern light, but the words made perfect sense. Especially the first sentence: "Many of us began maturing in complacency but were soon to be disillusioned." That's it in a nutshell, he thought.

He felt it was talking about him. Not poor Blacks in the inner cities, not poor whites in the Appalachians, not comrades or campaneros. It addressed young, middle-class, educated people at odds with the country they had thought was the best in the world. A confidence that had been put on edge by the threat of nuclear war and shattered by a real war in the jungles of South East Asia.

He read it from beginning to end, never once pausing to consider if he disagreed or didn't understand. The values, as she had said, were clear and repeated. Communalism, democracy, equality and open government. He kept nodding in approval as he turned the pages. It was positive, affirming and rational. Nothing soppy about free love. Nothing grandiose like the "overthrow of capitalism". The language was conversational.

Looking back at the cover, with its screaming slogan and clenched fist, he felt a twinge of doubt. He always thought of himself as an independent thinker. That's what scholarship, especially law school, was all about. An open-mindedness that permitted the pursuit of truth. The opposite of group solidarity.

'Must be pretty heavy,' Ted said, looking up from his book. 'Some political thing?'

'Yeah, something I picked up in town. Same old rhetoric, though. Flat as a pancake. Makes me appreciate Vonnegut all the more.'

He slid the pamphlet underneath the pile of books on his side table. He needed to keep some things to himself.

They took the children on what Ted called a "field trip" and he called a "forced march". They hiked for two days into the mountains, camping overnight, and on the third day reached their destination. A wide, shallow river.

They dug a pit in the sandy bank and collected wood. Ted showed the kids how to pitch a tent while he supervised the fire that cooked their lunch. No one complained about the person they got stuck with in a tent, and no one mentioned the sand at the bottom of the vegetable soup.

The kids said they wanted to go into the forest, but Ted told them to stay on the riverbank.

'Within shouting distance,' Ted added. 'If I call out and don't get a response, we're all going home.'

Satisfied with this compromise between freedom and supervision, the kids began to explore. They hauled boulders and added them to a cluster of half-exposed rocks, making a bridge across the river. On the far side, keeping to the bank, they gathered branches and leaves and built a lean-to.

When darkness fell, Ted called them in, all nine of them, by name. They put on sweaters and jackets and sat around a blazing fire, talking about what they had seen in the woods.

'This huge bear came out of the cave and…'

'Asked us if we wanted some supper.'

'We said we were hungry, and he invited us into the cave.'

'Where we saw a huge boiling pot…'

'But not as big as ours,' Ted said, getting up to lift the cast-iron container from the flames.

The two adults served the evening meal, and the kids joked that warmed-up canned corn beef "never tasted so good", but they did concede that the brownies were moist. Having cleaned up, they sat around the fire.

'Now, I'm going to tell you a story,' he said. 'Not like one of your fibs, though. This is a true story. A Pomo story.'

They huddled in a circle of warmth under the cold stars,

expectant faces glistening in the firelight. A screech split the silence, and Ted said it was a grey owl. Then everyone turned toward Steve.

'Long ago, before the world began, Coyote came and saw there were no mountains. No rivers. No trees. And no people. First, he created a mountain and sat on top of it, in a sweathouse.'

'What's a sweathouse?' Estella asked.

'A place where it's hot,' answered Billy.

'Yes, where you sweat. And Coyote stayed inside for a whole year. He began to sing. He sang to the east and to the west, he sang to the south and to the north. And as he sang, he plucked out his hairs and rubbed them together with his sweat. From that mixture, he created the sun and the sky, the rivers and the oceans. Last, he made the redwoods. He made them red because that is the colour of our blood. Because they are our relatives.'

He stopped and asked the children to continue the story in any way they liked. Estella said that Coyote married a bear and their children spread around the mountains of California. Marvin said that the children got married and lived in Mendocino. The story ended when another boy said that Coyote started fishing in the river, right where they were camped.

Two days later, he was in her room, with the late-afternoon light fading behind the single window. She sat on the edge of the bed, he in the desk chair, facing her.

'It made a lot of sense,' he said and handed the pamphlet back to her. 'Nothing I could disagree with.'

'Good. They are clear-headed people.'

'Do you know them?'

'I knew them.'

'You mean, you were part of the group?'

'Yes and no. But let's talk about what you read. You said you didn't disagree with anything. But did you agree with anything?'

She lit a cigarette and waited.

'Well, the goals, the values, they're what we all believe in. But I'm not sure how they're going to achieve that kind of a society.'

'That's always the question, isn't it? What to do?'

The words sounded familiar, something he'd heard in his Russian history class in high school.

She went to the bookcase and picked out another booklet, one with a slick cover and sophisticated graphics.

'This goes into the question of methods,' she said and handed it to him. 'Particularly the tricky one of when violence is justified.'

He noticed something odd about her eyes, as though each looked at him individually.

He spent more and more time in her room, discussing the books she gave him. Frantz Fanon and Herbert Marcuse, Rachel Carson and Stokely Carmichael. Together, they also read the latest publication from the group whose pamphlet she had first given him, going through it sentence by sentence, examining every angle, considering every implication for the anti-war movement.

He liked being in her room with its clean lines and square corners. He had adjusted to Ted's space, had even started using his friend's expressions. Back to the land, that's what they called it, and that's what he'd come for. To retreat. But now he found himself fitting into Sharon's orderliness and responding to her energy. Her clarity of expression impressed him. Probably a result of her legal training.

Mid-summer and still the temperature rarely climbed above seventy during the day or dipped below fifty at night. Unlike anything he'd ever known in New England or Southern California. At least there was no rain to speak of, just morning mist. No time like the present, he thought.

'C'mon,' he urged her. 'You need to get out of your office sometime. It's not good to stay cooped up all day.'

She had dreaded something like this. He was obviously the athletic type and, after all, they were in the middle of the woods.

It had all begun aged ten, when her mother declared her "skinny", and her father said she needed "beefing up". She never wore shorts and hated PE. And it only got worse in high school when her first and only boyfriend discovered the padded cups in her bra. She thought hiking was silly, but there was something in Steve's boyish enthusiasm she couldn't resist.

'All right,' she said, dragging out the words. 'Give me five minutes to finish this.'

'Meet you in front.'

He went back to Ted's place, put on his boots, combed his increasingly long hair and looked at himself in the mirror. It doesn't show, he thought. Not on the outside.

'Don't you have any other shoes?'

He was looking at her black pumps as they stood on the front steps of the house.

'No.'

'You can't go in those. You might break an ankle or something.'

'Don't be silly. These are fine.'

'No, c'mon. Let's ask Catherine. She must have something.'

He was tuning toward the door when she caught his arm. 'Don't. I wouldn't wear them anyway.'

He looked at her, the taut lips daring him to argue.

She stumbled but never fell on the trek up the slope to his favourite spot. Once or twice, she grabbed his hand for support, rewarding him with a warm smile. You can help me, it said, but only when I ask.

The woods were dry, leaves and twigs crackling underfoot. They stopped to listen to a piercing shriek, followed by short chirps.

'That's a sparrow,' he said, craning his neck. 'Probably a white-crested sparrow.'

'Ted teach you that?'

'Yeah. And a lot more.'

She nodded with what he hoped was approval.

They sat on his flat rock, listening to the waterfall. When she leaned in, he put an arm around her. She snuggled closer and he kissed her. The first kiss in over a year. The first since his girlfriend had left him during the teaching stint in Maine. And it was different. There was sexual desire, all right, but less impulsive. More controlled, like a step on a path.

Moving in with her prompted only smiles from the others. Gavin and Catherine didn't comment, maybe because he spent time in the house helping their youngest child with his reading. Sleeping together on the single bed was not as comfortable as the cot in Ted's cabin, but the electric lights and indoor bathroom made him realise how much he had missed those amenities.

He'd never lived with a woman before, and Sharon fascinated him. Her routine before bed at night, the hairband she wore when washing her face, the way she dressed in the morning and her unwavering schedule, including the thirty-minute reading slot before dinner. She didn't smoke dope or take any drugs, as far as he could see, just unfiltered Camels. The smoke didn't bother him, only the nicotine stains on her fingers. He was still a virgin and, at first, he was embarrassed. But she was gentle, coaxing and patient. He admired her, he desired her and, when he thought about it, he wondered if he loved her.

Ted hit on the idea of celebrating "Earth Day". He'd seen posters in town about such an event in San Francisco and proposed it at a Sunday morning meeting, where it won near-universal approval. Ted told him that was a rare thing at River Ridge. It was also unique in that everyone participated.

The day began, just after breakfast, with a meeting inside the barn, where Gavin spoke with the conviction of the convert.

'We have to stop the destruction of nature caused by human greed. And it's not what we say that counts, but what we do.' Heads nodded. 'Here, we live our philosophy, and our philosophy is our life.' Catherine brought her hands together in silent applause as he went on to declare that "consumerism is death" and to ask everyone to "give earth a chance". Fifteen-year-old Billy strummed his guitar, and everyone sang "This Land is Your Land".

When the voices faded, Ted set out the plans for the day. The commune was divided into groups of five or six, a mixture of adults and children, and told to come up with a one-word name for itself. After one group chose "Gaia", the others declared themselves "Pacific", "Redwood", "Arcadia", "Infinity" and "Space Travellers". This last was ruled inadmissible by the one-word-only rule, but the Travellers refused to back down and Ted conceded that it could be hyphenated.

Each group was given a hand-drawn map of the area where they were to find, draw and describe plants, trees and wildlife. They were also told to collect edible flowers, berries and nuts, and to bring them back to the farm, where they would be used to cook the evening meal.

'Save the earth,' Ted cried, when everyone was ready. 'We can't get off it.'

It was a chilly, misty summer morning in the woods, with only the ghost of a sun. Steve's group had a long trek, across the shallow river and up two high hills. He tried not to direct, letting the two children, one boy and one girl, take the lead.

He was curious when they stopped not far from the tree where Estella had been bitten. Beckoning him to come closer, they showed him a patch hidden in the thick undergrowth. The ground had been dug up and filled with woodchips, creating a growing bed for slender-stemmed mushrooms with dark brown caps and white spots.

'We take them and sit in the tree,' Billy said. 'Only us older kids, not the little ones.'

He was about to ask why they hid in the tree but realised that even kids in a commune had to have secrets.

The communally collected and cooked meal was a mixed success. Half-eaten portions of leafy soup and nasturtium salad were tipped into the compost heap, while the huckleberry pies disappeared within minutes of reaching the tables.

'That was fun,' he said later, inside the house.

'Yes, fun. Feel-good politics, I call it.' She had come in from the bathroom, towelling her hair after a shower.

'OK, it didn't change the world, if that's what you mean. But it was nice to do something together. This is a commune, after all.'

'Funded by our sugar daddy.'

'That's a bit harsh.'

'Don't get me wrong.' She had advanced toward the bed, where he sat. 'I like Gavin and what he's done here. But let's not fool ourselves. It's an escape, a place to hide.'

He looked up at her, standing in front of him, damp and unsmiling.

'For you, too?' he asked.

'For me, too.'

13

On a cloudless day in late July, he drove into Mendocino with the older man who usually came with him. Same division of tasks. He would go to the hardware store, post office and drug store (and not forget Gavin's newspapers), while his companion would buy the food and household items.

When everything was stored in the car, they allowed themselves an hour before returning to the farm. Normally, he would have gone directly to the bookstore, but he decided to walk out to the headland. Standing back from the cliff edge, and squinting into the sun, he spotted a rock arch poking up out of the water. Once part of the coastline, it had been carved out by the sea and was now detached. A fragment of the past and a marker of forces beyond our control.

He still couldn't figure it out. Two days ago, Sharon had asked him to drive her into town, not to buy things, but to make a telephone call. Why not use the house phone? She said it had to be a public phone and told him not to ask why. He had watched her in the phone booth in the parking lot on the outskirts of town.

Now, hands in pockets, he turned and walked back to the main road. It was her birthday in a few days. Mid-thirties, he guessed. Looking at and rejecting scented candles and soaps, he went to the bookstore, where he picked out a new hardback of *Middlemarch*. He remembered that it was a story about the evil of money and a woman who wants social change. He looked at the young Victorian heroine on the cover. Drab brown dress, thin lace collar, face half-turned from the viewer. It was also about thwarted ambitions. He put it back on the shelf.

The store was busy on that warm summer day, and the tourists seemed to stand in exactly the wrong place. He waited patiently for a man in Bermuda shorts and a woman in calf-length pants to shift down the aisle. Scanning the spines, he spotted three possibilities, almost side by side. *To Kill a Mockingbird*, *The Spy Who Came in From the Cold* and *The Invisible Man*. He chose the Harper Lee and asked Maggie to gift-wrap it. Folding and tying, she mentioned the upcoming election for county sheriff.

'You folks out there going to vote?' she asked.

'Ah, not sure. I might.'

'You should. It's grassroots democracy. The only thing that works.'

The post office was not crowded. He sent a letter to his parents, telling them he was working in a restaurant in San Francisco for the summer and had driven up the coast for the weekend, where it was beautiful. And, yes, he was reading law books in his spare time to prepare for Harvard. He would visit them soon.

Standing in line for stamps, he looked at the glass-fronted bulletin board. A red triangle warned about forest fires, a small flier announced a board of supervisors meeting and a psychedelic image promoted a music festival. There was also an FBI poster with a photograph of a desperate-looking woman wanted in connection with a bank robbery in Sacramento.

They celebrated her birthday with a chocolate cake baked in the kitchen and a bottle of wine bought in town.

'I saw the film,' she said after unwrapping his gift. 'And it made me cry. Not the injustice – though that was horrible – but the courage.'

He smiled and gave her a wine-scented kiss.

She sat on the bed propped up against the headboard, smoking, with the *San Francisco Chronicle* spread out in her lap. When Gavin finished with his newspapers, he gave them to her, one by one. 'Got to know what the imperialist media is saying,' she liked to say though he knew she also looked at the financial pages.

'Well, what do you know!' she cried.

'What?'

'The My Lai trial has been postponed. Again.'

Eyes on the paper, she didn't see his face. It happened every time he read or heard about the massacre. All of a sudden, he had not driven to California. He had instead reported for induction, gone through basic training and learnt to fire a rifle. He was tramping through rice fields and burnt-out villages.

He put his glass down on the desk.

'They can delay it, but we know what happened, don't we?' he said. 'They should all be on trial and convicted of murder.'

She heard the anger in his voice and lowered the paper. 'You're right,' she said. 'Everyone. All the way up to the top, including the president.'

'Killers, all of them,' he said, hissing through his teeth.

'They are. And we have to hold them to account.'

They locked eyes for several seconds.

In the barn, he wrote on an old blackboard that Ted had picked up a garage sale in Mendocino. The children stared at the unusual names. Alliklick, Lasski, Nongati, Whilkut and several more.

'OK,' he said, turning back to them. 'I want you write these names in your notebook. Be sure to get the spelling right.'

He watched the bent heads, floppy-haired and pony-tailed, bobbed and crew-cut. He heard the grunts and sighs until the last head rose.

'Right. Now, I want you to memorise those names. Try to get them in your mind.'

He waited ten minutes while they frowned and grimaced.

'Now, erase the names. All of them.'

'But…'

'Just do it, OK? Then I'll tell you why.'

They bore down hard with their erasers, removing the names and flicking away the rubbery crumbs.

'The names that you wrote,' he explained when they'd finished, 'are the names of the California Indian tribes that are extinct. You know what that means?'

One of the older girls spoke up. 'It means gone. Dead.'

'That's right. They lived but they no longer exist. Ex-tinct. Like ex-tinguished.'

'Like the dinosaurs?'

'Yes, only it happened recently.'

Over the next few days, he read to them about the coming of the trappers, loggers and gold diggers, the Russians, Mexicans and Americans. They learnt that the native population had plummeted by the early twentieth century. Murdered or converted, imprisoned or driven onto reservations.

'That's enough, don't you think?' Ted said one evening. 'How about something a little lighter?'

He agreed and spent the next week going over their American history essays with them, one at a time, reminding them of the importance of an introductory sentence and pointing out where a paragraph had strayed off course. The structure, he told them, was as crucial as the information.

'But what if the facts are wrong?' Billy asked.

'That's bad,' he said, 'but if you don't make your point clear, it doesn't matter if the facts are right. No one will be convinced.'

He wasn't sure he believed that anymore. Form over content, something he'd learnt in college and taught in Maine, seemed divorced from reality. Just words about words. Wasn't that what *To Kill a Mockingbird* was all about? The law was a formal set of rules necessarily elevated above the messy reality of everyday life. And sometimes, you had to break the rules to do the right thing.

'More My Lai news.'

She was on the bed, smoking and reading the paper again, while he corrected essays at the desk.

'What is it this time?' he asked, twisting around to face her.

'Most of the charges against the officers have been dropped. The court martial was obviously a sham. A total cover-up.'

'That's unbelievable. You mean, they're going to get away with it?'

'Looks like it.'

'But they killed hundreds of villagers. They can't go scot-free. That would be almost as bad as the massacre itself.'

'Well put. So, what are we going to do?'

Again, that phrase. Turning ideas into action.

'I don't know.'

He was on his feet, stalking around, frustrated by the limited space. She decided this was the moment. Putting the paper aside and crushing out her cigarette, she stood up.

'We can strike back,' she said. 'Let them know they *are* being held to account.'

'What do you mean?' He stopped pacing and leaned against the desk.

'I mean we can strike a blow against the military machine.'

'A blow? You mean a bomb or something?' Half-mockery, half-disbelief.

'Yes. That's exactly what I mean. A bomb.'

He shifted his weight and stared at her. That flicker of a smile, those uneven eyes and rigid hairline.

She came closer.

'Is it wrong to use force to stop violence? That's what you're thinking, isn't it?'

He gripped the desk behind him.

'Is it wrong to knock a man down who is about to hit a child? No. It is not wrong. It is never wrong to use force against an aggressor in order to protect the innocent.' She was standing in front of him now. 'And that is what we will do.'

'OK, OK. But a bomb?' He looked up at her, scrabbling for a lifeline. 'It could kill someone, make us no better than the military bastards.'

She brushed the hair from his forehead and spoke softly.

'We never kill anyone. We attack empty buildings at night and give warnings.'

'*We*? Oh, right. That phone call.'

'Listen, Steve. If you know the war is immoral – that killing innocent people is wrong – then you have a duty to act.'

Yes, he wanted to say, but I'm a coward. I avoid doing something because doing nothing is easier. But he kept silent and went back to the essays on the desk.

The new aluminium ladder made all the difference. He held it steady while Ted climbed up to the steep barn roof, and he continued to hold it while the older man stapled tar paper and hammered wooden shingles.

'Shit!'

He heard a scraping sound, saw a shingle fall and felt his heart leap. But Ted was still there, lying flat on the roof, the soles of his boots visible.

'You OK?'

'Yeah, yeah. Just smashed my thumb, that's all.'

He gripped the ladder while Ted climbed down.

'That'll last for a while,' Ted said, picking up the fallen shingle and tossing it into the barn. 'Until the next storm. Hey, why don't you get two beers from the house – I'm sure you can swing that.'

He didn't like beer much, but the cold and wet felt good on his tongue as they sat and sipped inside the cabin.

'Something on your mind?'

What could he say? He hadn't agreed to anything, had he? No, not in so many words. But that's what made it so unsettling. A tacit agreement. Another Molotov cocktail thrust into his hand.

'Sort of.'

'Out with it.'

'Well, I've been reading a lot of politics lately.'

'Sharon's stuff?'

'Yeah, mostly.'

Ted eyed him.

'And I've been going over it all in my head. Over and over.'

'Go on.'

'It boils down to one question. Is violence justified if it's done for the right reasons?'

'You mean, like taking out the PTA?' Ted's weathered features broke into a wide smile.

'I wish it were that easy.'

'The old ends-versus-means argument?'

'Yeah, I guess so.'

'You and Sharon thinking of doing something?'

'Maybe.'

'Something big?'

When he didn't answer, Ted took a deep breath and exhaled through his nose.

'I'd think long and hard.'

'I have.'

'Is it possible that someone might get hurt?'

'No. I mean, it shouldn't happen.'

'But it might?'

Again, no response.

'I don't know. It's your decision. I'll only say one thing.'

'What's that?'

'Make sure you're prepared for the consequences. Whatever they may be.'

14

Walter Gill always said that the army had given him a better life. He joined the forces in 1940, aged eighteen, and served as a sergeant in an all-Black tank battalion that fought in North Africa and Sicily, landed in Normandy and pushed all the way through to Germany. His only regret was that they didn't reach Berlin before the Russians. But he liked to say that the "greatest victory" was when his battalion helped liberate a concentration camp. He was in hospital at the time, having his face reconstructed, but that didn't matter. He still belonged to the unit, and he celebrated as if he'd been there. When the war ended, a ship brought him to the Presidio, an army base in San Francisco, where he began work as a cleaner.

That's also where he met his wife, Susan, a nurse in the hospital, and where he continued to work, gaining promotions in a desegregated military. Susan Gill also continued working on the base, rising to head nurse with a health insurance plan that covered them both. Soon, they were the proud parents of a baby boy.

Ronald was a handful. 'A very active little boy,' is how his mother put it. More than once she'd been summoned from the hospital to the nursery on the base because her son had caused a ruckus among his fellow infants. A reluctant Walter administered a belt to the backside and then put an arm around the boy.

Ronald changed when he went to elementary school, close to the family apartment in the Tenderloin district. Confident and articulate, he attracted friends, both Black and white, excelled at maths and did not disgrace himself on the basketball court.

The entrepreneurial streak emerged during high school, where he tutored less-able students for a fee. He used the pocket money to buy himself nice clothes, a proper watch and a stereo set. Walter felt his boy slipping away from him but was wise enough not to attempt to retrieve him. Whenever Ronald edged further away, he would swallow his pride and say to his wife, 'It's all right. All I want is for him to succeed.' He was not disappointed. Ronald graduated top of his high school class.

A two-year course in business administration led to an internship in a life insurance company. Aged only twenty-three, he set up his own commercial real estate and property management company in a tower block on the shores of Lake Merritt, in Oakland. He distanced himself from activism, especially the Black Panthers, whose headquarters were only a stone's throw from his office. "Misguided brothers" is what he called them. He voted Democrat because everyone he knew did.

Although his father never mentioned it, Ronald knew he wanted, maybe even expected, him to enlist. But he'd seen what the army had done to his father, a second-class citizen even when he was "liberating" Europe. They gave him a shit job back home. No, he wasn't going to fall for any patriotic crap and go to Vietnam. Three of his high school classmates had already come back in body bags. After the first, he found a doctor willing to write a letter certifying that he had diabetes.

After his business took off, he got married and helped his parents buy their first house, a modest bungalow in the Outer Sunset district. He didn't visit them as often as he would have liked, but he spoke with them on the phone every weekend. It was enough to know that they were happy.

His mother loved her job at Letterman Medical Centre, the renovated and renamed hospital on the base, whose ten floors were filled with the wounded brought back from Vietnam. She often thought how fortunate they were that Ronald had been granted a medical deferment. His father never said anything about that, preferring to avoid what he didn't want to know. But he often spoke about how the army "looked after its people".

Walter's only complaint was his daily commute. One hour by tram and bus through Golden Gate Park, and another hour back. But it wasn't just the time. It was also the not-so-subtle racism he experienced on public transport, not unlike his childhood in Georgia, where his father had been an errand "boy" for a grocery store. Fortunately, the battlefield taught him that he was as good as any man, and he proved that when he became manager of the cleaning unit on the base.

It was an honour, and well paid, though it also meant more hours. First to arrive and last to leave, he supervised all the cleaning work on the sprawling base, from the soldiers' barracks to the commanders' quarters.

The Officers' Club, with its restaurant, bars, kitchen and TV room, was one of the most important buildings. Here, everything had to be spotless by early morning, when the commander might show up for breakfast with a five-star general from Washington. That meant night shifts every night, and if the assigned person got ill or couldn't show, Walter filled in. 'After all,' he told his wife, 'I have my office in there. It's my patch.'

Located next to the kitchen, his office was little more than a converted broom closet, but it was his command centre. A row of ten clipboards hung from hooks on the back wall. Lifting one, he could see who was responsible for cleaning that area of the base that week. Also, what time they had clocked off the previous day and if there were any concerns, like short supplies or damaged equipment. That had been his idea, dividing the base into ten areas and rotating responsibility. 'Keeps the men on their toes,' he'd said to the procurement officer at the time.

If truth be told, he didn't mind staying through the night and going home in the early hours. He could play his radio more loudly. The music went off at midnight, but he had newspapers and magazines, and he liked to take a walk around the building and its grounds, picking up any litter and checking that the raccoons hadn't overturned the garbage cans again. His flashlight also exposed clandestine lovers in the bushes. Nothing was ever said, by either party, though he suppressed a laugh when they scuttled away, half naked and clutching their clothes. He always halted at the northern edge, near Crissy Field, where he watched the blinking lights from ships at sea.

He admitted to Susan that he did doze during those night shifts, but only, he added, to be more alert when he sat back up. The real treat, however, was going home at the crack of dawn, with light leeching into the sky. More beautiful than any sunrise.

On an unusually warm evening in March, he decided to skip the bus and walk home through the park. Almost fifty, he wondered if he should retire early, take his pension and move to a quieter place. Not that the Outer Sunset was noisy, but he'd always dreamed about living in a more rural place, maybe by the ocean. Bodega Bay to the north or perhaps Monterrey to the south. Property was cheaper, Ronald kept telling him. And property tax, house insurance and most other things. Susan, though, wasn't keen. 'We've got good friends and nice neighbours here,' she said. 'There's the park and the church, everything within walking distance.'

She was probably right. He wouldn't like living outside the city no matter how pretty it was. And maybe people in a small town wouldn't especially welcome a new Black family. All that was a smokescreen, however, for what was really bothering him.

Ronald, "the youngster", as he called him, was becoming a stranger to him. Wouldn't even go with him to see a baseball game, like they used to. Of course, he was consumed with his business and his family – that was only natural – but it was every evening and weekend. Never a minute's rest. Although Ronald's wife, Marilyn, didn't complain, he heard despair in her voice when they spoke. Susan suggested that they would be happier with a child. Walter wasn't sure what was cause and what was effect.

Ronald was doing well in his business, though, he reminded himself. And we get on all right. So, that's a blessing. He's just determined to succeed, which is what I want. But that kind of hellbent energy might be the death of him.

Alerted by a jangling bell, he stopped just in time to let the streetcar trundle past. 'Almost walked into that one,' he said to himself with forced levity.

Susan said she was sorry. She was dead tired from the hospital and only had time to pick up TV dinners on the way home. 'But it's your favourite,' she added, following him into the bedroom, where he took off his work clothes. 'Salisbury steak.' Walter grunted approval, gave her a kiss and stepped into the bathroom, where he looked in the mirror, assessing the closely cropped hair and small moustache. A little like his hero, Martin Luther King, though Walter was taller and heftier. A half-smile, half-grimace emerged when he touched his right cheek.

He could recall every detail of that blistering hot day. He had manoeuvred his tank into position outside the town in Belgium where the Germans had dug in. Under heavy shelling, he crawled forward with the rest of the unit, through mud and across ditches, until a sudden downpour created a deep hole and he got stuck. A shell smashed against the front of his tank, killing the driver and knocking him off the gunner's seat. Someone dragged him free before the flames got to him. Surgery rebuilt the left cheekbone but did not achieve symmetry with the other side. He liked to touch his skin and remember it all.

Attired in his pyjamas, he came into the living room, where Susan had set up the trays facing the new television – a birthday gift from Ronald. He was just in time for the start of a new crime series about the exploits of a retired sheriff in Nebraska who worked undercover, ferreting out fraudsters.

One sunny Saturday, Walter chose dark blue chinos and a flower-print shirt. Not too bright, though. The daffodils were a muted yellow on a green background. Susan had given it to him for Christmas, and he'd never worn it. 'Saving it for a special occasion,' he'd told her each time she asked. Well, this was special. His son and daughter-in-law coming over for a barbecue.

He made sure all the preparations were completed before they arrived. He had rolled the three-legged kettle out from the narrow strip of patio and onto the patch of grass they proudly called the "back yard". Having positioned it in the right spot, away from the hot afternoon sun, he cleaned everything: the inside of the black drum, the circular grill, the charcoal holder and all his cooking implements. He laid in charcoal bricks, checked that he had enough lighter fluid and looked at his watch. Plenty of time. The chicken was marinating in the fridge, beside the beer and coke. Susan was making potato salad.

Satisfied, Walter sat on the plastic webbing of a fold-up lounge chair and turned on the radio. The news led with a story about some scandal to do with the FBI. He sipped his beer and listened to details of how they had tried to infiltrate, disrupt and discredit various political groups in the US. Lost in the jumble of acronyms, he was happy to hear a familiar voice.

'Hi, Dad.'

In his tailored linen suit, Ronald looked lean and out of place in the somewhat scruffy back yard.

'Hi, Son. Didn't hear you. Traffic OK? Over the bridge and all?'

'We're here on time, aren't we?'

'Yes, like always. How's Marilyn?'

'I'm just fine, Walter.'

Ronald's wife had come out of the kitchen and joined father and son.

'And I'll be even finer when you've cooked that succulent-looking chicken Susan's got in there.'

She leaned in to receive Walter's cheek kiss and snuck a look at the open-topped barbecue.

'Right,' Walter chirped, 'let's get started.'

While his father fiddled with bricks, fluid and lid, Ronald strolled back into the kitchen.

'How's Dad been,' he asked his mother, still chopping and mixing.

Walter had twice been to the hospital in recent months, once after an asthma attack and once for chest pains. Each time, the doctor had recommended rest and reduced working hours, and each time Walter had said thank you. Back at the base, he worked as hard as ever.

'Oh, pretty good. But you know him. Wouldn't cut back unless you chopped off his legs.'

'Yeah, I know. I keep telling him to take a long vacation. I'm sure he's due one. But he doesn't listen.'

Susan let the long-handled wooden spoon come to a rest in the mixing bowl.

'Well, well. A man who's married to his work – you wouldn't know anything about that now, would you?' She caught her son's eye and smiled.

'C'mon, Mom. I'm young. I've got to hustle to make it out there. No pension like you and Dad. It's tough.'

'Maybe, but you could pay a little more attention to Marilyn.'

'I know, I know. We're going to LA next weekend – if things calm down.'

His mother snorted and bore down on the potato salad.

'Well, I hope you enjoy yourselves. By the way, any chance of some news on the family front?'

'Mom, just back off, OK? Everything's fine, but…'

Marilyn entered the kitchen and knew from the abrupt silence that they'd been talking about her.

'Can I help with anything?' she asked, patting her heavily sprayed hair. She liked both Ronald's parents but felt more relaxed around Walter, who seemed to accept her as a daughter, instead of a wife for his son.

'Let's see.' Susan sucked in her lips and looked around. 'Can you take out the plates and things?'

'No, I'll do it,' Ronald said. Good for them to have a little chat, he thought, and left the kitchen with his arms full.

He stepped through the sliding glass door and stopped. His father stood with his back to him, holding a long fork in his gloved hand and a bottle of sauce in the other. At first, it had been awkward, the reversal of roles when he began to help him out financially. Amiable and affectionate, his father was, first and foremost, a proud man.

15

She listened to his breathing. It had taken time to convince herself. Afraid of making a mistake, she had waited and watched for many months. And it was even more complicated because they were sleeping together. But that might be a good thing. Other couples had supported each other when things got difficult. She trusted him; that's what counted.

He grunted softly and turned over. The dark brown hair hung over his face, hiding the blue eyes. No, she told herself, it isn't entirely instrumental.

After breakfast, she asked a young woman to accompany her on the run into Mendocino. A person who, she knew, would spend time in the town's only gay bar before they returned. He had said he'd drive her, but she put him off, telling him not to set a bad example. 'Teacher shouldn't play hooky too often, should he?'

She took his car, though, and pretended to listen while her companion complained about her current partner, who was "too screwed up" to understand her needs. Once parked on the main street, they divided up the list. When everything was bought and packed into the car, Sharon looked at her watch. 'OK,' she announced, 'meet me back here at 3:00pm.'

She dallied beside the car, watching the younger woman walk down the street and enter the bar, before driving out of town, past the church and the water tower, to the parking lot. On that weekday in March, there were only about a dozen cars and no one in sight. Still, she sat for a full five minutes. Satisfied, she climbed out, slipped into the phone booth and dialled the number.

'Sebastian? It's Melissa. I've found someone. No, but he's solid. Don't worry. Now listen. First, you need to identify someone on the inside. Then get the materials but use cash. After that, get the van and the plates.'

There was a long pause while she listened to the other voice describe the surveillance work he'd done.

'Good. So, remember. First, identify an insider. Second, purchase materials. Last, steal a van and plates. I'll call again. Same time, same day, next week. *A luta continua.*'

She drove back into town, parked close to the original spot and sat for a moment.

Gabriel. She saw him in her mind's eye. Tall and gangly, with the ponytail he'd been wearing ever since she first met him in Cuba. Whenever she advised him to get it cut, as a "precaution", he chuckled and ran a hand down its sand-coloured length. He was reliable and tougher than his languid movements suggested. It will work, she told herself.

Going into her favourite café, she ordered a bacon-and-tomato sandwich and double espresso. She lit a cigarette and opened the San Francisco newspaper she'd picked up for Gavin. The story had already been on the radio, but she wanted the details.

A photograph captioned "Bomb Damages Science Lab" showed a partially destroyed building. The three-storey structure on a state university campus in the Midwest was a centre for army-funded research into weapon systems. According to the article, campus police had received a telephone warning minutes before the huge explosion and no one was injured, but the damage was extensive. No group had yet claimed responsibility. At a press conference, an FBI agent said that they "were conducting a thorough investigation" and that "the perpetrators would be hunted down and caught".

The curling smoke partially hid her taut smile. She looked around the café, mostly local people single and silent, or small groups talking and laughing. They knew but pretended they didn't because they didn't want to know. That's why she had to do it. Make them wake up and confront reality. History showed that it does happen. It just takes time. And effort.

She pushed her coffee aside and began to compose the statement in her head. Ten minutes passed before she pulled out her notebook and started to write. Two cigarettes later, she was satisfied with the opening paragraph.

> *Each act of resistance is a spark that can light a fire. And even small fires can spread and eventually, when they join with other fires across the world, they can burn down the whole rotten structure of imperialist, capitalist society.*

When she'd finished, it was nearly a thousand words long: just right. She would send it to an address in New York, where one of the members in the local unit was living undercover, though in full view. Her statement would appear on the front page of the next pamphlet sold on the streets. That's one thing she had insisted on from the beginning: they must make money. Some members received welfare, others worked part-time, and a few had parental support. She was one of them.

16

She could still remember the dinner-table conversations when she was a young girl. Her father, a trade union activist, and her mother, a high school teacher, discussed everything from the Korean War and nuclear bombs to civil rights and the space race. Seared into her memory was their anger at the Rosenberg executions. That's when she realised that there was an actual Communist Party in America, and that they were members. All through middle school and high school, she spent weekends marching and attending rallies. Mostly in New York, but also in cities along the eastern seaboard from Boston to Washington, DC. When her school friends went to a party on Friday night, she stayed home and made placards.

Until she hit seventeen.

'No,' her father said. 'I don't care. But you have to think of your grandparents and Uncle Benjamin.'

She had her hair styled in a bouffant, wore striped slacks, a tight sweater and lots of eye shadow. She had just told her parents that she was going to marry her boyfriend, who was three years older and studying for a degree in mathematics. A very nice "boy", her mother conceded, but not Jewish.

'You're too young, anyway,' she said. 'College has to come first.'

'I will go to college. I've already told you.'

They were in the living room of the apartment on the waterfront in Newark. From the sofa, they could see the Statue of Liberty. Her legs were crossed at the ankles, bobby socks rolled down, hands in her lap.

'You always talk about individual freedom, but when it comes to your own daughter, you're a hypocrite.'

'That's not fair, Sigrid, and you know it.'

'It's true. That's all I know.'

She had expected resistance. Her parents were not Orthodox, though they went to synagogue, sent her to Hebrew lessons and celebrated her bat mitzvah, which was considered progressive in the 1950s. But they were close to their own, more observant parents and to her father's older brother, who was a rabbi.

The argument ended in a standoff. She would wait at least a year, after which, she could do as she pleased. At eighteen, she could, in any case, marry without her parents' consent. She agreed in part because they couldn't stop her from spending nights with her boyfriend in his student accommodation at NYU. The feud with her parents simmered under the surface all through her senior year and only ended when the boyfriend went off to graduate school in California. They had drifted apart anyway, and she felt immense relief that she wasn't pregnant.

'I don't want to go to one of those elite places,' she said when it came time to apply to college. With excellent grades and high SAT scores, she had been advised to apply to the most prestigious women's colleges. 'They're just finishing schools, for rich kids.'

'Perhaps,' her father said, 'but don't let politics get in the way of your education. You should go where you'll find the most intellectual stimulation. The best professors and motivated students.'

He was the practical one. Her mother only said that she wanted her within "striking distance", whatever that meant.

'I totally agree, Dad. And I can get that in a big city university.

I want to stay in touch with things, you know. And I can't do that in some pretty little college town.'

Again, they compromised. She applied to and was accepted by the University of Chicago, on a full scholarship. It was exhilarating, going that far from home, by herself, on a train, and moving into her single room in an all-women's residence hall. Just five-minutes to a green park and the oceanic lake. Orientation week, during which she met other students as articulate and well-informed as she, ended with candidate Nixon sweating in front of television cameras.

'They're both stooges of the system,' she declared to the others watching in the common room.

'Only one's better looking,' someone said.

When the group giggled, she shrugged and pulled a face.

During her sophomore year, she changed her appearance again. Straight hair and no make-up, though she continued to paint her nails. She joined a campus organisation that led protests against segregated housing in the neighbourhood bordering the elite university. That was when she decided to become a lawyer.

That was also the summer, only months after the Bay of Pigs disaster, when she went to Cuba as part of a student delegation. Avoiding the government ban on flights to the island, they flew from New York to Prague and boarded an Aeroflot plane that took them non-stop to Havana. For two months, they visited factories and farms, learnt Spanish and sang revolutionary songs. Fidel Castro spoke to them before they left, but she was more impressed by Che Guevara, who held a two-hour meeting with the group. Even more important, she later told friends in Chicago, was meeting Kim, a Vietnamese woman in Havana. In a mixture of French and English, Kim told her about her parents and sister, killed by an airstrike, and her brother assassinated by US-trained Vietnamese soldiers.

When the group returned, immigration officials stamped their passports invalid because they'd defied travel restrictions. The group leader and four others were subpoenaed to appear before a federal grand jury. She escaped prosecution, but the trip earnt her a file with the FBI.

She graduated magna cum laude, went to Washington and heard King's "I Have a Dream" speech. En route back to Chicago, she stopped off in Newark and spent a week with her parents. Walking along the waterfront, she marshalled her thoughts while watching clouds play a game of hide and seek with the statue on the island.

She would go to Chicago Law School, but only to defend those who defied unjust laws. And she would support direct action against the state. The logic was simple. The racist, imperialist, capitalist society was immoral and had to be destroyed. Strike a blow, inspire others and the revolution will follow. As day follows night.

'But, Mom, sometimes it has to be violent,' she said at the dinner table. 'That's the only thing they understand. The only way to change the system.'

'I've heard all those arguments, for a long time. They don't make sense. You cannot bring about a more humane society by violence. It is a contradiction.'

'So, you think peaceful marches would have stopped Hitler?'

'C'mon, Sigrid,' her father said. 'That's absurd. Don't weaken your argument with false analogies.'

'OK, maybe that's not the best comparison. But the fact remains: only revolutions bring about fundamental social and economic change. This country had a revolution – I believe that's what it's called. So did France and Russia. Now Cuba and Vietnam.'

Her father shook his head. 'If you look closely, in most of those cases, the elites stayed in power by forging alliances with the middle class and sections of the working class. What we need to do is educate people and support democratic reforms.'

'I'll leave that to you, Dad. Meanwhile, I'm going to law

school to get the tools to fight the establishment on their own terms. And to win.'

After earning her law degree, she honed her legal skills by working for a civil rights organisation in Atlanta. Political rhetoric became reality when she joined a crowd outside a police station to protest a killing of a young, unarmed black man. The police charged, swung their batons and knocked her to the ground.

'No, I'm all right,' she told her mother over the telephone. 'I needed stitches, and they nearly broke my arm, but the doctor says I can leave hospital tomorrow.'

'Better come back here. At least for a few days.'

'I'd like to, Mom, but I've got things I want to do.'

'With your job?'

'Yes and no. Don't worry about me. I know how to take care of myself. Just give my love to Dad.'

Her air-conditioned office in downtown Atlanta was her fortress. High up, behind closed doors, she used her legal weapons to defend people under attack by the state. She was bent over a deposition when a light blinked on the intercom. She pressed the button.

'A Mr Randall to see you.'

'First name?'

There was a pause and murmur before the secretary spoke again.

'Mark. Mr Mark Randall.'

The tall man entered her office with a smile that was openly mischievous.

'*Buenos dias*, Ms Steinhouse.'

'*Buenas*, Mr Randall.'

They had been together on the Cuba trip but hadn't been in touch since. After a firm handshake, they sat side by side on chairs in front of her desk. He stretched out his long legs, which ended in open-toed sandals.

'Turns out our good friend Johnny – remember him, with the golden locks? – well, he was working undercover for the FBI.'

'Figures. Snitches are everywhere,' she said. 'But it all came to nothing in the end, didn't it? I could see a mile off that they'd have to drop the case.'

'The feds talk a good game but often don't know what they're doing.'

'True.'

'Enjoying your desk job?' he asked with a tiny smirk.

'Yes. It's satisfying, knowing you're beating the bastards at their own game, every day.'

With a nod, he drew himself up and leaned in toward her.

'It's safe here, right?' He waved a hand around his head in a circle.

'Of course.'

He looked around and hesitated. 'No. It's better if we talk outside.'

'OK,' she said, looking at her watch. '1:00pm. At Mason's. It's right across the street, next to a bank.'

As she worked on her brief, her mind kept wandering back to Mark. Self-assured, like he'd always been, but without the underlying levity. He even spoke with a different voice. Almost hoarse.

She found him sitting in a booth, reading a book. They ordered coffee and she lit a cigarette.

'Listen, Sigi. I'll make it short. The war has come home. A group of us are planning a series of actions. On the front line.'

She stubbed out her cigarette and pushed her hair back, behind her ears.

'OK.'

'And we need you, your legal skills and your determination.'

'What do you want me to do?'

'Meet with us. Next month, in New York. I'll give you the details later.'

She nodded.

'Oh, by the way, I've changed my name.'

'Why's that?'

'Safer, that's all. I'm Gabriel now. Gabriel Pennington.'

Three months later, in the fall of 1967, a bomb ripped through a police station in downtown Chicago. A telephone warning meant that there were no injuries, but the damage was considerable. In other cities across the country, a flyer appeared, claiming responsibility and declaring "a state of war against the United States of America". It was signed by the Fifth Column Brigade.

She called her parents to explain that she had quit her job and was working with a group dedicated to social change.

'I can't really say more than that. Except that I know I'm doing the right thing.'

'I'm sure you are,' her father said, 'but I hope you're not putting yourself in any danger.'

She hesitated. 'We're all in danger, Dad.'

'You know what I mean.' It was a reprimand. 'Just take care of yourself,' he said more gently.

'I will. And, I hate to say this but… I could use some money.'

'All right. We'll send a check.'

'No, don't do that. Use Western Union. The main office, here in Atlanta.'

Her parents read about the spate of bombings but never spoke about them. They barely talked to each other about their daughter, confining themselves to expressions of hope that she was "doing all right" and sending money when requested. They didn't expect to see her for a long time and wouldn't have recognised her if they had.

Climbing down from the Greyhound bus in San Francisco, she took a taxi to an address in the Tenderloin. Gabriel had said they were young, but the people she met there, three men and two women, looked like teenagers.

In the bathroom, she studied herself in a mirror. The short, spiky black hair would have to go. She had been seen and possibly identified. She needed a new name, too. She cocked her head to one side. Yes, Sharon is a nice name. Sharon Walker.

In front of the group, she laid out the framework of a plan agreed with Gabriel and the leadership in New York. She spoke slowly, with long pauses, allowing everyone to digest the details. It was ambitious, she said, but only bold action would stop the war. They asked questions and the discussion went on late into the night.

Lying in bed in the cold and damp apartment, she told herself that she could mould them into an effective cell. It would take months, but she could do it. She'd start small and build up.

The turbulence of 1968 – mass rallies across the country, two infamous assassinations and a presidential election – provided cover for the actions of her group in the Bay Area. It also brought increased FBI surveillance. When one of their "safe" apartments was raided, she decided to disband the group and disappear.

A woman she had met at San Francisco State told her about a commune. A model alternative society, except that its finances were in a mess. 'You might like it there,' she said. 'Just tell Gavin I sent you.'

Gavin couldn't believe his luck. He'd been thinking to give it another two months and, if things didn't improve, call in the auditors. Maybe wind the whole thing up. Now, this bright young woman was sitting across from him. Not just with a personal recommendation, but also a law degree and experience in running an office and handling budgets.

She was given a bedroom and a small office, converted from a storage room, on the ground floor of the house. On the first day, she sent a letter to the logging company, rebutting each of their allegations of trespass and threatening to sue them if they continued to "harass my client". Next, she wrote to the county Board of Supervisors to initiate Gavin's plan for an agricultural preserve. She also tackled the finances, from Gavin's house insurance to gardening expenses. She laid it all out on paper, with graphs, projections and recommendations for cost cutting.

Seeing the actual numbers, Gavin realised it wasn't as bad as he'd feared. It was the not knowing that had made him so anxious, especially the legal fees required to fight the logging company and work with the county. Sharon would do that for free.

She didn't mix much with the others, preferring to eat in the house with Gavin and his family. During any casual contact, around the grounds or at the twice-monthly group meeting, she was friendly but reserved. Ted said something about a gift-horse, and everyone agreed.

She didn't take walks in the woods, didn't even like them, but they provided the screen behind which she was able to recoup. She kept in touch with the surviving members of the group in San Francisco, using payphones and charging calls to false or stolen credit-cards. Posing as a casual visitor, Gabriel came up to see her, allowing them to make more detailed plans. They decided that the next target had to be high-profile and closer to the war machine. Back in the city, Gabriel did reconnaissance and phoned her with a recommendation, which she accepted.

About a year later, Steve arrived at the commune. In her only previous serious relationship, with a professor at law school, sex had been frequent and energetic, but without much passion. Steve was softer and less demanding. She could see that he'd been knocked off course and was struggling to regain his footing. Although his politics were naïve, beneath the confusion she sensed a strength, a commitment to do what was right. As the summer months passed and they spent more and more time together, she became convinced. With that final piece of the puzzle in place, she had called Gabriel from the payphone in the Mendocino parking lot and spelled out his three tasks. The insider. The materials. The van and plates.

17

'Sharon isn't your real name, is it?'

They were lying on the bed, side by side, reading newspapers.

'No.'

'What is it, then?'

He shifted his position so he could look straight at her.

'Well?'

'All right, Mr Inquisitor. It's Sigi. Sigrid Steinhouse.'

'So how did you become Sharon.'

'Simple. After the Chicago bombing, we heard that someone had seen us approaching the building. So we all needed new identities. When I came out here, to San Francisco, people helped me.'

'Helped?'

'It's called dead-child harvesting.'

He grimaced.

'No, nothing like that. You just search through newspaper archives for a death notice of a baby who died in the same year that you were born.'

'OK.'

'Let's say you find one who died at five months. You then go back five months and find the birth announcement. That gives you the place and date of birth.'

'Right.'

'Then you write to the local registrar and request a copy of that child's birth certificate – they're considered public information so anyone can get one. They send it and you have a birth certificate of someone who would be about your own age.'

He nodded, wide-eyed. 'So, Sharon Walker is a baby who died, what, thirty years ago?'

'Twenty-eight, to be exact. Anyway, once you have that birth certificate, you get a few photos taken and apply for a social security card, driving license, credit card – everything you need. Passports take a little longer, but you can get that, too.'

'But wouldn't they know that the person is dead?'

'No, because they don't match deaths with births, especially if they happen in different counties.'

'It's that easy?'

'Yes, that easy.'

Gabriel sat at an outside table, sipping his coffee and nibbling a cherry pie. He had a good view, across the street, of the Lombard Gate entrance to the Presidio. Lots of people came to look at the square sandstone pillars and the mounted canon, booty from the Spanish-American war. Just another tourist, he walked across the street and studied the inscription on the barrel as well as the images carved on the pillars. Eagles clutching arrows and a laurel leaf, the goddess of victory, crossed swords, plus rifles and canons.

By now, he knew everyone who sat in the guard box and checked passes for those who drove in or walked through the gate. He knew them by sight, when and how they came to work, when and how they left. Six of them, all men, in a dark blue uniform and badge. There were also two MPs flanking the entrance.

He chose the guard who worked the night shift on most weekends. Today though he was on the afternoon shift, which ended at six in the evening, when he usually went across the street to buy a burrito before going back into the base to get his car.

'Hi. I just wondered, is that any good?'

Gabriel was standing next to the man inside the café.

'What? Oh, this.' The man raised the greasy wrapping paper. 'Yeah, it's good.'

Mexican American accent.

'Hard to find good food around here nowadays, don't you think?' Gabriel smiled.

The man looked at him, curious but not alarmed. Just a talkative guy.

'You might not believe this, but I can help you make some easy money.'

The man turned to leave.

'I'm serious. $500.'

The man frowned and hurried away. Gabriel trusted his instincts and made the same offer, in the same way, two days later. When the man hesitated, Gabriel ushered him into a bar on the corner opposite the café.

They sat on faux-leather benches and drank ice-cold beer, their voices drowned out by the rock 'n' roll from overhead speakers. Gabriel learnt that the guard was an army reservist, married with two children, making $360 a month.

'So, here's an extra six weeks for you. And you don't have to do anything. You see, we're playing a prank on a friend, one of the officers in the base.'

The man squinted at Gabriel. Dark suit, pastel tie, hair tied back in a ponytail.

'That's right. You really don't have to do anything. Just let a friend of mine in.' Gabriel flashed a smile. 'Look, it's simple. My friend will come after midnight, in a van.'

The man narrowed his eyes.

'Not so simple. I have to write down his name and license plate.'

'That's fine.'

The name would be fake, and Gabriel doubted that the numbers on the stolen plates would be readable after the blast.

'But MPs patrol the base all night. If they see something funny, it's trouble.'

'What's funny? A van delivers kitchen supplies to the Officers' Club.'

'Not after midnight.'

'OK.' Gabriel tried to think quickly. 'Then, what could be delivered after midnight?'

'Cleaning supplies. There's someone on nightshift there, in the back.'

'Good. So, it's cleaning stuff. By the way, how often do the MPs pass by your guard hut?'

'After midnight? One, maybe two times.'

Gabriel made a mental note: probably the same for the Officers' Club.

'Right,' he said, 'you write the details in your notebook. You lift the pole, and you go back to sleep.'

Gabriel chuckled, but not the guard.

'A letter. He needs a letter.'

'What kind of a letter?'

'Authorisation. From the quartermaster.'

Gabriel hesitated. They hadn't anticipated that.

'Don't worry. He'll have a letter.'

The man eyed him.

'What is this prank? Who is your friend?'

'That's a secret. Has to be. Nothing special though, just a little surprise.'

The man took another sip of the beer, his eyes still fixed on Gabriel.

'When will this happen?'

'I'll let you know a few days in advance.'

'The money?'

'Half when I tell you the day and half on the night. My friend in the van will give it to you at the gate.'

The man ran a hand over his lined face. Could be thirty but

looks fifty, Gabriel thought. They finished their beers, stood up and separated on the street outside, beyond the reach of the speakers inside crying about a bad moon rising.

Gabriel climbed up Lyon St on the eastern boundary of the Presidio, past cream-coloured apartment buildings and up steep steps. Entering Pacific Heights, he saw tree-lined streets with single-family houses, front lawns and garages. And the occasional mansion. The city's old money: railroad money, shipping money and banking money. He stopped, turned around and admired the view across the ocean to the Golden Gate.

He guessed that the guard didn't believe him about the "prank", but he was pretty sure that he'd go through with it. His real concern was whether the man would keep his mouth shut afterwards.

He drew a detailed map of the Presidio and added estimated times for each segment: driving from the apartment to Lombard Gate; driving from the gate to the Officers' Club; setting the timers; exiting the base on foot; getting back to the apartment. He put the map in a manila folder, added a note with a single sentence – "I've found our friend" – and sent it to River Ridge Farm.

When Sharon called him a week later, he told her about the guard.

'Are you sure he knows exactly what to write in the ledger?'
'Yes.'
'What's his nightshift schedule?'
'Most Saturdays and Sundays.'
'OK, we'll wait for a weekend night that's going to be cloudy. You said there're lights on all the roads in there, but what about the footpaths?'
'No lights. They're dark at night.'
'What about night patrols?'

Hearing what the guard had said, she grew more confident. It was extremely unlikely that the MPs would pass the Officers' Club during the few minutes when the van was parked there. And she brushed aside Gabriel's concern about the guard.

'He won't talk,' she assured him. 'It would only make him an accomplice. He'd lose his job.'

'But they're sure to suspect him.'

'Yes, but it's not his fault if someone lied about what was in his van. And from what you say, he's not a self-righteous do-gooder who's going to sacrifice himself for a matter of principle.'

'No, I guess not.'

Still, he couldn't forget that the guard knew what he looked like.

'Now, listen. This is what happens next.'

She explained everything in detail. She had plotted each movement on her own hand-drawn map, based on the one Gabriel had sent. Running along the bottom was a timeline, again using Gabriel's estimates for each step. It would run like clockwork. In fact, she smiled to herself, it was clockwork.

One thing, though, she had not been able to anticipate.

'It's not an impediment,' she said to Steve, after the test showed she was several months pregnant. 'It's a sign. A good sign. Everything goes ahead as planned.'

'But what if…'

'No, there's plenty of time. It'll be fine.'

'Why didn't you tell me?'

'Because it doesn't matter. But didn't you notice?'

'No. I mean, you looked different but…'

'And now what do you think?' She tilted her head to one side, eyeing him.

'It's wonderful. But it's up to you, of course.'

'You are sweet,' she said and took him into her swollen arms.

They were in her room, late-afternoon sun streaming through the only window. After making love, they lay flat on the bed, side by side. When she lit her inevitable cigarette, he rolled onto his side, propped himself up on an elbow and faced her.

'Shouldn't you stop? For the baby?'

She pursed her lips.

'I read about it in the paper,' he continued. 'You know it's not good for you anyway.'

'You're right. I'll cut down.'

That was good enough. He needed something fixed, something to hold on to, to stop his mind from spinning around. He was still struggling with the Presidio plan and now this. He would be a father, but what kind of a father? Should he tell his parents?

They talked about getting married. He was ready, but she said no. No ring and no ceremony. Just mother, father and baby. They would be a strong family unit. That was how she saw the future. At night, in bed together, they tried to come up with a name after the ultrasound images showed a girl.

'Angela,' she suggested. 'In solidarity with the Panthers.'

'No, no,' he said. 'It's got to be Lucy. The one in the sky.'

They compromised on Rosa. History and beauty combined.

They made no announcement, but she stopped hiding her bump and patted it with uncharacteristic pride whenever anyone noticed. She got smiles from the women, advice from Catherine, and kisses from Gavin and Ted.

Another month passed before Gabriel called to say that he had the materials. Now, they needed to fix a date – only then would he steal the van and the plates. They waited until weather reports predicted a cloudy Sunday night in early April. She calculated that she had three or four more weeks. She could still go with him to San Francisco, supervise the action and make the warning call.

However, the contractions started early, and she had to stay behind. By some uncanny symmetry, the gestation of the child was aligned with that of the plan, and they reached maturation within days of each other.

Although she didn't try to explain the baby in quasi-revolutionary terms, she regarded the synchronicity as normal. That's how she viewed the world. Things were, and should be, linked, sequential, predictable. Cause and effect; thought and act. Without that connectedness, things were loose, chaotic, even dangerous.

18

Bending over, he kissed mother and baby goodbye on the Saturday afternoon.

'All set?' she asked, propped up in bed inside the house.

'Yes. Don't worry about anything. I'll be back by noon on Tuesday.'

'There's no rush. Take it slow, every step of the way.'

'OK.'

'And one final thing.'

She looked up at him with anxious eyes, something he had never seen.

'If anything goes wrong, anything at all, you abort.'

Driving south, he kept seeing those eyes. Could he and Gabriel pull it off by themselves? She had conceived it, nurtured it and made all the decisions. Even "recruited" him. He didn't like to put it that way, but that's what had happened. Or had he offered himself? He would never be sure, and now it didn't matter. Get this over with and focus on Rosa. River Ridge wasn't a bad place for a kid to grow up. At least, for the early years. After that, she'd go to a proper school. He'd get a teaching job or Sharon would get one as a lawyer. Or both.

Surely, she would agree. Being a parent changed things –

everyone knew that. Especially for a mother. He'd have to tell his own mother eventually. She'd probably like the name Rosa, but he wasn't so sure how she'd get on with Sharon. Later, he told himself, eyes glued to the road ahead. There's plenty of time for all of that.

Again and again, he reviewed everything in his head; the details she had drummed into him. He couldn't see any flaws. He swallowed hard and reminded himself that there'd be no one there at that hour and that Gabriel would make the warning call. That made him feel better. No deaths. He was anti-war because he was anti-killing.

The sun had dipped by the time he reached Jenner. She had told him to take the slower, coastal route because it was less conspicuous, but he was already behind schedule. Maybe he should cut through the mountains and get the highway at Santa Rosa. He stuck to the plan but began to wonder if all her timings were accurate.

More doubts crowded in as he neared San Francisco. Maybe the guard would get cold feet. Maybe he'd be sick and someone else would take his place. Maybe the alarm clocks would fail. Maybe he wouldn't get out of the base in time. And what about this Gabriel? Was he as reliable as she thought?

Gliding over the Golden Gate, he reflected that he'd been in the commune for almost a year and never gone further afield than Mendocino. This was his return journey, emerging from the woods and going back to what he had left. But he told himself it wasn't a U-turn or an admission of failure. It had purpose, a clear and compelling purpose.

He skirted the edge of the Presidio, looking hard, but saw only trees. Leaving the waterfront, he drove along a city street with stores and cafés, apartment and office blocks, a gas station and fast-food restaurant. He'd memorised the directions but didn't know the city well and was afraid he'd miss the first turn. Stopped at a light, he realised that was the street and put on his blinker.

He drove up a steep hill into a residential area and slowed down, hoping it didn't look strange on the almost deserted street.

Two more turns brought him to the place, an apartment building, two stories above a dry-cleaner's and directly across from Golden Gate Park. Quiet, even for Saturday evening. He waited in the car, as instructed, for a full five minutes. 'Just to be safe,' she'd said. He didn't notice anything unusual, though he wasn't sure what he was looking for.

Opening the car door, he heard voices and pulled it shut. Two men passed by, moving briskly down the sidewalk. Then silence. He waited another two minutes, got out and felt the cool air on his skin. It was just beginning, he thought.

He pressed the buzzer.

'It's me,' he said into the small, round grill. Hearing a metallic click, he pushed the door open, stepped into a dark space and searched for the stairs. Narrow and unlit, they led him to the top floor, where a man stood in a doorway. Slender in body, he had the identifying ponytail.

'Come on in, man. It's good to see you.'

They shook hands and looked each other in the eye. She had vouched for them, the one to the other, but now they were on their own. Gabriel stepped aside and gestured for him to enter. Probably ten years older, he thought.

The apartment was as tidy as a hospital ward. Not a book or an ashtray out of place, and curtains drawn across the bay windows. Gabriel said it belonged to a friend of a friend who was in Florida.

'Family holiday to Disneyland. Be back next weekend.'

He nodded and dropped his backpack on the sofa in the front room. He didn't ask where Gabriel would go afterwards. He never wanted to see him again.

'Too bad about Sigi,' Gabriel said. 'I mean, her not being here.'

Of course, he thought, she's Sigi to him.

'But it's fine. We can do this by ourselves.' Gabriel smiled, deepening the lines on his face. 'Baby doing well and all that?'

'Very well. Thanks.'

'Well, we're pretty much all set here.'

He looked around. 'You got everything?'

'I was just working on it. C'mon, I'll show you.'

Gabriel led him into a large bedroom. On the bed, on top of a handprinted batik bedspread, lay sticks of dynamite, dry-cell batteries, blasting caps, alarm clocks and coils of electrical wire. Everything loose, nothing connected. On the floor, a new backpack.

'I'll put it all together tomorrow. Thought I'd wait 'til you came.' Gabriel paused. 'You know, just in case.'

'Sure. By the way, where'd you get it, the dynamite?'

'Bought it off a farmer, near Modesto. One of our contacts knew him.'

'What about the van?'

'Whoa! You're beginning to sound like Sigi.' Gabriel's soft chuckle pulled the punch.

'Sorry, it's just…'

'Sure. Anyway, the van was easy pickings. A nice white one, near Alamo Square. Some dickhead left the keys in. Probably getting boozed up in a bar.'

'Where is it?'

'Two blocks away.'

'The license plates?'

'Got them off some rich asshole's Cadillac in Pacific Heights. Last night.'

He strayed over to the crib by the window and ran his hand over the smooth wood railing. Nice and old-fashioned.

'And the security guard? He's OK?'

'Yeah, yeah. Just relax, man. It's all set.'

'What about the cash?'

'I gave him half on Wednesday. You give him the other half when you go in.'

'Where is it?'

They went into the kitchen, where Gabriel opened a drawer and drew out an envelope.

'It's in there. Don't touch it. Just give him the envelope.'

'What about the envelope?'

'He won't keep it.'

'OK.'

'And remember, your name is Jones and you're delivering cleaning materials to the Officers' Club.'

They ate pizza and drank one beer each at a round table in the kitchen alcove. Below, on the street, they heard Saturday evening traffic and voices. Rather than talk, they watched the news on a portable television. Lt Calley had launched an appeal against his murder conviction. An American table tennis team was on its way to China in the first round of ping-pong diplomacy. The San Francisco Giants defeated the St Louis Cardinals six to four. The weatherman predicted a dull Sunday and a cloudy night.

'You take the couch,' Gabriel said. 'I can manage on the floor.'

'Can't we move the stuff off the bed?'

Gabriel saw he wasn't joking and bit back disbelief. 'Not a good idea.'

He slept well, exhaustion dulling the doubts that had receded after getting to the city and into the apartment. Being there, meeting Gabriel and seeing the dynamite had turned free-floating anxiety into specific questions. Doing it was easier than thinking about it. Still, he didn't know the city well and wanted to make sure of the route to the base.

In the morning, he asked Gabriel for the keys to the van.

'What for?'

'Just a test ride. Make sure there are no surprises.'

Gabriel stared at him. 'You driven a van before?'

'Sure.' Once, so it wasn't a lie.

Leaving Gabriel to work on the explosives, he went first to check on his car. She had told him to use it for the test ride, but he wanted to feel confident about the van. There was no parking ticket and Sunday was meter-free. The fuel gauge showed a little over half, more than enough to get back to Mendocino. He moved it to a nearby street.

The van was two blocks away. It felt strange. High seat, huge windscreen and big hump between him and the passenger seat. The shift lever was on the steering wheel column, not the floor, which was good, but he had trouble getting into first. Just take it easy, he told himself, as the gears ground and the van lurched. He slumped back and sat still for a minute, found the groove and slipped away.

The van handled well around corners, and he managed smooth stops and starts. Straight down Divisadero, through the Haight, up to Pacific Heights, left turn on Lombard St and there was Lombard Gate. Twelve minutes in the light traffic. He guessed it would be similar that night, possibly less.

He also needed to be sure of his escape route on foot. The segment inside the base – from the Officers' Club to the perimeter wall – was not something he could practise. But he could do the rest from the wall back to the apartment.

He parked the van and made his way to the section of the wall where he would exit the base. Not a specific point, just somewhere along the eastern boundary, as marked on Gabriel's map. He noted the low wall, easy to jump over, and chose a spot. Where Lyon St doglegged left, he climbed the steep stone steps straight up to Pacific Heights, continued down toward the park and back to the apartment. Fifty-one minutes. He would need about seven or so to get out of the base, after setting the clocks. Altogether, then, an hour back to the apartment.

Unlike other timed segments of the plan, that estimate didn't have to be precise. He just needed to get out of sight as soon as possible.

He took a bus back to Lombard St and sat at an outside table across the street from the entrance, where Gabriel had eaten his cherry pie. Scrambled eggs, coffee and a paperback allowed him a good long look. Two military policemen, one on either side of the entrance to the base. Khaki uniform, high black boots, visored cap and holstered pistol.

They went off duty at sunset when an all-night patrol, again two MPs, took over. Gabriel didn't know their exact route, but Sharon had said that the chances of them walking by the club during the operation were "extremely unlikely".

But not impossible. A van parked near the club at that hour would definitely attract attention, and he might get arrested. Maybe that wouldn't be so bad. Intention, he knew from his reading prior to not going to law school, wasn't in and of itself a crime. He'd be charged with trespass and conspiracy, but not bombing.

He watched the entrance. Cars, vans and Jeeps approached and waited for the horizontal bar to rise before going into the base. Drivers of civilian vehicles were questioned by the guard, who checked whatever papers they had and wrote on a clipboard. Army vehicles slowed down and were mostly waved through, presumably because the guard recognised the driver. Having passed the checkpoint, everyone proceeded up a road that bent to the left and disappeared behind trees.

He knew the club was farther up that road, in the centre of the base. Just under a mile from the entrance along that winding road. Six or seven minutes was Gabriel's estimate, which seemed about right to him. Especially in the early hours, with no other vehicles around.

He left Lombard Gate and walked down toward the bay, still skirting the base. The more he knew about the place, the better, she had said. Tall eucalyptus trees thinned out and were replaced by low-lying buildings, sand-coloured with red-tiled roofs. Barracks. For the men before they were shipped out to Vietnam.

He passed the Palace of Fine Arts and found a footpath that ran along the waterfront with unimpeded views of the Golden

Gate and Marin headlands. Hearing voices, he turned around. Across the road, young men were marching in rows on a grassy field. The closer they came, the clearer the call-and-response:

'You ain't got nothin' to worry about.'

'He'll keep her happy until I get out.'

'And you won't get home 'til the end of the war.'

'In nineteen hundred and seventy-four.'

'Sound off!'

'One, two.'

'Sound off!'

'Three, four.'

He retraced his steps, from the waterfront back up the hill, keeping to the perimeter wall of the base. When he reached Lombard Gate, he stopped to inspect the pillars and canon. With attempted nonchalance, he strolled to within a few feet of the entrance and peered in. The road curved away and out of sight. Quiet now. And in the dead of night, it would be like a graveyard.

He drove the van back, parked and walked to the apartment. The dry-cleaner's was closed and the sign on the door said it would open at 9:00am on Monday. When it was all over.

On the bed, he saw four bundles of dynamite, each held together by black duct tape. Wires connected each bundle to a dry cell battery, and the battery to an old-fashioned alarm clock, with a hammer and bell on top.

'Looks complicated.'

'It isn't,' Gabriel said. 'What you can't see are the blasting caps inside the bundles. That's what the wires are connected to. When the alarm goes off and the hammer strikes the bell, it completes the circuit and ignites the cap. And then... it explodes.'

He looked again at the bundles, the funny wires and funky clocks. Small things, almost toys. He would have to set the alarms. That's all.

'How much damage do you think it will do?'

'Can't be sure. But the closer you can park the van, the better.'

He nodded, though the location and layout of the club was only roughly indicated on Gabriel's map.

'Must have been difficult to get all this stuff.'

'Not really. Except the clocks. I had to hunt them down, in junk shops and garage sales.'

'Can I have a look?'

'Sure. They're not set. Not yet.' Gabriel's smile, intended to put him at ease, put him on edge.

He picked up one of the clocks and looked for the little wind-up handle on the back. It was there, plain as day.

'You're going to set them for 3:10am, right?' Gabriel said.

He nodded. He would do that at 3:00am, the same time that Gabriel would make the warning call, giving him ten minutes to get away. At first, Sharon had wanted him to set the timers for 3:05am because the longer the van sat there, the greater the chance someone might notice it. And because too much time after the call might allow someone to get to the van and defuse the explosives. But Gabriel had estimated it would take at least seven minutes to exit the base. So, she had said 3:10am.

'Think that's enough?'

'Plenty,' Gabriel answered.

'Does that take into account the fact that I have to set all four clocks?'

'Don't worry. She's thought of everything.'

'Of course she has,' he mumbled to himself. Except that I might fumble with the clocks. Or take off in the wrong direction.

19

They got up in total darkness, ate toast with jam and drank two mugs of coffee each. Gabriel wrapped the bundles of explosives in thick towels, put each in a plastic bag and the bags in the backpack. He made Steve repeat the details for everything: the route to Lombard Gate, what to say to the guard, where to park at the club and when to set the timers.

'Remember,' Gabriel said, 'you've got to do it at 3:00am exactly. That's when I'll make the call. If you're a little early getting to the gate, you can delay going in.'

'Right.'

They checked watches. It was 2:24am.

'OK, last thing. What's your exit route out of the base?'

That part of the plan, which had been put together from maps and information gleaned from the guard, was crucial. One wrong step in the dark and he would get lost in the sprawling base. Lost and captured.

'Ah, down the road and…'

'What direction?'

'Left, as you face the club.'

'Then?'

'Down some stairs at the end of the parking area and through the trees. Straight ahead. Avoid the roads. Over the wall, wherever I find it.'

'Perfect,' Gabriel said with a grin and put a hand on his shoulder. 'Just go nice and slow. Every step of the way. And I'll see you back here.'

He slung the heavy backpack over one shoulder and stepped toward the door. Hand on the handle, he spun around.

'You put the lantern in there, right?'

Gabriel nodded and he was outside.

Descending two flights of stairs, he didn't worry about the sounds he made. And he didn't look to see if anyone was on the street when he left the building and walked toward the van. He needed to feel relaxed.

The van was jammed in between a car and a motorcycle, only inches from the front fender. He decided on the motorcycle, shoved it off its kickstand and guided it down to the asphalt, with a loud crunch. A light appeared in a high window, and he heard a voice. He ducked back against the building. The light went out and he got into the van. Reversing to get out of the tight space, he slipped a gear and listened, in a cold sweat, to the whining scrape of metal on metal.

He took a deep breath, re-engaged the gear and pulled out, just missing the sprawled motorcycle. 'Damn it,' he hissed. Lost time already. Go to go faster. No, no. Slow and easy.

The streets were deserted and the lamp lights blinding bright, especially around the park and up through Pacific Heights. Two cars appeared from nowhere and tailed him down the Lyon St hill toward Lombard Gate. He pulled over and let them pass. Checking his watch, he saw he was a little ahead of time.

'Jones, cleaning materials, Officers' Club,' he mouthed, glancing at the envelope on the passenger seat.

The entrance was well lit, the sandstone pillars picked out in a garish yellow. He eased in and stopped. One of the MPs looked in his direction but didn't move. The guard came out of his hut with a clipboard. He looked older than he'd imagined, lines on his face and grey streaks in his hair. Was he the right person?

'Name?'

'Jones.'

'What you got in there?'

'Cleaning supplies, for the Officers' Club.'

The guard bent down to see the license plate and wrote on his clipboard.

'You got a letter?'

'Sure. Here.'

The guard looked at the letter, took the envelope underneath it and went back into the hut. Inside, he checked that the envelope had the right number of dollar bills. Only then did he enter the details in his ledger. It was 2:45am.

'C'mon,' Steve muttered in the van.

The barrier rose and he drove through. The curving road was lit by globes on lamp posts, but the trees were pitch black in the moonless night. Rounding the bend, he saw a stop sign that wasn't on the map. OK, OK, he said to himself. You're fine. Fifteen seconds at most. But why am I stopping? Just don't grind the goddamn gears.

The trees disappeared and he reached the centre of the base, landscaped like a shopping mall. Buildings squatted on all sides of a parking lot divided into sections by low concrete squares enclosing trees and shrubs. Nothing moved as he edged forward, looking for the club.

There it was, at the far end, where it was supposed to be. And where it was darker, away from the lamp posts. Only the front veranda and red-tiled roof stood out from the shadows.

It was now 2:53am. He guided the van around to the back and parked next to a windowless wall. So close that he couldn't have opened the door on the passenger side. Crawling into the back of the van, he flicked on the camping lantern, eased the bundles out of the backpack and lined them up along the inside of the van closest to the club. Sweat trickled down his neck and under his jacket.

Squatting in the cramped space, he heard only the pounding of his heart. His legs ached and he shifted to a kneeling position. 2:59am. He counted to twenty, lifted the first clock and checked it showed the correct time. He turned the knob on the back until the extra hand showed 3:10am and pushed in the alarm button. Same with the second clock. His fingers slipped on the third, but he managed it and the last one. Scrambling out of the van, he shut the door tight. Gabriel said that would increase the blast impact.

He hurried along the road, down the steps and through eucalyptus trees. Stumbling, he reached another road, but it seemed to loop back to the parking lot. Just keep going, he told himself, as he crossed that road and crashed through more trees. Seeing barracks with lit windows, he crouched and waited. The bombs would go off any minute.

A car engine roared so the wall must be close. He found it, scrambled over, banged his knee and limped up the hill. Everything was still and dark, except for the pale white glow of the streetlights.

Got to walk normal, he told himself, out of breath, pain searing through his knee. A yellow cab whizzed by, and he turned his face away. Halfway up the stone steps, he heard the explosion and looked back to see orange-smudged plumes rise in the night sky. Somewhere in the bay, a foghorn moaned.

At the top of the steps, with sirens tearing through the air, he bent his head and stumbled forward. House lights came on and dogs barked. When a front door opened, he darted onto a side street, off the planned route but still going downhill. That way he knew he'd hit the park or the Panhandle.

He crossed that narrow strip of grass, where a coyote scuttled away at his approach. On the other side, bodies encased in sleeping bags hunched themselves back into the doorway of a store. An old man in baseball cap and bomber jacket came shuffling toward him. 'Got a fag?' The hoarse voice followed him across the street.

Reaching the apartment building, he let himself in with Gabriel's key and sank to his knees. Pain shot through his leg, and he braced himself by slapping a hand against the wall. He dragged himself up to the top of the stairs, where Gabriel gave him a hug.

'Welcome back, man. Hey, you all right?'

'Yeah. Just my knee, that's all. Got to sit down.'

Gabriel helped him hobble to the sofa and found a damp cloth in the kitchen.

'Nasty,' Gabriel said, dabbing the bloody gash and fashioning a bandage with antiseptic and Band-Aids from the bathroom cabinet.

'Thanks,' he said, his bad leg stretched out on the sofa. 'Did you hear it?'

'I heard it all right! All the way over here. We did it!'

'Yeah,' he said, blowing out his cheeks, 'it sounded pretty loud where I was.'

'And right on time.'

'You made the call, right?'

'I did, but…' Gabriel pulled his lips into a thin line.

'But what?'

'No one answered. I called again. No answer then either.'

'Jesus Christ!'

'Calm down, man. There was no one there. We can celebrate. We just blew up an army base.'

After a few hours' sleep, they were in the kitchen, with coffee and muffins, staring at the radio. A large, brown portable with buttons on the top. His pain had subsided, and the adrenalin had drained away, leaving only exhaustion. At 8:00am, they heard the signature jingle followed by a sombre voice.

Early this morning, at about 3:00am, a bomb exploded inside the Presidio Army base in San Francisco, partially destroying a building. A cleaner working the nightshift was killed. No other casualties have been reported.

'Shit!'

He slammed his mug on the table, spilling the coffee. He tried to remember if he'd seen a light on in the building. The truth was, he hadn't even looked. No one should have been inside! he screamed in his head. No one!

'Hey,' Gabriel said from across the table. 'We did what we were supposed to. Not our fault if they don't even answer their phones. Incompetent assholes.'

He winced and listened to the end of the news report.

The FBI have launched a major investigation. According to a spokesman, they have several leads, but no one has claimed responsibility for the bombing.

'Not yet,' Gabriel sneered and left the apartment to make another call. This time to the *San Francisco Chronicle*. Covering his mouth with a hand, he said it was about the bombing and asked for the news editor.

He waited a minute before a gruff voice said, 'Yeah, what is it?'

'The Fifth Column Brigade has attacked the Presidio as part of our war against the US military machine. We demand an immediate withdrawal of troops from South East Asia.'

On his way back to the apartment, Gabriel bought a copy of the morning paper, with a front page dominated by the continuing story of Charles Manson's trial. He flipped through the rest of the paper as he climbed the stairs.

'Too late to make the *Chronicle*,' he said to Steve, still staring at the radio. 'But just wait for the *Examiner*.'

'Shut up!' he burst out. 'We… I killed someone; in case you've forgotten!'

'Look. It's not our fault. We made the call. They messed up.'

He felt a hand on his shoulder but shook it off. 'I'm going to leave now.'

'No, you stay put. Here with me. Like Sigi said. Today we clean up. Tomorrow, we clear out.'

They stayed inside the apartment, listening to the radio, watching TV, feeding the parking meter, heating up canned food and taking naps. The radio news kept repeating the same details, and there would be no TV news until dinner time. At 5:00pm, Gabriel went out and returned with a copy of the evening paper.

The headline – "Presidio Bomb Blast: One Death Reported" – was accompanied by a grainy photo of the damaged building. The deceased was named as Mr Walter Gill, 49, a war veteran who worked at the base as a cleaner. Married with one child.

'Don't worry, they won't get anything from that charred mess,' Gabriel said, pointing to a smaller photograph of what was left of the van. 'Even if the plates survive, which they won't, they're stolen. Remember?'

He sat down and read further. The bombs had ripped through the Officers' Club, destroying the back wall, collapsing the roof, blowing out the windows and scattering debris in every room: mess hall, kitchen, laundry, assembly hall, ballroom, bar, restaurant and cleaner's office. Although the van had been almost completely destroyed, forensic experts were checking for any possible evidence. Responsibility had been claimed by the Fifth Column Brigade, an organisation known to have committed other terrorist acts. The police and FBI were conducting a joint investigation and called on anyone who might have seen or heard something to contact them.

'What is this "Fifth Column Brigade" anyway?'

Gabriel looked up at him and, in that moment, saw something he hadn't realised before.

'It's just a name.'

'The name of killers, you mean,' he snapped and crunched up the newspaper, kneading it again and again, until it was a small, hard ball. He had been told that the bar and restaurant closed at

9:00pm on Sundays and that the staff left by 10:30pm or 11:00pm at the latest. No one said anything about cleaners because no one had thought about them.

'Hey,' Gabriel cried an hour later, shaking him, slumped on the sofa. 'Time for the TV news.'

The screen flickered into life, and he heard the sounds of men talking. Muffled and far away, like the bar on the night of the lottery. Grey figures drifted across the screen and Gabriel was saying something. He got up, went to the only window and pulled back the curtains. Above the park, the sky glowed with anger. He gripped the window frame and held on tight.

20

When Walter didn't come home at the usual time, she didn't get worried. Sometimes, he had to stay at the base for an extra few hours. She'd see him in the evening, after she returned from her shift at the hospital. She picked up her handbag and checked herself in the hallway mirror. The telephone rang.

'Mrs Gill?'

'Yes.'

'This is Commander Blake at the Presidio.'

'Good morning, sir.'

'I'm afraid there's been an incident here at the base. You may have heard on the news.'

'No, I… what incident?'

'There was an explosion.'

'Explosion?'

'Yes, a bomb. At the Officers' Club.'

Her heart leapt into her throat.

'Mrs Gill. I'm sending a car to pick you up. It should be there in ten minutes.'

Swallowing hard, she managed to squeeze out a few words.

'Our son, in Oakland. I need to call him.'

'Yes, of course. The driver will wait outside your house for both of you.'

Susan Gill sat in her front room. She did not turn on the radio or the television. She did not want to hear anything from anyone. It wasn't good news, that much was clear, but whatever it was, she wanted to see for herself. She sat bolt upright, hands gripped in her lap, eyes straight ahead.

When he arrived, Ronald guided her into the unmarked car parked outside. The drive to the base was quick, quicker than she wanted. The driver took them through the gate on the south boundary and straight to the hospital, avoiding the Officers' Club.

Commander Blake led them down a corridor and around a corner on the first floor of the new building. Although she knew where the room was, she'd never been inside. Ronald held his mother's arm as they followed Blake through double swing-doors beneath a black-lettered sign that read "Mortuary".

Blake introduced them to a woman in a blue surgical gown and blue gloves. Susan blinked in the glare from the overhead lights bouncing off the white tiled floor. The wall ahead of her had two horizontal rows of stainless-steel lockers, one above the other. Each had a heavy metal handle and a large number painted in black.

The pathologist pulled out the tray and guided it onto an adjustable trolley. Ronald took his mother's hand and they shuffled up beside the waist-high gurney. Standing on the other side, the pathologist looked at them, waited for a nod and unzipped the heavy-duty white bag. Only as far as the neck.

Something like a smile lay on his powdered lips, as if he were dreaming. His short hair had been oiled. She reached out a hand, let it hang in the air and brought it back to cover her mouth.

She did not cry or utter a word, not until they had been driven back to the house in the Outer Sunset. Once inside, she broke down and Ronald helped her onto the sofa, where she crumbled in a heap and sobbed. He made two telephone calls, rearranging his day. 'Whoever did this,' he said to no one, 'will pay.'

21

Miguel Himenes faced three men. Commemoration plaques and paintings of sailing ships hung on the wall behind them. The wooden filing cabinets in the corners had stood there since the mid-nineteenth century. Himenes knew Blake and thought he recognised the man on his left, who was introduced as the head of military police. The third man, the stranger, was the director of the Army Criminal Investigation Division (CID) for Northern California.

'Now, Mr Himenes, I think you know why we want to talk with you.' Blake's voice was calm, his words ladled out in a slow, steady rhythm.

'Yes, sir.'

'Good. I understand that you logged in a vehicle in the early hours of yesterday morning. Is that right?'

'Yes, sir.'

'And I've got your ledger here, somewhere.' He made a pretence of looking through things on his desk. 'Right. This is it, isn't it?' He held up a thick notebook.

'Yes, sir.'

He flipped through a few pages. 'OK, here we are. Yesterday, Monday, April 11. 02:45 hours. License plate – CA PXM 738.

Name – Mr Jones. Destination – Officers' Club. Purpose – deliver cleaning supplies.'

Blake looked hard at Himenes and held his eyes for a moment.

'Do you get many civilian vehicles entering the base at that hour?'

'No, sir.' His voice was little more than a squeak.

'Speak up, please, Mr Himenes. So we can all hear you.'

'No, sir. Not many at that hour.'

'How many?'

'I don't know.' The commander continued to look at him, expectant. 'Maybe two or three a month.'

'In fact, Mr Himenes, there are no entries at any time between 12:00am and 6:00am for three whole months prior to this date. So, tell me again, didn't it strike as strange that this van appeared when it did?'

'No, sir. I mean, he said he had a breakdown and delay.' Himenes had decided he needed an explanation. 'And he had a letter.'

'Oh, yes, the letter. You mentioned that to Lt Pearson, here, when he spoke to you earlier.' He tilted his head toward the military police officer. 'What kind of a letter?'

'Official stationery. The quartermaster's office.'

'And was it signed?'

'Yes, sir.'

'Whose signature?'

'I don't know.'

'You mean, you didn't actually look at it.' Blake's voice was just short of a sneer.

'No, sir. I did look. I just don't remember the name.'

'OK. Now, what about the driver? This Mr Jones. Do you remember him?'

'No, sir.'

'No? You can't tell us what he looked like?'

'It was dark, inside the van.'

'Well, how old would you say he was?'

'Twenty-five, maybe thirty.'

'Hair? Eyes?'

'I don't know, sir.'

'Was he white or black or something else?'

'White.'

'Good. Now, another thing, licence plate PXM 738 is registered to a Mr Witherspoon, not a Mr Jones.'

'I don't know about that, sir. That was the number.'

The commander narrowed his eyes and issued a cold smile.

'That will be all for the time being, Mr Himenes. You are now on temporary leave. You may go.'

After a brief conference with the others, Blake called the FBI office in San Francisco.

'Tom, I think you might be right. Our Mr Himenes is not entirely reliable. And CID are reassured that the perpetrators are not military men and are no longer on the base. They're turning the case over to you.'

'OK,' Thomas Callahan said in his impatient voice. 'Now, tell me what you've got.'

Frantic for the past twenty-four hours, Blake's own investigation had turned up little, aside from confirming suspicions that the license plates had been stolen and that the letter Himenes claimed to have seen had not originated from the quartermaster. The MPs on patrol that night had seen and heard nothing, until the blast. CID agents and SF police officers had begun to question residents near Lombard Gate. A forensic team had searched the guard's hut, where they found an envelope; they had also collected fragments of the van and taken photographs at the scene. All that had been handed over to the FBI, but lab test results were not expected for some time.

'Any hard evidence?' Callahan asked.

'Well, our MPs found footprints about two hundred yards from the club. They lead through a grove of trees to the eastern boundary wall. I've already redirected the house-to-house people to that stretch of Lyon Street.'

'Anything else?'

'Yes. Our people also identified the shoe size.'

'And?'

'Size nine. And they're pretty sure it's a Nike.'

'Good work, Commander. Let's stay in close touch.'

Callahan hung up and walked to the window. Tie askew, belt loose, sleeves rolled up to the elbow, he looked down at Market St Hundreds of feet were scurrying in every direction.

'Size-nine Nike. That narrows it down nicely,' he muttered.

Callahan already had his hands full. The mysterious death of a Taiwanese businessman, the ever-expanding scope of Mexican drug cartels and the slippery movements of a Soviet spy, plus the day-to-day stuff of robbery, tax fraud and petty crooks. Not to mention three terrorist incidents in the past year.

Scowling, he returned to his desk and reread the fax sent from Washington. He was instructed to interview "every person living within a two-hundred-yard radius of Lombard Gate". He'd decided it was best not to point out that half of that circle would be inside the base itself. He was also told to check on the anti-war protestors who had been arrested at Lombard Gate almost exactly a year ago. Mr Hoover, the fax informed him, did not think this was a coincidence, and he should consider those protestors as suspects in the bombing. Callahan shuffled papers and pulled out the list of the thirty-nine names. He shook his head and laid it aside.

'First things first,' he mumbled and picked up his telephone.

Half an hour later, he was looking at four of his best agents, all ex-military, one of whom spoke Spanish. He briefed them on the case, leaving out details and emphasising the need for results.

'We don't know if this bombing is linked to the others. But we do know who helped them get into the base. And your job is to find out everything you can about this guy.'

He passed around a photo.

'I want to know where he goes, who he meets and what he eats for breakfast. Everything.'

Himenes left the commander's office and walked past the cordoned off area at the far end of the parking lot. Police, firemen and men in suits were moving around, huddling in small groups, going in and out of what remained of the club. Some looked like they were being interviewed by newspaper and TV journalists. He wanted to go closer and get a good look.

He knew Walter Gill, not personally, but he'd checked his ID card many times when he came in through the gate. He wondered if he should go to the commemoration service on Saturday. It wasn't really a funeral, just a ceremony in the chapel garden, only a stone's throw from the club. He couldn't decide what would look worse – going or staying away.

He turned the key and waited for his old Buick to cough into life. During the twenty-minute journey across town, from the base to the Mission District, Himenes made two decisions. He would not go to the ceremony, and he would not spend the money. Not yet anyway. He'd give it to a friend for safe keeping, away from any prying eyes, domestic or otherwise.

He parked near Dolores Park and walked to his apartment, one of four units carved out of a single-family house that had seen better days. The money wasn't enough to get a better place, but he could offload his gas guzzler and buy something better. Used, of course, but still an upgrade. He'd look at ads in the paper. Just look. That couldn't hurt.

Even before he reached the landing, he saw his wife staring down at him. From the day he had brought her to the city, she had tried to get a job, but her poor English made that almost impossible. Even cleaners were expected to understand orders. They had married in 1955, when he'd gone back to his village in the mountains of southern Mexico for a family visit. Six months later, he returned to San Francisco with his bride and found a job at the Presidio, where he had trained before being sent to Korea.

'*Xa nuu?*' she asked. How are you?

'*Izyla.*'

They always spoke to each other in their native Zapotec dialect.

He showered, changed and sat at the table with a glass of cold beer and a plate of refried beans.

'Maria wants to go the movies on Saturday,' his wife said. 'I told her there's no extra money.'

'Oh, let her go,' he said. 'I can give her some. But only after she goes to her class in the morning.'

He had enrolled their sixteen-year-old daughter in a locally funded Saturday programme designed to help Chicano students get into university. She was smart enough, he told himself. All she needed was better teaching and more confidence. Berkeley had scholarships for kids like her. Her brother, just a year younger, was a different story, though. It wasn't even clear he'd graduate. But at least he spent his free time playing baseball, rather than with one of gangs in the neighbourhood.

'And while she's at the movies, let's go shopping.'

'Really?'

The last time they'd gone shopping together was at Christmas.

'You know, that new dress you've been asking for.'

22

All through that same morning, at breakfast and when they cleaned up the apartment, he hardly spoke. Now, he was standing at the front door, backpack in hand.

'Look,' Gabriel said, 'you said no one saw you go in or come out. Right?'

'As far as I know. That's all.'

'You'd know. So don't worry.'

'But people did see me when I got near here. On the street.'

'So what? That's a long way from the base.'

'But suppose one of them remembers me, goes to the police and…'

'Homeless people don't go to the police.'

'No, I guess not.'

'Listen. The main thing is: nothing links us to the bombs. And this apartment belongs to a friend of a friend. Besides, we don't know each other, do we?'

'No.'

'So cheer up. OK, that poor guy was in there, but that's not our fault. We called. Twice.'

'Umm.'

'It was a total success. Go back to Sigi and your new baby and relax.'

He managed a wan smile.

'And tell her I'll get in touch after a few weeks, when it all dies down.'

Halfway down the first flight of stairs, he stopped. It couldn't be that easy. They must have forgotten something. He started to go back, shook his head and plunged down the steps.

Outside, he shouldered his backpack and zipped up his jacket against the breeze. The sun was warming the late-morning air and the sky was clear. No fog or mist. Almost no one on the street. He wanted distraction, anything to short-circuit the constant self-doubt.

Seeing a ticket under the windshield wiper of his car, he felt his chest tighten. That meant a police record of the time and place. He ripped it out from under the rubber strip. It was a flier for a new laundrette.

He decided against going over the Golden Gate since that meant driving past the Presidio. It wasn't that someone might recognise him – that was crazy – only that he never wanted to go near the place again. He took the roundabout route, the Bay Bridge to Berkeley and over the Richmond Bridge, at the northern neck of the bay, to Marin.

Sharon would have followed the news, the bombing and the death. What should he tell her? That he hadn't noticed any lights on in those final minutes? Or that he hadn't even looked? Because there wasn't supposed to be anyone in there!

It's faster this time, he thought, as he sped along Highway 101. Past San Rafael and Petaluma, toward Santa Rosa and Ukiah. Heading north, escaping again. It was manslaughter, not murder, wasn't it? How many years for that? She ought to know. Jesus Christ! What the hell had he done? Like Gabriel said, it wasn't their fault, but he was the one who planted the things, not him. Accidents happen all the time. On roads, on stairs, on playgrounds. Why didn't he see any lights? Because you didn't look, that's why.

Continuing on 101 would be quicker, but he wanted to slow down. He turned off at Cotati and rode through the low mountains and along the Russian River to the coast at Jenner. Rocky headlands, a strip of sand and blue water stretching out as far as he could see.

Although the radio news concentrated on other stories, they never failed to mention the FBI investigation. But Gabriel was right. They had no way of identifying him. Even if fingerprints were found, they couldn't be traced to him. Wait a minute! Santa Rita. They had his prints, his name, his photograph and his parents' address.

He reached Mendocino in the late afternoon, decided against stopping to eat, continued past the town and took the turning into the woods. Bumping along on the dirt track, he came to the parking area, where he turned off the ignition and let his body go slack. Exhausted, he wanted to sleep right there, hidden among the trees.

She jumped up when he walked, ashen-faced, into her office. Coming around her desk, she embraced and held him close.

'I know, I know,' she murmured.

When he didn't respond, she pulled back and looked at him, hands on his shoulders.

'It's unfortunate and we'll issue a statement tomorrow expressing regret. But military bases are a legitimate target in war. You know that, don't you?'

He took a step back. 'Legitimate target,' he repeated, slowly, as if they were words in a foreign language.

'Yes. Like we said, we are at war. The war at home.'

The furrow between his eyes deepened to a knife cut. He had avoided one army only to join another.

'And the main thing is you've struck a tremendous blow. It's something to celebrate.'

'Where's Rosa?'

It sounded like an accusation.

'Asleep.'

He entered the darkened bedroom and approached the cot, where he heard soft sounds. Scooping up the tiny infant, he nuzzled her. The weight of the life in his hands felt heavy. So heavy he might drop it. He placed her back in the cot, knelt down and wept.

Watching from the doorway, she saw his shoulders rise and fall and heard him whimper. She stepped forward, bent down and raised him up. Hand in hand they stood, looking at their daughter.

'What's that red splotch?' he asked, pointing to her forehead.

'It's nothing. A temporary birth mark. The doctor said it will fade out in a few weeks.'

She squeezed his hand and led him back to her office. The straight lines and square corners, everything in place. Familiar and safe, where there was no blood. They sat down in chairs.

'Tell me what happened,' she said and lit a cigarette.

He hesitated, lips bunched, and then burst out, 'He made the call, twice. But nobody answered. That's what happened!'

'I see. That's unfortunate. But let's leave that for a minute. Just tell me exactly what happened from the time you left the apartment that night to the time you got back.'

He had gone over it many times in his head that day, driving up from San Francisco. Now, it came out with more detail as the words lined up and turned into a story, with a beginning and an end. The telling placed it at a distance, outside of him, something he had witnessed.

She waited for him to finish before speaking.

'The guard, at the gate. How did he strike you?'

'What do you mean? I hardly saw him.'

'What did he do when you gave him the money? Count it? Pocket it?'

'I don't know. He took it inside the booth.'

'Did he say anything?'

'No.'

She stubbed out her cigarette, grinding it hard.

'Now tell me about the phone call.'

As he spoke, he realised that he only had Gabriel's word for it. Maybe he hadn't called at all. Maybe he got nervous or got the timing wrong or called the wrong number. No, he wouldn't have lied. He made the call, all right. The stupid bastards just didn't answer.

'How is he?' she asked when he'd finished.

'Huh? Oh, he's fine.' Like you, he thought. 'Said he'd contact you in a few weeks.'

'Good. Come on, let's eat something. You must be starving.'

She heated up a casserole she'd made that day – using the house kitchen was one of her perks. They ate early, to avoid Gavin and his family, and retreated to her office with mugs of coffee.

For the next hour, they considered everything that could link them to the bombing. The explosives had been purchased with cash in Modesto; the clocks and wiring came from junk shops; the van and plates were stolen. Recovering prints from the van would be near impossible, and he confirmed that he'd left no prints on the money given to Himenes. No one, as far as he knew, had seen him going to or coming from the base. No one who could identify him, that is. The apartment was unknown to the FBI. Telephone calls had been made from a phone booth. Gabriel was in hiding and he was in the woods.

'By the way,' she added at the end, 'if anyone asks, you went to your sister's wedding in Sacramento.'

'But I don't have a sister, in Sacramento or anywhere else.'

'You do now.'

As usual, he was reading in bed before going to sleep. She sat down on the edge of the bed and waited for him to lower the book. He couldn't concentrate and felt annoyed, denied his moment of peace at the end of the day.

'Remember what I said about how I got my new name?' she asked.

'Yeah. "Dead" something.'

'Right. We're going to have to do it. Both of us.'

'Both of us?'

'Look, Steve. They'll throw everything into this. Agents, informants, house-to-house, phone taps, surveillance. Everything. We need new identities.'

'You mean, all that stuff with birth and death notices in newspapers?'

'Yes, and the sooner the better. Unlike me, you're not known to the FBI. But suppose someone did see you? Suppose they put pressure on the guard and crack him? Suppose they identify Gabriel? It's not impossible. We have to stay ahead of them.'

He let the book fall. *Ahead of them.* That made sense.

'So, what do we do?'

'I'll go to Ukiah. They've got old editions of the *Chronicle* in the library there.'

'Won't it look strange, leaving the baby?'

'I'll tell Gavin I've got to sort out some legal issues with the planning commission there. It shouldn't take more than a day or two.'

He had managed to evade Ted by staying in the house. In truth, he was exhausted and didn't want to face Ted or the kids. Sharon told Gavin, who told Ted, that he wouldn't be around until after lunch. He waited for as long as possible before walking out toward the barn.

'Wiped out from the wedding, huh?'

Ted was sitting on a stump at the side of the barn, whitling and keeping an eye on the youngsters building a treehouse.

'Sort of.'

He sat down on another stump and looked at the ground.

'Sacramento's a long way. You go by way of the Bay Area?'

Ted knew he didn't have a sister and, hearing the news of the bombing, would have put two and two together.

'Yeah, I did.'

'Well, it's good to have you back. Safe and sound.' A conspiratorial smile.

'Thanks. It's good to be back. Everything OK?'

'I think so. They might have done a bit more woodwork than homework, while you were gone, but I didn't hear many complaints.'

The shared laughter sealed their unspoken agreement. For half an hour, they planned morning lessons and afternoon activities. Just like always. Feeding off each other, different enough to generate ideas and similar enough to put them into practice. When they fell silent, Ted continued whitling while Steve watched the kids in the treehouse, sawing, hammering and laughing. Someday, little Rosa could be doing that.

'How's the baby?'

'That obvious, huh?'

'Like an open book.'

'She's fine. Already looks as determined as her mother.'

Ted nodded, still working on the piece of wood in his hands.

'What are you making?' he asked.

Ted blew off the shavings and handed it to him. The round disc has been scooped out in the centre, leaving only a vertical rib connected to the outer rim by two short legs.

'Thought you might like it.'

He looked at the peace symbol in his open palm.

'I can put a little hole in it,' Ted added. 'At the top there and run a bit of string through. Or leather. If you want.'

'I'd like that.'

'Which?'

'Leather, I guess.'

'Good choice. It'll last longer.'

It rained for two days, and when the sunshine returned, there was a celebration. It was a secret, withheld from the parents until the last moment during breakfast, when an enormous cake arrived from the house. The adults sang "Twinkle, Twinkle, Little Star" and the kids danced around, chanting, 'Rosa! Rosa!' Ted made a short speech consisting entirely of horticultural metaphors and ending with the hope that "this rose would bloom with love, beauty and courage".

The infant herself was in the house, fast asleep in her crib, with Gavin's teenage daughter in attendance. Steve gathered her up and returned to the barn, where, with a beaming Sharon, he thanked everyone and smiled benignly when their cake-choked mouths spluttered into a cheer.

Back in the house, she was walking around the bedroom, patting Rosa, when the telephone rang in her office next door.

'You take her,' she said to him. 'I think that's the bank calling.'

'I can't. I've got the kids in ten minutes.'

His voice was strident, almost belligerent. The strain, building ever since his return, had peaked with the outpouring of emotion during the surprise celebration.

'I know,' she said. 'I won't be long. But this is important.'

When the crying stopped, he laid Rosa in the crib and rocked her back and forth. Soothed by the movement, he began to think about what to teach the kids. He and Ted had made plans, but he wasn't sure he could or even wanted to pick up the broken threads. Rosa gurgled, spat and began to bawl again. "Rock-a-bye Baby" came to his lips so quickly that he didn't know he was singing until she was asleep.

That's it, he said to himself. We'll do lullabies. Find them in books, sing them, write them down and talk about why they're so popular. They can even write their own. And if they're any good, we can try them out on Rosa.

He thought about writing to his parents, who still believed he was working in a restaurant in San Francisco and were still waiting for him to visit. They would be overjoyed at having a granddaughter, but they'd insist on seeing her and meeting her mother. Better to keep it all buried. If one little corner got exposed, the whole thing would have to be dug up.

'All clear,' she said, coming into the bedroom. 'The bank is satisfied, and the kids are waiting for you. I'll keep an ear out for Rosa while I work next door.'

They had at least been able to agree on a schedule. She took responsibility during the mornings, burping Rosa, fetching the bottle and changing nappies. He did the same in the afternoons. They were supposed to alternate at night, but it always was he who got up.

'OK,' he said, managing to sound conciliatory.

'Ah, you need to ask Gavin's daughter to look after her tomorrow. I'm going to Ukiah. You know, our new names.'

23

The room buzzed with anticipation. The word had spread that someone from Washington had arrived to take charge of the investigation. A well-known special investigator with the reputation of being ruthless and disciplined. That's why, it was said, he'd cracked several high-profile cases, including the assassination of a big city mayor and a church bombing in Florida. He clearly had the backing of the Bureau, all the way to the top.

That was good news. Hoover's man could bring in agents from all over the western states. Where they'd house them might be a problem, but rumour was they had commandeered the top three floors of a downtown hotel. Anyway, it meant more resources, which meant a better chance of success, which is what really mattered.

Sitting beside the new man at the long table, Callahan looked out at the assembled agents. Mostly in their thirties and forties, a few with long hair, all with serious faces. He had a great respect for them and hoped it was reciprocal. He was glad that Washington had declared the bombing, officially known as "Presbomb", a major case and sent a senior investigator. But he didn't relish having to relinquish control. After all, he had the local knowledge and personal relationships with the police and Blake at the base. The orders given in the latest fax showed how out of touch Washington was. Worst of all, the new arrival had been given his office and he had to do with a smaller one that overlooked the parking lot.

Charles Bennett, round-faced and bald-headed, stood and surveyed the audience with his small eyes.

'Gentlemen,' he said, 'once again, we are faced with evil. Cruel and sadistic evil. And, once again, with your hard work and dedication, we will prevail.'

He paused and waited for heads to nod.

'I won't say more today because we have a job to do. We must identify and find the person who recklessly killed an innocent man, a war veteran. We must find this person and his accomplices and see that they face justice.'

Again, he waited.

'Just a word of warning. If I hear that anyone of you has spoken to the press without my permission, you will be fired on the spot. Understood?'

Murmurs of assent rippled around the room, and when Bennett sat down, there was spontaneous applause. Even Callahan couldn't help joining in.

After the men had dispersed to their rabbit-warren rooms, Callahan followed Bennett down the corridor and into the office marked "Special Agent in Charge". When Bennett sat behind the large desk and gestured to him to take a seat, Callahan swallowed his pride and pulled over a spindle-back wooden chair.

'I've read the reports,' Bennett said, 'but I'd like you to sum up the situation so we're on the same page.'

Callahan had expected something like this and spoke without hesitation.

'Last Monday, at approximately 2:45am, a white Ford van entered the Presidio base through Lombard Gate. According to the guard, the driver gave his name as Jones, said he had cleaning materials for the Officers' Club and showed a letter of authorisation. We have since established that the letter was forged, or never existed.'

'The guard might have lied?'

'Yes, sir.'

The honorific came out by habit rather than choice.

'Right. Now, what about the driver?'

'The only person, apparently, to see him was the guard at the gate. He described him as Caucasian, twenty-five or thirty years old. The van…'

'That's all? Nothing about hair, eyes, height?'

'No, that was all the guard gave us.'

'Not enough for an Identikit, then?'

'Probably not, sir.'

'Right. Carry on.'

'The van went up Lombard St, presumably turned on Presidio Boulevard and proceeded to the Officers' Club. That's the usual route. Here, sir, have a look.'

Callahan handed over a small, printed map, with the likely route indicated in red ink.

'Excellent,' Bennett said as he studied the map. 'Not far, is it?'

'No. Probably took about eight minutes, maybe less. The van was parked in the driveway on the right-hand side of the building. Just after 3:00am, four bombs – and possibly more – were detonated.'

'Any links to other terrorist attacks here in the Bay Area?'

'None that we know of. This is the first time the Fifth Column Brigade has claimed responsibility around here, though we know about their attacks elsewhere.'

'What about the explosives?'

'The usual. Dynamite triggered by alarm clocks. That's what lab boys say.'

Bennett pushed out his lips. 'I see. Now, tell me about the man who died.'

'Walter Gill. Head of the cleaning unit on the base. World War Two veteran.'

'Jesus. Married?'

'Yes. The wife is a nurse at the Letterman Hospital, here on the base.'

'Children?'

'One. A grown-up son, lives in Oakland.'

'No other casualties?'

'No, sir.'

Callahan then described the footprints and probable exit route of the bomber but added that interviews with residents on Lyon St near that part of the wall had produced nothing useful.

'What about the van?'

'The lab has identified it as a Ford Econoline. First generation, which means made between 1961 and…'

'OK, OK. Who owned it?'

'We don't know. Not yet. But it was probably stolen, like the plates, which are registered to a Mr Witherspoon of Pacific Heights. He reported them stolen on Monday morning.'

'All right. Main thing is to find out where the van was stolen. Send someone to every police station to check reports of stolen vehicles.'

'Every station in San Francisco?'

'Start there and fan out until we find what we're looking for.'

Callahan was about to say that thousands of vehicles were stolen every year in the City.

'Don't worry,' Bennett said, reading his expression. 'I'm bringing in more agents from all over the state and outside, too. Should be here tomorrow. Now, what about this list you mentioned?'

Callahan handed him the piece of paper.

'These are the names of the activists arrested last year after a protest at Lombard Gate. Some are known to our informants, so we keep pretty close tabs on them. Even identified one or two places they use as safe houses.'

'Enough for a search warrant?'

'Tough to get in this town. We'll need more evidence.'

'Right. Now, what about the guard?' Bennett had already been briefed on Blake's interview with Himenes the day after the bombing. 'Anything new there?'

'Not much, sir. A family man. Doesn't go out much, not on his own I mean. Modest living.'

'How many men on him?'

'Four.'

'Make it six. Anything unusual, I mean *anything*, I want to know. Immediately.'

'Yes, sir.'

'And now, you will accompany me on a little trip.'

It was grey and windy that April afternoon when the two men approached Lombard Gate on foot. They'd parked up on Lyon St and walked down the hill.

'Just here, sir,' Callahan said, indicating the spot where they believed the bomber had exited the base.

Bennett looked over the waist-high wall into the dense trees, and then up and down the street.

'No idea which way he went, right?'

'No, sir.'

Bennett continued down the hill to the entrance, where the two MPs on duty snapped to attention. The traffic in and out was thin but steady. Military personnel and civilians in cars, a delivery truck and a busload of schoolchildren. He ran a hand over the canon and read the plaque.

'Busy afternoon?' he asked the guard after introducing himself and Callahan.

'Not too bad, sir,' the guard said. 'I get a chance to catch up on the news and my reading.' He held up an Ian Fleming paperback and gave a toothy smile.

'OK. Let's see the ledger.'

Bennett flipped back to the night in question and studied Himenes' handwritten entries. Clear, flowing writing. Must have been calm, he thought. Probably had no idea what was happening.

'Ever have to turn people away? Because they don't have the right paperwork, for instance?'

'No, sir. Not very often.'

They retraced their steps up the hill to the parked car and drove back down to the entrance. The guard wanted to wave them through, but Bennett insisted that he enter their details in the ledger. On the short ride along the curving road to the club, Bennett tried to imagine that night when the white van took the same route. What was the man thinking? Was someone else hidden in the back, someone to set the timers? And who had planned the whole thing?

They parked in the central area and walked up to what remained of the club. Built in the eighteenth century as barracks for Mexican soldiers, the adobe and timber frame had been remodelled over the years, adding a second storey and a bell tower. It was now a charred shell.

Debris had been cleared away and police presence reduced. It was no longer a crime scene, just a building site. Bennett grimaced, as if warding off a bad smell. He could feel the pulse of the base around him. The clump of marching feet, the purr of Jeeps, the inaudible hum of offices. More than three thousand people. And now one of them was dead.

Back in his office, he wasted no time approving the text of a poster offering $10,000 for information leading to the arrest of the person or persons responsible for the death of Walter Gill. The only thing missing were the suspects.

24

Tight-lipped between his wife and mother, Ronald was angry. Angry that it had taken so long to release the body. Angry at the excuses: autopsy, protocol, paperwork. Angry that his father was dead. He hadn't wanted this kind of ceremony either, not with those bouquets piled up on a coffin. He'd wanted to do it at home, by themselves. With a minister, but that's all.

His mother had pointed out that, even though he didn't go every Sunday, his father loved church. Particularly singing in the choir at Christmas and Easter. Constructed soon after the earthquake, the church was more ornate than most in the neighbourhood. Carved pillars flanked the arched front doors, and the bell tower was topped by a cupola. Light streaming through the stained-glass windows fell on wooden pews and crimson carpets.

'What God creates God loves, and what God loves God loves everlastingly.' The minister paused for a moment and continued. 'Those words were true for Walter Gill before he died, and they are true for him today. However, even the truth of those words and the strength of God's love do not remove our grief or answer the questions we ask today.

'How can we carry on when a husband and father dies before his time? Not just dies, but is the victim of a criminal act? How, we ask God, can we live when death shatters our world, and nothing makes sense anymore?'

Ronald tightened his grip on his mother's hand. Death had made his father more, not less, present. He was again the protective, wise father, like when he was a child. After that, things had gotten confused. The years of political protest and police brutality, which Ronald did his best to ignore, had shaped him, nonetheless, and left him with a father he could not admire. The war hero rewarded with a cleaner's job became a humiliating symbol of servility.

Now, the death of that same man consumed him. It was devastating and undeserved. Tore his mother apart, destroying their plans for retirement and old age. It didn't help that the idiot who did it was white. He would make it up to his father, atone for all those years when he'd taken him for granted and even, in low moments, shunned him as a failure. Nothing would stop him from getting justice for the man who, he now realised, he had loved all along.

'Let us pray.'

Ronald fingered the thin gold chain hanging around his neck. A birthday gift from his wife, Marilyn. He stood when she did and watched the coffin as it was carried back down the aisle by four men, two in suits and two in uniform. One black, three white. What did that mean? The organ music soared, but he heard little above the deafening roar in his head.

'He was a very good man, your father.'

Ronald turned to see Blake standing beside him on the church steps. Blake was all right, as far as army brass went. He'd met him only a few months ago at the ceremony commemorating his father's thirty years of service, when the commander had given him a medal. It was still hanging, behind glass on the living room wall.

'A very good man,' Blake repeated, his brass buttons gleaming in the hazy sunshine.

'Thank you.'

'And I want you to know that we are doing everything possible to find out who is responsible.'

'Can you tell me anything? Anything at all?'

'I'm afraid not. But I will say that things look promising.'

Blake stuck out his hand and Ronald accepted it.

'Promising, my ass,' he snorted beneath his breath after Blake left him.

The hearse pulled away, on its journey five miles south, to a cemetery where the city's dead had been buried for the past hundred years. Marilyn guided her mother-in-law toward the unmarked police car that had driven them the few blocks from the house to the church.

'Wait a minute!' Ronald cried and rushed over. 'We'll go there in my car.'

'I'm ready to take them. Commander Blake's orders.' The young man in fatigues blinked as he spoke.

Ronald controlled his rage and said, 'That's all right. We will bury my father ourselves. Just tell the commander I insisted.'

25

It was always the same, Bennett later reflected. When a breakthrough comes, the surface weakens, and the cracks keep spreading until the edifice collapses.

'Got it!' the man shouted, bursting in without the deferential knock.

'Got what?' Bennett growled and looked up from the interview transcripts he had been trawling through since early that morning.

'The van! A white Ford Econoline was reported stolen two days before the bombing. Near Alamo Square. It's still missing.'

'Must be it. Where is that?'

'The Lower Haight. Some call it the Western Addition.'

Bennett blew out air. The multiple names and imprecise boundaries of the city's neighbourhoods had frustrated him from day one. 'What do you expect in a town full of potheads!' he'd bleated on the phone back to Washington.

He summoned his core team and tasked them with interviewing residents in the area where the van had been stolen. Equally important, they were to check if anyone on the list of thirty-nine activists was reported to be living in the vicinity.

In the Mission, Miguel Himenes squinted at the newsprint. As usual after the nightshift, he'd slept into the early afternoon, eaten a meal and was relaxing in the only comfortable chair in the apartment.

He'd been at it for days, telling himself he was only looking and not buying. But this offer was just too good. If he waited, surely the chance would be lost. It was a risk, he knew, but desire defeated caution. He'd been back on guard duty for almost a month, and the story had already disappeared from the papers. But the money was still there. All he had to do was collect it.

The man tailing Himenes that day was also reading the newspaper, or at least studying the baseball standings. He parked in a different place each time and used the paper for both cover and distraction. He only realised Himenes had emerged from the building when the battered Buick rumbled past him. Putting on his sunglasses, he pulled out and followed. When Himenes headed south, toward Bernal Heights, the man smiled. This was a new direction and might yield new information.

The Buick made two quick turns and parked in front of a recently renovated apartment block. Himenes disappeared inside. Could have a bit on the side, the man thought with a shrug and lit a cigarette. Only minutes later, Himenes came bounding down the steps and practically leapt into his car. 'Pretty quickfire,' the man said to himself with a chuckle.

The Buick went east, turned south on Potrero and kept slow until it chugged up the ramp and raced down the 101. Might be headed to Candlestick. The Giants were at home that week, but his target never been near there before. When Himenes sped past the stadium, the man wondered if he might be going to the airport. Was there an extradition treaty with Mexico? That might be exciting. He watched Himenes pull into a used car lot and drive out with a shiny, if somewhat mature, Pontiac.

The following morning, Himenes faced Callahan and another man across a metal table bolted to the floor, in a small, windowless room. Bennett watched through a darkened glass panel set into the wall and listened via a microphone hidden in the ceiling.

'Now, I'm going to ask you one last time, Mr Himenes,' Callahan's colleague said. 'Where did you get that money?'

Himenes was still in his uniform. He'd been detained as soon as his shift ended at first light. Agents had already questioned the man whom Himenes had visited for a few minutes in Bernal Heights and were satisfied that he had simply been holding the cash for Himenes.

'I got it from a friend.'

'What's his name?'

Himenes hesitated and looked at the duty lawyer sitting beside him, who shook his head.

'Mr Himenes, I'm going to give you some advice,' Callahan said. 'If you cooperate with us, things will go easier for you in court. Judges and juries like cooperative people, you see.'

They had checked his bank account. No unusual withdrawals, nothing to match the $550 in new bills that he'd paid for the Pontiac.

'Maybe you don't know this, but lying to us can land you five years in prison. So, just tell us who gave you that cash and we'll see that you are treated right. OK?'

Himenes looked at the lawyer and this time got a nod.

Straightening up, he brushed his dry mouth with the back of a hand. It all came out in a rush: how he'd been approached by a man after work and offered money for just letting a guy in and writing down a name.

'I didn't know anything about a bomb!' he cried. 'They said it was a joke.'

He bowed his head and began to sob.

Callahan ordered coffee and waited until Himenes had drunk his.

'OK. Now, you're cooperating, and we can wind this up. But I've got a few more questions first.'

Himenes raised his head.

'The guy who approached you, was he the same one who drove the van?'

'No.'

'Let's start with the first guy. Did he give a name?'

'No.'

'What did he look like?'

'Tall, thin. Dressed nice. Had a ponytail.'

'A ponytail?'

'Yeah, tied up in back. Like a girl.'

'Age?'

Himenes shrugged. 'Thirty, forty. I don't know.'

'Anglo?'

'Yes.'

'Thank you. Now, the other one, the guy in the van. What was he like?'

'I don't know. Like I told the commander, it was dark, and he was inside the van.'

'OK. Was he younger or older than the first guy?'

'Younger, I think.'

'Anglo?'

'Yes.'

After Himenes was taken into custody, Callahan sat with Bennett.

'I don't think he knows anything more,' Callahan said. 'Just got lured in by the money.'

'Could be.'

'So, if he didn't know what was in the van, we can't charge him with aiding and abetting.'

'No, but taking a bribe will get him five years, maybe more.'

Himenes spent the rest of the afternoon working with the FBI to produce an Identikit of the man with the ponytail. He was then released and told he would be picked up the following morning for his appearance before a magistrate. At home,

Himenes told his wife that he was helping the police with their investigation.

By noon the next day, the Identikit image was in the hands of local agents, who showed it to their informants. Two days later, they had a name. A name that was on the list of known activists. A man who, at the time of the bombing, was reported to have been staying in an apartment not far from where the van was stolen.

When he heard that last piece of information over the telephone, Bennett smacked the desk with his open palm.

'That's it!' he cried. 'Three strikes and you're out.'

26

After lunch, he decided to take a nap. It was a warm day and fetching Rosa's bottle throughout the night meant he'd lost sleep. Nearing the bed, he saw the San Francisco paper, tossed there by Sharon, who was working in her office next door. He heard soft grunting and looked toward the wicker cot in the corner. More groans drew him over. Rosa was squirming around, gurgling and spitting. He picked her up, burped her and walked in circles until she was quiet.

Laying her back down, he smoothed out the thin layer of fuzz on her head. Why was she born with so much hair? Because, he told himself, she would be precocious. A girl with waist-length hair and long strides. Scenes formed in his mind, the three of them walking hand in hand on a sandy beach, up a mountain and along a riverbank.

Fluffing up the pillows, he stretched out on the bed and opened the paper. The front page covered a large anti-war demonstration in the city's financial district, part of the May Day protests across the country. He grimaced when he read about the beatings but smiled at a placard, captured in a photograph, with the words: "Don't like bombings in America? You should see Vietnam".

He was about to turn to the page, when his eye snagged on a story at the bottom. "Bombing Suspect Arrested." He jerked himself up and read the short paragraph.

Yesterday, the FBI arrested Gabriel Pennington, thirty-three, in connection with the bombing at the Presidio which killed a man last month.

The article, largely based on information released by the FBI, went on to recount the known facts of the bombing. Continued on an inside page, it speculated on motives and added that a guard employed on the base had also been questioned and then released. The final sentence was the one he'd been dreading.

An FBI spokesperson confirmed that they were searching for the driver of the van that delivered the bombs and any of his accomplices.

Shutting his eyes, he grit his teeth and ground them until they scraped. Although he pretended otherwise, he had known, deep down, that this would happen. His thin layer of self-deception was ripped away, shattering an already shaky confidence. Not even four weeks had passed, and they were looking for him.

She saw the alarm on his face when he stood in the doorway to her office.

'Rosa…?'

'No. Gabriel.'

He handed her the paper and she read quickly.

'The guard must have talked,' she said in an even tone and lit a cigarette. 'The good thing is that Gabriel won't talk.'

'But the guard saw me.'

'Don't worry. You said it was dark and only for a second.'

'Yeah, but maybe he saw enough to identify me. Remember, they have my photo and fingerprints, from that time in Berkeley.'

'Yes, all right, but the van was destroyed, and you didn't touch the money. Even more important, we've got our new names.'

She began to pace around the small room, inhaling and blowing out smoke.

'But you need a backstory. I'll use my old one, but you need to create one.'

'I've memorised my new birthdate and place.'

'You need a lot more than that. People might ask where David Williams went to high school and to college. What jobs he had. Where his parents live. All those kind of things.'

'That stupid fucking guard!'

His shout was answered by a piercing scream. He glared at her with reddened eyes and went next door to soothe Rosa.

She was sitting down when he returned.

'She OK?'

He nodded.

'Good. Now, forget about the guard. We need to focus on ourselves. We'll leave here tomorrow, or the day after, at the latest.'

She was prepared for this, he realised, and had been from the beginning.

'Where to?'

'We'll drive to Seattle. People there will get us new passports and help us get over the border, to Vancouver.'

'Vancouver?'

'It's a big, liberal city. Like San Francisco. They can't touch us there.'

'How long can we stay?'

'Six months, no questions asked. We can settle there, too, if we want. Thousands of people have done it.'

'Settle? You mean permanently?'

Her eyes left his and sought a resting place toward the window.

'Yes. We're going to start a new life there.'

He was trying, as usual, to catch up with her. He'd known about people fleeing to Canada, even considered it himself after his army physical. The "second underground railway" they called it, after the one used by those fleeing slavery before the Civil War. And like that earlier route, there were chains of safe houses, stretching from the Eastern Seaboard up to Montreal and Toronto. In Maine, he had rejected the idea. Too far and too final. Now it was a fait accompli.

'I'll speak to Gavin this evening,' she said in a toneless voice. 'Tell him something about moving on. You can tell Ted the same thing.'

'What same thing?'

'That we are leaving, but you don't know exactly where. Nothing more, all right? Don't even hint at Canada.'

He didn't speak.

'Better go find him now. Get it over with. Say something like you're sad to leave but things have changed, and you're looking forward to setting up family life somewhere else.'

Walking toward the barn in the hot sun, he felt a flicker of hope. That's what he needed. A new life, with Sharon and Rosa, in a new place. River Ridge was great, but it was a dead end. One of them would get a job – lawyers and teachers were probably as much in demand in Canada as the US – and the other would look after Rosa. And when she was a few years old, they…

'Hi there!'

He looked up and saw Ted in the treehouse.

'Got to reinforce these boards. Be with you in a minute.'

He watched him align wood and hammer in nails. Always practical, doing things for people. A real teacher.

Ted climbed down and surveyed his work.

'It's looking really good, you know. I might even try sleeping up there myself. Hey, what's the matter? You look like you lost your teddy bear.'

'Something like that.'

Ted put a hand on his shoulder and led him over to the stumps beside the barn.

'Nothing to do with you and Sharon, I hope.'

He shook his head and looked away. 'No. It's just we're... going to leave, that's all.'

Ted nodded, two or three times, his head dipping lower and lower each time. Picking up a woodchip, he scratched lines in the dirt.

'That could be a good thing, you know. Where are you going?'

'I...'

'No, don't say. Sometimes it's best not to know.' Ted continued etching in the earth, head still bent. 'I bet Sharon's excited, though. I always sensed she was like a library book. On loan only.'

His dry lips cracked a smile. 'You're right, she is excited.'

'Well, I suppose having little Rosa might have put ideas into her head.'

He didn't reply.

'Any idea when you're going?'

'Tomorrow or the day after.'

Everyone watched as they crossed the grassy area dotted with wildflowers. Gavin and his family on the porch, others in the garden plots, Ted and the kids by the barn. It didn't happen often and when it did, there was no ceremony or farewell speech. It was better, they thought, to let the wound heal itself. But there were questions and comments, and sometimes tears. Not for Sharon, who everyone respected and no one knew. If there were moist eyes, they were for the shy young man who had never spoken an angry word and who had looked after the children like a parent.

They watched them walk away, he with the suitcases, she with the baby in a carrycot. The silence was broken just as they were about to disappear into the trees.

'Good luck!' Ted shouted and waved.

He put down the suitcases, pulled the wooden pendant out from under his shirt and held it aloft like a trophy. Few recognised what was in his hand and no one saw the strain in his face. Only Sharon, who whispered to him and waved to Ted.

When they reached the car in the parking area, she positioned the cot between them on the front seat, making sure Rosa was lying on her back.

'We'll get rid of this car as soon as we can,' she said. 'It's a liability. A footprint.'

Moving down the narrow dirt track, the car hit a rock and lurched to one side. She held on to the cot and he gripped the wheel. Should go slower, he knew, but adrenalin was pumping through him.

After what seemed like an hour, they reached the junction with the highway. Relieved, he came to a halt, the nose of the car poking out of the woods.

'She needs her bottle,' he said.

'Another hour will be fine. Anyway, we can't stop like this. It looks funny.'

They headed north on 101, the same two-lane highway that had brought him from Berkeley to Mendocino a full twelve months ago. Along the same coastal spine dotted with small towns and single-pump gas stations. The only difference was that the stretches of redwood and conifer forests between the towns were longer. He kept the radio low and the speed down. She kept her head straight, only turning when they emerged from fog and saw water. She was planning and he knew not to interrupt.

She'd said he shouldn't worry. They had their new birth certificates, social security cards and driving licenses. She said it again and again that morning, before they left River Ridge. They would be fine. All of them. Then why were they doing this? She'd said it was just to be safe. But it didn't feel that way.

'Ah, better take off that necklace.'

'But…'

'I know. Just keep it out of sight for a while. No point in advertising ourselves.'

They only stopped to refuel and feed Rosa. At gas stations, they took her out of the portable cot and walked around with her in their arms. While one walked her, the other used the bathroom, filled her bottle, bought newspapers, coffee and sandwiches.

'That your wife and baby there?'

The blonde, shaggy-haired woman in the store thrust her chin out the door behind him.

'Yes,' he said and took his change.

'You know,' the woman said, 'I heard someone say travelling is good for a child, specially a little baby.'

He hesitated for a moment. 'That's good to know.'

'Going far?'

'No, not really. Just a little family trip.'

The woman smiled at him. Lying isn't that hard, he thought. But should they be stopping so often, talking to people? Young man and older woman with a baby. Did people remember things like that? They might if they saw few customers and had a conversation with one of them.

'She's asleep,' she said, lighting another cigarette as he drove off.

'Hmm.'

'What's the matter?'

'Can't you stop smoking? It's not good for her.'

She wound down her window several inches.

'OK?'

'Put it back up a bit. It's too windy.'

She looked over at him but said nothing. He was drumming his fingers on the steering wheel, deep ridges between his eyes. Too bad, she said to herself. It would have been a good life together.

The Redwood Highway climbed, hugging a mountainside and running through thick forest. Rosa started to cry, and they stopped to change her, even though there was no emergency lane. He was struggling with the stiff nappy when a highway patrol car pulled up behind them.

'I'll handle this,' she whispered.

The officer strolled up to the passenger side and stood beside the open window. White milkman cap, grey-brown uniform, dark blue tie and a black holster on his hip.

'Good morning, Officer,' she said.

'Morning, ma'am. Your car is sort of sticking out here.'

'Yes. I'm sorry. We had a little emergency.'

The officer took in the carrycot, the man's sheepish grin and the dirty nappy in his hand.

'Oh, I see. Well, better hurry up.'

Heart in mouth, he somehow managed to fasten the snap on the clean nappy.

'There we are,' she announced. 'Everything's under control.'

Prompted by her sweet voice, the officer saluted and executed a tiny bow. She smiled and Steve drove off. After a minute, when he began to breathe normally, he roared with laughter.

Rocked by the movement and lulled by the low rumble, Rosa went back to sleep. As soon as they got inside the motel, though, she started to bawl and kept on bawling despite all efforts to soothe her. He walked her around the room, hummed tunes, patted her back and still she wouldn't stop. He handed her to Sharon, who was on the bed with a newspaper. After a single circuit, the child fell asleep in her mother arms.

'Morning, Mom.'

He was on a payphone across the road from the motel because she had insisted. He hadn't written home since the letter from Mendocino the previous summer. Only called three or four times and still not visited. His parents told themselves that they shouldn't worry. He seemed happy. 'Let him find his own way,' his father had said, though the cliché sounded hollow, even to himself.

'I know it's early, but…'

'That doesn't matter. How are you? That's all we want to know.'

'I'm fine.'

'Still working in San Francisco?'

'Yeah, same place. But the pay isn't great and I'm low on cash, so…'

'How much do you need?'

'Ah, could you send five hundred? I mean, if it's not…'

'Of course.'

'Thanks. Send it to Western Union in Seattle. I'm visiting a friend up here for a few days.'

They ate breakfast at a roadside café near Crescent City. Truckers, travelling salesmen, construction workers and high school students fuelling up on the morning of their final exams. Sitting in a booth beside a window, Rosa on his lap, they ordered pancakes. Just like a family on vacation, he thought, surveying the others, who paid them scant attention.

When the coffee came, she lit her first cigarette and looked through the local paper.

'Wouldn't be anything in there, would there?' he said.

'No, just checking on the weather. It's supposed to be misty.'

They turned off the coast road, headed inland and crossed into Oregon. Leaving California behind seemed like a cause for celebration. They had seen a few more "beetles" – their name for the black-and-white highway patrol cars – but, as she had said, "everything was under control".

Miles and miles of farmland took them to the Willamette River, where the Portland skyline hove into view. Reading the map, she told him to stay on the overpass, which carried them above the urban sprawl, over the Columbia River and across the state boundary into Washington.

Seeing his relaxed face, she told him her plan. Most of it.

He took the first exit, found a gas station and asked for directions. Five minutes later, he pulled into a lot that took up most of a city block.

'Now, remember,' she said. 'Just make it look like we're shopping around. No urgency.'

Despite the pretence of nonchalance, they accepted a low price for his old car, added another $150 and drove away in a sleek, cream-coloured Oldsmobile. The whole transaction had taken less than an hour.

He had been tight-lipped throughout, saying little to the salesman in the shiny suit, white shirt and no tie. He let her handle everything: haggling, paying the cash, showing her driving license and signing the papers. He only had to show the registration.

'Looks like a cop car,' he said with a smirk, as he eased out of the lot and onto a city street.

'Anything's better than that thing you had. Vega? Sounds like a vegetable.'

'You're wrong there. It means "speed" in Sanskrit. Very appropriate.'

'You know something? You're weird.'

He raised his eyebrows at her, and they both laughed.

'Let's see that license,' he said, stopped at a traffic light.

She handed it to him, and he read aloud. 'Judith Mason. 1833 West St, Lompoc Calif. 93448. Date of Birth: 19–08–42'

'Not bad. She even looks like you,' he said, handing it back. 'Only prettier.'

'But dumber,' she replied.

'Hear that?' He was looking down at the carrycot between them. 'Mommy likes to keep secrets. You better watch out.'

Following another half-night of sleep, they were skirting the Columbia River on the short and final leg of the journey. When the wide river bent west toward the Pacific, they followed the six-lane highway north, through open country, with a screen of trees separating them from the traffic coming in the opposite direction.

A mountain rose in the middle distance, snow-topped and shaped like an inverted cone.

'What's that?' he cried.

'Must be Mount Ranier,' she said, checking the map.

'Spectacular. No wonder everyone raves about Seattle. But where's the ocean?'

'Patience, patience.'

Half an hour passed, during which they said almost nothing.

'There it is,' he cried with boyish excitement. 'The *Pacific*. How appropriate.'

'Puget Sound,' she corrected him.

'Puget? Is that an Indian word?'

'No idea.'

He looked over at her blank face and when he turned back, the water had disappeared behind a wall of apartment buildings and office blocks.

'Straight ahead,' she said, following the instructions she had been given the night before over the telephone. 'Stay on the interstate, all the way to the overpass and over the bridge.'

Seattle must be Indian, he thought. And probably Tacoma. Not Vancouver, though. That sounds vaguely English, maybe from the French. But Spokane…

'Hey, slow down. It's the next exit.'

North Seattle reminded him of North Berkeley. Tree-lined streets, single-family homes, university campus and the ocean nearby. Except the houses were mostly bungalows and there were no hills.

'That's it,' she said. 'Over there.'

The grey-shingled, single-storey house had an attractive front porch and a dormer window. The red door swung open as they climbed the steps with Rosa and the suitcases.

A slim, bearded young man in jeans waved them in. And quickly shut the door.

'Welcome,' he said, not extending a hand. 'I'm Marcus. You found us OK? Didn't have to ask directions?'

'No. We came straight here.'

'That's good. A few months back we had to change houses because someone asked a policeman for directions.'

He felt a tightening in his chest. Soothed by the unceasing movement and rhythmic rumble of the road, he had begun to enjoy the journey, the freedom and the sometimes-beautiful landscape. Having reached their destination, he was confronted with the reason they were on the move.

'You've got food for two days,' Marcus said. 'And extra milk for your baby. And a crib. Do you need any money?'

He spoke almost without opening his mouth and pointing to various rooms.

'No,' she said and advanced into the living room.

It was spare but neat, with a blanket thrown over the back of the couch.

'Neighbours?'

'No reported problems.'

'Our car?'

'You don't need a permit to park here.'

'Good. When do we see Robert?'

'Tomorrow. I'll pick you up at 10:00am and bring a babysitter. Until then, don't leave the house. No telephone calls. No visitors. No music.'

'Radio?'

'Radio and television are fine.'

He listened to the rapid-fire exchange. Like lines rehearsed for a play. Although they had never met, the trust was implicit.

When Marcus left, they settled Rosa into the wooden crib in a corner of the living room. It was missing two slats but swung back and forth without much creaking. They stripped off their three-day old clothes, put them in the washing machine and took showers.

Lying on the bed in fresh underwear, he waited for her. There was a crack in the ceiling and the window frames needed repainting, but it felt better than the sterile motel rooms. Something like this, he said to himself, a little house would be nice.

She came wrapped in a towel and lay down beside him.

'We're almost there,' she whispered in his ear. 'A few days here, to put everything in place and then we can cross. And be safe.'

He looked into her pale blue eyes, inches from his, and saw that they were calm. He edged closer, put an arm over her chest and they slept, face to face, knee to knee.

'Who are these people?' he asked when they woke to a setting sun. 'Marcus and this guy Robert we're meeting tomorrow.'

'You don't need to know that.'

'But you know, don't you?'

'Yes.'

'Then tell me.'

'I don't…'

'Tell me,' he demanded. 'We're a family now.'

She cocked her head to the side, hair falling in a perfectly straight line and hiding one eye.

'OK. They're a unit of the Fifth Column Brigade.'

The name Gabriel had used to claim responsibility for the bombing. But he'd said it was just a name.

'A unit?'

'That's what they're called. We have units in sixteen cities across the country. About 140 people in all.'

'There's one in San Francisco, I guess.'

'One of the biggest, split into two. The City and the East Bay.'

'So, you were part of this group? Before River Ridge, I mean.'

'Yes.'

'And you still are?'

'We both are.'

27

It was a quiet neighbourhood, but he didn't sleep well that night. It wasn't Rosa, it was his own mind that wouldn't shut down. What else didn't he know? What would they tell Rosa when she was older? What could tell his parents now?

In the kitchen, he put on the radio and chose a sharp knife. Resting the blade on the little bump, he sliced through the orange and watched the two halves separate, revealing a colour so vibrant that, for a moment, it seemed alive.

'Good morning, early bird,' she said, coming toward him. 'Anything left for me?'

'No, not much. Just scrambled eggs, granola and orange juice.'

They ate and drank while listening to the radio. Atrocities in Bangladesh, a failed US space probe and the debate over an amendment to lower the voting age to eighteen. The jingle that signalled the end of the news and the beginning of the weather report prompted an exchange of relieved smiles.

'Seems like a good NPR station,' she said.

'Can you get it in Vancouver?'

'Probably. We'll find out.'

Bang on the hour, Marcus walked through the door and introduced a rosy-cheeked university student, who nodded through the detailed instructions about Rosa, while Steve wondered if she was a member of the "Brigade".

'Can I smoke?' the girl asked. 'In the kitchen. Not in there, of course.' She meant the living room.

'Sure. Why not?' he said, glancing at Sharon.

Marcus drove them to a three-storey house, farther away from the campus. A brick path led to stone steps, wrought-iron railings and white pillars. The door had slender stained-glass panels and a half-moon window above. She looked at him with an expression that said "not exactly what you expected, is it?".

In a pale purple shirt and dark maroon tie, Robert greeted and congratulated them on the Presidio "action". With brisk strides, he led them down a hallway to a room large enough to hold a captain's desk and a dining table with eight chairs.

'Please,' he said, gesturing toward the chairs.

They dragged two across the thick carpet and positioned themselves side by side, facing him. Steve couldn't help noticing that the man's silver-grey hair blended in with the shrubbery visible through the French windows behind.

'Your baby is being looked after?'

'Yes,' she said. 'Thanks.'

'Not ideal, but it does provide cover,' Robert said, looking at a tight-lipped Steve. 'Right, now tell me your situation. I know the big picture but not the detail. And be quick. I have forty minutes.'

Robert took notes on a yellow pad as she told their story. The planning and the surveillance, the bombing and the death, Gabriel's arrest and the guard's suspected role, their flight and intention to take refuge in Canada.

Robert put down his pen and pursed his lips.

'I fully understand your decision. But I want to know if you understand its implications.'

'What do you mean?' Steve stammered.

'You are going into exile and will probably never be able to come back and live in the US. That's what I mean.'

'Exile?'

'Look, you are both are high-profile targets. The FBI has mounted a major manhunt.'

'But we have new names, like she said.'

'The FBI will assume that. Do not underestimate them. You will be hunted day and night, even in Canada. Do not think the Canadian police don't cooperate with the FBI. They do. FBI posters are displayed in their offices all across the country.'

'Are we on posters here?'

'No, but you will be soon.' Robert fixed his eyes on him. 'Are you ready for this?'

'Yes,' she said.

'OK. Now listen carefully. This is how it works. You will enter Canada as tourists. A nice little family holiday. To Vancouver Island, you can say. The Canadian border officials might ask a few questions. Where and when you were born, for example. Nothing more.'

'Do we need to show passports?' she asked.

'No, not when entering or leaving Canada as tourists. Possibly when re-entering the US.'

'Re-entering the US? I thought you said it was exile.' Steve winced in confusion.

'It is and I'll explain in a moment. But why do you ask about passports?'

'Because we need new ones,' she said. 'We didn't have enough time to get them before we left Mendocino.'

'Right,' Robert said, drawing out the word. 'And you don't have enough time here either. However…' Leaning down, he pulled two dark blue covers out of a drawer. 'We keep a few on hand.'

He flipped one open and held it up.

'We leave everything blank until something like this comes our way. We can have it filled in fairly quickly.' He looked down at his notes. 'Judith Mason and David Williams, correct?'

She nodded.

'Dates of birth?'

She recited and Robert recorded.

'We also need a new birth certificate for our child,' she said, handing him a copy of the existing one. 'It has our old names.'

Steve looked at her, wondering why he hadn't realised that.

'The name should be Rosa Williams,' she said. 'Born in Pasadena, California. 10 April 1971.'

'Of course,' Robert said. The day of the bombing, an alibi. He wrote on his pad and jerked his head up.

'Marriage certificate?'

'No. We'll need that, too.'

'OK. Now, what draft card do you have?'

'1-A.'

'We'll get you a 4-F. It's our speciality.' Another self-satisfied smile. 'And we'll back that up with a doctor's letter. Are you OK with being subject to dizzy spells? Or would you rather be a homosexual?'

'Dizzy is fine.' Not far off the mark, he thought.

'You won't have to show the card when you go into Canada as tourists. But when you come back here, the US officials might ask for it. And Canadian officials might ask when you return there.'

Steve shook his head in confusion and slumped back in his chair.

'Another thing. They sometimes inspect cars at the Canadian border, so don't take much luggage with you. Leave it with us. You can pick it up when you come back.'

She nodded.

'Now, the crossing back and forth is like this.' Robert pulled himself up and leaned over his desk toward them.

'First, you go to Vancouver as tourists, a family of three. Then, you contact a group there – the Vancouver Committee to Aid American War Objectors. Marcus will give you the address and call ahead to let them know you're coming.'

He asked for a pen, but she gave him her smile of reassurance. Don't worry. Everything's under control.

'They'll help you get permanent residence there. The most important thing is a job offer in Canada. Once you get a letter of employment – they'll handle that too – you come back here, spend a few days and then go back into Canada with that all-important letter. But this time you don't go as tourists. You go as potential permanent residents.'

Steve looked at Sharon, who had settled back in her chair, smoking.

'I know it's a lot of information to take in,' Robert said. 'But they'll explain it all in greater detail in Vancouver.'

'We're going to become citizens?'

'In essence, yes. First, you get what's called Landed Immigrant Status, which gives you the right to stay and work in Canada. After five years, you can become a citizen.'

Steve pushed out his lower lip and nodded in approval. Citizens sounded better than exiles.

'OK. What about the car?' he asked. 'Should we get another one?'

'No, keep it. You should avoid any unnecessary transactions. They leave traces.'

'How long will this take, to get all the documents?'

'A week. Ten days at the most. We'll send over a photographer this afternoon for the passports.' Robert checked his watch. 'Right. Got to go.'

Steve looked at this man moistening his lips and straightening his tie, who held their fate in his hands. Off to an office in downtown Seattle, no doubt. Property development? No, life insurance would be more appropriate.

They all stood up.

'Just one more thing,' Robert said.

'What?'

'Get a haircut. And a decent pair of shoes.'

Marcus drove them to a whole foods store. On the way back, Steve asked him to take them to the Western Union office.

'That's risky,' Marcus said. 'FBI undercover agents have been crawling all around the city centre for the past few weeks.'

'We need some money.'

'But I thought you said…'

'We need more money.'

Marcus looked at Sharon, who didn't object.

'OK but be careful.'

Marcus parked several blocks away and gave him directions. He got the money and came back, without twitching or looking over his shoulder. He wasn't afraid because he had no idea what an undercover agent looked like.

At the small house on the corner, he opened the red door and stepped inside, his head spinning. Passport photos, Rosa's birth certificate, 4-F card, a doctor's letter. Keep the car, go to Vancouver, return to Seattle, back to Vancouver. Get a letter of employment and something called "Landed Immigrant Status".

She pushed past him and spoke to the babysitter, who was reading in the living room, with Rosa asleep in the corner. The girl shook her head at the five-dollar bill and said she'd be happy to help out whenever they needed her.

'Just tell Marcus.'

He opened a window to air out the kitchen, and she put away the groceries. He fed Rosa while she made a green salad and tuna fish sandwiches. They ate in near silence and listened to the news. Again, nothing.

Robert said they would be hunted day and night, and he realised that they would only know when it was too late. When they'd been caught. Hearing a cry, he picked up a warm bottle from the stove and went to the living room.

'We need to buy more formula and diapers,' he said, back in the kitchen. 'Good thing I got that money today.'

She did the dishes and he sat at the table, fiddling with an empty glass. Two plastic folders lay on the table, containing the new documents obtained while at River Ridge. On top, in his folder, he saw his birth certificate. He hadn't thought much about his new name; everything had happened so fast after the news of Gabriel's arrest.

'David Williams,' he said to her back. 'Sounds like a famous baseball player. I should be able to make up a good backstory. That's what you call it, right?'

Turning around and leaning against the counter, she saw the playful look on his face. This is a good time, she thought.

'Yes. You might not know it, but your wife, Judith Mason, had a very ordinary childhood. Born in Reno, her family moved to Los Angeles when she was seven and...'

'Met David in 1968 when they were students at Cal State Long Beach.'

'Yes. She was older, a graduate student, while he was just a callow undergrad.'

'And he was mightily impressed with her. After a short time, they got married and went on a honeymoon to Honolulu.'

'Wonderful.'

He was walking around the small kitchen, his face beaming.

'Judith went on to grad school and David began teaching at... Hold on. Can you get a degree in education at Long Beach?'

'Not sure. But you don't need one to teach in California. Any BA is enough.'

'OK, so he started teaching high school in... Pasadena.'

'Sounds good.'

'Where he was named teacher of the year. And where their darling daughter was born and given his last name – she lost that argument, by the way. Within months, he got a better job in...?'

'Anywhere except San Francisco and the Bay Area.'

'San Diego. Wait a minute. Couldn't someone check? I mean, they keep records at schools.' He slumped back into a chair. 'This isn't as easy as it seems.'

'It isn't easy, but you don't need to worry about that level of detail.'

'OK. So, they move to San Diego – not far from my parents' new place, by the way – where Judith starts a book club…'

'No.' She waited for him to stop pacing and stand still. 'No. That's not what happens.'

'OK. What does?'

'Judith dies in a car accident.'

He snorted in good-humoured disbelief but then saw the look on her face and sat down. She folded the dish towel into a neat square and placed it on the counter.

'I've made a decision.' The voice was flat, the eyes smooth as ice. 'After we come back here, to Seattle, I'm not going to return to Vancouver with you.'

'What do you mean?'

'I mean that you and Rosa will cross back into Canada and begin your new life there without me.'

He leaned back, flinching from the blow, and almost tipped over in his chair.

'But you can't…'

'Listen, Steve. You will tell Rosa that her mother died in a car accident.'

'No, no. This is crazy.'

'It is not crazy. I've thought it all out and it's the best thing to do. For all of us.'

'But you're her mother. You and I… You can't just leave us.'

Seeing his face collapse in pain, she wrapped her arms around his neck. In that awkward position, standing behind, she leaned down and kissed him on the cheek.

'I still have work to do,' she said softly. 'I'm sorry, but this is how it has to be. There's a war on and I cannot retreat. I've got to fight. For you and for Rosa.'

'No!' he shouted and jumped up, throwing her off and knocking over his chair.

'Steve, please.'

He stood, head down, throat dry. This would be another loss, another failure. One he could not accept.

'All right,' he managed to say. 'We'll forget all about Canada. We'll stay here. You and me and Rosa.'

'Not a good idea. Think about it. What kind of a life would she have with both parents living underground, always on the run?'

He slapped the table with an open palm. 'But what about us? What about me?'

'Don't worry,' she said, moving close. 'You'll be a great father. Because you will love her twice over and raise her to be a strong woman.'

He shook his head, again and again. It would be the culmination of all his bad choices. Hiding in a foreign country, raising a child on his own.

'Listen to me, Steve. It'll all work out. They'll help you with everything there, when you go back by yourself, I mean. A place to stay, a job and someone to look after Rosa. And I'll send money from time to time.'

He kept shaking his head. She had planned this from the very beginning, he realised, as soon as she knew she was pregnant. Maybe even before that. It was her contingency plan, in case they had to leave the country. He had gone along with it because he thought they would be together. A life in exile would be bearable because of her strength and conviction and common sense. But he couldn't do it alone, not with a baby.

Hot tears trickled down his cheek while she held him.

'Do it for me. Please. Look after Rosa for me, because I can't, and you can.'

Easing away from her, he gathered himself together, limb by limb, and spoke in short gasps.

'I'll try. And someday. After a few years. We'll get together again. Won't we?'

'I hope so. When it's all over.'

28

With Rosa's new birth certificate, their new passports, marriage certificate, 4-F card and doctor's letter, they resumed their journey north. Beyond the urban sprawl of Seattle, along the eastern edge of Puget Sound and into the now familiar landscape of the Northwest. A wide highway topped by an open sky and bordered by conifer trees.

But nothing was the same.

'If you're going to stay in the US, why are you coming to Vancouver?'

He had been thinking about this since she first announced her decision. But they had agreed not to discuss it during their stay in Seattle. They had concentrated instead on getting into Canada – what to buy, what to bring, how to dress and what to say at the border.

He waited for her to answer.

'Because I need to know you're settled there with Rosa. And, besides, like Robert said, it looks better. A family on vacation.'

Again, it made sense. Except it didn't.

The journey to the Canadian border took only two hours, with Rosa dozing the whole time. Approaching the red-brick building that housed US border control, they rehearsed again who they were and what they were doing.

They waited in a short queue, radio on, not talking. As they edged forward, she combed her hair and put on lipstick while he ran a hand through his new crew cut. Their turn came and he rolled down the window. In the heavy June heat, Rosa began to cry.

'Having trouble with the little one, huh?'

The chubby-cheeked officer peered in through the open window, ran his eyes over the back seat and waved them on.

In the no-man's land between two countries, a tall, white structure stood on a grassy strip. Its triangular lintel rested on two thick columns set yards apart, like an open doorway. He parked and walked up to it. Sea gulls, strutting on the wide swath, squawked and flapped away. He went close and read the inscription: "Brethren Dwelling Together in Unity".

'It's called The Peace Arch,' he said, back in the car. 'Built to commemorate the end of the War of 1812, when the border here was fixed.'

'Peace Arch. That's nice,' she said.

'Yes. And borders, too. They can be useful.'

The wait on the Canadian side was longer. Three separate lanes of cars and trucks were queued up in front of a building with half-timbered walls and a steeply pitched roof. It looked like an illustration in a Dickens novel. Of course, he chuckled to himself. It's British Columbia.

'Get ready,' she said sharply under her breath. 'We're next.'

He eased forward and stopped, less smoothly than he wanted. A grizzled officer laid his hand on the frame of the open window, poked his head a little too far inside and said hello. They returned the greeting and answered the questions they had been told to expect.

David Williams was born in Los Angeles. Judith Mason in Reno. The baby? There was hesitation, as each waited for the other to answer.

'Pasadena, California,' she said.

'Where are you going?'

'Vancouver Island. A week's vacation.'

'Whole week, huh?' The man pulled back and peered into the back seat. 'Where's your camping gear? In the boot?'

'No, we're staying with a friend.'

He recited the memorised address. Robert might be an arrogant asshole, but he was thorough.

The officer handed him a permit, good for six months.

'Enjoy your vacation,' the officer said and looked behind them for the next car.

He turned the key but the engine stalled, and again when he tried a second time.

'Easy does it,' she said and patted his leg.

The Oldsmobile coughed into life at the third attempt and seemed to glide forward, on its own, into Canada. She smiled at him, and he pulled his lips into a thin line.

Wide lanes cut through abandoned farmland and isolated clumps of trees. He was still struggling to accept her decision. 'Don't take it personally,' she had said. He'd just stared at her, dumbfounded. 'It's for the greater good,' she said. He had to admit that she had conviction and knew what she had to do, while he was only running away. And what she said about Rosa was also true. The child needed stability. That would be his greater good. Her happiness.

But he didn't like this story of her death. Couldn't he just tell Rosa that her mother had gone back to the US for work? Or to be with an ailing parent? Anything but a body mangled in a car crash. 'No,' she'd said, more than once, 'it has to be final. It's better for her that way. No false hopes of meeting someday.'

You mean better for you, he wanted to say.

'Not far now,' she said, looking over at him with that reassuring smile that revealed little.

They crossed a bridge, passed an airport, drove over another bridge and slowed down in the northwest corner of the city. A dense grid of narrow streets, two- and three-storey buildings, the occasional skyscraper and small park. They found West Hastings Street and their unmissable target.

A tall, slender building from the turn of the century, it had once housed financial advisors, stockbrokers, accountants and life insurance agents. Now there were small businesses, a local newspaper, a housing society and, on the fourth floor, the Vancouver Committee to Aid American War Objectors. VCAAWO.

'Remember,' she said as they climbed the interior stairs with Rosa in the carrycot, 'these people are not part of our group. They support "war objectors". That means draft resisters, evaders, even deserters. Some of them might individually agree with direct action, but the organisation does not.'

They entered a large space with no divisions or rooms, only areas of activity marked by desks and tables. An enormous monthly calendar, with circled dates, hung on a side wall. Next to it, daily tasks, with names and times, were listed in black felt pen on a whiteboard. It reminded him of his grade school classroom.

At one table, people were lettering signs, while others sat on the floor, stapling the signs to pieces of wood. Another group was sewing letters onto a long piece of cloth, and still others clipped articles from newspapers and filed them in a wooden cabinet. There was chatter, laughter and country rock playing at low volume on a stereo deck.

'David and Judith, right?'

The man with round, rimless glasses and a turtleneck sweater looked in his fifties. He led them to a corner with a trestle table covered in newspapers, magazines, clippings, scissors, rolls of tape, erasures, pens and pencils. A young woman, on the telephone, smiled up at them from the far end of the table.

When he tried to balance the cot on his knees, the woman cleared a space in front of her with a swift sweep of a hand.

'You can put the baby here, if you like.'

'Thanks. She's Rosa, by the way.'

'And I'm Emily.'

He handed the baby to her, and everyone smiled.

The man said his name was Benson and that he was "the counsellor". A wall behind him displayed large black-and-white photographs. Straw hats bending over in a rice field. GIs resting in a jungle. Helicopters hovering over a burning village. The other wall had similar-sized photos of demonstrations. One of them, he noticed, showed protestors on the Berkeley campus, with that helicopter above them.

'Welcome to Vancouver,' Benson said. 'How can we help?'

She told him how they'd met in Mendocino, their opposition to the war, his number in the lottery and their decision to seek refuge in Canada. Listening, he realised that the other story – meeting in LA and teaching in Pasadena – was for other occasions.

Benson tapped a pencil on the back of one hand, listening as he eyed Rosa squirming in the cot. He took pride in his work, helping young Americans evade the war. Most of them were principled, polite and grateful. He preferred not to dwell on the mentally unstable, the fantasists and the drug addicts. These two won't be difficult, he thought. But they'll need a slightly bigger place for the baby.

The pencil tapping stopped. 'You have any documents that will help?'

He handed over his fake 4-F classification card and doctor's letter, supposedly from a neurology clinic in San Francisco and signed by a Dr Mathew Salomon.

'A small problem,' Benson said, after glancing at them. 'The letter is dated after the card.'

They looked at each other. Robert wasn't quite the magician he fancied himself to be.

'Don't worry,' Benson said. 'We can fix that. They probably wouldn't notice anyway, not at the border.'

He mumbled a thank you.

'And the letter is good,' Benson continued.

'Good?'

'You see, it's tricky. You need something to justify the 4-F but nothing too serious – otherwise they won't let you in. If the US army won't take you, why should Canada? That's how they think.'

'Will they ask about my... illness?'

'Maybe, but we'll be prepared for that. More important is getting a letter offering you a job. Do you have anything from your last employer?'

He showed him a letter of recommendation from his headmaster in Maine. That was his father's doing, insisting that he get a letter when he'd finished – or when his father thought he'd finished – his year of teaching. Benson read the single-page typed letter and frowned.

'Nicely worded, but another small problem. It's got your old name.'

Cold fear crept over him. He wasn't any good at this. Sooner or later, he'd get caught.

'Can you do anything with it?' she asked.

'We should be able to touch it up.'

'Idiot,' he mumbled.

'Don't feel bad,' Benson said. 'You're extremely well prepared. Some people come to us with no documents, no money and no skills. And you've got a partner, a family. That helps a lot, you know, when you're settling into a new life. Stability is crucial.'

In the awkward silence, Benson coughed and continued.

'So, we'll get you that all-important letter, probably a job in a primary school here.'

His eyes lit up. 'Really? When do you think I could start?'

Benson shook his head. 'It'll be a forged letter. But once you're here, you can look around for a real job. And we'll help of course. If not teaching, maybe something else.'

Another silence.

'By the way, how much money do you have?'

'Not a lot,' he said.

'Four hundred US,' she said.

'Right. We'll get a bank statement prepared, something closer to fifteen hundred. They don't like poor people at the border. By the way, when you get back here, we'll help you find an apartment and give you $25 a week. For the first month. Then you're on your own.'

At the far end of the table, the young woman holding Rosa looked up at Benson.

'Of course, you have a child, so it's thirty a week. Sorry, that's all we can afford.'

'It's very generous,' he said.

Benson made a telephone call, spoke for less than a minute and turned toward his newest wards.

'Good news. I've got a comfortable place for you to stay for now. Nice people.'

With more and more Americans coming to him every week, Benson wished he had a bigger staff. They just about managed as it was, surviving on donations and the goodwill of supporters, some of whom took in resisters as lodgers or offered apartments at reduced rents. He took great satisfaction in finding the right place for everyone, but it wasn't easy.

'Now, when you return – you do know that you have to go back to the US and come back here?'

They both nodded.

'Good. When you return, we'll see about finding a more permanent place for you.'

'Thanks,' he said, 'but I'm not clear about how we do this… going back and forth.'

'It is a little complicated, so let me explain.'

She lit a cigarette and he started to take notes.

'When you come back, you're going to apply at the border for what's called Landed Immigrant Status. They'll interview you and grade you on different criteria – age, education, knowledge of English, employment potential and so on. All you need is fifty points out of one hundred.'

'Can you go a little slower, please?'

'OK, but everything's explained in here.'

Benson handed him a thick booklet entitled *Manual for Draft-Age Immigrants to Canada*.

'You won't have any trouble getting those fifty points,' he continued. 'You get ten just for your age – between eighteen and thirty-five – another sixteen for your college degree. One for your year of teaching. Ten for your English. Ten for the employment letter. And as many as fifteen for what they call "personal assessment".'

'What's that?' she asked.

'Motivation, resourcefulness – things like that. Based on an interview. It's arbitrary, but David should do fine. Mind you, some border officials are ex-military and don't like Americans escaping the draft. So keep the hair short and the pants long.'

He nodded.

'One last thing. I have to ask, are you married?'

'We have a certificate,' she said. 'Is it advisable?'

'It is. A married couple, especially with a child, will score well in the personal assessment and...'

'The thing is, I'm not coming back with them. Not at first. We decided that I'll join them only when they're settled, with a job and all. Easier that way.'

She spoke without emotion, a lie so convincing he almost believed it.

'I see.' Benson started to pencil tap again.

'Is that a problem?' she asked.

'No. Once David gets landed status, he can sponsor you.'

He bit his lip to keep from speaking.

'However, if he crosses over without you, I strongly advise that you leave the child here. It wouldn't look good – a single man with a baby. They don't like anything out of the ordinary, anything unconventional.'

'Leave her?' he asked.

'With me.'

They turned toward the end of the table, where the young woman was still holding Rosa. She had been speaking on the telephone but hung up abruptly.

'I'd be happy to look after your baby. My mom and I do it a lot, for people in your situation.'

It was a handsome house, the red-brick exterior trimmed with black window frames. High hedges separated it from the neighbours, and a low wooden gate barred the entrance to the driveway. No cars on the street, and no houses on the other side. Only a sizable public garden with grassy parkland.

They stood on the paved walkway leading to the front door.

'Just remember,' she said, 'when you return, it'll be some kind of apartment.'

He glared at her.

The wife and husband owners were both lawyers whose children had moved to other parts of the country and were happy to welcome American war resisters and offer free legal advice. Their guests, who stayed on a separate floor but ate dinner with them, usually left after a week.

A tall, wispy figure in slacks and loose-fitting cashmere sweater opened the door. Helmet hairdo, long nose and glasses hanging from a cord around her slender neck.

'What a beautiful little girl,' she cooed, peering into the carrycot.

The house tour ended upstairs in the nursery, across the hall from the guest bedroom. The two women watched, and exchanged smiles, as he placed sleepy Rosa in a white-wicker cot raised on legs.

'We kept everything,' the woman said, 'even after our children had grown up. Kept it for our grandchildren. But nothing so far. Just bad luck, I guess.'

He mumbled commiseration while she turned toward the

window and looked out across an expansive backyard. Did Benson tell her I was going to leave them? she wondered.

'We've also arranged a babysitter for you,' the woman said, recovering composure. 'Someone we know well.'

'We're extremely grateful.'

'It is Emily?'

'No. Not Emily, though she is wonderful. No, this girl is a neighbour. *Sans politique.*'

The woman issued a tight smile. She and her husband often talked politics with their American guests. Intense, even heated, those discussions made them feel part of the struggle.

Back downstairs, she excused herself, saying that she was leaving and would be back in the late afternoon.

'My husband is out of town for a few days. So, I'll cook something for us. Just make yourselves at home. There's plenty of things in the kitchen if you're hungry. And milk in the fridge for your baby.'

'That's very kind. I think we're ready for a nap,' Sharon said with a smile that he was already beginning to miss.

The lawyer grabbed a slim, leather briefcase and was halfway out the door. 'Oh, you can put your car in the driveway. Just use this,' she said, pointing a brick-shaped device at the little gate, which swung open.

In the morning, after giving instructions to the babysitter, they set out on their own. Following Benson's advice – "Best way to get to know this city is to use local transport" – they took a bus into the city centre, where they sat in a café and read newspapers. Nothing there or in the day-old copies of the San Francisco papers they found in the public library. They walked through a small park and browsed in a bookstore. He hated the inertia and the waiting, and her everything's-going-to-be-fine expression grated on him.

Later that afternoon, they entered the office in the narrow building and saw Benson with a group of young men and women.

'They're his students at the university,' Emily explained. 'Sometimes they help us out.'

'That's nice. You're a hard-working group, that's for sure,' he said.

'Ironic, isn't it?' Emily said. 'This place was built for the Stock Exchange, and now we're using it to help stop a capitalist war.'

The phone rang and Emily excused herself to answer it. In the room buzzing with activity, he picked up a pamphlet while she lit a cigarette and surveyed the room.

Benson joined them a few minutes later.

'Sorry, I was helping them with a project. Everything OK with Mrs Kenney?'

'Yes. She's wonderful. Even arranged for a babysitter and lent us a pram.'

'Good. Getting to know the city, I hope.'

'A bit.'

He waited but they didn't say more.

'I don't have anything for you. Not yet,' Benson said, tapping away with his pencil. 'I'll call when I have. Save you from coming here every day.'

'OK, but maybe we could help,' he said, gesturing around the room.

'Thanks, but we have enough volunteers. And frankly speaking, your time is better spent getting to know your new city.'

Back at the house across from the park, they found Rosa asleep and the babysitter reading.

'I'll use her when I come back,' he said. 'She's just right.'

'Yes, but she lives out here,' she said, 'and your apartment will probably be near the office. And Emily.'

29

The long days of enforced togetherness became burdensome, alleviated only by Rosa's antics and their hosts' lively conversation. No news from the US was good news, which they acknowledged without words while listening to the radio. Mornings were dragged out in the library, bookshops and cafés, while afternoons were consumed by pushing Rosa's pram through parks. They particularly liked Stanley Park, a sprawling rainforest on a headland jutting out into the harbour, though they often ended up on different paths or sitting on separate benches.

On the ninth morning, they were summoned by Benson.

'Here it is!' he cried, waving a piece of paper, when they entered the office.

Sitting down, Steve glanced at the letter from the Vancouver School Board. 'How did…'

'We have friends in most departments in city hall,' Benson said. 'It doesn't harm anyone, and it serves a good cause.'

Steve read that Mr David Williams was offered a full-time position at Dwight D Eisenhower Primary School starting in September at $9,880 a year. Canadian dollars, he knew, were more or less the same as American. They would be all right, Rosa and him. And later, maybe years later, Sharon would join them.

'It's a new school,' Benson said. 'Opened just last year. So, who knows? They may actually have a real job soon.'

'Yes, of course,' he mumbled, light fading from his eyes.

'That's great,' she said and squeezed his hand.

'Now, let's work on the questionnaire,' Benson enthused. 'The one you have to present at the border when you come back.'

They spent an hour filling in the lengthy form, while she smoked and read the pamphlets on the table. Benson then advised him on how to dress: a jacket is fine, better than a sweater. How much cash to bring: $200 or $300 is good. And how to handle the interview, which was subjective and could sink him.

'Be polite, even deferential,' Benson counselled. 'Don't pretend you've never heard of draft resisters. Don't make any political statements. And don't, for god's sake, mention the VCAAWO.'

That afternoon, their last in Vancouver, they went again to Stanley Park. They sat together this time, holding hands, and watched the sun set over the water. With the lines drawn and the date set, he could fix his mind on what came next. If only he could get a real teaching job, maybe Vancouver wouldn't be so bad. He'd get used to being alone. Come to think of it, he'd been by himself a lot during the past two years, teaching in Maine and even at River Ridge. When he took walks in the woods, she was never there.

They left Rosa with Emily and drove back to the border. A flash of passports, a glance at the Peace Arch, a wave of an arm and they re-entered the United States of America. He tried to steel himself, to match her detached efficiency, and speak of the present as if there were a tomorrow. Marcus again met them at the house in Seattle, smiles all around.

In the morning, they were early – she was always early – and he fidgeted on the polished wood bench in the ornate ticket hall. They'd already said their goodbyes. Still, he tried to say something about staying in touch.

'No, don't do anything like that.'

'I mean a phone booth, or a letter forwarded from somewhere else.'

'No, Steve. Please, listen to me.'

The face framed by straight hair remained untroubled. She had thought it all through, long ago.

'Don't do any of that.'

'OK, not at first. But later, when things cool down.'

'No, not then either. Remember, when she grows up, you will tell her that I died. A clean break.'

An ugly, hurtful phrase.

'I know,' she said. 'But it's best for all of us. Trust me. You'll be fine. And so will Rosa.'

When the southbound train was announced, they walked out to the platform. Beside the carriage, she went up on tiptoe and kissed him. He held her until she withdrew and disappeared.

He spent one more night in the small house and awoke before daybreak. Alone at that hour for the first time since they'd left Mendocino, he realised something. He could call it all off. Cross back over the border to Vancouver, as planned, but collect Rosa and return to the US. Just go back to River Ridge, where she'd grow up with other kids. Safe in the woods. Sharon could visit from time to time. Not perfect, but better than being separated forever.

But would she visit? Probably not. Besides, it was risky. He might be tracked down and hauled away. Leaving little Rosa all alone. Crazy to even think about it.

He drove to the large house and met the immaculately attired Robert. When he started to explain Sharon's absence, Robert produced his all-purpose smile.

'Yes, I know. She's gone back to continue her work.'

He narrowed his eyes. They had planned it together, before she even told him.

'Where is she?'

Robert's expression told him not to ask any more questions.

'One thing, though. A slight change of plan. The FBI are all over town. Walking the streets, asking questions. At the train station, too.'

He felt his chest tighten.

'I sent a message yesterday, but you'd already left for the station. And I didn't send anyone there to warn you because that might have alerted the watchers.'

He hadn't noticed anything at the station. Too preoccupied. But she would have spotted them, he was sure of that. And she hadn't let on because she didn't want him to worry.

'They're looking for draft resisters, showing photos and asking people.'

'Photos?'

'Don't worry. Not photos of you or Sharon.'

Not yet, he thought. It's only been six weeks.

'Still, it's best if you don't cross the border at the Peace Arch. Go instead to Abbotsford. It's only about fifty miles from here. But far fewer cars and less surveillance.'

As he drove out of Seattle, he considered another idea. He could bring Rosa back to the US, go to his parents' house and turn himself in. His parents would take care of her until he got out of prison. Again, not ideal, but when he got out, he and Rosa could live together in the US and by then, Sharon would… No. If he turned himself in, the FBI would find out about River Ridge, trace Sharon and put her in prison. He couldn't do that to her.

The Abbotsford crossing was not as quiet as predicted, though most of the cars seemed to be commuters going to work on the British Columbia side. The others looked like American families on vacation. Sitting in the long line, he again rehearsed the details of his new identity: name, date of birth, place of birth. Speaking aloud to himself, he recited the name of the school in Vancouver where he had been offered a teaching job and the name of the doctor in San Francisco at the bottom of the forged letter.

He cleared his throat when asked about the nature of his visit.

'It's not a visit, Officer. I want to settle permanently in Canada.'

'I see,' the officer said. 'Park over there, next to that blue van, and go inside.'

He sat on a plastic chair in a small reception area with walls displaying colourful posters proclaiming "Beautiful British Columbia" and "Year-round fun for Everyone". Happy people skiing down mountains, fishing in rivers, bathing on beaches and hiking through woods. One showed a young boy staring up at a totem pole carved in the shape of a bird's head and wings.

He was shown into a room commanded by a uniformed official, who gestured toward a chair without any greeting. He sat and looked up to see a moose head glaring down at him from the wall behind the desk.

'Now, why in the world would a young educated American, like you, want to emigrate to Canada?'

This was the type of ex-military officer Benson had warned him about.

'I think it has a lot of opportunity. And it's beautiful. I like nature.'

It didn't sound too bad, even to himself.

'Lots of that in your own country.'

'Yes, sir, but I like adventure. Change. A challenge.'

The man pulled a taut smile. 'Challenge? You're not wrong there, son. Now, let's see your questionnaire.'

In neat handwriting, under Benson's supervision, he had answered all thirty-four questions, beginning with his name and ending with a declaration that the information he had provided was "truthful, complete and correct".

The rock-jawed officer ran his eyes over the form, grunting once or twice. Steve tried to avoid looking at the moose.

'Teacher, huh?'

'Yes, sir.'

He handed over the letter of recommendation from Maine, hoping the man wouldn't scrutinise it. He barely looked at it.

'And you have a job offer here in Canada?'

'Yes. It's a wonderful school, right in the middle of Vancouver.'

The officer read the letter.

'How are you going to support yourself? This job doesn't begin until September.'

He dug out his wallet and showed the wadge of twenty-dollar bills he had managed to save.

'And there's more in my account,' he said, handing over the falsified bank statement.

'OK. Now, you're coming here, or wanting to come here – it doesn't have anything to do with the Selective Service, I assume.'

'No, sir, it does not.'

'Still, you wouldn't do anything illegal, would you? I mean, concerning your duty as an American citizen.'

'No. Of course not.'

The officer's jaw loosened when he showed him the 4-F draft card.

'What's the problem?' the man asked, leaning back in his leather chair.

'Mental health, sir,' he squeaked. 'I lose it sometimes. You know, when I get nervous.'

'Like now?' A tiny crack of a smile.

'What? Oh, no, sir.'

'You got any documents for this?'

The officer mumbled through the doctor's letter and paused before reading the last sentence aloud: 'Although Mr Williams does sometimes suffer from bouts of dizziness, this does not in any way prevent him from being a productive citizen.'

Laying the letter down, the officer looked hard at him, as if trying to spot the site of his mental instability.

'OK if I call this Dr Salomon?'

'Sure.'

'Right now?'

'Yes.'

He swallowed hard and tried to keep his eyes on the man. Robert had explained that if border control called the San Francisco number, a woman would say, 'Twin Peaks Neurology Clinic,' and summon "Dr Salomon". Salomon would speak with a gravelly voice and enough medical knowledge to answer questions concerning the medical condition of David Williams. That's how it was supposed to work.

The officer stared at him, his hand hovering over the telephone.

'That's all right, Mr Williams,' he said and handed back the letter. 'You may now enter the Dominion of Canada with landed immigrant status. After five years, you may apply for permanent citizenship and obtain a Canadian passport. I wish you good luck.'

Too late for that, he thought as he drove off. After a mile, he eased onto the hard shoulder and stopped. Open farmland and rugged mountains in the distance. Canada. A cold country, and a kind of prison, no matter how you looked at it. He should have been finishing his first year at Harvard Law School. Instead, he was in a strange country, on the run from the FBI, with no job prospects and a six-week-old daughter to raise.

He lowered his head until it rested on the steering wheel. Tears trickled, then gushed as he let out a howl that racked his whole body. Everything was gone. He'd probably never see Sharon again. Or his parents. Unless they came up and visited him. But then the whole humiliating truth would have to come out.

A gust of wind from a passing truck rocked the car and forced him to grip the wheel. Raising his head, he saw a bridge in the near distance. He pulled back onto the road and stayed in the slow lane, crossing the bridge over the Fraser River and heading toward Vancouver.

First thing was a job. His dollars, even with whatever Sharon might send, wouldn't last long, and Benson's subsidy was only for a month. He couldn't ask his parents to send money to Vancouver, not without some explanation. How bad could it get? A damp apartment. Utilities cut off. Whatever happened, he would not let Rosa suffer. Never.

He found West Hastings St and climbed the stairs in the narrow building. Benson was in conference with two people, but Emily greeted him with a hug. Rosa lay in the carrycot on the table next to her.

'Welcome back!' she cried. 'She's such a delight.'

The telephone rang and, for a moment, he thought it must be her. Checking up, just to be sure.

'VCAAWO. How can I help?' Emily chirped.

When he peered into the cot, Rosa burped, opened her eyes and spread her lips in a crooked smile. Lowering his head to hers, he whispered his promise. He continued to watch her while listening to Emily's crisp replies, Benson's hushed tones and the volunteers' bursts of laughter. Thank god for these people, he thought. Where would I be without them?

'No problems?' Benson asked when he got free and slid over to him.

'None whatsoever. I just followed everything you said. Thank you.'

'Great. And little Rosa here looks happy as a clam – very much like a clam, in fact. Now, let's see. Here's the address of your apartment. As I said, it's free for the first month, by which time we hope to find a job for you.'

'And if that doesn't happen?'

'Let's be positive.'

The apartment was only a short walk away, above a noodle shop in Chinatown. Emily put the carrycot down and held the door open as he lugged his suitcase up the uncarpeted stairs. Although the furniture was worn and the appliances on their last legs, the rooms were clean and bright. He laid Rosa in the dropside crib and waited until she closed her eyes.

'The telephone needs reconnecting,' Emily said when he

joined her in the living room. 'But the utilities are working. Sorry, but there's no freezer. I think Americans…'

'That's OK. I don't need a freezer.'

'How's the crib? I mean, it's a bit old-fashioned.'

'It'll do fine. Rosa doesn't like fashion.'

'Ah, just you wait.'

She flashed a smile, so different from the office.

'Anyway, remember I can babysit whenever you need me. And I can look after Rosa at our house if you need to go away or something.'

'Thank you, Emily.'

Her face beamed, his body tingled, and he would have kissed her, but she thrust the key into his hand and said goodbye.

He heaved the case up onto the bed and began to put things away. Pretty much the same clothes he'd brought with him from Maine and all the worse for wear at River Ridge. His long-sleeved button-down shirts, one blue and one white, plus a red-and-black L.L. Bean, were hung in the narrow closet, along with a pair of chinos and two jeans. His winter coat was still serviceable, but he'd sold his only suit in Seattle to get extra cash.

Black leather shoes, acquired per Robert's advice, were arranged on the closet floor, next to the hiking boots bought in Mendocino. A wool sweater and a cotton sweater, t-shirts, underwear and socks went into a dresser drawer. Underneath them, he slid the plastic folder with his documents, some forged, the others authentic but fraudulent.

He opened a sealed envelope, drew out Ted's necklace and stared at it before hanging it around his neck. In a second envelope, he found the photograph taken in a Seattle studio before the first crossing to Vancouver. His arm around Sharon's shoulder, Rosa in her arms and impossibly white mountain peaks in the background. He told himself he'd get it framed.

He slept well for the first time in almost a month and spent the morning making breakfast, feeding Rosa and finding CBC on the radio. When she fell asleep, he dashed out and bought newspapers at the corner shop. Only twelve minutes in total, he saw, checking his watch when he returned. She was still asleep, but the silence spoke of an emptiness.

By the time he buzzed Emily in, he had fed Rosa again, made himself a sandwich and taken a nap.

'Any news?' he asked her.

Although he knew it was far too soon for Benson to have found him a real job, he couldn't stop himself from asking.

'No, but he's working on it.'

Inside City Hall, he scanned the white index cards pinned to a cork board behind glass. Some were typed, others handwritten, and none would have worked for him, even if he were eligible. The school board wanted applicants with "previous experience in the BC school system". And many of the openings were for teaching English as a second language, a skill he did not have.

Returning to Chinatown, he wandered into The Magic Turtle, a bookstore where the walls glistened with green paint. New and used books were displayed on free-standing shelves that divided the room into separate areas. In the "Health and Family" section, he thumbed through a book by Benjamin Spock and smiled at the advice to be both "lenient and courageous with your infant". But not with "your infantry", he imagined the famous baby doctor saying.

'How old is your child?' the woman asked at the counter as he paid for the book.

'Nine weeks and four days.'

'That's the right book, then.'

He always knew her exact age because he knew when he had killed a man.

Weeks slid by unnoticed, except that he was granted formal permission to stay in Canada. He wanted to celebrate, but with whom and for what? He'd lied to his parents and to his headmaster, and he'd been lying ever since. To everyone he met, even friends like Benson and Emily. Before long, he'd have to lie to his own daughter.

He went to Stanley Park, where he walked out to the wooded headland and stared at a bridge heading north. All so familiar, but the Lions Gate was not the Golden Gate. He guessed she was in the Bay Area. The news was full of bombings across the country, and the Brigade had claimed responsibility for some, but you could never be sure. Six people had been injured in one, including two policemen. No one had died.

The $50 she sent him through Western Union helped pay the rent. But Benson's money had stopped, and his own cash was dwindling. He thought about asking parents, but he didn't want to pile up more lies.

He grew a beard. 'Economising,' he told Emily, though it was a precaution that Sharon had advised. Emily said he shouldn't "let himself go" because it wouldn't look good when he applied for a job. They ended up in bed, but the lovemaking was not a success.

'I guess I'm better at babysitting,' she said.

'And maybe I should stick to being a dad,' he added.

On a Saturday, hurrying to get to the library before early closing, he stopped someone on the street to ask the time.

'Excuse me, but do you have…?'

'I don't give money to beggars.'

He shuffled off and looked at his reflection in a window. That's when he saw the "Help Wanted" sign. Brushing down his longish hair and smoothing out his beard, he entered and realised it was a toy shop.

The job was part-time and only until September. He admitted that he didn't know much about toys but said that he had a "young" daughter who liked games. He seemed to win over the manager when he mentioned that he'd bring in his recommendation from a private school in Maine.

He shaved off his beard, cut his hair, sold his suitcase and bought second-hand corduroys and another white button-down shirt. Not mint condition but a definite improvement on his usual attire. As soon as he entered the store on Monday morning, he felt lighter, dancing through the day, smiling with customers and exchanging parenting stories.

Back in the apartment, he kissed the departing Emily on the cheek and nuzzled his daughter until she squealed with delight. The flickering hope in his heart grew brighter. I can get through this, he said to himself. I can and I will.

Things did in fact get better when another call brought him to the office on West Hastings St.

'Finally got something for you,' Benson said. 'A job advertised by City Hall. We know the councillor involved, one of our supporters. He's waiting for you to apply.'

'That is good news.'

Although he had begun to like Vancouver, the prospect of no income had been terrifying.

'Yes, I just hope your expectations aren't too high.'

'Of course not. I think you know me well enough now.'

Kindergarten teaching or a low-level office job would be fine.

'What is it?'

'You have a driving license, don't you?'

'Yes.'

'Canadian?'

'Got it a few weeks ago. Why?'

'They need a driver for the municipal waste-collection service. They're expanding out into the suburbs.'

'Driving a... garbage truck?'

'That's it. Go down to City Hall right away, to the Department of Health, and fill out the application form.'

A week later, he was speeding south toward the river at daybreak. He had estimated it would be only a ten-minute drive, but it was already more than fifteen and he was overwrought.

When Emily had come through the door before 6:00am that morning, Rosa was crying and he had panicked.

'I can't be late,' he said. 'Not on my first day.'

'Don't worry,' Emily said. 'She's not crying. She's laughing.'

Why didn't I know that? he asked himself, charging through a red light.

He found a parking place at the depot and reported to the controller's office. A burly man checked his papers, entered something in a ledger and gave him a key and a metal token with a painted number.

'That's for your locker, that's for your uniform, and this here's Mike.'

He turned to see a smaller man in the doorway.

'He'll show you the ropes and be your trainer for the first week.'

The uniform was light brown with broad yellow bands on the sleeves and bottom of the legs. Scratchy on his skin, but warm enough and brand new.

'That's one good thing about this job,' Mike said as he led him out to the yard. 'You don't have to worry about dressing for the office.'

The fire-engine-red truck was large and square, its praying mantis arms sticking out in front. High up in the cab, he listened and watched as Mike took him through the dials and gadgets. He'd never driven anything like it and the gear shift looked menacing. Mike pushed a button, the motor roared and the chassis rumbled, setting his nerves on edge. Yet when the behemoth moved forward, the ride was smooth.

'These ones are new,' Mike said. 'City coughed up the dough last year. Part of the "green agenda". Whatever that is.'

By the end of the week, he was steering the beast around on his own. Any problems, he asked his swamper, the guy who stood on the metal plate at the back and handled the bins. And who assured him that their patch in north Vancouver was "easy street".

Mostly detached houses, few parked cars and bins properly placed on the sidewalk.

The work was monotonous. He stopped the truck, the swamper jumped off and slotted a bin into the tipper. He pushed a button; the arms lifted the bin up and angled it so the refuse fell into the open top of the truck. Empty four or five bins, advance a hundred yards, stop, wait for another few bins, push the button. Again and again. Four hours of hissing pistons, groaning arms and crashing trash. And three more after lunch.

The precision and repetition soothed him. The anonymity, too. Alone in the cab for most of the day, he listened to music on the radio. Plus, the pay was good with a decent pension plan. And Rosa was growing day by day. Did she miss her mother? Emily said she didn't think that was possible.

30

Ronald swept aside the newspaper with an angry hand and crushed out his cigarette. Why hadn't he been told instead of having to read about it in the paper? Could it be because the dead man and his son were Black?

He rifled through his address book but couldn't find the number until he remembered it was under "F". Dialling, he looked out the picture window on the fifth floor, at the jagged skyline on the other side of the bay. It is good news, he conceded, but not good enough. Pennington is not the murderer. Not the one who has to pay.

At midday, he was riding high above the water on the Bay Bridge. The Golden Gate always struck him as a beautiful toy, whereas this was an impressive feat of engineering, with a longer span, allowing him to feel he was going somewhere.

He'd spoken to his mother on the telephone, not telling her much but making sure that her cousin from Redwood City was there to keep her company. And saying that he would stop by later that afternoon. She never spoke of her pain, but it was obvious. Although her bereavement leave had ended, she had not yet recovered. Had, in fact, missed several days at the hospital recently. 'It's nothing, son,' she said. 'Just feeling a little tired. That's all.'

Well, I've got energy for both of us, he thought, swooping

down into the heart of the city, where, once again, he got trapped in a maze of one-way streets. He swore aloud as he negotiated his way through trams, busses, taxis and cars – not to mention pedestrians – flowing in both directions on Market St. For some reason, he could never find the garage he knew was nearby. He promised himself he would take a cab next time.

Parked but still fuming, he straightened his tie and marched up to Market. All around him, post-earthquake brick and stone had been replaced by steel and glass. Except for the Federal Building, a granite-grey colossus ornamented with tall columns and horizontal divisions. Going around to the back, he found the entrance he wanted beneath an angry-looking eagle clutching the required arrows and olive branch.

He strode down high-ceilinged corridors wrapped around an open courtyard and lost his way. Swallowing his pride, he asked at the reception desk, rode in an elevator with bronze doors and followed signs to room 335.

Bennett greeted him with professional politeness.

'Thanks for making the trip. I was going to call you but…'

'Skip the excuses, please, and fill me in.'

'OK, but I can't tell you everything. We have protocols, you know.'

'Please just get on with it.'

'Right. Gabriel Pennington's trial has been set for November. As you know, he's been charged with conspiracy to murder and commit arson. We're confident of a conviction.'

'What kind of a sentence will he get?'

'Hard to say. He's got a good legal team and…'

'How many years?'

'We'll ask for life.'

'But?'

'He could get as little as five to eight years.'

'Jesus Christ!'

'I know, I know. We're closing in on the bomber, though.'

'Tell me.'

'There's not much evidence from the van itself. The steering wheel, which is where we had hopes, looks like a charred pretzel.'

That was Bennett's favourite phrase, already used several times when talking to the press and his agents. Unlike them, Ronald Gill did not smile. His father had looked all right in the coffin, but he knew he'd suffered terrible injuries to his body.

'Nothing there, but we did get fingerprints from the envelope passed to the guard.'

'OK. So, what's happening right now?'

'We have more than sixty agents working the case, here in the Bay Area. There's also a nationwide alert.'

Ronald leaned forward in his chair and put a heavy hand on the man's desk.

'But how are you going to find him? What do you know about this person?'

'Like I said, I can't share details of our investigation with you.'

'Listen, he killed my father. I have a right to know.'

'Please, Mr Gill. I understand your feelings, but I hope you'll appreciate that secrecy is the key to success in this business.'

Ronald managed a twisted smile.

'I can say this,' Bennett said. 'Whoever he is, he will have made a mistake. We will find that. And then we will find him.'

Ronald looked at him. Short-cropped hair, flowery tie, raisin-like eyes. He wanted to believe him, but driving back to Oakland, he began to consider other options.

What Bennett did not reveal was that Gabriel Pennington had refused an offer of immunity from prosecution if he named his co-conspirators. Even that prospect of evading many years in prison did not sway him. Still, during hours of interrogation, he had let slip a "she". Not the van driver, of course, but a person who must have played an important role.

Bennett dispatched a dozen agents to the San Francisco Health Department. Assuming that the woman they were looking for would be in her twenties or thirties and had probably changed her name during the past twelve months, they trawled through requests for copies of birth certificates made during the past year for girls born between 1941 and 1951. Working around the clock, it took them two weeks to compile a list of sixty-three such requests.

Switching over to the Department of Motor Vehicles, the agents cross-checked that list against applications by women for a driving license during the past year. They came up with four names. Those matching names might belong to different people, Bennett allowed, but not the matching signatures. The Sharon Walker who had applied for a copy of her birth certificate had also applied for a new driving license. Again, possibly above board. But further checks established that the Sharon Walker born in May 1942 had died five months later.

Bennett's eyes lit up as he scrambled through the files on his desk. He'd seen that name somewhere. He dug up the list of the thirty-nine activists and saw that one of them was indeed Sharon Walker.

But where was she now?

'Still here in the Bay area?' Bennett suggested.

'Unlikely. Not if she's smart,' Callahan said.

'Mexico?'

'I don't think so. Our college-educated radicals don't like refried beans. No, the preferred route from here is north, to Canada. Usually Vancouver, via Seattle.'

'OK. But what about before the bombing? She had to be in touch with Pennington. So, not far away.'

'True. Could have been anywhere, including here in the city. But, again, I'd bet it was somewhere to the north. Lots of places to hide up there. Especially in the mountains.'

'Where's that map?'

They divided Northern California into eight regions and assembled eight teams, each with four agents. The teams were given one month to find Sharon Walker. Bennett wanted to call Ronald Gill but decided to wait. Having a name was a breakthrough, but he wanted to actually find the woman first.

The Mendocino team split up and stayed in two different B&Bs in the town. One group posed as old college classmates on a reunion, while the other said they were looking for a friend they'd lost contact with. When a week of sightseeing and casual conversation produced nothing useful, the second group moved further up the coast to Fort Bragg, where they stopped at the botanical gardens and got into a conversation with a waitress in the café.

'If you're looking for your friend,' she said, 'you might try some of the communes around here.'

Within an hour, they had seven names, though some had no address, just "near South Fork" or "in the mountains towards Willits". Rejoining the other group, still in Mendocino, they divided up the list. River Ridge was the first commune visited by the agents posing as old classmates.

'Yeah, we're up from LA to get some fresh air,' one of them explained at the breakfast table. 'You know what it's like down there.'

They had arrived late the previous day and, like all visitors, had been given a cabin to stay in for a week.

'What part of LA?' Ted asked, pausing between spoonfuls of granola.

'Glendale.'

'You go to Glendale High?'

'Yeah.'

'Same as my daughter. She's about your age. When did you graduate?'

The two agents looked at each other.

'We didn't,' one said. 'Not from Glendale. Our parents sent us to a private school for the last two years.'

Before Ted could ask what private school, the men excused themselves and left the table.

All that morning and afternoon, the visitors worked in the gardens, eager to learn how to plant snap beans and sow corn seeds. By nightfall, the gossip was they were good workers.

And they were at it again, after breakfast the next day, weeding in the warm sun.

'People must love it here,' one of them said to a long-term resident. 'I guess most of you stay a long time.'

'Not everyone.'

'Oh? How's that?'

Back in San Francisco, the agents told Bennett and Callahan that a woman called Sharon had left River Ridge in early May with a younger man named Steve and a newborn baby.

'Left all of a sudden,' the commune member had said. 'No one saw it coming.' And no one knew where they went, though an older man said he'd heard them talk about Florida.

'Early May,' Callahan repeated with a satisfied smile. 'When we arrested Pennington. Must have thought we were getting too close.'

'It's her, all right,' cried Bennett. 'And maybe the bomber, too. I'll send Drake up there right away.'

Ted enjoyed his breakfast, even more than other meals. Something about the freshness of the fruit mixed in with his granola. He also liked listening to the voices rippling around him, especially the high-pitched laughter of young children.

It was already warm that morning and promising to be hot, perfect for picking peas and tomatoes.

'I thought I'd cook that goulash tonight,' the woman next to him said. 'You know, the one…'

A teenage boy burst in, out of breath.

'Some men are coming,' he managed to say. 'In suits and ties.'

Senior Special Agent Drake hadn't counted on the march through the forest and didn't like looking flustered, his cheeks red and armpits dripping. Especially when entering a drop-outs' commune.

He halted his posse of three on the edge of the clearing and surveyed the terrain. Gardens, cabins, grassy paths, a weathered barn and a big house. By now, half the community had gathered outside the barn, staring at the suited men who had huddled a hundred yards away and were staring back at them.

'Right. Go see what you can find out from that crowd,' Drake ordered. 'And I'll have a little chat with Mr Wheeler.'

Moving down the slope toward the barn, one of the agents slipped, fell, and doubled his humiliation by scrabbling around to retrieve wrap-around sunglasses, to the delight of his audience.

By the time Drake reached the porch, Gavin's wife had opened the front door.

'Morning, ma'am. My name is Drake. FBI.' He held up his badge and was about to pocket it, when she asked to see it up close. Drake raised an eyebrow but complied without saying what he thought.

'I'm here to speak to Mr Gavin Wheeler. Is he at home?'

'Yes. He's my husband. I'll get him, if you'll...'

Drake brushed past her and into the sunlit interior, admiring the furnishings and quality flooring. Not bad "for a hippie pad".

Gavin was standing in the hallway, his anger tempered by bewilderment.

'I assume you have a good reason for this intrusion.'

Drake took in the man's height, thick silver hair and patrician air.

'I am sorry for this unannounced visit, Mr Wheeler, but yes, we're here for a good reason. We need to talk to you about some of the people here.'

'Because?'

'Because a man was killed a few months ago in San Francisco, and we have reason to believe that two people here were involved.'

Over the years, Gavin had been contacted by the police concerning people at River Ridge. Usually divorce and child custody, sometimes drugs and theft, even assault. But never murder.

'I see. Perhaps we'd better sit down. Would you like something cool to drink?'

'Yes, thanks.'

Gavin gestured to a Lincoln rocking chair. 'I'll be just a minute.'

He turned and saw his wife approaching with glasses of lemonade. He took the glasses and handed one to his seated guest, dropped down in the matching chair and raised his glass in a mock toast. Drake drained his in two gulps.

'Well, now, that hit the spot.'

'You said you were interested in two people,' Gavin prompted, anxious to get the man out of his house.

'Yes. A woman named Sharon Walker and a man called Steve. Though they might have used other names. Here's a photo of the woman. Do you recognise her?'

Gavin took the enlarged, grainy photograph, reproduced from the driving license application, and appeared to study it.

'No. I don't think so.'

'Really? We understand that she stayed here for almost two years. Lived here in your house and had an office. She was your accountant, wasn't she?'

Gavin shrugged. 'I'm afraid you've been misinformed. People around here can be imaginative, especially after consuming certain substances.'

Drake did not return the smile.

'I don't think so, Mr Wheeler. We were also told that she became involved with a younger man, Steve, who arrived last year. They lived together, here in your house. And they had a child, before leaving suddenly in early May.'

'Like I said. Some of us around here like telling stories, especially to figures of authority. I think they call it "false leads", don't they?'

Drake scowled. 'Mr Wheeler. I suggest that you cooperate and tell us the truth. Because, if you don't, I will return tomorrow with a search warrant and tear your house apart.'

'And what would you expect to find?'

'Things you can't even imagine.'

Gavin lowered his eyes.

'Listen. You are not under suspicion. We consider you an innocent party, not complicit in whatever crimes they may have committed. But you should also know that lying to us is punishable by a fine of up to $10,000 and five years in prison.'

Gavin looked at his wife, standing in the doorway. Her face persuaded him. In fact, he had wondered about Sharon. Hard working and reliable, and private. Not just guarded, but impenetrable, professional-level secrecy.

'OK,' he murmured.

'Good. Now, take another look at the photo, please.'

He pretended to take a second look. 'It could be her,' he said in a near-whisper.

'Could be or is?'

'It's her.'

'Thank you. She called herself Sharon Walker?'

'Yes.'

'Only that? No other name?'

'No.'

'And what about the man called Steve?'

'He came last year. Nice guy. Taught the children.'

'His last name?'

'Not sure. Cooper? Something like that.'

'Were they married?'

'Maybe, but I don't think so.'

'Why not?'

'I don't pry into people's private lives, OK?' Angry with himself, Gavin was trying to row back from what he'd already said.

'All right, all right. Just tell me about them.'

While Drake collected details of appearance and character, his agents had little success with the crowd at the barn. When asked questions, they all, one by one, excused themselves and went about their morning routine. That didn't unduly bother the agents, who were immune to rejection and joked among themselves about the collective amnesia of the "inmates".

However, there was one person who they hoped would be more forthcoming. And from the detailed description given by the undercover agents who had visited before, they had little trouble finding Ted.

'I understand you heard them say they were going to Florida. Is that right?'

'Yes.'

'Anything more you can tell us?'

'She said Gainesville.'

'Why was that?'

'Usual reason. A job. Teaching for him. She was going to be a *hausfrau*.'

'What about the baby?'

'What about her?'

'Did she have a name?'

'Of course.'

'What was it?'

'Meredith. Means "great" in Welsh.'

'Is that so?'

Ted ignored the sneer. 'Yes, you see Welsh is a Celtic language, which unlike Germanic...'

'Did they ever talk about San Francisco?'

'No. Not much that I remember, anyway.'

Ted was sitting in his favourite spot, on a stump beside the barn, whittling. The agents stood around him in a semicircle, admiring, despite themselves, his deft hand movements.

'That's funny,' one said. 'Because they both came from there. From San Francisco, I mean.'

Ted shrugged.

'Did they strike you as committed radicals?'

'Radicals?'

'C'mon, Mr… what is your name?'

'Ted is all.'

'OK, Mr. Ted. You know the type. People who go about destroying property, even killing people, to achieve their political goals.'

'You mean the US army?'

'Very funny. So, they were radicals then.'

'No. They weren't like that all. They had Meredith. They loved her. That's what mattered to them.'

Back in the house, Drake had finished collecting information about Sharon Walker and the man known only as "Steve".

'I'll leave now,' Drake said to Gavin, 'but I'll send an artist up here tomorrow. To work with you to create an Identikit of Steve. It won't take long and…'

'That won't be necessary,' Gavin's wife said. 'Just hang on a sec.'

She returned with a black-and-white Polaroid photograph.

'That's him,' she said, pointing to a man holding up a fistful of wild flowers on Earth Day.

'Thank you, Mrs Wheeler. Thank you very much.'

When Drake brought the results back to San Francisco, the mood was triumphant. Not only had they traced Sharon Walker, but they also had the first name and an image of the man they believed to be the van driver.

Within a week, they had matched the photo of "Steve" with a photograph of Steven Collins in the Alameda County police files. The clincher came when his fingerprints on file matched those on the envelope used to pass the cash to the guard. A federal grand jury soon issued indictments. Collins was charged with second-degree murder and Walker with conspiracy.

Job half-done, Bennett was summoned back to Washington.

31

The receding heat left a thin haze, turning the sunset a washed-out pink. Mr Collins eased down the freeway exit and onto the coast road, where he switched off the air conditioner, pushed a button and watched the windows slide out of sight. With a breeze blowing in off the water, he could smell the salt air. After his transfer from Pomona last year, he'd bought a new car, and he enjoyed the short ride from the Anaheim office to his new house on the ocean.

Sales figures had been impressive since his appointment as general manager and he was due a few weeks off. Mexico, he thought. Maybe October, when it was a little cooler down there. He knew a man in Merida, on the Yucatan peninsula, who'd invited him for a stay. Catherine would like that; Mayan temples and history. Steve might come, too. He loved history as much as his mother. Only he seemed to be moving around a lot these days. Hard to say where he'd be then.

Turning off the highway, he noticed a black car in the cul-de-sac. When he parked in his driveway and climbed out, two men from the car approached him. They both wore dark suits and hats, even on that warm evening.

'Excuse me, are you Mr Collins?'

'Yes. Who are you?'

His voice was uneven. There'd been a recent spate of burglaries in Dana Point and the surrounding area.

'We're from the FBI, sir,' the tall one said. 'I'm Special Agent Jenson and this is Agent Poletti.'

Mr Collins stared with disbelief as the man opened a wallet and held up his badge.

'We'd like to talk to you about your son, Stephen.'

'What's happened? Is he all right?'

'Well, sir, that's what we don't know. But we'd like to ask a few questions, if that's all right.'

'Yes. Of course.'

Both men looked at him. Inside?

Limp with confusion, he managed to push open the unlocked door and call his wife's name. She came up the steps from the sunken living room, where she'd been reading, and stopped in the hallway. The visitors held their hats by their sides.

'These men are from the FBI and, ah, they want to ask us about Stephen.'

Mrs Collins stiffened, like a guard dog, in the narrow passage.

'Good evening, ma'am.' The tall one executed a slight nod, while his partner remained behind him.

'Good evening to you,' she said icily.

'Yes, you see we have reason to believe that your son might have been involved in an incident that we are investigating. We'd like to talk to him. But we've been unable to locate him and thought you might be able to help.'

'Incident? What incident?' she asked, rubbing the wrist of one hand.

'Perhaps we could sit down and talk.'

Mr Collins ushered them forward, down the steps and into the living room, with a panoramic view of the darkening ocean.

The couple sat on the sofa and the men perched on matching upholstered chairs, angling them toward the married couple.

'Please, gentlemen,' Mrs Collins said. 'Tell us why you are here.' The voice remained stone cold.

'Well, it's like this,' the tall man began. 'We suspect your son was involved in a bombing that occurred in April, in San Francisco. At the Presidio army base there. You may have heard about it.'

Husband and wife looked at each other, incomprehension on their faces.

'A bomb?' Mr Collins said.

'Yes, explosive devices were detonated in the base and a man was killed.'

Mr Collins opened his mouth but found no words, while his wife narrowed her eyes.

'You have made a mistake in coming here,' she said through clenched teeth. 'My son would not get involved in something like that.'

'I understand your shock, Mrs Collins. Really, I do. But…'

'But what?' She dug her fingernails into the piping on the sofa cushion and stared at him. 'What do you understand?'

'Let me ask you a question, if I may.'

Silence.

'Do you know where your son is? Or where he has been for the past five months?'

'Yes. He's working in San Francisco.'

'He's in San Francisco now?'

'I don't know. He was in Seattle on vacation.'

The two men exchanged glances.

'When?'

'A few months ago.'

'How many months ago?'

'About three.'

'And how do you know this? Did he write or telephone?'

'We spoke on the telephone. He calls every so often.'

'I see.' The tall man edged forward. 'Has he ever mentioned Mendocino? Or a place near there, called River Ridge?'

'No.'

'Ever mentioned a female companion?'

'Excuse me?'

'A woman friend. Ever talk about one?'

She looked at him, hard. 'Do you have children, Mr...?'

'Jenson.'

'Any children, Mr Jenson?'

'Yes, a boy and a girl.'

'Well, Mr Jenson, I don't suppose you'd expect your son to tell his mother all about his love life, do you?'

Jenson's partner coughed and leaned forward.

'This is important, ma'am. Did he ever speak about a woman, maybe a girlfriend?'

'No. He did not.'

'So, just to be clear,' Jenson summed up, 'your son called you from Seattle about three months ago.'

'Correct. Now, if you will excuse us, we would like to have the rest of the evening to ourselves.'

'Of course. Just one last question. Did he give you an address in Seattle?'

'No,' Mrs Collins said and stood up. 'Goodbye, to both of you. I hope you find who you're looking for. But it won't be our son.'

32

Standing in the post office in downtown Oakland, she eyed the poster with practised calm. The names "Stephen Collins" and "Sharon Walker" were printed in large block letters above grainy, reproduced photographs. His wasn't much of a likeness and, although hers was sharper, she'd recently dyed her hair a different colour. But was her face recognisable? Several people waiting with her glanced at the poster and some seemed to read the small print: "Interstate Flight; Destruction of Government Property; Murder; Conspiracy".

She readied herself. One pair of eyes swivelling from the wall to her and back to the wall would be enough. 'Ah! The parking meter,' she'd cry and rush out.

She shifted herself out of sightline with the poster and shuffled forward. Smiling at the woman behind the Wester Union counter, she told herself to get glasses. When she'd filled in the form and handed over the money to be sent to David Williams, she smiled to herself. Good thing we both changed our names.

No posters appeared in public in Vancouver, but the local papers carried news from south of the border, especially crime stories. Especially FBI stories. He bought his usual paper from the corner shop after getting back from work in the early afternoon. Inside the apartment, he exchanged a few words with Emily, checked on Rosa and took a nap. Later, eating a sandwich at the kitchen table, he opened the paper and saw the poster, accompanied by an article about the bombing and the investigation.

He studied the photo. No, they wouldn't recognise him at work. The hair was longer and the name was different. They wouldn't make the connection at the depot because they wouldn't be looking for it. Benson, on the other hand, would because he'd seen them together for a whole week, and he'd see past the name.

Climbing the stairs at West Hastings St, he wondered what kind of a reception he would get. To everyone there, including Emily, he was a draft resister. Now, he was wanted for murder.

He was greeted with looks as undecipherable as those on the faces of a returning jury. Was it contempt or anger? For the bombing or for his deception? Was that a hint of sympathy on the pinched lips of the student volunteer? He smiled at them all, even the stone-faced Emily, as he walked to Benson's desk.

'Emily, can you take that package to the post office, please?' Benson said.

'Sure.'

Benson gestured for him to sit down.

'Let's have it,' he said, almost without opening his mouth.

'Well, after Kent State, it just seemed like we had no option. The war…'

'Spare me the lecture, OK? Just tell me what happened at that army base.'

He had several versions in his head. One for the police, if ever necessary. One he might tell Emily. Another for Rosa one day, and possibly his parents. And one for himself, which he kept revising.

He told Benson the Emily version. A bare outline, without names or dates, and nothing about River Ridge. Just preparing the bombs, transporting them to the base, setting the timers and escaping into the streets of San Francisco.

'My friend called the base with a warning,' he said at the end, with little more than a whimper. 'Twice. But no one picked up. That's why someone was killed. It was never, never our intention.'

Benson nodded.

'I believe you. But I hope you understand that we can no longer be seen to support you. You can't come here, to the office.'

'I understand.'

'The apartment's OK since you're now paying the rent.'

'Thank you.'

'I suppose your fiancée won't be joining you,' Benson said without sarcasm.

'No.'

'Well, I wish you well. Just look after yourself.'

'What about Emily? Can she…'

'That's up to her.'

He trudged back down the stairs and out onto the street. On his own, even more than before, and even more exposed.

33

Although the church was the same, the gathering was smaller and the mood more reflective. Commemoration rather than mourning. The young pastor, golden hair flowing over her shoulders, stood in front and recounted Walter Gill's life with soft words. His childhood in rural Georgia, his decorated military service, his long, happy marriage, his stellar record of employment at the Presidio. His pride at being a father.

After leading the family and friends in prayer, she stepped aside.

'Go on, Mom,' Ronald whispered and helped her rise.

She wore a black dress, black gloves and black hat, hair swept back from her round face. At five feet and three inches, Susan Gill was not tall but she held her head high when she spoke.

'Twelve months have passed since Walter was taken from us. We have endured with God's blessing, and we will endure with His strength. I have lost a husband. My son has lost a father. And this city has lost a good man. But we remember always his kindness and his courage. And we pray that the Almighty will bring justice on this earth.'

A murmured chorus of "Amen" rose above the recorded organ music. Ronald took his mother's arm and guided her down the aisle and through the wide doors. He had not realised how infirm she had become. Thin and unsteady, she needed more than a hand to navigate the steps. Her smile, when they reached the flat sidewalk, was a mask.

They stood in the shade of a laurel tree, a rare comfort in the barren Outer Sunset, and waited for a nephew to bring the car around. Ronald nodded as relatives and friends consoled him, but his eyes never moved from the large blue birds painted on the church wall, their wings stretched high and wide like angels.

His father had been part of the US army for thirty years, from the age of eighteen, when he'd enlisted to fight in Europe. Coming home a hero, he'd been given a job as a cleaner. Now he was dead, killed by some self-righteous radicals. Stupid white kids who believed their own fantasies. "Innocent victim" is what the papers said, and that was true, technically, but he was part of the military that the bombers had targeted. Even if he wasn't in uniform, he was proud to be working on the base.

'Time to go, Ronald.'

He drove back to the house, where a few family members and close friends gathered. The funeral and burial had been a time of numbed mourning, but now, a year later, in his mother's house, the absence was more conspicuous than ever. The sherry and cake, the murmured condolences and warm hands, only deepened his despair. After everyone left, he made sure that his aunt was staying the night before he said goodbye to his mother. Still wearing the hat from the church service, she was exhausted but dry-eyed. As they embraced, he told her that he would help God to bring justice.

He had been considering the idea for a while, but on the drive back to Oakland it became a decision. It wasn't as if no progress had been made. Far from it. He cast his mind back to last summer when he'd had high hopes. The FBI had arrested Pennington, got indictments against Collins and Walker, and launched a manhunt for them. But they were still at large.

Ronald's most recent meeting with Callahan had deflated him. He'd listened with growing impatience to a description of the army of agents, network of informers and range of surveillance methods, including phone taps and stake-outs at addresses in major cities.

'And what have you found?' he had asked.

'I'm afraid we don't have anything concrete. Not yet. But we are continuing to follow up leads all the time. And rest assured, we…' The towers of the Bay Bridge caught the light of the setting sun as Callahan's time-worn promise echoed in his head. '…we will find these people and they will face the full force of the law.'

The case had stalled, and the string of apologies only confirmed his suspicion of incompetence. It wasn't just Callahan, though. According to the papers, Hoover's sudden death had left the whole organisation in chaos. High-profile cases had been dropped and suspects released without charge as attention shifted from domestic to international terrorism.

He also blamed himself, for letting hope get the better of judgement, for believing – because he wanted to believe – that the FBI would find his father's killer.

In the darkened space of the lower deck, shadows slanted between gaps in the one-way traffic. He twisted his lips and held them tight until he emerged into the sunlight at the other end. He wouldn't tell his mother – that would only cause her more distress – or his wife. She was already fed up with his "obsession".

Trouble was, he didn't know what to expect himself. The best private investigator would not come cheap, but he had no other option. If this Collins had evaded the FBI for a whole year, why not five years? Or ten? Didn't matter, though. He wouldn't stop until the man had been caught.

Next day, Ronald drove back to San Francisco with renewed expectation. A friend had been impressed by an agency he'd hired to handle a car insurance claim. 'And they don't just do insurance, fraud and divorce,' the friend had said.

Ronald couldn't help smiling as he walked up to the Flood Building on Market St, where the office was located, only two blocks from the FBI office. He hoped it was miles apart in getting results.

'You can't miss it,' the secretary had said on the telephone, and she was right. On a corner where two streets meet at an acute angle, it stuck out like the projecting bow of an ocean liner. Inside, its marble walls, high chandeliers and metal elevators shone with turn-of-the-century elegance and solidity that had survived the earthquake.

Mr Anderson, head of the San Francisco branch, wore a pinstriped suit and a closely cropped goatee. The chair he offered his guest was covered with bottle-green leather and studded with brass buttons. Coffee and cigars were brought in and sent back.

When the door closed, Anderson rested his elbows on his desk and steepled his fingers.

'Now, Mr Gill, how can we help?'

After Ronald outlined the case in a few rehearsed sentences, Anderson asked him to start over and tell him everything he knew. Ronald spoke for twenty minutes, consulting his timeline and his notes from conversations with Callahan.

Anderson took no notes. 'It's all on tape,' he explained, pointing to an innocuous-looking black box on his desk. And he asked no questions, nodding only twice. Once when his client declared his determination to "do whatever it takes" and once when he had finished.

'This is my plan. I will dispatch five teams, each led by a senior investigator and each to a separate region – the Bay Area, Northern California, Southern California, Oregon and Washington.'

'Someone said they went to Florida.'

'Let the FBI chase that goose.'

'But how do…'

'Trust me, Mr Gill. They almost certainly went north. You said Collins' parents had a call from him in Seattle.'

'Do you think he's still there?'

'Perhaps. I don't know.'

'Suppose he went to Canada?'

'I'm afraid we're not licensed in Canada, but we do have contacts there. I can alert them.'

'Alert them?'

'Give them the relevant information.'

Ronald pulled a sceptical face.

'Don't despair, Mr Gill. My agents will scour every town and city, from Canada to Mexico.'

'How long will this take, this scouring?'

Anderson fended off the mockery with a pleasant smile.

'I can't honestly say. But one thing, Mr Gill. We need to be patient. Unless I underestimate these people, it will certainly take months, possibly years, to find him.'

Ronald breathed in and out heavily.

'Are you prepared for a long wait?' Anderson asked with his grey eyes.

'I am.'

'Good. I will select our best people, the ones who do not give up. And they will get to work immediately.'

'What about costs?'

'We have a daily rate of $200 plus expenses. Or we can agree a fixed fee.'

They negotiated a fixed sum and a retainer.

'What about a reward, for the guy who finds him?'

'No, Mr Gill, we do not work on the basis of a contingency fee.'

Ronald wrote a check, signed the contract and left.

Anderson called two weeks later.

'Yes, Mr Gill. In Santa Barbara. Our man spotted a couple with a young baby, checking into a hotel. The names don't tally, of course, but the descriptions do. We'll have them followed and I will report back to you as soon as I know more.'

Ronald picked out a plastic pushpin from the square container on his desk. Using a fine-tipped felt pen, he wrote "1" on the pinhead and stuck it into "Santa Barbara" on the large map taped to the wall behind his desk. In his new notebook, he put "1" in the left-hand margin and entered the date, time, location and physical descriptions of the sighting.

Over that summer of 1972, Anderson's people made progress. Armed with xeroxed photos of the fugitives, they trawled streets, cafés, hotels, restaurants and shopping malls, asking random people if they had seen the faces. Hour after hour, day by day, they plodded on, meeting with denials, dismissals and worse. Then someone would make a positive identification, usually the pair together, sometimes only one of them. Every sighting was recorded in his notebook, and Ronald added a star if a baby was mentioned.

The numbered pins in the map on the wall looked like stepping stones. But to where? Most were in the Bay Area, others around LA, some in Seattle and Portland, and a few scattered in smaller towns. Nothing over the border in Canada. Anderson might be right. The direction of travel was probably north. But maybe they would circle around and come back down south. He just needed more pins to see the pattern.

34

In Vancouver, he read that peace talks had resumed in Paris and more troops were being withdrawn. 'Benson will be out of a job soon,' he had joked to Emily, but she saw the light dim in his eyes.

It was the beginning of the end. The end of everything that had led him to where he was. The war was drawing to a close, protests were fewer and smaller, and direct actions had virtually ceased. People were moving on – even Sharon was probably doing new things – but he was stuck. Even if the FBI had scaled back its manhunt, he'd gone underground through a trapdoor that he couldn't open.

The early morning knock on his door startled him. Emily had a key, so it wasn't her. He opened the door and saw Benson, perspiring.

'Come in.'

Benson sat while he made coffee and brought two mugs to the kitchen table.

'You doing all right?'

'Yes. Emily's a great help.'

The space between them shrank, their heads leaning forward, each drawing the other closer. Benson pushed up his wire-rim glasses and coughed.

'I thought I'd stop by since we can't meet at the office.'
'Thanks. What is it?'
'Well, a guy came in yesterday and said he wanted help. But I could see right away he wasn't genuine. I can tell, you know.'
'What did he want?'
'He was asking too many questions, looking around like he was going to buy the place.'
'OK.'
'Thing is, he switched tact and said he was looking for a friend who'd come to Canada to escape the draft. Gave a description that fits you. "He's got a little baby, too." That's what he said.'
'Did he give a name, the person he's looking for?'
'Steve Collins. The name on the poster.'
'What did you tell him?'
'That I couldn't help him. Told him to try Montreal. "That's where most people go," I said.'
'What did this guy look like?'
'Mid-thirties, I'd say. Well-dressed, shortish hair… and spoke with what I think is a southern accent.'
'FBI?'
'I don't think so. They don't operate up here. Maybe someone hired by a private investigator.'
'I see.'
'I'd be extra careful for a while. He won't go to the depot, of course, but better stay inside as much as possible.'
'For how long?'
'Hard to say. At least a week. These guys don't hang around for very long.'

After Benson left, he wondered if he should dye his hair or wear glasses.

Sitting back down with the newspaper, he noticed that the curtain was moving. That wasn't possible – the window was closed and latched. But it *was* moving. He could tell by looking at the fixed window frame. Impossible, yet the dark purple cloth was swaying back and forth, like a pendulum. He rushed over, grabbed the curtain and held it still.

It was his day off, so Emily came later that morning. She was devoted to his child, almost too devoted, and he wondered if Rosa might think she was her mother. He also felt confused about the time they ended up in his bed. It wasn't guilt – she had been as keen as he was – more embarrassment. Even with Sharon's guidance and patience, he never seemed to enjoy sex. It was a performance, usually not a very good one, and he didn't like failure.

He gave Emily a peck on the cheek and went to his favourite café, in the Gastown district. Surrounded by cobblestone streets, historic buildings and boutique shops, it was a hippie neighbourhood and the site of a riot the previous summer when police broke up a "smoke-in" to promote the legalisation of marijuana. He could smell cannabis even now, sitting at a sidewalk table.

Maybe that would help. Smoke a joint now and then. He'd tried it while in college and smoked a few times with Ted in the cabin. Better than getting drunk, but he didn't really like the loss of control and feeling tired after. He preferred to sip a beer and let his mind wander.

Pedestrians flowed past him, short and tall, thin and stout, shuffling, hurrying and bustling. He saw leather shoes, open-toe sandals, two-inch heels, knee-high boots, tennis shoes, flip-flops and brogues. Trousers and shorts, skirts and dresses. Legs sliced through the air, carrying their owners, each one of them, to a destination.

He walked to the harbour and all the way out to Stanley Park. Along the paths through the woods and out to the headland, where he found an empty bench. High above the water, a flock of starlings wheeled into view, hundreds of them, dipping and swerving in uncanny syncopation, shifting shape without breaking apart, like mercury sliding on glass. Tears rolled down his cheek.

The late-summer sun was a white disc that failed to burn. The winter will be harsh, he thought, even on this temperate coast. But in the spring, Rosa will have her second birthday. More bodies swept by him. Joggers, hikers, cyclists and dog walkers. Suddenly they all stopped and bunched up on the path. A woman knelt beside a man on the ground, raised his head and screamed for help. He had seen it before.

The sirens got closer and louder. Looking over his shoulder, he ran in what he thought was the right direction. Dizzy from the pounding in his ears, he took refuge among the trees.

When he climbed the stairs and opened the door, he was drenched in sweat. Emily rose from the couch to greet him, but he rushed into the bedroom and stood beside the crib. Bending down, he lifted the sleeping child to his chest and sang a lullaby cobbled together by the children at River Ridge.

'Sleep, baby, sleep,
'Your mother's here to keep you warm,
'And your father's in the woods,
'Sleep, baby, sleep,
'The moon's here to protect you,
'And guide you through the night.'

Watching from the doorway, Emily smiled in silence.

PART THREE

35

'What happened to Emily?'

'She got married and moved to Ottawa. I never saw her again.'

Rosie considered this, stood up and went to the large window at the back of the living room in Castlegar.

'Is that it, then?' she said, spinning around. 'Nothing else you haven't told me?'

'No.'

'OK. But why didn't you tell me before?'

'I don't know. At first, you were too young. And then, after a while, it just didn't seem necessary. You were happy and…'

'Ignorance is bliss.'

'No. Well, maybe a bit of that. It was just easier to continue as we were.'

'Easier to lie, you mean.'

'It was what she wanted,' he half-shouted. 'She said it would be better for you. Better than knowing you had a mother who left you.'

'And you accepted that?'

'No, I argued with her. But it didn't matter then, did it? Not until you got older.'

'And how old was I when you told – no, lied – to me about the accident?'

'Eleven.'

'Pretty young. But you could have told me the truth. Or something like the truth. "Mommy's in America. Yes, she loves you, but she has work to do." Something like that.'

He took two steps toward her. 'You don't understand. She didn't want to leave things like that. She wanted finality. A dead end.'

'You keep saying it was her decision. But when you told me, it was your decision. So why didn't you tell me the truth then?'

That's what had nagged him for years. Why hadn't he just said that her mother was alive in America? That she was a political activist who had left them because… That's where he faltered. He couldn't find the words to explain it.

'I don't know. Maybe I thought she was right. Better to make it final. Besides, it was easier, that's all. We were happy together, the two of us, and I didn't want to complicate things.'

She glared at him, arms across her chest.

'Complicate things?'

'You know, introduce a new person into your life. Our life. I'd learnt to live without her and I didn't want to rake all that up again. It was in the past.'

Rosie returned to the panoramic window and stood with her back to him.

'So,' she said, turning around, 'let me get this straight. I was born in Mendocino, not Pasadena. My mother is not dead, she abandoned me. Together, you bombed an army base and killed a guy. Then you fled to Canada, and she went back to America. Is that about it?'

'I didn't *kill* him. It was a terrible accident.'

'But you set off the bomb, didn't you?'

Silence.

'Didn't you?'

'Yes! Yes! We were responsible for his death. And I don't need you to remind me, all right?'

He slumped down on the sofa. He had imagined how this would be, the moment when she learnt the truth. Imagined it so many times he wasn't sure this was the real one. He'd expected shock, even anger, but not mockery and accusation. Fearing he'd lost her, he sat so rigid that his body ached.

Head down, he still noticed the light released from the window when she moved. Looking up, he saw her come toward him, felt her hand on his shoulder and grasped it. A full minute passed.

'Right!' he cried. 'There's something I want to show you.'

He came back with the photograph from his dresser drawer, still unframed.

'It's the only one I have.'

The man held a baby wrapped in a blanket, its face hardly visible. She could just about recognise him though, smiling beneath the long hair and bushy moustache. The woman beside him stared out at her with piercing blue eyes and straw-coloured hair falling straight to the shoulder, like a waterfall, her lips held short of a smile.

'How old was she then?'

'Let's see… about thirty.'

She looked again, this time more closely.

'Is that your necklace?'

'Yes. Ted, my friend at River Ridge, gave it to me. Way back then.'

'And that's me?'

'None other.'

'So, 1971?'

'Yes. In May.'

'After the… bombing?'

'About a month after. We were in Seattle, on our way to Vancouver.'

'Running away?'

It was a question this time, not censure.

'Yes.'

She put the photo aside and they sat back down on the sofa.

'And that's what the binoculars are all about?'

'Yeah.'

'Because you're still running?'

'Sort of. I might still be on the wanted list. I'm not sure. There aren't any posters now – they stopped that a long time ago.'

'But they'd arrest you if you went back to the US?'

'Only if they found me.'

She brought her legs up underneath her on the soft and leaned in against him.

'So, tell me the real reason we left Vancouver.'

He looked out into space and took a deep breath.

'Hard to explain. I sometimes get this feeling.'

'Like what?'

'You notice things, things that are unfamiliar and then recur. Cars, faces…'

'You got scared?'

He blew out air. 'I guess so. After Benson mentioned that private investigator, I was always looking over my shoulder.'

She wrinkled her nose, as if trying to ward off something unpleasant.

'And you feel safer here, in Castlegar?'

'I think so.' He was chewing his lower lip. 'Maybe they'll never find me because we changed our names back then.'

'Oh, yes, the names. You're not David Wiliams, are you? You're actually Stephen Collins. And I'm not Rosa Williams. I'm Rosa Collins.'

'Well, it depends on…'

'Where's my birth certificate?'

He brought it out from his bedroom.

'But this says I'm Rosa Williams.'

'We changed it to match my new last name.'

'OK, so where's the original one, with my real name?'

'Ah, we didn't think it was a good idea to keep it. It might be found and…'

'And then the whole pack of lies would unravel. That's what you thought!' She was on her feet again, shouting. 'And then you'd have to face up to what you'd done. So you just lied to me all this time. Even about my own name!'

She stomped off into her room and yanked down the blinds, cutting her finger. Lying on the bed, she sucked away the blood and fought back the tears. She slid a cassette in her Walkman, put on the headphones and turned up the volume.

Tuxedo wandered in and jumped up on the bed. Stroking his thick black-and-white fur, she felt her own body slacken, though her eyes remained narrowed. She wasn't Rosa Williams. Never had been. Her whole life was based on a lie. Everything. And now it had all collapsed and lay like rubble at her feet. She wasn't sure which piece to pick up first, which piece could bear the weight of truth.

She took off the headphones and tossed them aside. Face flush, temples throbbing, chest damp with sweat, she padded over to a window. Prising open a space between the slats, she faced pitch-black, except for murky yellow streaks drifting down from the streetlamps.

She wondered if her mother was right. Maybe it had been better to think that she had died. That her father had moved to Vancouver because he needed a new job and that his bouts of anxiety were normal for a single parent. That his binoculars were for birdwatching.

She turned around and looked at the terrarium on her desk, a present from her father when they'd left Vancouver so abruptly. To assuage his guilt, she guessed. The orchids and cacti on the windowsills had been her idea. She had hoped to create what she called an "indoor garden". Now, as she picked out the shades of green and purple, she wasn't sure.

She only heard the knocking when it became banging.

'Come in.'

His head popped through the half-opened door.

'Hungry?'

'Yeah, I guess so.'

He took a step inside the room, eyes avoiding hers, hands on the door frame.

'It's tuna pasta bake, I'm afraid. Not exactly your favourite. But…'

'That's fine, Dad.'

During dinner, they managed to keep up a conversation. Mostly what she was doing in the creative writing club and when she expected to hear from the University of British Columbia. Her grades and SAT test scores, she said, were probably enough to get in, but she still had to pass her exams at the new school.

'Exams in May – isn't that a little early?' her father said.

'They call them "senior exams" because they're the marks that universities use to make a final decision on whether or not to accept you.'

'OK. When will you hear from UBC?'

'A week or so after the exams, but I've got a lot of revising to do. And right now, I'm not sure about anything.'

He opened his mouth twice before speaking.

'I'm really sorry about all this, Rosie, but it doesn't change anything between us. I mean, it's just the same as always.'

'No, Dad. It changes everything. My mother is alive. There are three of us now.'

Shadows had crept into the corners of the kitchen, and she thought of the little house in Vancouver, half hidden by trees. The place where she had lived her whole life, the life which now seemed all wrong.

'Where is she, by the way?'

'No idea. We haven't had any communication since we separated. That was eighteen years ago. I don't even know what name she's using.'

She looked at him. 'But do you know people who might know or could find out?'

He hesitated. 'Maybe.'

The woman in Castlegar public library was reassuring.

'Those newspapers are held on microfiche in Vancouver,' she said, 'and they're very efficient about sending them to us.'

During a break from exam revision in the library, Rosie got out an atlas. An enormous thing, which she carried in both arms over to her table. Leafing through, she found maps of western Canada, northwest America and California, but all on separate pages. Nothing allowed her to see Vancouver and California together, to understand how they were connected.

Studying the California map, she found Pasadena without any trouble. She'd never thought much about where she'd been told she was born, only that it was near Los Angeles. She was about to give up on Mendocino when she spotted the tiny dot on the coast. Maybe her mother was there.

She waited for her father's day off to ask for the car.

'OK, but what about the shopping?' he said, laying the newspaper in his lap. He couldn't say no, not after what he'd told her, and he didn't ask where she was going.

'I'll pick up whatever we need,' she said, buttoning her coat and taking the car keys.

'Be careful. It's still icy in spots.'

She glided through the town and across the bridge, heading north along the fast-flowing river. The valley widened and the mountains drew back, blurring into a patchwork of white and green. No towns, just scattered houses set back from the road, a lumber yard and a warehouse.

She parked beside a long lake, climbed out and began to walk in the cold air. Hearing honking, she looked up and watched an arrow of black-necked geese pass overhead. Back from their winter feeding grounds, she thought, somewhere across the border. From the maps, she knew it wasn't far. About thirty kilometres, half an hour by car.

The microfilm arrived quickly, but the bulky reading machine was awkward to use. After a roll of film had been fixed on the plastic spindle on the left, the film was threaded between glass plates and into a slot in the empty spindle on the right. A light beneath the plates projected images onto a large plastic screen, each image showing one page of newsprint. The film was advanced by turning a small handle on the righthand spindle, but the movement was jerky, and she found it difficult to position the film so that she saw the whole page, while also adjusting the magnifying lens.

She fiddled and wiggled until she could read the pages of the *San Francisco Chronicle* for April 1971. The photograph of the damaged building was shocking, but the public outrage was even more disturbing, especially the Letters to the Editor. "The killers are traitors and deserve to die," one declared. There was also a photograph of the dead man's wife and son, standing in front of their house. Dignified, she thought, her throat tightening.

She hurried to the library every day after school and got home later than usual. She told her father it was exam revision, and he didn't probe further. By the time she'd worked her way to the end of April, the story of the bombing had retreated to the back pages and soon disappeared altogether. Sort of like my parents, she thought. "The trail has not gone cold," the last article declared. "It had never been warm in the first place."

'Did you find what you were looking for?' the librarian asked when Rosie handed back the box of film.

'Yes, I did,' she said with a grim smile.

She walked home, hunched up in her parka. The sun had retreated from the streets and hovered on the mountain tops. Head bent to the winter wind, she trudged through town and up the hill, unable to forget the photograph of the widow and son. Gasping for breath in the cold air, she steadied herself by grabbing a lamp post.

She found her father reading in the warm living room.

'You're really putting in long hours, for your exams,' he said, not unkindly. 'When exactly are they?'

'Two weeks from yesterday.'

'Are you ready?'

'I think so.'

'Good. But are you ready for spaghetti?' he said, falling back on their well-worn phrase.

36

Susan Gill looked at her husband across the dining table. Should she tell him? He'd gotten angry the last time. Still, she had to do something. His secretary had called again that afternoon, asking if he were ill. 'Sorry to disturb you, Mrs Gill. It's just that he had an appointment this morning at 11:00am.' She decided not to mention it.

It had to be this business with his father. She could understand his grief. It had been horrible, devastating, and, worst of all, completely out of the blue. Here one moment, gone the next. But that was a long time ago. She'd hoped, back then, that the funeral would allow him to move on, but it hadn't. The birth of their daughter brought back to her the cheerful and confident man she had married. But that didn't last. Inexorably, like an addict, he returned to his pursuit and even hired a private investigator. That much he told her, but little else. Certainly not the financial side of it all. Anderson's fixed fee was renewed each year, with the result that Ronald had paid him a staggering amount of money.

'Michelle's been accepted at Stanford,' she said when they'd finished eating. She'd hoarded that morsel all dinner long, planning to use it to put him in a better mood. 'She's out celebrating with her friends.'

'Good,' he managed to say. 'She deserves it.'

They'd invested a small fortune in tuition at a private school in San Francisco. Now they needed even more to send her to Stanford.

'Do you think we should apply for a scholarship?'

His face turned cold. 'No. We don't need any help from anyone. Besides, we wouldn't qualify.'

Again, she decided not to challenge him.

'By the way,' he said, getting up from the table. 'I'm flying to Seattle for a few days. Business.'

Sanders, the man who had replaced Anderson, had advised against it. Yes, the sighting was credible but there was nothing he could do by going up there. Might even get in the way. But Ronald was tired of staring at the pins on his map and convinced himself that he needed to be there. A man had been seen with a woman and a teenage girl. Everything fit: the ages and the descriptions. The agent had even managed to capture the man's face in a blurry photograph.

37

They stuck to their tacit agreement not to talk about it, and she didn't feel close enough to anyone at school. She thought about calling her best friend in Vancouver but didn't want to go through the whole thing on the phone. There was the school counsellor, who had recommended the creative writing club and given her advice about university, but maybe she would feel compelled to pass on the information to the police. And what about her own obligations? Was she required to inform on her parents? Was withholding information a crime in itself?

She was in the library, in her corner at the back, where no one disturbed her. She should have been preparing for her geometry exam, but the widow and son would not let her. Each time she looked down at the textbook, they were there.

Screwing up her face, she began to write the letter she had written a hundred times in her head. "To Whom It May Concern. It has come to my attention that a man wanted by the FBI is…"

He would go to prison and be an old man when he got out. She'd probably be married by then, maybe have children. Would they be able to start again? Would he ever forgive her?

She tore the paper into tiny pieces and threw them into a waste basket. Opening her textbook, she focused on the diagrams, trying to lose herself in the lines and angles, where the answers were numbers, not words.

She waited until it got dark before walking home. That would minimise the amount of time she would be with him. She wanted it to be like before, when they'd shopped and cooked together, watched the same programmes and sometimes gone to a film. Now they kept apart even on weekends. He did the shopping, most of the cleaning and cooking, while she holed up in the library and her room. Exams were a convenient cover.

She shivered in the cold air. Writing that letter would have been as bad as what her parents did, even though it might have been right and for the same reason. Their desire to stop the killing and hers to atone for a killing were both were morally unassailable. In the abstract, that is, before you considered the human damage. It was a mess and sometimes she wished she'd never been told the truth about her mother.

When she came through the door, he was watching television. Alone. Like in Vancouver, only there he had someone from work he went to hockey games with. Here, his isolation was more exposed. But it's his own fault, she muttered to herself.

'I've got dinner ready,' he said, rising from the couch.

At least he didn't know what she'd almost done. That was some consolation.

'OK, I'll be there in a minute.'

He didn't ask any questions, just placed a warm plate in front of her and waited for her to finish. Then he brought her tea and his coffee and sat down opposite.

'We need to talk.'

'OK.'

'About your plans, I mean.'

She sipped, unsure what he would say.

'I think going back to Vancouver will be good for you. Seeing your old friends and all.'

He hated the idea of being alone, though he had known it

would happen sometime. But this gulf between them would make it worse.

'Yeah, we're planning a party there in September. If we all get in, that is.' A nervous laugh.

'That's what I wanted to talk about.'

She put down her cup.

'The school counsellor called this afternoon. She's worried about you. Apparently, your teachers have been saying you're not engaged, forgetting homework. Stuff like that.'

She shrugged.

'Rosie! This is important. What's going on?'

'What do you think?' she cried, scrapping back her chair and retreating into her bedroom.

Ten minutes passed. He knocked softly and inched the door open. She was on the bed, on her stomach, plugged into her Walkman. She lifted her legs, held them in the air and let them fall, one at a time. Up and down, one and then the other. He watched for a moment and closed the door.

She wasn't listening to the music. Pulling out the earphones, she watered her plants and stared at herself in the mirror, once again hating her frizzy hair. She opened the geometry text and looked at the triangle with the value of two angles given. What was the value of the third? Exactly.

At breakfast, she found a note on the kitchen table.

Sorry. My fault for not appreciating the shock of everything. See you this afternoon. Love, Dad.

She made her own breakfast, cleaned up the kitchen and went to school, where she tried to concentrate. Back home from the library, she sat and waited. When he opened the door, she was already in the hallway.

'You're right. As usual,' she said with a tiny smile. 'I have to work harder, especially on geometry.'

They went arm in arm into the living room and sat down.

'How far behind are you?'

'Way far! There's only a week left and if I don't pass, UBC might reject me.'

'That's what the counsellor said. But she also recommended a tutor, out at the college.'

'Won't that be expensive?'

'Don't worry, sweetheart. It's just for a week.'

'Thanks, Dad. I really appreciate it.'

'Nothing more important than going to a good university.'

He would have expanded on that advice, as he'd done many times in the past, but it wouldn't sound so convincing now.

'I know. But there's something else that's even more important to me.'

'What's that?'

She saw that he was unprepared, settled on the sofa, hands on thighs, lips holding a smile. But she didn't know how else to say it.

'I want to meet my mother.'

He froze, his face drained of colour.

'Out of the question.'

'But…'

'No,' he said, rising to his feet. 'And that's final!'

His words thundered against the window and ricocheted around the room.

'Dad!'

'I'm not going to discuss it. Do you hear me?'

She brought it up again at dinner, and he dismissed it again.

'Didn't you hear me the first time?' he snapped.

'Yes, but I'm not going to stop until you at least agree to discuss it.'

He inhaled loudly and pushed his plate aside.

'Now listen to me. Meeting her, or trying to meet her, could be a disaster. For both of you. These things never match expectations.'

'I don't have expectations.'

'Rosie, she doesn't want anything to do with us. That's clear enough. She probably thinks contact would be dangerous. And she's probably right. She usually is.'

She appeared to listen, then hit back with rehearsed counterarguments.

'How do you know? You haven't had any contact for eighteen years. Maybe she's been waiting for you, or me, to get in touch.'

'That I very much doubt.'

'OK. But she can always just refuse to meet me, can't she?'

His lips moved but no words came out.

'I'm sorry to say this, Dad, but you're stuck in the past. I can understand that, a little, but this is my life. My future.'

He looked at her moist eyes and reddened cheeks.

'OK, but I still don't think it's a good idea.'

'Why not?'

'It's dangerous. Don't think they don't know about you. They probably even know your name.'

'But not my last name.'

His look made her smile.

'See? I'm learning. And they don't know what I look like either, do they? Plus, I've got my Canadian passport, so I can cross over and back without any hassle.'

'I just don't like it.'

She got up and came around the table to him, bent down and brushed his cheek with hers.

'I know, I know. But maybe this can be good for you, too. Not just me. I mean, you've lived with this long enough, don't you think?'

Too choked to speak, he reached up and found her warm hand. Rising, he pulled her to him and held her tight.

All through the next day, at work, he thought about what she'd said. It had the ring of truth, damn it. He was trapped in the past. Contact with Sharon might be just what he needed. Might lead to something, a new start. Maybe she'd come and live with them in Canada. Or maybe he could... no, that was impossible.

She said it was her future, and she was right there, too. His fear had dictated her life for too long. Their lives had been inseparable – she was safe only if he were – but that couldn't last. Somehow he had to disentangle her need to grow from his need to hide.

He was probably no longer top priority these days. The FBI's attention had been diverted to Russian spies and corrupt US congressmen. But that didn't mean they'd forgotten about him. That he was free to move about. Any illusions he'd entertained had been shattered by the arrest of a man in Nova Scotia wanted for a murder committed in Philadelphia twenty years before.

And he couldn't stop her from going – he admitted that to himself – not if she was really determined. All he could do was make sure it was safe. But he had no idea where Sharon was or how to contact her.

'Hey!' his swamper screamed, sitting next to him in the cab. 'You nearly ran over that guy on the bike. What's up with you today?'

'Nothing. Just tired.'

'I'd say you had a fight with your wife, except you don't have one, do you?'

'I have several. All secret.'

That was his standard reply. No one in Castlegar knew about his past, not even that his wife had "died". Only that he had a daughter.

When he got home in mid-afternoon, Rosie was still out. At the library, he assumed, so he picked up the binoculars and scanned the street from the kitchen window. Nothing unusual. The same cars he'd seen most days since they had arrived a month ago. That didn't mean much, though. Sometimes they didn't sit in their cars. Just passed by late at night.

38

He was stumbling through a rainstorm, in dense woods, holding it tight, afraid it might squirm loose and run away. He'd never see it again. He held tight, but not too tight. That would hurt it and make it try to wiggle out. He couldn't see much, just wet black trees. No path, no escape. 'Hold tight,' he kept saying. 'Don't let it go.'

Hearing the front door slam, he awoke and scooped up the newspaper that had fallen off his lap. He tried to compose himself, but she was already standing before him.

'Rosie, I'm not sure this is going to work. I've no idea how to find her.'

'What about the guy you planned it with?'

He shook his head. 'I don't know where he is either.'

'In prison?'

'No, no. He got out years ago.'

'So, he might be in San Francisco?'

'Maybe.'

'What's his name?'

'Gabriel. Gabriel Pennington.'

'OK. I have an idea.'

He listened, tight-lipped. She had the momentum, and they came to an agreement.

A few days later, he again heard the door slam and readied himself. This time, her face was shining.

'It's all over! And I'm sure I passed.'

'Wonderful. That's really great!'

After their hug, she pulled back and held out a piece of paper. 'Here are the names and numbers.'

'But we agreed…'

'Yes, not to *talk* about it until exams were over, and I didn't.'

He looked at the sheet torn from a notebook. Eighteen Penningtons and their telephone numbers had been gleaned from the San Francisco telephone book ordered through library loan. One name was followed by a "G".

He muttered something and shook his head. When she'd told him her idea, he'd hoped the telephone book wouldn't arrive or there'd be too many Penningtons or none with a "G".

'You realise this is a wild shot,' he said. 'And even if we do find her, you can't go now, before school is out.'

'OK, here's the deal. You make contact with him, but I'll go only after, or if I get admitted to UBC.'

'OK, but what about school?'

'It'll be late May, deadtime.'

He drove into town at dusk and turned into a supermarket parking lot. The phone booth, a new one with see-through panels, stood in a far corner. This is probably unnecessary, he thought, but who knows?

He dialled the number.

'Hello.' A woman's voice.

'Hello. Is Gabriel there?'

'Yes. Who shall I say is calling?'

Clipped, professional tone. A wife?

'An old friend.'

'Just a minute, please.'

He counted to ten. Twenty. Thirty.

'Who is this?'

'It's me. Steve.'

He held his breath in the silence.

'Steve? Jesus! What the…?'

'Yeah, sorry to call out of the blue. But I need to talk to you.'

'Where are you? No, don't say. You're on a payphone, right?'

'Yes.'

'Got a pencil?'

'Just a second. OK, go ahead.'

'Call me in fifteen minutes on this number.'

Steve waited and called the number.

'What the hell is this about? Be quick.'

'Do you know where Sharon is?'

'Look, I'm not involved in any of that anymore, all right? Paid my dues, didn't I?'

'I understand. I just want to contact her.'

'She's not in the open. All those actions after the Presidio – that was her.'

'It's nothing to do with that. There's someone who wants to meet her.'

'Who?'

'Her name's Rosa. Just tell her that.'

He was nervous. The call was taking too long. 'Tell her Rosa wants to meet her.'

'OK. Call back on this same number. 6:00pm. Next Wednesday.'

He hung up and saw how dark it was outside. In the well-lit booth, he might as well have been on stage. But the parking lot was empty. Black and shiny, even though it hadn't rained. Stepping out, he heard a loud voice behind him, like someone shouting his name. He turned. Two teenage girls walked into the supermarket, shrieking with laughter.

He trusted Gabriel to be careful, but he kept muttering to himself as he drove home. It was not a good idea. Not for any of them. It was risky for Sharon, and possibly for him, and could be disastrous for Rosie. He considered telling her that it was someone else, a Gary Pennington. Or that Gabriel had refused to cooperate.

'Was it him?'

She was standing just inside the front door, quivering with the expectation that he'd warned was unrealistic.

'Yes, but he didn't sound optimistic.'

'What'd he say?'

'Told me to call him next Wednesday.'

'Good.' She used both hands to smooth back her hair. 'I know it'll work. I just know it.'

'This is serious business, sweetheart. Let's be sure about it before we do anything we regret.'

Her indulgent smile suggested that she wasn't going to turn those words against him.

'OK,' she said, 'but things have changed. It's not like when you were, you know, doing stuff.'

'Maybe.'

'I've been meaning to say this for a while.'

'That I'm trapped in the past? You already have.'

'No.'

'What then?'

'Just that you don't need those binoculars anymore.'

Now, it was he who managed a smile.

'You mean the birds have flown?' he said.

'Something like that.'

He brooded at home and at work. Sharon was cautious. Maybe she'd say no and that would be the end of it. Maybe Gabriel wouldn't be able to contact her. Or, thinking it was too risky, maybe he wouldn't even try. And even if a meeting was arranged, he could still try to talk her out of it.

At her urging, he had the old Seattle family photograph framed and hung on the wall in the living room. At first, it made him uneasy and he avoided looking at it. After a day, he couldn't stop looking.

The second call was shorter than the first. Gabriel said that Sharon had agreed to meet Rosa "in principle". She could stay with him, in his house, and should plan on at least a week. She should wear a red scarf and come by train. Safer than by air, no passenger lists. Steve was to call him on the house phone when he knew her travel details.

'Why the hell didn't you tell me she's your daughter?' Gabriel said at the end.

'I left that to Sharon. That was our agreement,' he explained. 'By the way, what's her name now?'

'I don't know. And I'm not sure she'd want me to tell you if I did.'

Rosie received a letter confirming her admission to UBC. The following day, her father bought her ticket and called Gabriel with the date and time of her arrival in Oakland.

'You're going to miss a whole week of school, aren't you?' he said to her, as a last-ditch protest.

'Just send a note, saying I'm ill or something.'

'OK. Any particular disease you prefer?'

'Ah, let's avoid cancer. Pneumonia might be good.'

He drove Rosie on the long journey, through the Cascades to Vancouver, where they took separate rooms in a hotel and spent the next day wandering about like tourists. On West Hastings Street, he pointed out the tall building. He was about to take Rosie up to meet Benson but saw that the building had been converted into luxury flats.

They got a bad night's sleep and met in the bright breakfast room. Buffet style. They took a table in an alcove and talked about the weather and the too-soft beds. Until she pushed her teacup to one side.

'There's still one thing I don't quite understand.'

'What's that?'

'You could have gone back with her to the United States, right? I mean, you and I could have gone with her.'

'I could have. In fact, I wanted to.'

He didn't tell her that they had rejected the idea because it would have meant her growing up with both parents in hiding, always wary, always on the move. He didn't tell her because he didn't want her to feel she was responsible for that decision. And he didn't mention the other reason he didn't go back with her mother. That, unlike her, he was a political coward.

'So she convinced you to stay here, in Canada?'

'You could put it that way.'

'How would you put it?'

'I'd say that when you love someone, you do things you wouldn't ordinarily do.'

They drove in silence to Pacific Central Station, walked through the high-arched portico entrance and found US Border and Customs. Waiting in the queue, he repeated his advice.

'You can trust Gabriel but keep your wits about you.'

As he spoke, he heard an echo of Sharon's words to him before he drove from Mendocino down to San Francisco all those years ago. But this was his own daughter. He couldn't quite believe what was happening.

'OK, but remember, I don't have binoculars,' she replied.

'Ah, but those eyes of yours are pretty sharp.'

'Any words for my mother?'

He had been thinking of little else.

'Just that I hope she's doing well.'

After showing her ticket and Canadian passport, she turned, waved and disappeared through swinging doors to the platforms. Very much the young lady, he thought.

The sun was warm by the time he climbed into the Volvo and headed back to Castlegar. Seven or eight hours, with only the radio and his misgivings. Should never have allowed this, he kept thinking. But what good would it have done to stop her?

In a few months, when she's at university, she could go on her own, without telling anyone. It was bound to happen sometime. Besides, she's smart and Gabriel will look after her.

Rosie had never been outside British Columbia and never travelled anywhere by train. She tried to get some sleep but only stared out the window until she got off in Seattle, where, amid the confusion on the platforms, she nearly missed her connecting train. Bound for Los Angeles and San Diego, the Coast Starlight didn't touch the coast until it reached the Bay Area, but it did rumble under a starry sky.

She edged her way down the narrow aisle between high-backed seats, until she found one free by a window. Not very comfortable, she thought, settling on the slippery blue-and-red-striped vinyl upholstery.

No one was in the aisle seat next to her, so she squirmed around, curled herself into a ball and closed her eyes. She dozed on and off, bought a sandwich from the rolling trolley and read chunks of her novel, *Cat's Eye*.

When she awoke, it was pitch-black outside. She checked her watch. Almost 10:30pm. What am I doing, she asked herself, hurtling pell-mell through the night, ignoring warnings and trying to repair the past all by myself?

Most of the other passengers were sleeping, some snoring. Squinting in the glare of the interior lights, she noticed a man watching her from the seat across the aisle. Her father had warned her about such men, but surely he had meant the police or perverts. Not this type.

She pursed her lips and turned toward the window but saw only his reflected face. Only one way out.

'Excuse me,' she said. 'Do you know where we are?'

He lifted a watch from his vest pocket and peered at it. 'Should be near the California border. We passed Klamath Falls some time ago.'

'Oh, thanks.'

'Where're you going? If you don't mind my asking.'

His pinched, weasel-like face intrigued her. At least forty, maybe fifty, but something told her he was harmless.

'Oakland.'

He nodded. 'Home?'

'Sort of.'

A specific place. Boundaries, something solid, unlike the limitless blackness outside. It'll be fine, she told herself and again dug out her novel. At first, she'd been disappointed to discover that the title referred to a marble, not an animal, but the story drew her in. Deeper and deeper, into her own childhood memories. Had she buried them or just forgotten? She couldn't be sure, only that now they smarted like half-healed wounds. And knowing the truth, she was able to name what before she had only felt. Abandonment. Loss. Betrayal.

She put the book down and faced the blank window. She was separated from her father for the first time in her life. She was about to meet her mother. She was going to university. A convergence, where things were coming together. Even her father seemed to be more malleable, or maybe she was just more forceful.

Suitcase in hand, eyes alert, she slid past noisy families on vacation and entered the ticket hall. It was cathedral-like, with high, arched windows, carved stone lintels and sunlight slanting across the polished floor.

'Rosa?'

He had spotted her right away, not just by the scarf but because she was standing still, looking around. A refugee, of sorts.

'Hi. I'm Gabriel. Your father's friend.'

He was tall and slim, matching his ponytail, but looked older than her father. It was the creased face and deep-set eyes.

'Hi. Thanks for meeting me. It's Rosie, by the way.'

'OK. Here, let me take your suitcase. You must be exhausted.'

Sleepwalking is how she later described it. A fevered mind guiding a numb body. She was high up in the air, weightless, on a slender strip of concrete swaying between tall towers. A city skyline emerged through the clouds, and she knew something special would happen.

Unable to wait any longer, she swallowed hard and turned to him.

'Do you know when I can meet my mother?'

'Monday. I'll give you the details later, OK?'

Forty-eight hours. Then the gap of eighteen years would close.

Neither spoke as they glided over the water and sluiced down into the streets, where she was assaulted by the rush hour honking and jostling.

'Getting there,' he said when they entered a residential area.

It was more densely packed than Vancouver, and the houses, Spanish stucco and ornate Victorian, seemed older.

'So, how's your father doing up there in Canada?'

They had stopped at a traffic light. She let the pieces settle in her mind.

'Oh, he's fine. We've been there a long time now, so it's pretty much home.'

'I hear Vancouver is really nice, a little like San Francisco.'

She turned toward him, trying to read his expression.

'Yes. It is nice, but we now live in a smaller town. Much different and I miss Vancouver. A lot.'

How are we going to get through this, she wondered, without mentioning the past?

'I hope this isn't inconvenient – putting me up, I mean.'

Gabriel laughed. 'No, not at all. We have a guest bedroom.'

He didn't mention that his two daughters would be sharing a bed for the next few days.

Halfway up a hill on a leafy street, the house was small but tidy. Painted a cream colour, with gold trim on the peaked roof, it had flower boxes on the windowsills and an immaculate front lawn. Steep concrete steps led to a door inset with stained-glass panels of tulips and leaves.

'It's not usually this quiet,' he said, shutting the door behind them. 'My wife's at work and the girls are at school.'

'What does your wife do?'

'She's a lawyer. Mostly civil rights. We met during my trial.'

'Oh.'

'You know all about that, I guess.'

She nodded.

'That was our little joke, you see. Our deal. If she didn't get me off, she'd have to marry me.'

His smile seemed to blend in with the light streaming through the many windows.

'Anyway, you must be starved. Can't imagine the food was very good on the train. Overnight, wasn't it?'

'Yes, but I'm fine.'

'Nonsense. How do you like your eggs?'

He told her as she ate. Her mother had agreed to meet her on the Berkeley campus. On the other side of the Bay.

'She said Monday at noon. At the Campanile. That's the tall tower in the centre of the campus. Can't miss it. That's why she chose it, I guess.'

'But how am I going to recognise her? I've a got a photo, well, a xerox of one, but...'

'She wants you to wear the same red scarf. She'll find you.'

'But what does she look like? And what's her name? I mean, what she's calling herself?'

'Let's talk later. You look tired.'

He led her up the stairs and gestured down the hallway.

'We all share the bathroom, so I'd take advantage now if I were you.'

Her room on the top floor had a skylight. She pushed it open and craned her neck from side to side but couldn't see the ocean. Only houses and treetops.

39

Ronald picked up the telephone on the first ring.

'Yes, that's right, Mr Gill. A girl with a suitcase. College age, he said. Pennington brought her home in his car. We're keeping a close watch. As close as we can. Yes, will do.'

Replacing the receiver, Ronald swivelled around and scanned the map on the wall. The pushpins now obscured the names of major cities in California, Oregon and Washington, and a few others across the rest of the country. He'd stopped putting up new ones for lack of space, as well as belief, and hadn't written details in his ledger for years.

This new information was in a different category, though. It brought everything right back to where it began, to San Francisco. Was that the pattern he'd been searching for in those pins? A circle.

Sanders had been keeping tabs on Pennington ever since his release from prison. Just one man, who occasionally parked down the street from the house in Noe Valley. Nothing interesting had been reported. Until now.

Who was this young woman he'd brought home? As far as Ronald knew, Pennington did not have a younger sister. Could be a niece or a friend, of course. Or maybe someone connected to his wife.

He winced. Susan was about to leave him. She said she'd wait until their daughter had settled in at Stanford in September. Michelle would be eighteen, so they wouldn't have to go to court over custody. Then, Susan would pack up and clear out.

He wasn't surprised. Over the years, she had never challenged him about what he was doing, only what it was doing to them. There had been that low point when he cancelled the trip to Hawaii to celebrate their tenth wedding anniversary. When he said he had too much work, she said, 'You mean one of your idiots thinks he's found him. And you're off on another wild goose chase.' They had ended up screaming at each other, leaving their young daughter in tears at the dinner table. After that, they learnt to speak with icy politeness and avoid his "business affairs".

With every year that passed, though, he grew more and more unhinged. The business suffered and she noticed the shrinking bank balance. When she told him she was leaving, he'd pleaded with her, but not too strenuously. Truth was, it would be easier to see this thing through on his own. No constraints on his time or his money.

He walked to the window and looked across the bay at the City. Noe Valley. Nice neighbourhood. Pennington had done well for himself. Married a lawyer, had kids and kept out of trouble. But everyone slips up.

40

Standing at another west-facing window, Sharon tilted her head and frowned. She could usually see a sliver of water and the Golden Gate, but heavy fog had rolled in early that morning and stayed put. She had not been surprised by what Gabriel told her on the phone, only that it had taken so long. And she was surprised at how quickly she had agreed to meet her. Of course, any contact that came through Gabriel had risks attached, but she'd given him detailed instructions. She'd been doing this for most of her life and didn't make mistakes. Besides, she had to admit that she was curious.

But why now? What had Steve told Rosa? And where was he? She hoped he wasn't foolish enough to be using their daughter as a decoy, to lure her out of hiding and attempt a reunion.

She felt safe in her converted loft apartment on Berkeley's South Side. High up, with no exposure to neighbours, the apartment had its own entrance, an external staircase at the back of the large house. The owner, who lived alone on the two floors below, was pleasant and kept her distance. The only regular visitors to the house were the people who came on the first Monday of the month, for meditation. 'Buddhist boots,' she said to herself each time she heard them tromp through the house.

After leaving Steve in Seattle, she had not gone back to River Ridge. Assuming the FBI would trace her to Mendocino, and deciding that a crowd was the best cover, she had returned to the Bay Area, where she stayed in a series of safe houses, planning actions across the country but only travelling to the actual location to oversee the final hours.

All that had stopped a long time ago. When the war ended, internal divisions weakened the group, some leaders were arrested and others turned themselves in, knowing that the illegal methods of intelligence gathering would force the government to drop charges. The Presidio indictments, however, still stood and she continued to live the life of a fugitive, relying on new identities, constant vigilance and her parents' money.

She spent most of her time editing a radical magazine that advocated revolution by every means short of violence. *Action Now!* had a tiny office tucked into a courtyard off Telegraph Avenue. She avoided going to the office, barely ten minutes away, except to deliver her articles and the proofs of those written by others. The monthly publication sold well in big cities, especially around university campuses, where a new generation of leftist, feminist and gay groups debated direct action as a means for social change.

The loft was her home. Where she could sleep without an ear cocked for a knock on the door. Where she made calls from her own telephone. Where, on most days, from her window, she could see a slice of the bay.

She didn't mind living alone – she was used to that – and publishing the monthly magazine provided the right amount of contact with others. Lately, though, she'd begun to feel that it was all too sedate, her ideas inert on a page and she on a leafy street with an organic café and a yoga centre within walking distance. And everyone in Birkenstocks.

Turning away from the window, she went to her desk, tucked under exposed beams, and lit a cigarette. She twisted her lips and reread the first draft of her lead article. There had to be a logical link between the massacre in Tiananmen Square and the victory by Solidarity in Poland. She only had to find it.

41

Rosie found him in the kitchen, leaning against a counter.

'Sleep well?' he asked as he pulled the slender stick out of the leather barrette, shook his long hair free, gathered it together and fixed it back in place.

'Yes. And long, it seems.'

'Yeah, they get off early, to school and work.'

She had enjoyed meeting his wife and daughters but felt more relaxed when she was alone with him. More focused, no need to pretend. His wife knew why she'd come, but in front of the children, they kept up the story that she was the daughter of an old friend who was visiting San Francisco. That was easy because it was largely true.

'Got the house all to yourself.'

She knew the words were wrong as soon as they came out.

'Yep, I'm the househusband. Had a hard time getting work after I got out. Understandable – who wants to hire someone connected with a bombing and a killing?'

She kept her head low.

'Was it really hard? Being in prison, I mean.' She was thinking of her father.

'Not too bad. I was lucky, served only three years. In Dublin, on the other side of the Oakland hills. Nice weather when we were outside in the yard. Inside, group therapy was the worst. But I learnt to control my mind. That was the key thing.'

She nodded.

'Being out wasn't so easy either. I went through a few programmes to get "skilled-up" – that's what they call it. I had my BA, so they put me in construction, of course. It was a nightmare.'

He laughed and she looked up at him. A warm, broad smile on his weathered face.

'Driving a garbage truck, like your father, would have been a piece of cake,' he continued. 'But now I'm gainfully employed as father and housekeeper.'

'And chef,' she added. 'What's for breakfast?'

Later that morning, he dropped her off at Union Square and she spent the day on her own, acting as the tourist she was supposed to be. Went into Macy's, as instructed, looked around and located the back exit, wandered down Market St and rode a cable car to Fisherman's Wharf. She walked past Fort Mason and along the waterfront to the Palace of Fine Arts. Looking across the traffic, she could see the red-tiled roofs of the Presidio barracks. That was as close as she wanted to go.

She smiled all through the conversation at the dinner table that evening. Even the young girls joined in, especially when talking about the wildfires in Yosemite. Gabriel's wife entertained them all with a story about a man who wanted to hire her to find his missing pet snake, prompting jokes about her being a "slippery" lawyer and references to Gabriel's reptile paranoia. She laughed with them, a normal family, and cried that night in bed.

Again, it was just the two of them for a late breakfast. When they'd finished, he handed her a handwritten map, each segment of her journey numbered and timed.

'Now, listen carefully,' he said.

He paused after each step to make sure she'd understood. She wanted to write it down, take notes, but he said no, it's better to remember it. Besides, the map tells you everything.

'Don't worry,' he said at the end. 'It'll all go smoothly. Any questions?'

'What am I supposed to call her? What's her name now?'

'You don't have to know that.'

She got into a taxi, wearing a light blue linen suit, stockings and flat shoes. It was a last-minute decision. Having first decided on jeans and a sweater, a voice inside her advised against it. For one thing, the suit would go better with the scarf. Another dilemma was whether to paint her fingernails, as she normally would for any kind of occasion. She decided against that, too. 'Not very revolutionary,' she told herself with a squinty smile.

'Good luck and be careful,' Gabriel said and waved her off.

About what? she wondered as the sleek cab raced down a hill. She was just a young Canadian citizen on a visit to the Bay Area. No one knew her or why she had come.

She took the creased photo from her bag and studied her mother's face. Would they hit it off from the very beginning? Maybe she wouldn't like her at all. She hoped they could at least accept each other. Find something to build on later, when they were used to being mother and daughter. Not the same as with her father, of course, but something that would grow stronger over time.

Leaving the taxi, she walked into Macy's. Slipping past shoppers, she threaded her way between display counters, went out the back entrance, marched three blocks to Market St and disappeared into the BART station. Underground, she stood away from the ticket counter and waited for five minutes, scanning the faces streaming down the steep flight of steps.

This is ridiculous, she thought. How would I know if someone was following me? Besides, this actually makes me look more conspicuous.

She boarded an eastbound train and felt exposed when she saw it was almost empty. Men's eyes flicked over her. She wished she'd brought a book or her Walkman. The rumbling got louder and louder as the train picked up speed and passed through the dark tunnel under the water.

On the other side, she checked her watch. 11:31am. On schedule. At Rockridge, she stepped out into the bright light of the East Bay. Disoriented for a moment, she consulted the map and went down the stairs to streel level, where she climbed into a taxi.

She got out at Oxford Street, walked along the crescent-shaped entrance to the campus and turned onto a footpath that led through a grove of redwoods. A straight path, rising slightly. That's what Gabriel had said. Keeping going straight, up the hill. 11:46am.

Coming the other way, down the path, people brushed by her, their voices piercing her thin layer of protection. Frightened for the first time, she averted her eyes in the wooded shade. She could turn around, make some excuse and go back to Gabriel's house.

Red-tiled roofs came into view, then grey granite facades with high-pillared porticos. The path became a paved walkway bordered by lawns. Up ahead, the Campanile rose into the sky like an obelisk. Slender in its beauty, it drew her forward.

She came to a small plaza formed by another walkway, crossing from right to left. People hurried in all directions, stood in knots, sat on the grass, talking and laughing. Raucous and invasive. Everything out in the open.

Six minutes to go. She took the scarf from her handbag and tied it loosely around her neck. Checking that it hung in full view, she took a deep breath and strode up toward the tower, which grew taller as she approached.

Shallow steps led to a brick-paved area around the tower, a sort of patio with wooden benches and plane trees in square, raised beds. She clutched her handbag and steadied herself. A group of Japanese tourists, all women in floral-print dresses and holding tiny umbrellas, were listening to a guide. Other people crossed the patio area, most without stopping.

She sat on one of the benches. Perspiration trickled down her neck and back. Squinting into the sun, while trying not to stare, she tracked everyone who entered the paved area. It was a good place to meet. Exposed, easy to spot someone, but quiet where you could sit and talk.

'Are you Rosa?'

A woman stood in front of her. About the right age, but the wrong face.

'Yes,' she stammered as she stood. 'I…'

'I know. Unfortunately, she isn't able to come today.'

Rosie opened her mouth but didn't speak.

'She said to tell you that she is very sorry but that she simply can't be seen with you. She said you'd understand. And to give you this.'

Rosie took the envelope and watched the woman move quickly away, not down the hill, but off to the left, behind a large building, presumably the direction she had come from. For a minute, she thought of following her.

Gripping the envelope, she walked back down the slope, trying to control herself. Why had her mother agreed to meet if she thought it was too risky? What had changed her mind? Reaching the footpath, she felt the cool shade of the redwoods and slowed down. She opened the envelope and read the typewritten note:

Meet me at 2:00pm, Wednesday, day after tomorrow, at the Rose Garden in the Berkeley hills.

No name and no signature.

Might have expected something like this, she thought. Still in hiding. Like Dad.

Bells rang out from the Campanile and people began to flood up and down the path. She jammed everything, including the scarf, into her handbag and hung her head. Why am I doing this? Why couldn't I just have ordinary parents, even a dead one?

42

'We followed her, all right,' Sanders said. 'She tried the old Macy's trick, but that doesn't work anymore. Then she took the BART, went to the campus and met a woman there. No, it wasn't her. They only spoke for a moment and then separated. We don't know who it was. Our person couldn't follow them both, could he? She went back to the house in Noe Valley. Yes, that's what I think.'

Ronald made notes as he listened, his smile widening with each detail. The sighting of the unknown woman didn't warrant a pushpin, but it might be more important than all of the others put together. When he hung up, he shoved back his chair and lit a cigarette. Watching the smoke curl up above him, he wondered if Sanders was right. Pennington's guest, the one who went to the campus, could be the daughter. Right age. But what was she doing here? Was Collins in the Bay Area, hiding in plain sight? Whoever she was and whatever she was doing, they would follow her and find out.

43

Rosie hadn't planned it, but when the idea came it was irresistible. She had a free day, and she had the address from the newspapers she'd read in the Castlegar library. She told Gabriel she was going shopping downtown and to the fine arts museum on the Marina. She'd be gone all day, but not to worry, she'd be home in time for dinner.

The walk was longer than she'd expected, up and around Twin Peaks, and down into the Sunset District. She got lost a few times, but once she reached the grid of numbered streets, she had no trouble locating the house. Painted mint green, it was in a packed row of bungalow-style houses. No front lawn, only a driveway and a garage, with a bay window projecting out above it.

The blinds were pulled down and she could see no sign of life. In fact, the whole block seemed inert. No passing cars, no one on the sidewalk, no kids at play. She was about to leave when a woman approached, walking a dog that sniffed its way to her shoes.

'Are you looking for someone?' the woman asked. Friendly, concerned, like a retired teacher. 'I mean, I know everyone on this block.'

'Oh, no. I'm just talking a walk. And stopped to rest.'

'Well, enjoy your walk. If you continue down this street, you can see the ocean in another five minutes.'

She watched the woman and dog climb steps and enter a house two doors down. Probably about the same age, she thought. Maybe she's got a dog, too. For company. But she's got a son, she remembered. So, she's all right.

She thought about crossing the street and knocking on the front door. 'Hello, I'm the daughter of the man who killed your husband. I wanted to say sorry. He really didn't mean it.'

Two kids raced down the street on bicycles, front wheel raised in the air, hands-free, arms crossed over their chest. She walked away, down the treeless street, back the way she'd come. At the first corner, a black car, parked on the side street, pulled out and followed.

The fog burned off and she began to perspire as she climbed a hill with thin woods on one side. 'Ridiculous,' she said to herself. 'Why come all the way out here?' Like a voyeur. But she knew the answer. She wanted to know all the details. Everything.

The house in Noe Valley, trim and prosperous, was a welcome sight. Inside, father and daughters were sprawled out on the floor, playing a board game.

'C'mon, Rosie,' the youngest girl cried. 'You can help me.'

'I don't know. I'm tired and…'

'But you said you're going to university!'

Gabriel looked up at her with a "got-you-there" expression.

'OK,' she said, tossing her handbag on the couch and plopping down beside the six-year-old. 'Let's see if we can beat your father and sister.'

By the time Gabriel's wife came back, she had thought hard about animals that do not jump, which planet was closest to earth and what letter was not in any of the names of the fifty states.

At dinner, the pasta casserole and green salad were mixed in with a discussion about the break-up of the Soviet Union and plans for a family vacation to Lake Tahoe. She slept with an ache in her heart.

She opened her eyes before sunrise. Her father would be up now; coffee and toast and off to work. She hadn't spoken to him since leaving Vancouver almost a week ago. 'No phone calls,' he'd said. He had been against the idea from the beginning, and with good reason. She could see that now.

This time she chose jeans with a blouse and casual shoes. More natural, more like herself. She was studying Gabriel's new map, when he came into the kitchen.

'Go the same way,' he said. 'Macy's, BART, Rockridge. Then a taxi to the Rose Garden.'

'OK. What about the red scarf?'

'It wasn't mentioned, was it?'

'No.'

'I'd wear it anyway, to reassure her. She might have left it out on purpose, as a test. In case someone else got hold of the message.'

Rosie nodded. She followed the logic – her mother didn't know what she looked like – but sometimes it felt like a game. One she was learning to play. No matter what, though, she was determined to see it through.

It started badly. The taxi was late and got stuck in traffic. Gabriel had allowed for delays, but the cab was hardly moving. The driver swung down a side street ('Don't you worry. I know this town like the back of my hand,') and found himself blocked by road construction. She bit her lip and told herself to calm down. He backed up and looped around to Union Square.

The rear doors in Macy's were closed. Hurrying back to the front, she knocked into a woman and stopped to apologise. Out the door, she raced to the BART station, where she scrabbled in her bag, hunting for her purse. The scarf got in the way, and she swore loud enough for people to look over at her. Even when seated, and gliding under the water, she heard her heart pounding.

From Rockridge station, the taxi zipped up into the hills behind the campus, past a football stadium and along a winding road. The driver let her out and said he'd park nearby.

The Rose Garden had no gate or ticket booth. The entrance was a semicircular extension of the sidewalk, overlooking the garden with views of the bay and Marin County. Steep steps led down the hillside, banked with rows of flower beds, and into an amphitheatre of roses.

She was ten minutes ahead of time. Walking down the steps, she heard voices and wandered over to the tennis courts at the bottom. Two middle-aged men, bandanas holding back their long hair, grunted and prowled as they whacked a ball back and forth. She climbed back up to the entrance and sat on a bench. Cars slowed down and some stopped, engine running, to see the view and take photographs. It was 2:04pm.

As with the Campanile, she could see why her mother had chosen this place. Not for its name, though that was nice serendipity, nor for its part in the progressive WPA in the 1930s. She had selected it because it was easy to spot someone who might be watching you. And it was quiet, like the rose garden of a monastery, a place for whispered secrets.

She adjusted her scarf and wished she'd worn a thinner top, something sleeveless. Loud voices broke out. School children, mostly Black and Hispanic, the boys in shorts and blazers, the girls in skirts and knee socks, surged past and poured down the steps.

In the emptied space, she saw a woman who looked familiar. That was silly. She'd been in the area only a few days and mostly in San Francisco. Still, she thought she had seen her somewhere.

She left at 2:40pm and found the taxi, parked down the road.

'Back to Rockridge station?' the driver asked as he turned down the radio.

'Yes.'

44

'No, Mr Gill, she didn't meet anyone, but she looked like she was waiting for someone. Yes, that's right. Stayed for forty minutes and went back. Same route. What? You mean the woman who met her on the campus? No, she wasn't there either. Right. Same routine. Yes. As long as it takes.'

Ronald chewed on his lower lip and reached into the little square box on his desk. He'd had to devise a new system for the daughter and settled on red, instead of black, numbers on the pin heads. He now had several of them in the wall map, clustered around Noe Valley and the Berkeley campus. It looked promising.

45

She had opened the front door, hoping that Gabriel would be there. But she was alone in the silent house, with nothing except the realisation that she had been stupid. Stupid from the very beginning, thinking that she could undo the past and join what had been severed. The offer to meet her had just been another one of their little spy games.

Gabriel came in half an hour later, arms full of brown paper shopping bags.

'So how…'

'She didn't show. I waited a long time. Red scarf and all. She just didn't come. Again. Probably never planned to.'

She was sitting at the kitchen table, fingering a mug of lukewarm tea. Head down, hiding reddened eyes.

He placed the bags on the counter and sat down opposite, rested his forearms on the table and placed one hand on top of the other.

'OK. Take me through the whole thing. You went the same way as before, right? Macy's, BART, taxi.'

'Yes, except in Macy's the back door was closed.'

'OK. When you got to the Rose Garden, did you notice

anyone unusual? Anyone who didn't look like they were interested in flowers?'

She thought about the visitors, the schoolchildren, the tennis players.

'No, I don't think so.'

'Try to remember.'

'Well, a lot of cars stopped for the view. Some took a long time before moving on.'

'OK. Anything else? Someone who didn't fit.'

'Well, there was a woman who looked familiar.'

'You'd seen her before?'

'Yes, but I don't… Wait a minute. She was in Macy's. I bumped into her, in fact.'

'And again at the Rose Garden?'

'Yes. She seemed to hang around the entrance area.'

Gabriel leaned back in his chair and took a deep breath.

'I think that woman was following you.'

'Me? But how?'

'They know where I live and would have known you were here. We took precautions – that roundabout route – but it doesn't always work.'

'But my mother, why didn't she turn up?'

'I think she did. She was probably in one of those cars that stopped on the road. She saw the woman and realised the meeting had been compromised.'

Rosie nodded. She wanted to believe that's what happened.

'What can I do now?'

'I don't know. If I'm right, she wanted to meet you, but now…' He shook his head.

'Can't you contact her again? Ask for another meeting?'

'I can try but I wouldn't expect much.'

Rosie spent the next day, her last unless Gabriel had good news, at the Museum of Modern Art. Her eyes strayed from the paintings and sculptures, restless in their search for someone who might be watching her. She locked eyes with a young man, who smiled and turned back around to study a Matisse portrait.

By the time she got back to the house, a thick fog had settled over the city, reducing streetlights and headlights to murky blurs. It was midnight in mid-afternoon. Going into the kitchen, she found Gabriel reading the newspaper. Just as she was about to ask, he raised his head and shook it in commiseration.

When he saw her off at the Oakland train station the following evening, Gabriel made her promise to give his best wishes to her father.

'Thanks for everything,' she said. 'I can see that you would have been a good friend to him.'

'I still am,' he said with a smile. 'And when you see him, be sure to tell him everything.'

46

She hardly slept on the train that night, dozed through much of the next day and reached Seattle at dinner time. After a change of train and another three and a half hours of travel, she arrived in Vancouver in total darkness.

She never doubted that he was there, even when she couldn't see him through the crowd. And when he caught her up in his arms, she did not hold back the tears. She had not found her mother, but she felt closer than ever to her father. Knew him from the inside. His fear and his need for love.

'So, how did it go?' he asked, arm around her shoulder as they walked down the platform.

'Let's talk about it tomorrow,' she said. 'I need sleep and you look exhausted, too.'

He led her out of the terminal, surprisingly crowded at that hour, and along a well-lit walkway to the car park.

'Same place as before, OK?' he said, pulling out of the station.

'Sure.'

They ate a large breakfast, talking only about the weather and Tuxedo, before beginning the seven-hour trip. The same journey they'd made three months earlier. When her only worry was that she wouldn't like Castlegar.

He waited until they had left the city and reached the four-lane highway running beside the Fraser River.

'I guess you didn't have a good meeting.'

'Why do you say that?'

'It's obvious. You'd be bouncing with joy if it had been a success.'

'Probably right. But it's worse than that.'

He kept his eyes on the road and listened while she told him what had happened. The route, the scarf, the aborted meeting on campus, the handwritten note and the no-show at the garden.

'Gabriel thought I'd been followed.'

He shifted his eyes toward her.

'Is that what he said?'

'Yes.'

'Tell me exactly what he said.'

'He said the meeting had been "compromised".'

'Why would he say that.'

'Because a woman I saw in Macy's also turned up at the garden.'

'Are you sure?'

'Yes.'

'OK. Then what?'

'Gabriel contacted her again, to set up another meeting, but she refused.'

'Refused?'

'Yes. He thinks my mother was at the garden, watching from a parked car, and left when she saw that woman.'

He ran a hand through his hair. Probably someone working for a private investigator. If they were on to Rosie, they would have tracked her to Seattle and to Vancouver, where they would have had someone watching at the train station. That meant they had his license plate number, probably taken photos and would get his name soon. Fortunately, he had not updated the registration to the Castlegar address.

'Dad, what's wrong?'

'Huh? Oh, nothing. Just thinking.'

He eased over into the slow lane, letting cars and trucks roar past while he tried to focus.

'Do you want to see her again?' she asked. 'Just as friends, I mean.'

He hesitated. 'Of course I do. But I can wait.'

'For what?'

'Until she's ready.'

'Ready?'

'To come up here. And join us. She can, you know, any time.'

'Then why not now?'

'Because she has unfinished business there.'

Here, too, Rosie thought, and slumped back on the seat.

His eyes flicked to the rear-view mirror. He doubted that anyone would tail them this far out of Vancouver. But if someone had been at the station, the car details and photos would be passed on to the FBI, who would contact the Canadian police. Everything would be sent to stations and mobile units across the province. And people hired by the PI would continue tracking him.

'You know what it was?' she said.

'What?'

'This whole mess. It's just because I was stupid, thinking I could change things.'

Not many alternative routes to choose from, he realised. Got to get rid of the car, that was the main thing.

'You were not stupid,' he said, forcing himself to concentrate on spoken words. 'But you're right. Things don't change that fast.'

The satellite towns were far behind them now. Rolling along a two-lane highway, through forests, past gas stations and trailer parks, he felt relief. Even exhilaration. It was another escape.

'Let's eat,' he said, spotting a café beside a motel.

They had the place to themselves, and he chose a large table. After ordering, he spread out the road map.

'What's that for?' she asked. 'You know the route, don't you?'

'Yes, but we're going to take a little detour. Just to be safe.'

'From what?'

'You were followed down there and they might have followed you to Vancouver. To us.'

She squeezed her face hard.

'I'm really sorry, Dad. It's all my fault.'

'No. It isn't. We decided this together.'

'Not really. You never liked the idea, but I insisted. Remember?'

'Doesn't matter now.'

'Yes, it does because I'll probably never see her. I've ruined it.'

'Look, she probably wanted to meet you. But it didn't work out. That's all.'

She thought for a moment. 'All right. But what's this detour?'

'We'll take another route. Add an extra day. No more.'

'What about Tuxedo?'

'Don't worry. We'll telephone the Martins and tell them to feed her until we get to Castlegar.'

Holding back her questions, she watched him study the map. His eyes, stone-hard, sent a shiver down her spine.

He drove east for an hour before turning onto another highway that headed north. Two and a half hours later, he stopped at a motel on the outskirts of Kamloops. He chose it because it was on a slight hill and the parking area was right beside the highway.

'Say, I wonder if you can help me.'

He produced a disarming smile for the woman at the reception counter.

'Sure. You've paid in advance, so I owe you.'

He wrote down the directions and led Rosie to their room. Inside, sitting on one of the twin beds, she watched in silence as he again studied the map.

'Rosie,' he said, folding it up, 'you've got to trust me. Some of this might seem unnecessary or foolish. But we need to take precautions.'

She looked up at him, the only thing between her and the chaos she felt all around her. If she didn't trust him, what was left?

47

'Sweet dreams, buddy.'

The man grinned and turned to his partner. They were parked just off the highway, on a side street, from where they had a clear view of the motel and the brown Volvo. Having spotted it from their lookout at a major junction, they had followed it north to Kamloops. Now they saw the light go out in the motel room.

'Get some sleep. They won't be going anywhere before daybreak,' the man said. 'I'll wake you in a couple of hours.'

When his partner closed his eyes, he lit another cigarette and turned on the radio, keeping it low. No point in depriving himself of his favourite music.

48

'Dad, it's 4:30.'

'Shsss. Get up and get ready. Don't turn on any lights.'

Fumbling in the dark, she dressed, used the bathroom and picked up her suitcase. He was at the door, peering through a tiny crack. Half a dozen cars in the motel parking lot, a few parked on the road. Nothing moved in a darkness relieved only by the blinking motel sign.

They crept across the asphalt. He opened the car door, and the sound of metal scraping metal shattered the silence. He froze and looked around, turning full circle. Only a muffled roar in the distance. They got in and he closed the door with a soft click.

He released the parking brake and put it in first, but the car didn't move. She pantomimed with her hands. When he nodded, she got out and pushed from the back. The car began to roll, and she jumped inside. He guided it out of the parking area and down the hill, where it gathered pace. After a hundred yards, he switched on the lights, turned the key, put it in second and pulled away with a whoosh that wouldn't have woken a dog.

'Can we talk now?' she asked in a low voice.

'Sure, but I want you to lie down in the back. It'll be light soon and they're looking for two of us.'

He drove into the town, stretched out along a river. Pale light leaked onto the hills, a delivery van slipped in beside him and people appeared on the sidewalk. He kept his face averted and told her to keep her head down. Stopped at a traffic light, with only one other car, they were exposed.

He drove at a crawl, maybe too slow, but there had to be an all-night diner somewhere. He didn't know where to look and didn't want to ask, just kept turning corners on unfamiliar streets. It would look strange, if anyone was watching.

The neon sign said "Moonlite All-Nite. Best Burgers in BC". Not Edward Hopper, but it would do. He came back with coffee and donuts in a cardboard carton that he stowed on the front floor mat.

More traffic and pedestrians now. The sun was above the hills, spilling light at sharp angles, though much of the crouching town remained in shadows. The used-car place was on the outskirts, again exposed, but with fewer eyes around. He parked on a nearby cross street.

'We'll have to wait here until it opens. At nine.'
'Jesus! Almost four more hours.'
'Sorry. Just lie down and sleep.'
'Won't that look funny, us sleeping here?'
'Maybe, but we don't have a choice.'

ABC Car Sales spread itself over a large corner lot. Cars, vans and pick-ups lined up like toys on a game board and, above them, a painted sign promised "Cash Sales". He pulled up in front of the box-like office and entered with Rosie.

The dealer, in pinstriped shirt and braces, greeted them with a smile that turned sour when they said they wanted to sell, not buy. After test-driving the sturdy old Volvo, the grin returned.

'You know what they say.' He pulled the unlit cigar from his mouth and handed over the cash. 'First customer is special. So, have a wonderful day.'

'Thanks. Can you call us a taxi?'

On the short ride to the rental agency, he tried to calculate how long the money would last. $2,600 plus a few hundred in the bank in Castlegar. Not very long.

'Oh, yes,' the clerk behind the counter said. 'We offer a good discount for a full week's rental. And you can return it to any of our offices all over the country.'

He chose a four-door Chevrolet, handed over $100 as a deposit and signed the papers.

'Where to now, masked man?' Rosie asked with a smirk, as he adjusted the rear-view window. She'd decided it was easier to play along rather than demand answers.

They listened to the radio, each lost in their own thoughts, oblivious to the dun-coloured fields and the hint of hills. Two hours of small towns, until a long lake led them to a populous area with business parks and suburban housing.

'Look!' she cried.

Up ahead, flashing lights and traffic backed up on both sides of the road. His jaw tightened when he saw the cars, royal blue with white front doors. They were nearing Kelowna, still a long way from Castlegar. Turning around wouldn't look good. He thought about getting off the highway and taking his chances on side roads but wasn't sure where that would land him. There was only one route through the mountains and the turn-off for that was straight ahead, in the middle of Kelowna. Besides, he wanted to get on with it.

'Don't worry,' he said, slowing down. 'The car they're looking for is in Kamloops.'

'But they know what we look like, don't they? I mean, if they took photos like you said.'

'That was only the night before last. It'll take more time before any photos reach here.' He had no idea how those things worked, but he needed her to remain calm. 'Just sit tight and smile.'

They joined the queue, backed up a quarter of a mile from the checkpoint.

'What if they ask stuff?' Rosie said.

'What *stuff*?'

'Who we are, where we're going?'

'Simple. We are father and daughter. David Williams and Rosalind Williams from Vancouver. Just visited my parents in Kamloops and we're taking the scenic route back home.'

'You better do the talking.'

It sounded plausible. His license still had the Vancouver address. But suppose they asked for his fictional parents' address? Pine St, he thought. Every town in Canada has one.

The queue crept forward.

'It's taking a long time,' she said. 'Looks like they're asking lots of questions.'

He went over the story in his head, again and again. They would be looking for the brown Volvo, but suppose they wanted to see his registration? How could he explain a rental from Kamloops? He could say his car had broken down. No, better to say he left his car in Vancouver because they had been driven to Kamloops by his parents and he'd rented a car to go back to Vancouver. No, too complicated. Just say…

'Dad, we're next.'

Grinning like a clown, he handed over his license. The officer studied it and cocked his head to one side to check that the photo matched the driver. He waved them through.

'See? We're fine.'

Not for long, though. Soon, the photos would be everywhere, and they'd find out that he'd sold the Volvo and rented a Chevrolet.

He had two, maybe three days at most.

49

'Hello, Mr Gill. Good news and bad news.'

Ronald listened, smoking and making notes.

'It's him all right. We know from the photos taken at the train station and outside the hotel in Vancouver. Matches the ones we have from Santa Rita and Mendocino.'

'What about the girl?'

'It's his daughter.'

Ronald banged his hand on his desk.

'Why the hell didn't you arrest him, then and there?'

'You know perfectly well why, Mr Gill.'

'Right, right. No arrest powers in Canada. How convenient.'

Sanders ignored the sarcasm. 'We have people on the ground there, following them. We are also liaising with the FBI and they're in touch with the RCMP. An arrest warrant and extradition order are in process.'

'How long will that take?'

'The warrant should be issued tomorrow. The extradition order a little longer.'

'OK. Where's he now?'

'They headed east from Vancouver and spent the night in Kamloops.'

Ronald scanned the map of Canada spread out on his desk.

'And then?'

'That's the bad news. They slipped away early this morning.'

'What?'

Another loud bang on his desk.

'I know. It's our fault and the men responsible will be disciplined. But don't worry. They won't get far, not in that backwater. All our contacts and the Canadian police have their photos. Full face and clear as a bell.'

'They know the car, too, right?'

'Yes, but if I know this guy, he'll get rid of it.'

'OK. And if he buys another one, how will you trace him?'

'Easier than you think, because in British Columbia the plates stay with the person, not the car.'

'I see. Different car but same plates.'

'Unless he doesn't buy a car.'

'What do you mean?'

'He might rent one. But there aren't many places around Kamloops and my men are already checking. If he rents, we'll get the car and license plate number.'

'Then what? Search for him all over the state?'

'Province, Mr Gill.'

'What?'

'It's a province, not a state.'

'Yeah, yeah. State, province, what the hell difference does it make? How are you going to find him? That's the question. You don't know where he's going!'

'We think Calgary. As soon as we know what car he's using, we'll notify the FBI, and they'll pass the information to the Canadian police. They've got radio cars all over British Columbia and Alberta. He won't stay hidden for long.'

Ronald Gill hung up and looked at the map. Those two provinces were twice as big as California, Oregon and Washington put together.

50

Castlegar in June did not resemble the town they had first seen in March. The outer frame of forested hills and frothing rivers had not altered, but the picture itself had. There were flowers everywhere: by the roads, in hanging baskets, beneath windows and on windowsills. The streets bustled with shoppers and the playing fields teemed with screaming youngsters.

His face expressed Rosie's thoughts. Both wanted to say "Home, sweet home", but they knew it was neither. She bought food and newspapers, and he went to the bank. Back in the car, he rifled through the *Vancouver Sun* – if their photos had been published, they'd have only a few hours. But there was nothing, not even a story.

'Dad, when are…'

'Look down, quick!' he hissed, raising a hand to cover his face, eyes on the rear-view mirror.

He waited until the RCMP car passed them and disappeared in traffic. Looking over at Rosie, he saw the fear in her eyes.

'It's OK,' he said. 'We just need to keep low, that's all.'

The house at the end of the short street was cold. Rosie picked up Tuxedo and buried her head in the thick fur, murmuring excuses and trying not to cry.

'We should thank the Martins for looking after her. I'll go over right now. OK?'

It was the kind of thing they both needed. Simple, practical, easily agreed and immediately done. When she returned, they finished a pizza and faced each other at the table.

'You know what I have to do, I guess.' He was trying to sound matter of fact, but it came out as condescension.

'No, I do not know.'

'I can't stay here. It's only a matter of time before they find me.'

Rosie was chewing her lower lip.

'I've got to leave tomorrow, or the next day at the latest. First thing is…'

'Dad. I've thought a lot about this. I'm going with you.'

He reached out across the table and took her hand.

'No, sweetheart. They want me, not you. You have done absolutely nothing. You are going to graduate and start university in September. You can stay here until then.'

'While you just take off? Leave me and disappear? I've already had one parent do that, you know.'

'Rosie! This is different. You're an adult. You can take care of yourself.'

'I don't have a single cent.'

'Don't worry about that. I'm going to pay everything in advance and send money every month.'

'Like my mother did when I was a child?'

His face hardened. 'Something like that. I've been saving up.'

She knew the cash from selling the car wasn't even enough to cover tuition fees for one semester, let alone living costs. But she didn't argue about money.

'I'm going with you. I don't care about graduation. It's a mere formality anyway. And I can defer university until… you get settled.'

'No. It's better if we separate, for our own safety. Two people are easier to find than one.'

'Could be, but I'm not letting you go on your own. It's that simple. And you can't stop me from coming.' A defiant smile spread across her lips. 'Can you?'

He looked at his daughter and saw a woman.

'No, probably not.'

'Besides, it's all my fault. If I hadn't gone down there, we wouldn't be in this mess.'

'Well, we could take that a *little* further back and say that if I hadn't gotten involved in…'

'No, Dad. What happened back then was an accident. No one could have foreseen it. I know you did it for a good cause.'

'You really think that?'

'Yes, I do. I've read a lot about what was going on then. You know – the war, the riots, police brutality, government cover-ups, and all that. It must have been, I don't know, frightening.'

He hesitated, trying to recall what he had felt.

'It was scary, but we were trying to stop something that was so wrong. Killing people thousands of miles away. Just plain wrong.'

The words caught in his throat. He rarely thought about any of that now. He had taught himself to forget it, as part of his cover. And after a few years, when his new life became his only life, it was locked up and sealed away.

'You felt you had to do something,' he said. 'You know, like an obligation.'

She rolled the word around, testing it.

'I need some coffee,' he said. 'Want some tea?'

'No, I'll have coffee, too.'

He brought two mugs to the table and again they faced each other.

'OK,' she said. 'Let's have it. What's the plan?'

'It's simple, really.'

She took a sip and eyed him.

'You've always wanted to meet your grandparents, haven't you?'

Listening to what they would do and where they would go, she heard exhilaration in his voice and saw light in his eyes. The tired look and worried words were gone. It all sounded good, but she didn't like having to leave Tuxedo behind.

In the morning, he drove the rental car down the short street to the main road and turned right, away from the town. Cars honked and whooshed by as he crawled along, searching for the dirt track. He'd seen it dozens of times before, but where exactly was it? He couldn't recall a sign or anything, just a gap in the trees. Must have missed it, he decided, and turned around.

It was easier to spot coming from that direction. He followed the narrow track deep into the woods, no idea where it led. Up a slight incline and around a bend, maybe the other side of the high hill they saw from their house. Branches scratched the car as he pushed through dense undergrowth. It was taking too much time, but he couldn't reverse and go back. A clearing appeared with an abandoned cabin. He left the car and walked the four miles back to the house.

She was sitting at the kitchen table, cat carrier by her side, listening to her Walkman.

'Get rid of it OK?'

He nodded and called a taxi, which dropped them off at a rental agency in Castlegar. He told her to choose a solid car with lots of room. 'Who knows? We may have to sleep in it.' She paid cash for a Ford Bronco and a week of unlimited mileage. Same surname, but it was common enough and the female first name might buy them a little extra time.

At the pet rescue centre, she filled out a form and said goodbye. She knew it had to be done but that did not stop the tears. Then he drove them into town, parked and told her to meet him back at the car.

'Excellent,' he said an hour later, assessing her long auburn hair and sunglasses with large square lenses.

'And you look very distinguished,' she said. 'In fact, short hair suits you, Professor, though the grey is a little premature.'

Could become pure white before long, he thought.

'I think that car was there before,' Rosie said as he turned off the main road and onto their short street.

He looked at the black sedan, admiring her sharp eye while also regretting that she, too, had been cursed.

'It's OK. I saw it when we first moved here.' Better to lie than to make her more frightened than she already was.

They left at first light, one suitcase each, with clothes, shoes and personal items. He chose the framed photograph, his binoculars and two long novels. The peace symbol went into the plastic folder with their documents. No point in advertising ourselves, he thought, recalling Sharon's words. Rosie packed a writing notebook, an album with snapshots of her with friends in Vancouver, her Walkman and her tapes. She also convinced him to let her take a box full of textbooks. It was all stored in the rear space of the SUV, along with pillows, blankets, dry food, bottled water and flashlights. Everything else was left behind.

He cast a last look around the house. Neat enough, he thought and realised how wise it was to have rented and not bought the place. It had been instinct rather than decision, in case he was tracked down.

He had deliberated about which border crossing to use. Paterson, due south, was the closest. Nelway, further east, would be less crowded and possibly less obvious. He chose Paterson.

They ate breakfast at a roadside café, where he made sure she had her documents to hand. An hour later, they were riding down a country road through a narrow valley untouched by the morning sun. Ahead, the squat building with a flat, projecting roof looked more like a gas station than an international border crossing.

'It's open,' he said with relief. It was just 7:00am and he had expected to wait. 'Let's switch.'

As she guided the Bronco forward, they watched the uniformed officer approach each car. The tall man bent down and angled his wide-brimmed hat in through the car window, spoke with the driver, straightened up and waved them forward.

Rosie checked her wig and looked across at the old man in the passenger seat. He gave her a reassuring smile. "Don't worry," it said, "we've rehearsed it enough."

'Morning, miss. Travelling far?'

'No, Officer, just down to Northport for a few days.'

'Holiday?'

'Yes. My father here's a car fanatic, but he's never been to the racecourse there. It's a belated birthday present.'

The officer took a step back and looked into the storage space behind the seats. The assortment of items he saw made him frown. People were funny, always prepared for an emergency.

'When are you coming back?'

'Not sure. We might go to Spokane and see some friends.'

'Well, have a safe journey. And you, sir, enjoy the racing.'

She drove through an old wooden farm gate, hooked open to a post on the side of the road. A hundred yards ahead, a red stop sign and traffic cones formed lanes, one for cars, the other for trucks. An American flag hung from a weathered pole next to a glorified cabin.

He guessed they'd have the photos here, on the US side, but might not yet know about the car.

'Good morning.' The voice was stern. 'Driver's license, please.'

The officer saw that Rosa Williams was born in California in 1971 and now resided in North Vancouver. Her hair was different, but he'd seen that many times before.

'Long way from home, aren't you?'

'Yes, Officer. My father and I are on a little vacation. We love the mountains. We're going to explore the Cascades down here.'

'Your father, he's also Canadian?'

'Yes.'

'Passports, please.'

Mr Williams had aged quite a bit, but the officer didn't comment. It wouldn't be polite.

'OK. Have a nice trip.'

Five miles beyond the border, they switched places again. She took off her wig and sunglasses and plugged in her Walkman. He dug out his peace necklace and hung it around his neck. 'No point in hiding this now,' he said, with a wink. 'Not in the Land of the Free.'

They kept the radio low, mostly country rock, until they heard the only song they both liked, when she said, 'You probably don't know it but…' He completed their well-honed routine by adding, 'She's Canadian!' Laughing like little children, they let themselves get lost in the lyrics of "Both Sides, Now".

Heading due south along the Columbia River, he drove past Spokane and crossed into Oregon, where he made a decision. Instead of going west to the coast, he turned east and then south again, slicing through Idaho and straight down into Nevada.

They drove for eight hours, one at the wheel, the other dozing. They monitored the radio and newspapers, ate badly and soaked in hot showers. Nevada became California, with more scrubland and brown hills. Red-rusted box cars stood in train stations marooned in the sand.

She looked across at him. A hint of a smile, lips drawn tight, eyes straining down the two-lane highway. Did he know what he was doing or was he just running blind? Maybe his parents' house was part of a larger plan. He always had a plan. But what could it be? She felt her chest constrict. She had to protect him.

'Dad?'

'Yeah?'

'What will happen if they arrest you? I mean, how many years would you spend in prison?'

'Hard to say.'

'Like Gabriel?'

'No. He wasn't actually there. I was. They'd try me for second-degree murder.'

'Isn't there something called manslaughter?'

A trailer truck rattled past them, rocking their car and kicking up a dust storm. He waited until he could see clearly.

'Manslaughter is when there's an accident.'

'But it was an accident. You didn't intend to kill anyone. The phone call proves that.'

'Yeah, but they said we should have done more to check there was no one in the building. Said it was negligence. "Dangerous disregard for human life". And they're probably right.'

'So, what's the sentence for that?'

'Anything up to life.'

51

Ronald had decided to talk to him in person. The telephone created too much space and too many gaps, leaving unexplained details and unasked questions. He brought his notebook of sightings over the years and his timeline of events during the past few days.

'Now, let's see if I have this this right,' he said, perched on the edge of a chair in Sanders' office. 'He sold his car in Kamloops and rented a Chevrolet.'

'That's it.'

'How do you know they're in this country?'

'From my contact at the FBI. They checked the two most likely border crossings and one of the guards remembered a father and teenage daughter named Williams.'

'He recognised them? From the photos?'

'No. He wasn't looking at them because it wasn't the right car. But it was same name used to rent the car in Kamloops.'

'What kind of car was it?'

'An SUV. And, no, he didn't write down the license plate number.'

'So, how are you going to find them?'

'We have photographs and names and a rough description of the vehicle. Plus, they are travelling together. That increases our chances. A lot. More important, they are now in this country, which means we can employ all our resources.'

'But this country is huge! They could go anywhere.'

'Yes, but there is one obvious destination.'

Ronald looked puzzled.

'Money, Mr Gill. They'll need money. And my guess is that there's only one place they can be sure of getting it.'

52

They spent their third and last night near Mojave.

Waiting for her father to return the key to the desk, she scanned the morning desert. Shades of ochre and peach, wind-blown scrub brush and stunted Joshua trees. And in the distance, a streak of crimson. Hugging herself to keep warm, she realised she didn't want the journey to end.

'Beautiful, isn't it?' he said, coming up behind her.

'Yeah. And not a bad place to hide, either. No one would look here.'

She had a point. They might guess where he was headed, but he needed money and a car. And he wanted to see his parents, and for them to meet Rosie. His arm around her waist, they stood together and watched the colours change.

'Better get going,' he said.

'OK. But are you sure you're doing the right thing?'

'It's the only thing.'

The tops of the hills that surround Los Angeles to the north came into view. Closer up, they looked like sand dunes, or burial mounds, but soon they were riding through well-watered towns with wide streets and leafy trees. Until a roaring freeway, four lanes on each side, took them down into the heart of the sprawling city.

The parking lot was as large as two football fields and dotted with slender palms. He found what he wanted and brought the Ford Bronco to a stop between two haulage carriers. Even if they knew what car they were looking for, it wouldn't be easily spotted.

Suitcases in hand, the two travellers entered the red-tiled building. A middle-aged man and a young woman. They stopped for a minute while he spoke to her. She moved away and got the tickets while he bought a newspaper. After a sandwich in the café, they walked out to the platform.

Father and daughter, the woman thought, sitting down next to them on the wooden bench. Probably on vacation. They don't talk to each other much, though, and the man keeps looking around, like he's waiting for someone. Of course, his wife, the mother.

'Going far?' she ventured, unable to bear the silence any longer.

'Oh, not really,' he said, avoiding eye contact. 'Just a little trip.'

The woman executed a half-turn to face them.

'Me, I'm going to San Diego. My mother's ill and my dad, well, he's not really up to much these days. You know how it is.'

'That's too bad,' Rosie said.

'Yes, he's been in and out of hospital for months. You just don't know what's around the corner, do you?' No reply, so she added, 'Medically speaking, I mean.'

'Yes, and not just that,' Rosie said.

He gave her a tiny shake of the head.

'Where did you say you were going?' the woman asked.

'Mex…'

A whistle tore through the air. Grabbing Rosie, he hurried down the platform and into a carriage. They found aisle and window seats, stored their cases in the overhead rack and sank down.

'Almost there,' he said.

'Do you think they'll find us there?'

'I don't know. We'll leave as soon as possible.'

When the train lurched forward, he closed his eyes. Seven days on the run had exhausted him. Making decisions, second-guessing really, and trying to reassure Rosie while not wanting to think beyond the end of the day. But the hardest part, he knew, lay ahead.

They got off at San Juan Capistrano. A typical early summer day on the coast of Southern California. Warm and getting warmer, the heat trapped beneath a hazy sky and a fickle sea breeze. He rolled down the window in the back seat as the taxi raced past shopping malls, housing developments and gated communities. The land of wealthy retirees, health fanatics, senior surfers and redundant movie stars.

He tried to picture the house. He'd stayed there just once, in the summer after graduating from college and before teaching in Maine. His parents had moved to Dana Point a few months earlier, leaving behind the old house with the swimming pool on the mesa, and the bomb shelter next door. The new house was also on a cliff. A higher one.

He remembered how proud his father had been, showing him the new house and pointing out that it was only one of four in the cul-de-sac overlooking the ocean.

'What do they know about me?' she asked, next to him in the taxi.

'Nothing. I've only spoken to them half a dozen times since you were born. On the phone. And that was years ago.'

Rosie blanched.

'Not because of you,' he added. 'But because they would have had the house watched, probably tapped the phone and intercepted letters. I sent messages every six months or so, through an old friend in Berkeley. Just to say I was OK.'

'Did you tell them about me?'

'No,' he squeaked. 'And not about your mother, either.'

'But they know we're coming now, right?'

'No, Rosie. They do not.'

The taxi came to a stop at the discreet sign warning that "unauthorised vehicles" would be towed away. The driver turned around, saw his passenger nod and eased through the narrow gap in the brick wall separating the private street from the busy highway.

He barely recognised his father, stooped shoulders, heavy jowls and snow-white hair.

'Hello, Dad.'

'Stephen?'

After eighteen years, and with different hair, his son was almost as unfamiliar.

'Yes, it's me.'

'But what…'

'Can we come in?'

'Yes, yes. Of course.'

Laying a tentative hand on his son's shoulder and trying not to look at the young woman, Mr Collins guided them through the door. Inside, they put down their suitcases and stood with him in a mute triangle.

'Who is it?'

His mother's voice. From the sunken living room, she climbed three steps and came into the hallway.

'Hello, Mother.'

The book in her hand fell to the floor as she rushed forward and embraced him. His father wrapped his arms around them both, and they clung to each other, sobbing and shaking, releasing the pain of many years.

'This is Rosie,' he said, pulling away. 'My daughter.'

'Your…'

'Sorry for all of the surprises, but I'll explain everything. Including the silver hair.'

'Doesn't matter, doesn't matter,' his father muttered, wiping his cheeks.

His mother continued to stare, speechless, at Rosie, who

pushed her lips into an apologetic smile. His mother had also noticed his necklace but didn't comment.

'Let's go sit down,' his father said and turned toward the living room.

From where she stood, Rosie saw the ocean. Following Mr Collins through an open-plan kitchen and down the three steps into the living room, she placed a hand on a glass door.

'May I?' she asked.

'Sure. Go ahead,' Mr Collins said.

She slid the door to one side and stood on a redwood deck, facing the sparkling water. Looking down, she two hundred feet of rocky projections and scrubby vegetation. Below, on the horseshoe-shaped beach, sunbathers lay on towels and toddlers played in the sand. No audible voices, only the muffled roar of waves rolling in and tumbling over. She gripped the railing and breathed in deeply.

Back inside, she found her father and his parents sitting around a coffee table, talking quietly. Three tumblers lay untouched on the thick glass top.

'Rosie, how about a glass of water?' his father said, standing up. 'Or a beer?'

'Water's fine, thank you.'

She sat down on the couch next to her father.

'Stephen says you're going to university this fall. You must be excited,' his mother said.

'Yes. It's been a long time, preparing for exams and all.'

'What subjects are you interested in?'

'I'm going to study English literature and creative writing.'

'You've already decided?'

'Yes. You can apply for a specific degree course. I think it's different here.'

'Very different,' his mother said, with emphasis.

The glass of water arrived in a moment of strained silence.

'We could use some rest,' he said when Rosie had emptied her glass. 'It's been a long journey.'

They carried their suitcases down a flight of stairs to a lower floor: two small bedrooms and a shared bathroom. Each bedroom had a sliding glass door leading to a deck, like the one above, only smaller and closer to the cliff face. Leaning out, Rosie touched the silver-leaved bushes and orange-tipped succulents.

When she awoke, it was mid-afternoon, with sunshine pouring in through the glass door. Stepping out again, she saw her father on his deck, only a few feet to her right, scanning the horizon with his binoculars.

'C'mon, Dad!' She laughed. 'They're not coming by boat.'

Startled, he lowered the field glasses and smiled back at her.

'Can't we stay? It's so wonderful here.'

'No. We have to leave. Soon.'

Back inside, Rosie lay on the bed and put a tape into her Walkman. As the music floated through her, she saw Tuxedo's little face peering at her through the grill in the cat carrier. And the face of her best friend in Vancouver, who had planned a party for everyone in September.

53

He showered, changed and went up to the ground floor. Neither of his parents were around. Alone in the spacious, sunlit interior, he felt exposed. Avoiding the deck, he looked for a newspaper.

When Rosie came up, he fixed sandwiches, and they sat on wooden stools at the breakfast counter.

'No radio,' she said in a low voice.

'No. I'll ask if…'

A metallic scraping sound made him stop and listen.

'Dad, it's nothing.'

He ignored her and went to the front door. Opening it, he saw his father weeding the walkway.

'Get some sleep?'

'Yes.'

'Your mother is out shopping. Should be back soon. Let's wait for her.'

'OK. Is there a paper somewhere?'

'In my office. Next to our bedroom.'

The four of them assembled in the living room, his parents on the sofa, he and Rosie in matching upholstered armchairs. The sun, now drained of heat, was riding the horizon. No one turned on any lights.

'It's been so long I can't remember what I told you. Or how much of it was true.'

'Just tell us everything, from the beginning,' his mother said.

'That's easy. The starting point was the draft, when I was teaching in Maine. I didn't get a high number, like I told you. I got seventy-five, which meant I'd be sent to Vietnam for sure.'

'Harvard Law School, didn't they allow for that?' his mother said.

'No. They did away with that deferment a couple of years before.'

'I see.'

'So, I had a medical – you wouldn't believe how ridiculous it was – and passed with flying colours. Of course.'

'You were inducted?' His father was trying to be precise, to get the sequence clear, while his mind was whirling, not knowing what might come next.

'No, that was just the physical. I didn't wait for the induction letter. Just left the school and headed out to San Francisco. Berkeley, actually, where I stayed with a friend.'

'Berkeley,' his mother repeated, as if it was an explanation.

'And then, well, I don't know how to explain it all. It was a long time ago and…'

'Just tell us what happened.'

'Dad, a lot happened. It's not that simple.'

'OK, you were in Berkeley. What did you do there?'

'Well, I got a job, but I also got caught up in the protests on campus. One thing led to another and… I got arrested.'

His parents' eyes widened.

'With dozens of others. We spent a night in jail. Just one night. It happened all the time.'

'Were you part of one of those groups?' his mother asked.

'No. It was pretty spontaneous. There were groups, of course, but I didn't join any.'

The sky darkened, pulling the light from the room and drawing them closer. This isn't so bad, he thought. More like sharing secrets than admitting to lies.

'Then I left Berkeley and went to this commune, near Mendocino. It seemed like a good idea, to get away from everything.'

'How did you find it?' Rosie asked, speaking for the first time. 'You never told me.'

'I can't really remember. Someone must have told me about it. Things like that happened back then. Big decisions were made quickly.'

He described River Ridge, living in Ted's cabin, teaching the kids and walking in the woods. Then Sharon, falling in love and becoming a father.

'You didn't get married?' His mother struggled to keep her voice neutral.

'No. Lots of people didn't. It wasn't a big issue.'

'Where is she now?'

'I don't know.' His eyes slid toward Rosie. 'Probably around San Francisco somewhere.'

'Go on, son,' his father urged. 'We need to hear it all.'

He blew out some air. 'OK. Then we planned the bombing. Well, Sharon did. I went down to San Francisco – she stayed back because she was pregnant, with Rosie. Anyway, I stayed with this guy in San Francisco. He did all the wiring and everything, and bribed a guard to let me in. I drove the van inside the base and set the timers.' He swallowed hard. 'Then I ran.'

And haven't stopped running since, he thought.

'Someone got killed in there, right?' his father said.

'He shouldn't have been there,' he said, raising his voice. 'Not at that hour. That's what we were told. And the other guy made a warning call, but no one picked up the phone.'

Rosie reached over and took his hand. The groove between his eyebrows had deepened to a knife-like cut.

'That's the truth. We never intended to hurt anyone.'

'I believe you, son,' his father said. 'But what were you doing there in the first place? Exploding a bomb in an army base – that can't be right, can it?'

'It was different then, Dad. We wanted to stop the killing in Vietnam. Senseless killing of civilians.'

'Whatever you thought you were doing, Stephen, it was wrong.'

His mother nodded.

'But it was an accident! Can't you see that!'

He stormed off, downstairs to his bedroom, and Rosie followed.

'What are we going to do?' his mother asked when they had gone.

'What do you mean?' his father replied.

'I mean, should we call the police? Aren't we supposed to if we know something?'

'Maybe. Which means we should have called the police as soon as he arrived.' He swallowed hard. 'But I'm not going to do that. He's our son, for God's sake!'

'I know that, Jim. But he killed a man.'

It was dark when his father came down and asked if they wanted to join them for dinner. In the dining area upstairs, the night added stillness to the silence. Rosie sought out the pinpricks from the ships at sea.

'It's not much,' his mother said, handing around plates of roast chicken and steamed green beans. 'But I'm sure we're all hungry.'

They've talked it over, he thought, and decided to let it rest, for the time being.

'It looks good. A lot better than one of Dad's disasters,' Rosie said. 'But don't tell him that,' she added in an exaggerated whisper.

They all laughed and began to breathe more easily. Everyone chewed the beans, passed the gravy boat and worked hard at cutting the chicken without pushing it off the small plates.

'We could use some wine, don't you think?' his father said and rose without waiting for an answer.

Four glasses of red were poured and sipped as the meal progressed. When coffee and biscuits appeared, they moved back to the living room.

'So, what happened next?' his father said.

'Mind if I ask you a question first?'

'Of course not.'

'Did the FBI contact you?'

'They did. They came here after… what happened. They were very polite and very insistent. We told them what you'd told us. That you were travelling in Europe with your girlfriend.'

He nodded.

'Where were you, by the way? That was in the summer, I think.'

'We were in Vancouver by then. Rosie and me. Her mother had gone back to the US.'

'She left you with a baby that was only a few months old?' his mother said.

'Six weeks.'

'And she hasn't made contact since?'

He turned to Rosie with a "you answer" look.

'No. I've never met her. She's…'

'She's a committed activist. Social justice and world peace. She felt an obligation to continue her work in this country.'

'Obligation?' His mother snorted. 'What about her child?'

'Look, Mother. I don't want to get into all that, OK? Rosie and I have our life together. That's what you need to know.'

'All right, I'm sorry.'

'So, you were living in Canada, you and Rosie,' his father said, picking up the thread. 'And everything you wrote to us and all those messages from the friend in Berkeley – none of that was true?'

'I wanted to tell you the truth. I really did.'

'I'm sure you did. So please tell us now,' his father said.

He described their life in Vancouver. Rosie growing up in

their modest house, him adjusting to a new city and driving a garbage truck, which prompted tightened lips from both parents. He couldn't bring himself to mention the change of names and identity.

'The house was really nice,' Rosie piped up. 'Almost hidden in the woods, like a fairy tale.'

'Did you get involved in any politics there?' his father asked.

'No. I got help from a group of people who supported draft resisters, but I didn't do anything.'

'Because you were in hiding?'

'Partly.'

'What happened to bring you here now?' his mother asked.

'What happened is, Rosie decided she wanted to meet her mother. And about two weeks ago, she went to San Francisco – we have a friend there who keeps in touch – but…'

'It didn't work out,' Rosie cut in.

'No. And when Rosie came back to Canada, I realised that she'd been followed.'

'Followed?'

'By a private investigator. Which meant I was being followed, too. So, we left and came here.'

'To escape from the police? From being arrested?'

'That's one reason.'

'And the other?'

'I wanted to tell you everything, the truth about what happened. And for you to get to know Rosie.' Choking on his words, he looked straight at his mother. 'That was the worst thing of all, not telling you that you had a granddaughter.'

His mother mumbled something that sounded like acceptance.

'Well,' his father said, 'it's great to have you here. Both of you.'

Behind the smiles, the unasked thing had grown larger and larger.

'Do you think they'll find you here?' his mother finally asked. 'This private investigator, or the police or whoever?'

'I do. We have to leave. Tomorrow or the day after.'

54

The telephone seemed to ring with urgency. Sanders, ready for bed, looked at it with suspicion. Laying his cigar in a glass tray, he grunted and picked up the receiver.

'This is Rodgers, in Anaheim. I've got something for you. Where you been all day?'

'Up in Sacramento, getting nowhere with a custody case. Anyway, what've you got?'

'You were right about the house in Dana Point. He and his daughter came there in a taxi today.'

'When?'

'About noon.'

'You sure it's them?'

'Oh, it's them all right. I got a good view of the house from the beach. Those new binocs are super.'

'OK. Take up a position just down the road. If they leave, call me.'

Sanders hung up. Too late to call his contact in the FBI office. He'd do it first thing in the morning.

55

Buttering toast, she stopped, knife in mid-air. Alerted by her, he put down the paper and listened. A car engine died. A car door slammed. Footsteps crunched on the concrete. They faded and went next door. He unlocked eyes with her and picked up the paper.

Rosie went for a walk along the beach, his mother took her car shopping, and he sat with his father in the living room. Mr Collins hadn't really looked at his son since he'd arrived the day before. Not with all the tension.

'What are you going to do?' his father said. 'When you leave here, I mean.'

'Not sure. I could probably get another job driving garbage trucks. I've got a letter from my employer, in Vancouver.'

'That's good.'

'Just followed your advice.'

His father screwed up his face into a question.

'From before. Remember? When I left the school in Maine.'

'Oh, yes. What about teaching? There are always teaching jobs.'

'I don't think so. It's been too long. Wouldn't look good.'

'No, I suppose not.'

A short silence.

'But where will you go?'

'I don't know.'

'Don't know or won't tell me?'

'Dad, it's better if you don't know.'

His father nodded but only because he couldn't speak. He was struggling to keep hold of his son. He looked the same, despite the hair and the years, and his voice was familiar, but all those years of hiding and lying had knocked the stuffing out of him.

'What about Rosie?' he managed to say.

'She'll go back to Vancouver. To university. She's got friends there.'

'That sounds like the right idea.'

'The problem is, she doesn't want to. Says she won't let me go on alone.'

'She's a nice girl.'

'Yeah, but it's no life for her. Trailing along with a fugitive father.'

His father heard the bitterness in his voice.

'I've got to leave her behind somehow. I'm thinking I'll just say I'm going out shopping, or something, and not return.'

'No, Stephen. Don't do that. Don't lie to her. Together, we'll convince her to stay behind.'

'OK, but… could she stay with you? At least for a little while?'

'For as long as she likes. And we'll handle her university expenses and all that. Send her a monthly allowance.'

'Thanks, Dad.' He hesitated. 'And there's something I need.'

'What?'

'A car.'

'A car? OK. I guess you could take mine.' The words came out slowly, one by one. 'That would be easiest.'

'Thank you.'

'The registration card is there, in the glove compartment. Do you have a license?'

'My Canadian one should be good for a while. I'll get a new one when I settle down.'

They both nodded, thinking that through from different angles.

'What about money? Do you have a bank account?'

'I've got a few hundred dollars with me. Nothing left in the bank.'

'Let me see what I can do.'

'Thanks again, Dad. Better do it today, though.'

Later that afternoon, his father handed him an envelope stuffed with hundred-dollar bills.

'Don't mention this to your mother. She won't like the idea of the car, either, but that can't be helped.'

'I wish she could understand a little more.'

His father lowered his head and then looked up at him.

'Listen, Stephen. You don't know what these years have been like. Waiting. Hoping. Not knowing. The messages you sent didn't change that.'

'I…'

'Your mother practically went into hiding herself, not seeing her friends. She couldn't face them. Because they knew, of course. Your name was in all the papers.'

'I'm really sorry.'

'And it got worse. Someone in the post office actually said "Where's that killer son of yours?" After that, she stayed home most of the time.'

He closed his eyes.

'It got better as time went on. But she never really got over that.'

He went below, out on the deck and stared at the ocean. He had tried hard not to imagine what it was like for them. Because he'd known, underneath, that it would have been terrible. Their son and only child, talented and ambitious, wanted for murder. He had to spare them the humiliation of him being arrested in their house, police cars outside, the neighbours watching. And the stories in the papers and on television.

He looked across the cove, at the houses on the other side of the cliff. Some of them seemed tilted, out of alignment. He squinted and tried to correct it but felt dizzy and pulled himself back from the edge.

56

They were in the kitchen again, alone, suitcases in the hallway. After breakfast, they would say goodbye to his parents and be off. That's what he'd told her the night before, after he'd failed to persuade her to stay behind. When she'd asked where they were going, he said it was a surprise.

'Somewhere nice?'

'Of course. Sunny all year round.'

Now, in the semi-darkness, he waited for her to finish eating. Then she'd brush her teeth and use the bathroom, like she always did. When she was downstairs, out of sight, he would drive away. It would be hard, not saying goodbye, but he had to leave her because it was the only way to make sure she was safe.

'Last night, you said somewhere warm, right?' she asked between mouthfuls.

'Correct.'

'OK. I'm thinking Mexico. But do we need a visa?'

'We can…'

They heard slamming car doors, thudding steps and banging on the front door.

'Stall them for a while,' he whispered.

'Where are you going?'

But he was already downstairs. The banging got louder. His parents came out of their bedroom, and Rosie rushed to them.

'Let me do this,' she said. 'Just go into your room.'

Stunned, they padded back and closed the door.

'Just a minute,' Rosie shouted at the front door. 'I'm getting dressed.'

She took a deep breath, counted to twenty and opened the door. Two men in dark suits and ties. One was tall and suntanned. The other, young and muscular.

'Good morning,' she said, blocking their entrance and vision.

'Morning, miss. We're from the FBI,' the tall one said and showed his badge. 'We'd like to speak with Stephen Collins, alias David Williams.'

'Mr Collins? He's still in bed and…'

'Step aside, please. We have a search warrant.'

Pushing by her, they glanced at the suitcases and advanced down the hall into the kitchen area.

'Where is he?'

'Mr Collins is in there,' she said, pointing to a room at the end of the hall.

The tall man gestured with his head and his companion hurried toward the bedroom. Opening it, he saw an older couple in pyjamas, backed up against the wall.

'Excuse me, but we're looking for Stephen Collins.'

'Well, he's not here,' his father said with as much defiance as he could muster.

The man swung an arm through the built-in closet and threw open the door to the ensuite bathroom.

'No one,' he reported back to the tall man, who glowered at Rosie.

'He was in there. Before, I mean,' she said.

The tall man told the young one to go downstairs while he searched the rest of the house. His parents appeared in the hallway wrapped in robes, faces drained, huddled together like lost children. Rosie gave them a confident smile. Don't worry. He's OK.

'Not there,' the young man said, back upstairs.

'OK, here's what…'

The crackle of a walkie-talkie froze them all. The tall man put it to his ear.

'You sure? Right. Cordon it off.' Then to his companion. 'You stay here, with them.'

He ran out, across the cul-de-sac and down the sidewalk, toward the bottom of the hill.

Rosie said she needed the bathroom and went downstairs. From the deck, she saw a small knot of people on the beach and police officers trying to hold them back. From the corner of her eye, she noticed the tall officer from the house come striding down a paved boat ramp, his arms swinging from side to side, in rhythm with his swaying tie.

She grabbed the binoculars and trained them on the gathering near the base of the cliff. Fingering the knob, she adjusted the focus and brought the scene into sharp relief. The tall man had pushed everyone aside and she could see what he saw. A body face-down in the sand. He knelt down and turned it over.

Covering her mouth, she staggered back inside and saw his necklace lying on top of the dresser. Why would he…? She thrust it into a drawer and raced upstairs. She had to tell his parents before the police did.

His mother was sitting at the dining table, staring straight ahead, his father behind her, hand on her shoulder. Their eyes swivelled toward her when she appeared on the top step. Behind the fear, she saw their shame. FBI in the house, police cars outside, sirens screaming everywhere. That's when she knew why.

'I need to talk to my grandparents for a moment. Alone, please.'

The young man in the hallway shrugged. She ushered them into their bedroom, closed the door and faced them.

'What is it?' his father said. 'What's happened?'

'I saw him,' she said, struggling to still the beating of her heart. 'On the beach, beneath the cliff.'

'You mean...?'

'I don't know. He wasn't moving.'

She led them down the hallway, past the young man, through the living room and out to the deck. From that higher point, they had a better view than she had from below, but the spot where she had seen the body was obscured by police officers and ambulance crew.

The thump-thump of a helicopter made them look up. It hovered for a few seconds, dipped its nose and dropped down on the sand. The police stepped aside, and the paramedics stepped in. Hands on the railing, Rosie and his parents watched the practised drill, the manoeuvring, the shifting and the coming to rest. A slight pause before the paramedics lifted the stretcher and carried it to the red-and-yellow air ambulance. Lifted by whirling blades, the helicopter rose unsteadily, tilted to one side and drifted away.

His parents were driven to a hospital in San Juan Capistrano, where the identification took all of ten seconds. When the metal tray was pushed back into the wall, his father bit his lip to force back the tears. 'He was a good boy, a good boy,' he kept muttering, as his wife took him by the arm and led him away.

As soon as they came in through the front door, Rosie saw the devastation on their faces. She advanced, arms spread, and all three locked themselves in a tight embrace, their bodies shaking despite their coiled limbs.

'I think we could use something to drink,' Mr Collins said.

He poured two tumblers of scotch, hesitated and looked at Rosie. She shook her head.

They sat in the living room, husband and wife on the sofa, granddaughter in a chair. Rosie squinted at the light streaming in through the sliding doors and wished for the blessed cover of night. She listened while they talked.

'How could it happen?' his mother said, hands clasped in her lap. 'Yes, he did something terrible, but he didn't deserve to die like this.'

'He slipped and fell. That's all,' his father said.

'No, they drove him to it. Barging in here, frightening us.'

'He was trying to escape. He knew they were coming. He told me yesterday.'

'But he was never going to be able to get away. He must have known that.'

Rosie lowered her eyes. His mother was right. He knew the house and the cliff, and he would have had a plan. A final escape, at the point of no return.

'He was a wonderful dad,' Rosie said. 'You wouldn't know that, of course. How could you? But he was. Always supporting me, making sure I was all right. We…' She choked on her words. 'We were really close. Without my mom, you see. The best dad in the world.'

57

From his office window, Ronald watched the morning fog. Having swallowed the high-rise buildings across the bay, it was advancing on Oakland. Back at his desk, he looked down at the sales contract on a six-storey apartment block. Something about the purchaser's loan didn't seem right, but he couldn't concentrate on the figures. Lighting a cigarette, he allowed himself to smile.

This was the day he'd been waiting for. After eighteen years, a broken marriage and an ailing mother who had never recovered. After all those sightings and predictions had evaporated into thin air. There had been that screw-up when they lost him somewhere in Canada.

But yesterday Sanders had called to say he'd been located in Southern California.

'Where?'

'Better for me not to say. But you can expect positive news soon.'

'When?'

'Tomorrow. Noon, at the latest. I'll call you when I know something.'

He checked his watch and saw it was already past 10:00am. He began to pace around the office, wondering if he should call

Sanders. But what good would that do? He decided to go over again and see him in his office. He grabbed his suit coat from the hook behind the door, shoved an arm into a sleeve and got tangled up, like a straitjacket. He swore so loud he almost didn't hear the telephone.

'Good morning, Mr Gill. Positive news, like I said.'

'He's been arrested?'

'No. He's dead.'

'Dead?'

'Yes. In Dana Point, south of LA. When the Feds went to arrest him at his parents' house, he tried to escape and fell off a cliff. Broke his neck, they say… Mr Gill, you still there?'

'Yeah, I'm here.'

'Now, what about his accomplice, this Sharon Walker?'

'I'm not interested in anyone else.'

'You sure?'

'I'm sure. I'll send you a cheque tomorrow.'

'No rush. Pleasure doing business with you, Mr Gill.'

Ronald hung up and looked at the map on his wall. Pins everywhere. His eyes followed the latest trail, east from Vancouver to Kamloops and south to the border at Paterson, where the guard had remembered their names. He didn't know what route they'd taken to Dana Point, but he assumed it went through Los Angeles, so he stuck a pin there, where it joined a forest of pins.

He was dead. No trial, no reckoning. Was that what had driven him all this time, the need to see him punished? Or had he just wanted the whole thing over and done with? He would go on buying and selling property, he would try to patch things up with Marilyn and he would make sure their daughter did well at Stanford. He wouldn't tell his mother – it wouldn't bring her closure because her loss would continue.

Opening his top desk drawer, he found the large red pin. The one that didn't need a number. The one he'd been saving. He'd never heard of Dana Point, but Sanders said south of LA. He placed a finger on Los Angeles and slid it down the coast, past Huntington Beach, past Laguna Beach, until it rested on a little bump. Probably a beautiful place, he thought. Parents' house right on the ocean. He had felt anger and hate for a long, long time, but there was only relief when he pushed the pin in and whispered.

'End of the line.'

58

In her loft apartment, Sharon opened the *San Francisco Chronicle* and lit a cigarette. That was her daily routine. After a morning spent editing the next issue of the magazine, or writing her editorial, she would go down and find the paper stuck halfway into the metal mailbox on the front porch. The woman who owned the house always left it there for her after she'd finished it. Like Gavin, Sharon thought each time she picked it up. Then she would climb back up to her apartment, angle her armchair toward the window facing the bay and read the paper.

She blew out smoke and scanned the front page. A photo of men and women in formal dress accompanied a story about a society event in the City. She twisted her lips and turned the page. Bombs in Northern Ireland, economic collapse in Egypt, drought in the Central Valley and scandal in the property market – an apartment complex in Oakland had been purchased using a loan secured with insufficient equity. She was about to turn the page again, when her eye snagged on a headline near the bottom.

Placing her cigarette in the ashtray on the floor, she drew the paper closer.

> *Man Dies in Orange County Cliff Fall*
>
> *Eyewitnesses in Dana Point said a man fell from a seaside cliff early Monday morning. "The death does not appear to be suspicious," Orange County Sheriff Bill Walsh announced. The man was airlifted to a nearby hospital, where he was pronounced dead later that same day. The deceased has since been named by the Orange County Coroner's Office as Stephen Collins, forty-two, lately of Vancouver, Canada. According to the police, he was staying with his parents when he fell from the cliff at the back of their house.*
>
> *Sheriff Walsh also confirmed that Mr Collins was wanted by the FBI for a bombing on an army base in San Francisco in 1971, which resulted in a fatality. In an official statement seen by this reporter, the FBI took credit for locating the suspect, adding that "criminals will always pay for their crimes". A funeral service will be held in San Juan Capistrano later this month.*

The paper fell from her fingers. Staying with his parents? That was stupid. They must have been on to him in Canada, and he'd had no other way. Maybe that was why he'd sent Rosa to her. To get help.

Head in hands, she fought against a scream that escaped as a squeal. She had loved him. Loved him from the very first, and even more after he took care of their child. It had nearly killed her to leave them, but she had convinced herself it was the right thing.

All that had been buried, deep in the distant past, until Gabriel called a few weeks ago. A bolt from the blue. Her daughter, her grown-up daughter, wanted to see her. She knew it was risky and should have said no. But she couldn't. She desperately wanted to meet her. And then, at the Rose Garden, she saw the watcher and left without a word. If she had met Rosa, she could have helped, could have found him a safe place to hide. And he'd still be alive.

She walked to the window and searched for the water through the haze. 'Where am I?' she asked herself. Steve dead, Gabriel married, and she a journalist, surviving on handouts from her parents. Despite all the hard work, all the risks and the damaged lives, they had not achieved much. Maybe they had shortened the war. Maybe not.

The new world that she had fought so long to create had not been born. Only flickered into life during the acts of defiance that were intended to engender it. The movement had been crushed by the force of history, the very thing in which she had invested so much.

59

The Mercury Society was located in a modest, refurbished house on a palm-lined street. Flat-topped bushes crowded close to the white clapboard façade, with only a small gap allowing access to the front porch. And only a discreet sign in a corner of the lawn corrected the impression that this was simply another family residence in San Juan Capistrano.

A wood-panelled hallway led to a round room with a dome roof and curving pews. His parents, both in soft grey, sat in the front row with Rosie, who wore a black dress bought the day before. No one else was present as they had decided it should be invitation only.

The eulogy was given by a young man in a shiny suit and slicked-back hair. He narrated the high points of the life, emphasising what the parents had emphasised to him. Stephen's life was one of great promise. He was a gifted student and talented athlete; a young man who loved teaching and inspired students. Caught up in the "turbulence of those times", he made mistakes, "acts of compassion that went wrong". He lived his last years as a dedicated father and hard-working citizen. His death was an accident that left parents without a son and a daughter without a father. Stephen should be remembered for his early achievements.

Neither his parents nor Rosie spoke. Tears trickled down the drawn cheeks of the parents, while Rosie held them in check by balling her hands into fists. All three were still struggling to construct a chain of events and apportion responsibility.

After hymns and prayers, the wooden coffin was lifted and carried out of the circular room and into the cremation chamber. Out of sight. There was no organ and no music.

Back in the California sun, on the front steps, the three family members were confronted by reporters, photographers and camera crews. During the days between the death and the funeral, the *LA Times* had dug back into the past, located and interviewed key people – retired Commander Blake, ex-guard Himenes, retired FBI agent Callahan, retired private investigator Anderson and Mr Ronald Gill. Gabriel Pennington had declined to cooperate, as had Walter Gill's widow, but an old photograph of her with her son was reproduced to accompany an article that appeared in a Sunday supplement. "1970s Radical Dies after FBI Manhunt" was widely read and discussed. Most, though not all, of the facts were accurate, but explanations for the Presidio bombing – attribution of motives and identification of factors behind the "terrorist act" – were guesswork. That's what angered Rosie.

Mr Collins told the reporters outside the crematorium that he had nothing to say. Shepherding his wife and granddaughter with one arm, he flung the other out in front, as if to sweep away the crowd like a pile of papers. He marched his family through the throng and down the pavement to the parked car.

No one spoke until they were inside the house, in the living room, facing the ocean.

'Well,' Mr Collins said, 'I thought that young man spoke with… dignity.'

'Yes,' his wife replied, staring into the middle distance.

He looked at Rosie, who excused herself and went downstairs to her room, where she lay on the bed. As her body slackened, the peace necklace slid from her tightened fingers. Looking at it, she told herself that he was not "a misguided idealist" or a "self-serving terrorist". He was her father, who had raised her on his own, practically since birth. Who had supported her in every step she took. And whom she loved more than anyone would ever know.

The following day, the *LA Times* printed a large photograph with the caption "Family Mourns Death of Bomber Son". His parents stood with bowed heads, while Rosie stared out with defiance. Some readers assumed she was the dead man's widow.

'But you can't go back to Vancouver now. Not on your own. Not after what's happened.'

Mr Collins and Rosie were sitting on the deck off the living room. The tide was in, waves sloshing and gurgling on the beach below. Closer to the cliff, families, couples and individuals basked in the midday sun. No trace remained in the sand, hard-baked by the summer heat.

'Please don't worry about me. I'll be fine. I have lots of friends there.'

He scratched his neck. What did he know about an eighteen-year-old girl, even if she was his son's daughter?

'But who's going to… I mean, you don't have any family there.'

'Dad has friends, though.' That sounded better than saying she'd count on her friends' parents. 'Besides, university will be good for me. Give me something to do. If I stayed here – I mean, you're very kind – but what would I do? I don't know anyone.'

'I guess you're right. But we will only let you go on one condition.'

'What's that?'

'I gave some money to your father. I want you to have it. Take it and open a bank account in Vancouver.'

'That's very generous. I don't know how to thank you.'

'No need for that. You're our family.'

She left Dana Point with a promise to call them as soon as she reached Vancouver and to return for a visit at Christmas. Saying goodbye on the doorstep, she was surprised by the force of his mother's embrace. The granddaughter taking the place of her son.

The taxi penetrated the grey air of central Los Angeles and dropped her at the station. The train left on time that morning and she settled into her seat thinking of the long journey ahead. With a change in Seattle, she would reach Vancouver about 10:30pm the following evening. Resting her head against the high seat, she watched the industrial yards flash by and reached for her Walkman.

No one knew. Not the man reading across the aisle, not the woman smoking next to him, not the teenager looking bored next to her. Her pain was her own. A deep, dumb bruise that had not receded as the days passed. It had only grown larger, filling the expanding space between his death and the present. And all the time crushed by guilt, knowing that if she had not tried to see her mother, her father would still be alive.

She listened to an Irish woman sing about lost love. Outside, she saw the flat-roofed houses and windswept streets of a high desert town. Just like when they drove down into Los Angeles, a little over a week ago. She had known then that it would not turn out as he had led her to expect. But she had been too frightened to acknowledge what she saw, a desperate man too proud to show he was defeated.

She told herself that she would go to university. That's what her father wanted. Money would not be a problem. His father – she couldn't quite bring herself to say "my grandfather" – would pay her fees and send a good amount every month, until she graduated. And then she would make a life for herself. Maybe as a lawyer, like Gabriel's wife. Life without her father would be tough, but her friends would help. She knew they would.

Roused by a juddering stop, she peered through the window. Passengers on the platform. A tall woman with a dog. Another with three small children. More people got off than on the train, and her carriage was less crowded. An older man and woman took the seats across the aisle. She smiled at them and began to consider something that had been at the back of her mind ever since boarding the train. 'Just a small diversion,' her father would have said.

It was dark when she stepped down from the high carriage. This time, no one was waiting for her in the ornate reception hall, so she marched out and told the taxi driver to take her to a "good hotel" in San Francisco.

'You want a view?'

'Sure.'

'Then it's the Fairmont, miss. That's tops.'

In the morning, she pulled back the curtains and saw what he meant. A cityscape with blue-grey water and a hazy coastline in the background. A white tower, tall on a hill amid a clump of trees, drew her attention.

'Coit Tower,' the waiter said in answer to her question in the breakfast room. 'It was built in the 1930s to remember all the firefighters who'd died here. There are beautiful paintings inside, too. Well worth a visit.'

She went in the other direction, south toward Noe Valley. Probably should have called but she didn't have the number. The little house trimmed with gold and cream looked a world away from the sprawling house on the cliff.

Gabriel showed little surprise when he opened the door.

'Sorry to show up like this, but…'

'No, no. It's fine. Come in.'

They got as far as the kitchen.

'You know what happened?'

'Yes.'

They were standing a few feet apart, at the breakfast table. The newspaper, coffee mug and plate of half-eaten toast reminded her of that final morning. She laid a hand on the table to steady herself.

'It's just that…'

'I know, I know,' he said in a soft voice and guided her to a chair.

He made eggs and more toast while she sat and watched. The man who had made the bombs. The man who had spent time in prison. Happily married, with children and a future.

'Eat first and then tell me,' he said, putting a plate in front of her.

She ate quickly, jabbing her fork and biting hard. When she'd finished, he cleared the table and sat down opposite.

'It all started when I got back to Vancouver. Dad thought you were right – that I'd been followed to the Rose Garden. And he guessed they'd have someone in Vancouver, watching when I met him at the station.'

'So what did he do?'

She told him the story. Changing the route and leaving the motel at daybreak, selling the car and renting one, going through the police roadblock and ditching the car in Castlegar, renting another and driving to LA, taking the train to Dana Point and the taxi to his parents' house.

'How long did you stay there before…?'

'Two days. It was all so quick. They showed up just when we were about to leave.'

'He fell trying to escape?'

She squeezed her eyes and shook her head. 'I don't think so.'

He wanted to ask why but saw that it was still too painful.

'I should have known they'd be watching this house,' he said.

'No. No. You're not to blame. It was my own stupid idea of wanting to seeing my mother.'

'That was not a stupid idea.'

'Maybe not in itself. But in this case…'

'In this case, we all made mistakes. That's the truth, Rosie. Every single one of us. From the very beginning.'

She raised her eyes to him and managed a half-smile.

'You know something, though. He thought it was probably a private investigator – not the FBI – who was watching your house and followed me.'

'A PI?'

'Yeah. Hired by Walter Gill's son.'

Gabriel stroked his ponytail. He had been watched, even long after serving his sentence and leading a normal life. Would it stop with Steve? Or would this man exact revenge on everyone involved in his father's death?

'Makes sense,' he said and got up. 'Coffee?'

Again, she watched him. Patient and precise hand movements, measuring, filling, pouring. Maybe he could be like an uncle.

'And now you're going back to Vancouver?' he said, returning with two mugs. 'To university, right?'

'Yes. But first, I want to see my mother.'

Gabriel placed his mug on the table.

'I'm not sure that's a good idea. Especially if you're right about what happened last time.'

'That's what I wanted to ask you. Would the private investigator still be watching you?'

'I don't know. Maybe not, but the FBI are probably still interested in your mother.'

'Then it's up to her, just like before. Anyway, I want to try. I need to see her. Now more than ever.'

He studied her. The frizzy hair and slightly pudgy face. She looked older than he remembered. Or maybe just more determined. Like her mother.

'But I don't want to cause you any more trouble,' she said, misreading his hesitation.

'That's all right. They can't do anything to me. Not anymore.'

'So, will you contact her?'

'I'll call and see what she says. But wait a minute – where are you staying?'

60

Rosie was cossetted in the warmth of Gabriel's family. She kept up with their lively conversation, she laughed with them and was called "Big Sis" by the daughters. She also took long walks from Noe Valley to Twin Peaks and through Golden Gate Park, where she spent a day in the Asian Art Museum. She didn't go the additional half hour to the Presidio, where it had all begun. One parent dead, the other in hiding.

On the morning of the meeting, she put on jeans and a short-sleeved, pale blue blouse. She decided it was best to just be herself this time, no matter what. No red scarf either, but she was again headed for the Campanile on the Berkeley campus.

Leaving the house, she saw a man, idle across the street. She'd seen him before, somewhere on her walks. He stood still, looking down, as if he'd dropped something. But when he lifted his head, she wasn't sure. She skipped down the steps and into the taxi.

She'd gone over everything with Gabriel, just like before. The route and the estimated time of each segment. Taxi to Union Square, BART across the bay to Berkeley and walk to the tower. No shenanigans at Macy's this time.

She checked her watch at the semicircular entrance to the campus. Twelve minutes to go. The footpath through the redwoods was almost deserted on that Sunday afternoon in late June. As she advanced up the slope, familiarity gave her confidence. Sunlight filtered through the trees. A quiet beauty. Maybe she could switch and study here. It would be closer.

She continued straight ahead and crossed the intersection at the heart of the campus. People moving in all directions, their voices fading in the open air. She saw the tower. Tall, too tall, it looked fragile.

She climbed higher, past the library, to the red-brick area around the base of the Campanile. She found a bench and sat down in the shade. Two minutes before the hour. Her breathing slowed while she watched a group of tourists, whose language she couldn't identify. Scandinavian? She stood up and went back down the slope, circled around the library, climbed back up and sat on the same bench. As instructed.

She waited.

'Hello.'

It was the young woman who had met her before.

'Let's go. She's waiting for you.'

She led Rosie behind the tower and along a path that dipped into a ravine with a wooden bridge over a dry creek. On the other side, the path straightened and ran through a grassy area where the concrete buildings were new and square. No redwoods or eucalyptus.

They crossed a busy one-way street on the southern border of the campus and walked down a quiet road. Past a café, a xerox place, a vintage-clothes shop and a row of student apartment buildings. Her guide did not turn around. The apartment blocks gave way to single-family homes, brown shingle and red brick, with chimneys, porches and lawns. Some had flower beds and shrubbery, others palm trees and yucca plants.

The young woman stopped and gestured to a driveway beside a tall house with a raised front porch. At the back, hidden from the street, Rosie found an exterior wooden staircase that zigzagged up, like a fire escape.

She began to climb. The stairs were sturdy but narrow and

steep. On the first landing, she saw fuchsias and geraniums blooming in terracotta pots.

'Hello, Rosa.'

She craned her neck, almost lost her balance and gripped the railing.

'Hi.'

'Take it slow. It's a long way. Good exercise, though.'

At the top, on a small deck, she stood face to face with her. Not the same as the photograph from Seattle. The shoulder-length hair was bobbed with a fringe, and the pale yellow had become dark brown. Even the eyes looked darker. She wouldn't have recognised her on the street, but close up, she felt she knew.

When her mother held out an arm, Rosie hesitated, unsure whether to lean in for a kiss or a hug.

'Come in,' her mother said, not moving.

Inside, she stood and turned in a slow circle, taking in her mother's world. Bare floorboards, exposed beams, skylight and a high-peaked ceiling that sloped low at the walls. It was large and mostly open plan, with a kitchen area to one side and a sleeping area at the back. No clutter and no artwork anywhere. Only a poster of Rosie the Riveter.

'It's nice. Really nice.'

'Have a look around.'

She walked to the front, to the little window with a glimpse of water and hills. Dad would have loved it, she thought.

Sigi followed and stood beside her.

'I love it here. High up and quiet, with a nice view.'

Rosie looked around for binoculars but saw none.

'Would you like coffee or tea?'

'Ah, either's fine.'

'Come on, Rosa, which do you want?'

'Coffee, I think. By the way, it's Rosie. I mean, that's what I'm called.'

'Oh, I'm sorry. I… didn't know.'

At a round wooden table, Rosie sat in a metal-tubed chair with black wood armrests and a webbed cane seat.

'They're from Sweden, the chairs. Comfortable, don't you think?'

'Yes. Very.'

She watched her at the kitchen counter. Brisk, unhurried movements. Like Gabriel. No words either, no pitter-patter to fill the silence. So different to her father.

Bringing a tray to the table, Sigi sat down, poured coffee from the cafetiere and handed her a mug.

'I'm sorry about those other times when I didn't show up. On the campus and at the Rose Garden.'

'That's OK.'

'The campus meeting was just a test, to see who you were. And then, at the Rose Garden, I saw someone. Probably a PI – sorry, a private investigator – or one of their people. They're easy to spot when you know what they look like.'

'That's what Gabriel thought. And my father, too.'

They both went silent, allowing Sigi to study her face. More like him than me, she decided.

'And when I got to Vancouver, he was afraid I'd been followed there – or tracked – whatever they call it. Really dumb.'

Sigi smiled but did not disagree.

'What happened after Vancouver?'

'We went back to Castlegar.'

'Where?'

'The town where we live. Lived. A long way from Vancouver. We only moved there a few months ago.'

'Why was that? Was he worried?'

'Yes. Nothing definite. Just a feeling he had. That's what he said anyway.'

'So, from Vancouver, you went to Castlegar by car?'

'Yeah, but Dad changed course midway.'

She told the story of their escape a second time, adding more details and finding more names for her emotions. Sigi lit a cigarette and listened with the slit of a smile. She'd taught him well.

'What name was he using?'

'David Williams. Same as always.'

'I see. No time to change it. That's often the problem.'

'What do you mean?'

'Well, a border guard might have remembered that name. Did you show your passports?'

Rosie tried to remember. 'I think so.'

'Why did he go to Dana Point?'

'I guess that was the only place he could think of, where we could stay, I mean.'

'That sounds right. And his parents? What about them?'

Rosie hesitated.

'Let me guess,' Sigi said, stubbing out her cigarette. 'They were shocked, but they took him in.'

'Something like that.'

'Where was he planning to go after Dana Point?'

'I don't know. "Somewhere sunny" is all he said. Maybe he didn't really know himself.'

'And what about you?'

'He wanted me to stay behind and go back to Vancouver. But I told him I was going to go with him. I wasn't going to let him go on alone.'

Sigi reached out across the small table and put a hand on hers.

'I can see that. You'd stick with him.'

Rosie heard regret in her voice.

'And the morning that he died… tell me what happened.'

'It was early. We were having breakfast, about to leave. The police came, or the FBI. I don't know. He told me to stall them and ran downstairs. They looked around and went into his parents' bedroom. They were really scared.'

'Then what?'

'I went downstairs, to see where he'd gone. There's a deck there, above the cliff. I saw his body on the beach.'

'He slipped and fell?'

'Must have. It's high and rocky.'

Sigi looked at her. The FBI and the police would have known about the house and the cliff. And he would have known that they knew. Known that escape was impossible. She could see that Rosie had reached the same conclusion, but neither of them put it into words.

'Terrible, just terrible. I'm so sorry,' Sigi said.

She got up and edged around the table. When Rosie also stood, Sigi held her, wet cheek on warm chest. She had wondered if she would recognise her. Maybe her eyes or her smell. Wondered and hoped, but nothing had been familiar. Until now, skin on skin, rocking her back and forth, like she'd done until the day she left her.

She kissed the top of Rosie's head and stepped back. Startled and off balance for a moment, Rosie stumbled into a chair. Sigi poured more coffee and pushed a plate of biscuits across the table.

'I don't know what you think of me. Probably not very much. But I want you to know that it was not an easy decision, what I did back then.'

Rosie squinted at her through moist eyes.

'It was wrong, in one way, of course. But I had to fight against that immoral war. Killing innocent people, thousands and thousands of them. Bombing them and burning them with napalm. Our country was doing that day after day.'

'I know. I read a lot about it, after Dad told me what happened. Why we were in Vancouver.'

'But you're still wondering why I left.'

Rosie didn't reply.

'I could have stayed with you and your father in Canada. But then neither of us would be doing anything to stop the war. I just couldn't accept that. And – this is the key thing – I knew your father would take care of you.'

A single tear rolled down Rosie's cheek.

'I saw that from the very beginning. During those few weeks when we were all together. He doted on you. Always watching, making sure you were all right.'

Rosie squeezed her eyes tighter.

'It should have been me,' Sigi said. 'Who died, I mean. I should have realised that he wasn't cut out for that kind of life. He was too trusting. Too gentle.'

Sigi brushed the fringe from her forehead.

'Anyway, I'm so happy that you kept trying to find me, because I've wanted to say all this to you for a long time.'

'I wasn't sure what you'd think. Me coming here, out of the blue.'

'I think it's wonderful.'

'You do?'

'Yes, I think we'll be good friends. Very, very good friends.'

Rosie smiled and wiped her cheek.

'You see, I don't have friends, not really. Not the way I've lived. Always on the move, changing names and places. I had lots of "comrades" and "contacts", but that's different. There's a few people I trust. Like Gabriel. But I don't even really know him, and he doesn't know me.'

'Never shared fears or secrets?'

'Exactly. I didn't have any fears, not back then, because they were liabilities. And secrets were our stock and trade, so they lost their allure. Personal secrets, real secrets, didn't exist.'

'What are you doing now? Here in Berkeley?'

She described her semi-underground life, the magazine and its campaigns, including the current one to elect a leftist congressman in the upcoming state elections. Rosie noticed that she didn't mention a partner or any kind of relationship.

'I wish I could just take your father's place,' she said at the end. 'Go back to Vancouver with you and set up a life there, together.'

Rosie had been thinking the same thing.

'But I'm still on the wanted list. Not top priority anymore, but still under indictment. I could be spotted at the border. Then what? I'd be in prison, and you'd be completely alone. No, it's safer not to cross borders. Besides, if we take precautions, we can meet like this from time to time. And maybe, if things change, we could spend more time together.'

Rosie nodded. Her mother, she could see, would never be free of the past. And neither, therefore, would she.

'I could visit you here, I guess.'

'Yes. We'd have to be careful, but it could work.'

Sigi's face brightened as she imagined possibilities.

'Am I what you expected?' Rosie asked.

'Honestly, I don't know what I expected. But you're a brave person, I can see that. And maybe a little stubborn. Like your mother.'

Smiles turned to laughter.

'Now that we've got that settled,' Sigi said, lighting another cigarette, 'what about you? What are you going to do?'

Rosie told her about her place at university in Vancouver.

'How are you going to manage? Money, I mean.'

'My grandparents are going to handle that.'

'That's nice. Your father always said they would support you, in the end.'

'You never met them?'

'No. That wasn't possible back then. And it wouldn't be safe, even now. Besides, I don't think they have a high opinion of me. The older woman who corrupted their wonderful son. Led him astray.'

'They never said anything like that.'

'Not to you, of course. But in a way, it's true. I did influence him. Because he loved me.'

'What do you mean?'

'I mean if you love someone, really love them, that changes you.'

Rosie considered this.

'You two never got married, right?'

'Yes, and that's another thing they wouldn't have liked.'

'What about your parents?'

'They've always been supportive. Haven't approved of everything I did, of course, but we share some basic principles.'

'Where do they live?'

'New Jersey. You could meet them. They'd love it. They know all about you.'

'Wouldn't that be risky?'

'I don't think so. The FBI don't know my birth name and don't know who my parents are.'

'Do you keep in touch with them?'

'By telephone. I haven't seen them for more than twenty years. I've been waiting for an excuse. And now I have one. You.'

'Another set of grandparents sounds good. I always like to have a spare.'

'Very wise.'

They laughed again and eyed each other, not warily, like at first, but with a recognition of resemblance.

'So, I was wondering what should I call you? What's your name now?'

'I change it every seven years – like repainting a house. But I want you to call me "Sigi". Sigrid Steinhouse is my real name.'

'All right. But I might want to use "Mom" sometimes.'

'Please do.'

'Oh, I'd better go,' Rosie said, glancing at her watch. 'Gabriel doesn't like anyone to be late to his dinner table.'

'Let me know when you get to Vancouver and settle in.' She wrote down her number and handed it to Rosie. 'Call me and I'll call you back on a payphone.'

'OK.'

They held each other in a long embrace, until Rosie broke off.

'Almost forgot,' she said and dug into her shoulder bag. 'I think he would want you to have this.'

Sigi took the wooden peace symbol and closed both hands around it. Bunching up her lips, she fought to find the words.

'We tried, you know. We really tried hard.'

Following her mother's directions, she went down the quiet residential street to the first corner and turned left. Full of joy and anticipation, she didn't notice the man and woman in a parked car on the other side of the street. A light breeze cooled the afternoon sun as she continued down the sloping sidewalk and reached Shattuck Avenue, the shopping and business centre, thronged with people moving in all directions.

Her head was reeling. Back to Canada, but not Castlegar. To university in Vancouver. She saw herself in a dorm room, alone. Probably weren't allowed to have pets. Visiting her mother in Berkeley wouldn't be hard. She could combine it with a trip to Dana Point. Maybe she should change her name back to Collins. She'd look into that when she had time. Her father had been too trusting. He shouldn't have died. Shouldn't even have gotten into that kind of life.

Nearing the BART station, the flood tide of rush hour threatened to overwhelm her. She managed to disengage and become a spectator, watching herself blend in with the chaos around her. The flux of so many lives, all headed somewhere. A river plunging down a hill, eddying around rocks, swirling sideways and backpedalling, but in the end, surging forward. Until someone draws the wild card, the luck of the draw that's beyond anyone's control and changes a life from failure to success, or the reverse. The worst thing, in the latter case, is that by the time we recover, we are already past the point of no return.

She threaded herself back into the crowd and disappeared down the steps to the station. Sitting in the train as it rumbled beneath the water, she thought of what lay ahead. Her mother was not the easiest person to be with – not by a long shot – but she had a sense of what her father had seen in her. Unflinching honesty and not an ounce of pretence. Yes, she could learn to love her.